THE NATURAE SERIES

RISKING DESTINY

Discover a villain's creation in this Viking Age Prequel
Order your copy now **www.books2read.com/riskingdestiny**

DESTINY AWAITING

The enemies to lovers Prequel, escape to Agincourt where averting a
war between their races and their countries, Aioffe and Tarl's battles of
the heart are destined to fight with faith and hope itself.
Order your copy now **www.books2read.com/destinyawaiting**

DISRUPTING DESTINY

Book 1 – A country torn apart, lovers caught in the middle in the
early Tudor age.
Order your copy now at **www.books2read.com/disruptingdestiny**

ANARCHIC DESTINY

Book 2 – A forgotten heir, a queendom in crisis… chaos will reign as
Bloody Mary makes her move for power.
Order your copy now at **www.books2read.com/anarchicdestiny**

www.escapeintoatale.com/books

This book is written in British English.

Copyright © 2023 by Jan Foster

Published by So Simple Published Media
   First edition March 2023

Cover Design
   www.getcovers.com

Paperback ISBN: 9781916340824
E-Book ISBN: 9781916340893

www.escapeintoatale.com

Dedication

For my parents, Will and Cherry - the first enemies to lovers story I was told, and over fifty years later, still the most enduring and inspiring to our family.
With much love and thanks, especially for never being too cross when you discovered me reading under the covers by torchlight as a child, when I should have been sleeping!

Destiny Awaiting

By Jan Foster

THE NATURAE SERIES

CHAPTER 1 - CRASH LANDING

She'd left it too late to pull out of the dive. Her body collided with the fir top, covering her in dislodged icy clumps of snow. All forward momentum halted. With the trunk out of reach, Aioffe tried to steady herself inside the woody prison by pushing all her limbs out wide.

It seemed to work. She had time to draw in a calm breath. Then her wings gave way. As her body slid down the branches, her frozen fingers failed to grasp the dark green spiky tufts. Tumbling through the tree, the translucent panes of her appendages shredded into tatters.

Halfway down, she hooked a thicker branch with one hand, then froze, dangling. Before she could grab another hold, the supple wood sagged, then cracked.

Her numb fingers lost their grip.

"Ow." Her bare foot broke the thin, icy layer, twisting against the frozen earth beneath as her body weight followed. Having deposited its cargo in an ungainly heap at the roots, the branch pinged back with a whoosh.

Aioffe opened her eyes. A clump of snow plopped onto her head, a final insult.

Her quarry, a lone squirrel which had been sitting atop the tallest fir in the copse in an otherwise desolate land, now leant up on its haunches a few feet away. For a moment, its russet fur quivered as it examined her with curious eyes. They stared at each other silently, then it tilted its neat head at her and hopped off.

"Next time." She sighed as she caught sight of her battered, numb wings.

She needed to feed. The squirrels' Lifeforce would have been sufficient sustenance to return home with. Injured, she needed something more substantial to heal herself. Her wings twitched; the breeze whistled through the holes, tickling as sensation returned. There would be no flying away from the island with them so shredded. Her ankle throbbed in protest at the prospect of walking. Not that one could walk across the sea.

She swallowed, hearing her mother's voice in her head, 'One such as you should never leave. If you must, then never travel alone. And never be seen.'

And never find out anything, Aioffe always mentally added. Never be free. Never discover. Never live a different life than that which her mother, and the rest of the fae, demanded of her.

After following the squirrel's tracks across the flat white landscape with her eyes, Aioffe turned on the ground and peered through the cluster of trunks surrounding her. Her heart sank as she watched for a few minutes. No other prey hopped or flew into sight. The silent sun had begun its descent, twilight would soon fall.

Where the land dipped into the horizon to the west, a stone cross peaked into the orange sky. A slate roof hugged into the curve of the coast; its adornment jutted up like a beacon towards the water. From the air, this small island had appeared uninhabited, but the whitewashed building was worth considering as shelter against the long winter night ahead. At the very least, it had a roof.

She crawled to the edge of the copse and gazed across the other side of the expanse. In the distance to the east, a tall, square building dominated a ridge. A lone tower atop a mound at its base rose only half as high as the trees in Naturae, and cast a long, dark shadow towards the coastline. Centuries ago, the Vikings - invaders, and destroyers from even further North -

proclaimed their dominion over these islands with castles and brochs. Aioffe's mouth dried. Perhaps some were still used by those who ruled here. Stone constructs were so different to the treetop dwellings of her kind. The prospect of exploring them piqued her interest, despite her fear of discovery.

"Perhaps don't stray too close to them, then," she muttered to herself. Entanglement with people - humans - would likely get her in more trouble.

With hawk-like eyes, Aioffe stared at the tower, the low building, then the tower again for a few minutes. She didn't spot any movement or candlelight inside the small windows of either building. A gust of chilly sea wind whipped a loose strand of hair across her cheek. She needed to move, and now, before darkness fell.

Wincing as she stood on her sore ankle, she shook the last of the snow from her head. Her wings, shredded and aching, dropped behind her back, so she tucked them out of sight underneath her heavy cloak before setting off.

As she limped down the slippery incline towards the whitewashed building, the silence of the desolate land was broken only by the crash and rattle of waves, lurching from the Sound to the pebbled beaches between this island and the next. She caught a braying of seals from the cove below and her stomach rumbled. Now they come to shore! Typical of her luck - given her current speed, by the time she made it down there, they would probably have gone back out to sea. Her priority now was shelter.

As she approached the single storey building, a cluster of upright stones jutting from the grass, decorated with carved inscriptions, caught her attention. One was a more recent addition, judging from the absence of moss on its light grey face. The slate was graced with a cross within a circle above the writing, like the one on top of the roof, as if the symbol were the most important thing to announce. A freshly turned earth mound extended from the slab's base. Her nose wrinkled. Decay emanated from the soil where turf had yet to grow.

Weariness and pain swept over her, and she leaned against the stone. Her fingers traced the indentations of lettering as she caught her breath. Humans lived such short lives; how strange that they would place their bodies under ground when their life ended. Their souls freed to roam wherever they wanted without earthly ties.

A noise interrupted her pondering. Her head shot up and she stiffened. A chink of metal? Despite her extraordinary hearing, nothing further sounded. Aioffe snorted, dismissing the sound as her own knife, holstered, and hanging from her belt; it must have bashed against the slab when she moved. She shook her head; how silly she was to spook herself when she had seen no signs of anyone alive on the island so far.

A flagstone path led to the building entrance. Her ankle throbbed from the unfamiliar exertion of walking. When she pushed the heavy wooden door, it swung open with a creak.

A furtive movement in the shadows at the back of the room made her blink, then, another chink sounded. She gasped.

The light from the slit of a window behind lit upon blond hair. His face furrowed as he turned towards her. The bag he held clanked to the floor, then his hands curled into fists.

Aioffe's mouth dried as she stared at the human through the drifting dust. He was trapped, like her, in the last beams of sunlight.

CHAPTER 2 – CAUGHT IN THE ACT

Dropping the bag with the silverware inside had only served to announce Tarl's deceit. He might as well have put his hands up and surrendered. He blinked and cleared his throat, hoping to shift the girl's azure focus from his flushed face, but her stare was unwavering.

"I'm sorry to interrupt." Her soft voice had a peculiar lilt, as if she were from far away shores. Indeed, with her white blonde hair wild about her pale, heart-shaped face, not to mention those peculiar wide eyes, she certainly looked foreign. Her skirt and cape were in tatters and, although muddied, their fine fabric suggested wealth and position. Her skin bore no lines. The lack of cap and wildness of her hair was child-like, even though she had physically developed feminine curves. She seemed barely a woman, more of a girl and probably not much younger than himself. As such, no threat to a man.

"What do you want?" He hadn't meant to be so gruff, but his tone made her shrink into the door frame. "This is sacred property."

"Is it?" she said. "Why?"

He drew himself taller, frowned, then bent down to pick up the sack. Who doesn't know what a church is? "It's a church. Of course it's sacred." She was still examining him; he could sense those peculiar eyes roaming over his person. He blustered, "And it's closed except for worship. On alternate Sundays."

"Then why are you here?"

"I'm here to…"

Tarl's mind blanked of an excuse under the woman's curious

gaze.

It was no use. He fell silent.

There was no excuse to be made. Not really. He glanced at the sack in his hands, weighing heavier with his guilt.

"I was just wondering," her voice caught. "I might rest here a while."

"A while?"

She shrugged, then looked at him again through lowered eyelashes.

"Why are you out so late? I've not seen you before, and I thought I knew everyone on this island, and Rousay."

She scanned the stone threshold; her shoulders drooped as his mind whirled. He had heard nothing in the village about new arrivals. Such an event in the sleepy Orkney Islands was definitely worthy of gossip. He would welcome a change of conversation. Anything to turn the debate away from his mother's recent demise.

He stepped away from the altar table and frowned. "Are you lost? Do your family know where you are?"

Defiant, the girl still did not meet his eye and for a moment, he was torn. His instincts fluttered a warning, and goosebumps rose on his arms. The strangeness of the intruder could mean trouble, as if he wasn't in enough already.

But she looked so pitiful, all shredded, slight and wild. Silhouetted by the open door with the white snow behind her, she seemed so very small. So alone.

And different to anyone else he had ever met in all his seventeen years. Her face, or her accent, perhaps? He wasn't sure quite what it was about her, but his heart thumped another signal, and he took a step back. Guilt made him snap back, "Well, whomever you are, you shouldn't be here."

Those blue eyes flicked to his and narrowed. "And yet you are. What are you doing here?"

He wondered why this stranger kept asking him about his business? Had she no respect? "I'm collecting something. That's all."

His bluff didn't quite ring true, but he rolled his shoulders back and gathered himself up to his full height. She was just a girl. What could she understand of a grown-up's obligation to support a family?

"Is there a good reason why I cannot rest here?" Her voice was soft, yet with a steel-like determination behind it. "It's so peaceful, and I am so…" She sagged against the door. "Tired."

Tarl shook his head. "I don't consider that a good idea."

"You don't need to stay. I won't be a bother. If you need to leave, that is."

"I think you should go before the priest comes to lock up." He had planned to be gone long before that happened. Delaying with her might cost him the tide.

The girl tucked her front teeth over her bottom lip and pushed herself from the door frame. Her face creased with pain as she turned to the opening.

"Are you hurt?" he asked, and glowered.

She shook her head and pulled open the heavy wood. Her slim fingers tightened on the edge as she stepped outside.

"You are hurt." Goddammit, now he would have to help her, or she might tell someone about seeing him. He took her elbow and ordered, "Lean on me."

She yanked her arm back, then glared at him. "I'll be fine."

How peculiar she was. Defiant. "No," Tarl caught sight of the lowering sun. "It's nearly sundown. I'd better get you home."

Her lips tilted up, just enough for him to understand that she thought the prospect of a dark, cold night was irrelevant.

"I don't think that's going to be possible," she said. "But thank you for the offer."

He grimaced. "You can't stay outside in the winter night-time." Tarl pressed his lips together, then offered, "Just tell me where you want to go, and I'll get you there."

"But that's just it, you see." Her smile turned to what he could only have described as mischievous. "I am where I want to be."

"Hah! Who would want to come to Wrye?" He scoffed. "Nothing ever happens here. Barely anyone but the seals live here."

"You're here? In this… place."

"The church?"

She nodded. "Church, yes. And those upright stones outside with the…" She paused, her eyebrows crossing as though searching for the right word. Then she shrugged. "What is your word for them?"

"Gravestones?" He bristled. Did she know nothing of faith and burial customs? She definitely wasn't from Scotland. The way she talked with an accent yet didn't know what things were called – that was foreign behaviour. Tarl hadn't met many people who weren't born here, and only overheard occasional travellers once or twice. Maybe she was from the continent. Yes, that must be it. A visitor. A traveller. That made sense.

She continued, "Yes, with the writing on. Are they names? Of those who have passed into another life?"

Tarl took her elbow again as she limped forwards.

"Yes. A better life." This time, she did not shake herself free of him. The sack clanked against the wood as he guided her out. Keeping her distracted might be the best plan. Anything to get away from the church. Quickly.

"This better life. Where is that?" She gazed at him, and his brows furrowed even deeper.

"Heaven. Unless you know of somewhere better?"

She tugged her arm aside from his, then tentatively stepped out from the low porch onto the thin layer of snow.

"Heaven," she said quietly, almost to herself.

He closed the door behind them, then looked at the sky. Of all the times he could do with fresh snowfall to hide his tracks, but the clouds had dissipated. Across the horizon before them dimmed a pink-orange sunset. As spring beckoned to warm the chill of these windy islands, it was ever more likely to rain instead; this crisp, clear day would become a distant memory.

Already, he wanted to forget the day he had chosen to commit a sin. Not even being a good samaritan would absolve him of theft. From a church.

As the young woman turned her pale face towards him, a shadow darkened the pathway.

CHAPTER 3 – BUSTED

Shooting from under bushy eyebrows, the steely glare of a brown-robed vampire sent a chill through Aioffe. Seen only from afar before today, her skin tingled as a terrifying understanding of her predicament dawned. The surprise and speed of his approach suggested advanced years; indeed, he wore the wrinkles of many centuries. This must be the priest the boyman had threatened would arrive, but was the human aware of the kind of creature the Church protected?

Irrespective, the fact that he was a vampire posed an added complication. She consciously stilled her broken wings lest the human notice their quivering underneath her cape.

"Father McTavish!" The boyman exclaimed, dismay in his voice.

The priest's blood-red lips curled, drawing back to reveal a yellow-toothed sneer. "A little far from home, aren't we?" A gravelly voice barely contained the vampire's hostility, but she didn't know whether it was aimed at her or the human.

Aioffe raised her gaze to meet his.

"Oh yes, little thing, I smelled your filth. For you... are not altogether like others, are you?" He paced, almost leisurely, on the flagstone path. His feet crunched the ice crystals as beady eyes shot between Aioffe and the human.

The boyman took a step forward. "I found her in the church, Father." His earnestness caused Aioffe's jaws to clench.

Aioffe clenched her fists as the priest glared at the human, roaming his tall stature up and down. Although obviously keen to hand her over to the enemy, the boy was a casualty of the situation. He was not to blame for her intrusion. She was the one at fault here, having broken the first rule of the Vampire-Fae Sation Wars Treaty - never expose oneself to the humans.

The priest growled, "Which you, Tarl Smythson, should not have been in either. I know you, as I know everyone in your village. And I have heard of what happened to your mother."

The boyman paled. At least Aioffe knew his name now.

"God rest her soul," the vampire added sarcastically. "Except..."

"I have a right to visit," Tarl protested. "My family..."

"You and your family have no rights," the vampire interrupted. "There is a substantial payment to be made before you have 'rights,' as I recall."

The boy hung his head, chastised, yet his hand tightened on the sack.

"So that does not explain quite why you are here at all? Unless you thought perhaps to settle your family debt with items which already belong to the Church?"

She may have been right to question earlier, but that didn't help their situation now. Ownership of objects was something which she knew humans prized, but how did that work with an institution's possessions? She recalled how a Fae Elder spat as he derided the Catholic Church that was 'for the people,' yet was wealthier in coin than the majority of the human population.

If she'd had not been looking, she would've missed the quick sweep of the priest's arm. Tarl's body was flung backwards towards the rough stones of the doorway as if weightless. Mid flight, his fingers released his treasures.

His head struck the door frame with a loud thud, then he crumpled to the ground. Metal objects tumbled out of the bag - a silver cup, a candlestick and a small bejewelled cross on a wooden base.

Paying no heed to his victim or the spoils, the ancient vampire advanced. Grabbing her arm, he stared at her features as he squeezed. Probing her as if he had no idea who she was. What she was.

She noticed a thin film of grey covered his pupils as his gaze darted around her face, as if to avoid the fog which coloured his vision.

Aioffe understood then what the priest's real problem with the human was - a vampire unable to influence a human with a gaze was a vampire weakened. They needed their pupils to mesmerise the humans into forgetting the very recent past. Ancient or not, this vampire was still strong and fast, and probably hungry. His usual abilities could not solve the problem of human exposure for either of them.

And that made him more dangerous.

A flash of uncertainty crossed his face as the priest sniffed deeply, then his lips curled into an expression of distaste. As his eyes narrowed, Aioffe's stomach dropped. Before she could process the implications of him knowing precisely who she was, the vampire's fingers were at her throat. She gasped for air. He hissed, baring his teeth, and showing a chipped but still lengthened incisor.

"Let go of me," she wheezed.

The vampire responded by ripping her cloak from her shoulders. She stiffened as his icy hand then slowly slid over her shoulder. The lascivious movement made her shudder.

"You should fly on home, little thing. You have strayed too far."

Aioffe pulled herself back from his grip, leaning unintentionally on her sore ankle. A spasm of pain seared up her leg. She bit her lip to prevent the faelore curse which threatened utterance, but, her flinch did not escape the priest's notice. His brows lowered as a thin smile stretched his parchment skin. "Unless you cannot…"

A few feet away, Tarl groaned. Both vampire and fae heads whipped around. He propped himself up on one arm and shook his head, as if that would clear his mind.

The priest turned back to Aioffe, his tongue touching the tip of that broken incisor. The stench of his breath, foetid between yellowed teeth, hit her delicate nose. "Perhaps you need to feed?" His head jerked towards the boyman. "I can understand the appeal."

Her mouth dropped open. "I would never!"

"Oh come now," the vampire replied. "It would be our little secret. A favour from me, for a favour from you, pretty thing." His fingers squeezed her throat as his gaze roamed down her legs.

Aioffe guessed the priest's intentions, and her stomach churned. A vampire could not be trusted. Not to keep a secret. Not ever. Her fist rose and her toes curled into the ground. She tried to pull from the ground's magic, but the flagstones of the path would not yield.

She walloped the priest around the head.

The vampire's skull barely registered her strike. His fingers tightened on her neck in response, then she was lifted. Her feet scrabbled briefly in the air, before she too was thrown backwards. She hit the grave mound, flared wings snapping on impact. Her spine jarred. All air in her ribs was forced out by the blow.

Before she could catch a breath, the vampire was on top of her. Snarling. Teeth bared. With one hand holding her down, he crowed, "Or perhaps you have other reasons for being here?" His head lowered and he rasped into her face. "The Fae do not need to know what happens in my province, spy!"

Then his other hand tore at her skirt. "Spies do not go

unpunished," he spat, as he ripped the fabric, clawing until his fingers found bare flesh.

Aioffe shrieked, then thrashed against him. The shrill sound carried away over the land, unanswered. Pain and indignation fired her fight, but centuries of mistrust between their kinds fuelled his strength. His weight bore down upon her fragile bones.

She screamed anew at the agony shooting through her entire body.

His hand shot up and clamped over her mouth.

Her eyes widened as a hand gripped the priest's shoulder.

CHAPTER 4 – SAVIOUR?

"Father!" Tarl said. His fingers clamped on a bony shoulder, and he tried to drag the village priest off the girl. Surprised by the resistance he met when trying to wrench the man off her, Tarl redoubled his efforts. For an old guy, he had quite a grip. Another heave, putting all his years of pulling bows and hammering at the forge into it, and the Father's fingers released her. Despite the snarl, Tarl shoved him across the grass. He was surprised by how light the priest was, given his strength.

As the Father's body rolled over the flagstones, a dull snap accompanied his howl of frustration. Father McTavish's head spun around, a wildness and confusion in his eyes. "You dolt!" he screeched.

In one heartbeat, the priest shifted from sprawled on the ground to sitting. He glanced down at his knee. A thin hand fluttered towards it as if to ease a pain.

Tarl stared at the outline of the priest's leg underneath his cassock. The calf stuck out at an unnatural angle. Oh Holy Mary, what had he done?

"You don't know what you are doing, boy!" The Father's arm rose, wavering, and pointed at the young woman. "This 'thing' is not what you think."

"I have prevented you from committing a mortal sin, Father." Tarl hung his head. "I am sorry for my violence." From the corner of his eye, he noticed the girl shook; her fingers sinking into the soft soil of his mother's grave.

The priest's expression darkened with fury as he glanced down at his wonky leg. With a sigh of irritation, he lent over and straightened it.

Tarl winced and wondered at how Father McTavish didn't pass out from the pain of resetting his limb.

With a burst of energy, the priest's hands reached for her again!

"No!" she shouted, scrabbling back on the earth.

"I know that Our Lord would not want you to tarnish your conscience." Tarl's hand shot out and grabbed Father McTavish's shoulder, to restrain him from further indignity. Perhaps by this act, his own tarnished and deceitful soul might be in some way salvaged.

With a potency that must have come from the Almighty himself, the priest jerked himself into a crouch. Tarl gasped. His head whirled; how could the old preacher recover so quickly? Father McTavish barrelled past, shoving him off balance. Tarl stumbled on the icy flagstones and fell.

Tarl promptly righted himself on all fours and looked over his shoulder.

The priest had reached his target. Hunched over the slim body on the snow, he ripped the shoulders of her dress down. She screamed and batted his hands away, to no avail. A tearing sound, and the front of her shift fell open, exposing perfect, pale breasts. Tarl's blood began to boil; the preacher seemed determined to abuse the girl despite a witness! But then, the Father grabbed her arm and flipped her torso around.

Hanging from her shoulder blades were what could only be described as wings! Tattered, as one might see on a dying butterfly, with panes which shimmered in the lowering light. Long and flaccid, the appendages which - had she been standing - would stretch down to her feet.

They quivered against her naked back as the girl's head

bowed.

Tarl's mouth hung open as he gaped. Torn between fascination and revulsion, he couldn't drag his eyes from the shredded appendages.

"See?" Father McTavish leered. "Different."

Tarl swallowed, repulsed by both the Father's attitude and yet, his own disgust clenched his stomach.

What was she?

She raised her head, glaring at the priest as she cried out, "Why are you doing this?"

"Because in nakedness you cannot avoid the bare truth. He," the priest's eyes flicked towards Tarl, "should see what he is so keen to defend… before he dies for it."

"Dies?" Tarl said, stupidly.

She shook the blonde tresses away from her face. "He does not have to die. This is not his fault. My presence here has nothing to do with him."

The priest kept his grip on girl's shoulder as he sneered, "Tarl Smythson is nothing but a thief. A liar. A concealer of witchcraft. For these sins alone, he should die anyway." Father McTavish glanced at him then spat, "Now, he is involved in matters which do not concern him. He dares to injure a man of the cloth."

Tarl's heart thudded as the priest said with absolute conviction, "The human has to die."

Shame and confusion flooded Tarl's face, which he could not avert or push away. The Father spoke the truth about being a thief and a liar. Even trying to prevent the priest from committing a carnal sin had been a paltry effort to make up for his own wrongdoings. But to call him a human as if he were any different? It dawned on him that the girl with wings wasn't the only thing inhuman person.

"The boy won't say anything," she pleaded. "He doesn't

know much."

Tarl's stomach dropped. He'd intended to defend her and now she insulted him? What didn't he know? And calling him a boy - who did she think she was?

The Father shrugged as his gaze flicked between Tarl and the girl. "I cannot 'persuade' him to forget any more. Such is the curse of old age. He is a risk to both of us. Besides, he is only one."

As the priest's upper lip curled, Tarl noticed his unnaturally long teeth.

The girl jumped up, her shredded clothing falling from her like a skin being shed. She stood naked, bar a belt and a knife sheath. On top of his mother, like an angelic statue only seen in the most expensive of burial grounds.

Tarl gawked. He could not help it. Her slim, pale body seemed to glow from within, then her wings awkwardly rose behind her. She limped towards him, not taking her eyes off the priest and holding her arms out to ward away the Father. As if her fragile, slim physique would somehow protect a man of his size!

Father McTavish cackled again. "Do you really think you can escape the same fate as Tarl here, little one? Protect him?"

Tarl frowned. The Father sounded like he was toying with them. A cruel hunter playing with its prey. But, he was a priest. A holy man ordained before God. Now, the Lord was showing himself to Tarl in the strangest of ways, and he didn't know what was right or wrong or who was what.

Stood in front of him, the girl-angel's enormous wings would have eclipsed his view of the Father were they not translucent and shredded. She was broken. But Tarl could do no more than just stand there. Spellbound. Was she some kind of angel, like those painted on church walls?

Father McTavish sneered. "You cannot fly, or run. Even if

you did make it home, somehow, you have broken the Treaty several times over. They will not want you back."

"You don't know how wrong you are," she whispered.

"Am I? There are only us three here." His head cocked. "Your death, and his, won't be remarkable."

Tarl's mind raced. Whatever she was, she did not deserve to die for him. He was not worthy, as the priest said. And, despite everything he had done, he did not wish to die, as the priest threatened. Not without the opportunity to atone for his sins.

Yet, he couldn't unsee what was before him. He blinked, for if this were a vision or a dream, surely it would stop soon. However peculiar this girl was, she still seemed to think he needed protection. He didn't know how to feel about that, or anything about this strange situation, so he shoved his questions away. Emotions were not something he had time to indulge in.

He glanced at the disturbed soil mound. Why had she chosen that particular grave to dig her fingers into? Was her appearance some sort of omen? Or, had a knowledge of another world driven his mother to her death also?

CHAPTER 5 - A DEAL NOT TAKEN

Aioffe's mind raced, along with her heart. There had to be a way out of this situation without anybody dying. Although the vampire could not focus, and thus influence Tarl as well as he might have, he was still strong enough to pose a threat to both of their futures.

Her injuries prevented her from fleeing. That much was obvious to them all. But she would heal in time. She could not die; it took a great deal more than a twisted ankle and shredded wings to kill a fae. Or a vampire.

But why did she care about the human, someone she had met only minutes earlier? Vampires considered humans as simple bags of blood. She supposed Fae might equally view them the same way as their blood was rumoured to be equally satisfying for her kind, more so perhaps than the animals she fed from, but human lives were so much more than just the Lifeforce they emitted. Alive, Tarl could sustain her with his Lifeforce, if necessary. Dead, he was of little use to her. Dead, he became a victim of her behaviour, which she would have to live with. His imminent demise would linger on her conscience for the rest of her eternal life.

What was the vampire doing here, anyway? She could understand his animosity towards her kind - the Sation wars of millennia ago were still relatively recent to an immortal. There was a strong chance this ancient one had been involved. But, exposing both their natures to a human also broke the treaties created after the vampires had won control over the human population of this realm. So, in effect, Aioffe reasoned, the priest was the creature in the wrong here.

If she could escape this situation, she would be absolutely within her rights to bring this matter to the Council and expose him. She shuddered inside at the prospect though, because that would therefore mean revealing her own negligence, and misbehaviour, in travelling here. She also was exposed to the human.

But the vampire didn't know that she had snuck away from Naturae. It was the only advantage she had.

"Priest," she said, and drew her shoulders back as she straightened. "If you expect that there will be no repercussions for you, you are wrong. My absence will be noticed. If you are so blind as to think no-one knows where I am, you are more foolish than I gave your kind credit for. Age does not equate to wisdom, perhaps. My superiors cannot ignore this breach of the Treaty. They will not forgive my death. If I fail to return, then your kind's lairs, these churches, will be the first places they'll look. As this is your territory, you will be the first to pay the price."

The priest's head tilted, a thoughtful expression creeping over his face. His lips pursed and his gaze shifted quickly to Tarl, then back to her. "Fae. Young fae. It is clear you are young. Otherwise, you would know there is a far easier way to resolve this matter. Between ourselves."

His eyes narrowed as they looked past Aioffe's shoulder, then lingered on Tarl. "If we dispose of him."

"Father!"

From behind her, the shock in Tarl's voice rang in her ears. It reminded her he was an innocent, caught up in the history of their races.

"We will both leave, then. Say nothing more about what has occurred here," she quickly countered. "The human could move elsewhere. One of your kind can help him forget what he has seen, I'm sure. I will leave. You go about your business, and that is all. As if this day had never happened."

There were no guarantees that the vampire would abide by such an agreement, she knew, but perhaps it would give her time to remove Tarl from their predicament. Alive.

The priest mocked, "You suggest he just disappears off? Away from all of Orkney? To where? Have you seen him? With his build, he's more likely to get picked up to fight, and die, in Henry's war like all the fools his age, long before another of my kind can assist. He gets to salvage what little is left of his conscience in the service of a supposedly Godly and Just war. He'll perish anyway. Meanwhile, you flap off home and keep your mouth shut for evermore?" He shook his head as if the plan had virtually no merit.

"Why not?" she challenged. It sounded like a reasonable idea to her. Better than the other options available to them.

The vampire then sniggered. "What would I get from that?" His head dipped, just enough for her to realise he was serious. "No. There can be no alternative deal. The boy, a criminal, dies. Now. Caught in the act of stealing from the Church. Still holding the evidence. His death is justifiable to my superiors. Yours too, if you choose to tell them about this incident, that is. Which I doubt you will. Or can. And therefore, all mention of this evening's transgressions disappears as well."

His eyes glittered, then roamed over her nakedness. He had no intention of letting either of them remain alive, she suspected. Trust a vampire to keep a deal? Did he really think her so naïve?

Aioffe felt Tarl push past her wings. Without warning, he launched himself at the priest. Stupid boyman, he had no idea what he was dealing with!

Father McTavish dissolved into mocking jeers at Tarl's ineffective attempts to grab his arms and pin him down. She spurred herself into the fray. A human alone would not be strong enough to contain the ancient one.

In Latin, the universal lexicon which both Fae and vampire knew well, the priest goaded her as his limbs dodged Tarl's grasp.

There was only one language a creature such as this could understand. Pain. Inescapable pain. She kicked, then grabbed his injured leg. With the knee bent, she forced him to the ground, then sat on the limb.

"His eyes, don't look into them," she shouted at Tarl.

The vampire's screech tore through the air as she pushed her weight onto the joint, leaning onto the newly healed break.

Tarl followed her lead and plonked himself astride the vampire, their backs to each other. The priest's limbs wriggled, flailing, trying to get a purchase on the flagstones with which to toss either one of them off his skinny torso. The vampire screamed, an animalistic yelp of agony as she dug her fingers into his flesh. She heard a crack from behind her. The scream died away, then the leg fell slack, all resistance gone.

Aioffe looked over her shoulder to see Tarl raise his hands up.

"Oh God. Oh God oh God…" he muttered. "What have I done?"

"Broken his neck?" She said, hopefully.

"He… He sounded like a dog," Tarl stuttered out. "Like a hunted animal. In pain. I just…"

"Put it out of its misery," she said, nodding her head. At least he had compassion, even if he wasn't to know his actions wouldn't be the end of the vampire's long life. It might buy them some time.

Tarl nodded. "I didn't mean to."

"You did. And that's all right," Aioffe said, standing up, shifting her weight onto her uninjured ankle. She put her hand on his shoulder - not to comfort him, but because she felt lightheaded with the activity and low on energy. If nothing else, she needed some form of crutch, otherwise she would topple back onto the vampire.

"I killed a man of the cloth." Tarl shook his head.

He seemed to have forgotten the leg break, which had healed once reset. So too would the Father's neck. For a moment, Aioffe wondered if he might start to cry. He swallowed; a funny bump dropped his muscled neck and into the hollow above his collarbone.

"He wanted you dead. And, you were defending me." She let her note of wonder and curiosity hang as she studied the icy blueness of his eyes. Her body leaned towards his, unbidden. Calling out for his Lifeforce. She blinked and pulled back.

"Whatever he was, he has gone to a better place without blemish." he said. "At least I prevented a priest from sinning right before his death." He nodded rigorously. "He might not have said his last rites, but at he can go to heaven without tarnish on his soul."

"He isn't dead," Aioffe snorted and looked towards the coastline. "I'm not sure where he is precisely, as I don't know what happens next to their kind." She turned back to look at Tarl, still tantalisingly close. Too close.

"I broke his neck. I'm not sure how much more dead he can be."

Aioffe raised her eyebrow. "There is a way to be sure." She reached for the knife in her belt.

He frowned at her with disappointment clouding his eyes. The Lifeforce emanating from the boyman fizzled, disappeared as if it had never been there.

Aioffe glanced at the vampire, whiter than the displaced snow around them. "He is not dead," she repeated. "Because vampires aren't 'alive' to begin with."

It was disconcerting to disillusion a human. Used to disappointing her mother, the Court, pretty much everyone she knew, Aioffe realised that she didn't want to disappoint this boyman. Not when his Lifeforce, his essence, had been so strong. So... tempting. "We could just secure him. While we decide what to do next."

"We? There is no we to decide anything." Tarl reached up and removed her hand from his shoulder. Aioffe wobbled. "Have you no conscience at all?" he said.

"Have you?" Aioffe frowned, not entirely sure what a conscience was.

"Of course I have!" He huffed as his eyes flared. Between his legs, the Father's torso twitched. "Is that normal for a dead person? Or whatever a vampire is."

"How many times do I need to tell you? He's not dead. Or normal." She sighed. "I'll explain when we are safe. Please, if you don't want me to make sure he is properly.... gone... then let's just tie him up somewhere, or trap him at least, and go."

Tarl shook his head. He looked at his hands, bewildered. "No. I need time to figure out a better plan."

Time was not on their side. It grew darker with every passing minute, and the Father McTavish would rally quickly. In pain and hungry, she was dangerously close to the edge of her temper. She limped away. "I should point out," she called over her shoulder, "that he will need to feed. To restore and heal. On human blood. And you are the nearest."

She sighed. He was handsome, honourable and compassionate, certainly, but his race was clearly doomed if they couldn't accept the blindingly obvious. She began to see why her mother had always cautioned against involvement with humankind.

CHAPTER 6 - HOLE-Y

Feed on human blood? What in the name of heaven and hell was she talking about?

In the lowering light, Tarl stared at the Father's pale face. His fault. A life he had stilled through not tempering his instinct to put an animal out of pain, by snapping its neck with his too powerful arms. But now, grey lips hung open and no breath escaped. Black eyes, vacant and lifeless. His own face twisted with revulsion. How could the Father still live? His neck was broken. You didn't heal from that sort of injury.

But the Father - a vampire apparently - had healed before. Tarl was sure that the priest's leg had been fractured, yet he'd just straightened it out and resumed his attack. And that twitch of his torso - or could it have been some sort of end-of-life spasm? Tarl hesitantly poked his finger at the thin grey skin. He jabbed again, the coldness of the man's face not lost upon him. How could he cool so fast? The air was chilly, but it had only been minutes since his death, surely?

"You see those long teeth of his?" The girl's voice called back as she lurched away. "They're weapons. For feeding with, like an animal. Don't get too close or you'll end up one of them as well."

He didn't want to look at her. Her nakedness and strangeness. Being sat on top of a cold body was terrifying enough. He held his finger on the flaccid skin this time, fighting his disgust. Then he pushed with the tip of his digit up to reveal the inside of the Father's mouth.

Goddammit, she might have a point. Literally. The canine

teeth were unnaturally long. Although missing its point, the enlarged incisor curved like a dog's.

Tarl's head shot around, searching for the girl. Woman. Angel. Thing. Freak. Whatever she was, she'd been right; this priest was not the same as he was. Not human. Which explained his unusual speed and strength, and healing. But he hadn't moved in a while. He must be dead.

Tarl looked back down between his knees at the body, thinking he should stand up and do something with it. Bury it maybe. But then what? Just ignore the fact that he'd stolen from the church, then killed a priest. Met a girl with wings. Killed a priest. Killed. A. Priest. Tarl shook his head. A vampire, she said.

But was he really a priest? He certainly had not behaved like one ought to. How had he not noticed after eighteen years of the Father's preachings?

And the girl. She was so odd.

Angelic.

Peculiar.

Yet, what if she was right?

As if answering his question, Tarl heard a hiss. He frowned. Had he shifted his weight on the body somehow? Forced air from its chest to escape into the night?

"Come closer…"

There it was again, and Tarl was sure this time. The hiss bade him closer.

He glanced at her retreating back. Her wings obscured her naked form as they dangled behind her. No, it had not come from her; it was definitely from the Father. He bent his head a little down.

"Closer…"

Yes. Definitely coming from the immobile grey lips.

Relief almost caused the knot in his stomach to loosen, but

not quite. Naïve he might have been, but dumb, no. She had warned him, and so far, at least in her last words to him, she'd been right. Those teeth were killers. Weapons. And no-one dead hissed. "Not in a million years, Father."

He shouted after her, "Hey! What do I do then?" He felt foolish enough asking, but maybe she could offer some advice. "Hey! Come back!"

To be sure the priest didn't wriggle away in the meantime, he moved his hands so one pinned the vampire's head while the other clamped down on its chest.

Nearly out of sight, he saw her stumble, but she didn't respond or return. Tarl looked back at the thing beneath his thighs.

A rattle of breath being drawn in panicked him. What had she suggested? Secure him. With what, though? They were on Wrye, for God's sake, where nothing ever happened. Barely anyone came or lived here. There was only the broch - the old, abandoned Castle of Cubbie Roo - and the church close by. Having emptied the chapel of anything of value, he doubted there was a handy chain or pair of cuffs lying around for such an occasion.

His gaze fell on the priest's belt. Using the hand which held down the shoulder, Tarl yanked on the knotted rope. Feeling around the waist, his fingers found the knot and began to work it loose. He dared not take his attention from the preacher's head, in case it made a sudden movement, somehow, and lunged for him. His thighs tightened. Goddamn that girl.

Finally, he tugged the belt free. He threw both the priest's arms up above his head, being careful not to move the skull back into alignment. As he stretched his body over the Father's head, he paused. If the neck wasn't as broken as he thought, if those teeth were as sharp as he feared, his stomach was but a head-reach away. No choice, but with haste, Tarl wrapped the cord around the wrists.

"You will have to run far away, boy," the priest whispered. Tarl felt a chill on his stomach skin. "For the Church will extract their payment one way or another, be sure of it. You can never return home. Not now. I know what you have done, and I will not... be.... silenced."

"If anything happens to what remains of my family, I will know where to look. I will not be silenced either, for I will shout to the whole world which priest broke the faith. Broke those Treaties she was talking about." Tarl replied through gritted teeth, as he tied the belt into a knot at the base of his palms.

Holding the hands firmly above the creature's head, Tarl leaned in. The grey pallor seemed pinker and Tarl's lips tightened.

The Father's eyes shifted to the side, searching to meet his, although his skull could not move. Tarl held a suspicion that were he to connect with the priest's gaze, there would be a shift in the balance of power. Also, she'd warned him specifically not to look into the Father's eyes.

"Is that a risk you want to take?" Tarl said. "I don't see you have much choice in the matter right now but to keep your silence."

"You. Saw. Her." The Father enunciated, "and a Christian like you knows she's an abomination. Such a creature needs to be dealt with by the proper authorities."

Tarl wrinkled his nose; he was not like this priest either.

"Take her... to the Bishop of Norwich," The Father whispered. "In England."

"What on earth for?" Tarl had not fully considered what to do about her presence on these islands. And, she was the only other who knew of the sins he had committed. Could he trust her to stay quiet about it? Could he trust Father McTavish?

In a voice that was almost normal, commanding even, the

Father said, "The Bishop will know what to do… He will reward you for your services. He might even say a Mass for your mother, as thanks for bringing a fae spy to the attention of the Church. A Church which protects its flock. A faith that endures all challenge. And that can guarantee the souls of those who follow the righteous path will go to Heaven. That is the price for my silence and your soul, Tarl Smytheson."

Could he trust a man of the cloth, even when he was also not human? Tarl wavered, his hands pausing in tightening the knot as he contemplated. In the last hour, everything he thought he knew had been turned on its head. Yesterday, he would not have considered himself a thief, or a would-be killer.

That damned girl. She'd caused this situation. Delayed him. Made him commit worse sins than those which he'd been prepared for.

The only sliver of hope lay in if Father McTavish spoke the truth; that more senior Church leaders could deal with her and absolve his mother of her sin as well. The prospect offered comfort.

The priest's hips jerked underneath him, startling him from his thought process. Tarl had to do more than tie him up. Perhaps again, she was right; the priest had to be trapped so Tarl could escape. Buy himself some time. To think. To work out who was right.

"Why hesitate, boy? Free me, heal me, and we can both claim the prize," the thing hissed. Its legs twitched as they tried to get purchase on the slippery slabs underneath them.

To heal this priest meant certain death, if 'feeding' was involved. If the girl was right, again.

Tarl stretched his leg back, over the top of the cassock, pinning the limbs down. Holding scrawny wrists with one hand, Tarl pushed himself on his other leg, into a stand, dragging Father McTavish up with him. Then he stepped back, pulling the rope bindings closer to the ankles. A horrible, grating sound turned his stomach as the Father's head lolled forwards; disjointed bones rubbed bones, then hung, still, at that twisted, broken angle.

He looped the ends of the rope belt around the creature's scrawny ankles, fingers knotting as fast as they could to hog-tie the torso. He suspected it would only delay his captive, but it was the best he could do with such little help. As soon as a final knot was complete, he straightened, holding the belt in a tight grip.

The priest weighed as much as a man his size ought, but Tarl's broad chest and strong biceps lifted the priest clear from the ground. With a grunt at the effort of carrying the body, specifically its head, far away from his own person, Tarl staggered up the pathway. A lifetime wielding a hammer and bow added to the adrenaline coursing through his muscles, making short work of the few steps back to the church. He kicked open the door with his foot.

The priest's eyes flew open, his grey lips rasped something unrecognisable. An enchantment, Tarl wondered, as a chill of fear swept over him. He listened again in the stillness of the room. The priest mumbled in Latin, a verse he recognised from many a Mass, and Tarl breathed a little easier.

"'*Cognovit Dominus qui sunt ejus*,'" the Father repeated. "The Lord knows who are his, as Paul told Timothy. Go to England. Advise the Bishop, Father McTavish sent you, and hand her over to be dealt with," the priest said, louder this time. "Tell no-one else what you have seen but him. Perform this service, keep the faith, and your tainted soul - and your mother's - can be saved."

It was as if this priest knew the torment upon his soul which Tarl suffered, yet kept buried. Tarl considered that perhaps by having entered holy ground, the priest was regaining his strength and recovering faster than any normal person ever would.

There was nothing about this situation which could save his own soul now. He glanced down at the brown clothed bundle dangling from his hands, trussed like a pig ready for the spit. By doing this, he was surely destined for the fires of Hell. Tarl gritted his teeth as he hastened through the dark, cool building. Deal with one problem at a time, and what happened to his soul upon his death was something he could consider when he was safe.

His cargo fell silent, but that didn't mean he'd died, Tarl now knew.

The small room to the back of the chapel seemed most appropriate as a gaol. Windowless, barely more than a cupboard, the only thing left in it was the altar-cloth and some cleaning rags. This was where he had found the silver, the very items which led to this predicament and his downfall. He wished he'd not been tempted; the cruelty of hindsight gnawed at him but he pushed it away. Emotions were for weaklings, and he needed to focus on the present.

He flicked the latch up with his knee, then hooked the door open with his boot. As the wood creaked open, he tossed his burden in as soon as the aperture was wide enough. He didn't stop to see where the flung priest ended its skid across the flagstones, but shoved the door closed. The latch clicked down, but it wouldn't be enough if the thing got free of its ties. Tarl rushed to the altar and, with both hands, pushed the heavy cupboard over, blocking the Father in.

After crossing himself in the vain hope of forgiveness, he ran out of the church. He paused in the doorway to throw the silverware back into his sack, then tied the drawstring ends to his belt. Tarl's head throbbed as he straightened, right where his skull made contact with the frame. As he rubbed the sore, he glanced around, weighing up his choices.

He could, despite the threats the Father made, go home and

pretend nothing had happened. For a while, until a better plan could be devised. His mother's soul would still be in limbo, and, even if he melted down and sold the silver as planned, it wouldn't cover the debt for his mother's burial and reparations from her trial. But, Father McTavish would eventually escape, find him, and nothing would have improved. Very probably life would get much, much worse. He would have to leave anyway.

If he could find the girl, and take her to the Bishop as the Father had suggested… He might not be able to return home, but at least the debt would be wiped clean. Masses could be said for his mother. God would rest her soul in peace then.

But England was a long way from home. Tarl had never been further than the mainland of Orkney before. Few people did. And taking a captive? Especially one as unpredictable as her? As odd as a girl with wings? A fae, was she called?

Tarl rolled his eyes. He didn't entirely trust the Father, but for all of his eighteen years, he had trusted in the Church. Believed in its righteousness, the teachings of compassion, and of trusting in the Lord to choose the right path. Until today, nothing had given him cause to question it. Not even his mother's death wavered his faith. He glanced towards her grave, as if she could reassure him that he had done the right thing.

His mouth dropped open. The mound was covered. Not with snow, for that had long since melted under the heat of the tussle, but, right in the middle where the girl had ploughed her fingers into the ground, blooms as blue as her eyes trailed across the bump. Tiny flowers with flashes of hopeful yellow in their centres.

Forget me nots.

"As if I ever could," Tarl muttered under his breath. "Or anything about this day." He searched in the direction she went, but the horizon was empty. His heart thudded when, from inside the church, he heard a howl.

He had to find her. Fast. And deal with her before she could cause any more trouble.

CHAPTER 7 – BEACHED

As Aioffe limped away, heading for the coastal path which dropped steeply to the sea, she grimaced. The pain in her ankle irked with each step, compounded by increasingly irritating pangs of guilt. She shouldn't have left Tarl on his own.

He was strong. But human.

He had been warned, she argued with herself. He had no clue about what he was dealing with. An ancient vampire. Not that she really knew much about them either. Her life thus far, all several hundred years of it, had been spent in the exclusive company of Fae. An expert is only someone who knows one more thing than the next person, and she knew vampires recovered quickly, moved fast, and lived forever. They were always hungry for blood. Any blood. The Sation wars had taught the Fae that.

She should have stayed. Helped. Solved the dispute.

Tarl was a temptation; that was the heart of the problem.

The scent of his Lifeforce when he had surged forward to protect her, while she was trying to defend him, had almost overwhelmed her. Suddenly, the urge to pull it from him had grown too much to bear. She knew her body needed Lifeforce to heal, and thus solve her quandary about getting home, yet her heart and head held her back from giving in to the craving. A craving unlike anything else she had ever experienced. To draw as much Lifeforce as she required would take a beast of approximately human size, but she could not bring herself to ally with a vampire. To do what that horrible priest suggested and get rid of their mutual witness by feeding from him seemed wrong. Unfair. Tarl had tried to help her, and all she craved, with an ache which had engulfed her entire body, was his essence.

He might have satisfied both of us, her ankle throbbed in answer, searing through her attempts to quell its nag. Maybe, if she was at full strength, she could have prevented the vampire from taking his deadly share.

Maybe not.

The human's life was not hers to toy with though. "I am not that person," she muttered, setting her sights on the horizon. "I will not be."

She tripped and fell abruptly, sprawled once again on the turf. Goodness, this land was bumpy. Her wings fluttered in response but they only reminded her of their uselessness. Aioffe put her head up, pursed her lips, and looked out to the choppy sea ahead of her.

Aioffe stood, trying not to bear weight on her ankle. Her hands, thighs and chest dripped from the mist which rolled across from the Sound, dampening the grassland beneath as dusk fell. Why hadn't she grabbed her costume when she left? 'Foolish child,' her mother's voice echoed in her mind. But clothing had been the last thing on her mind; getting away from the temptation of Tarl seemed more important.

"A fish will have to do. Or a crab," she told herself. Or perhaps a seal. Yes, a nice, fat seal. That might be big enough.

They were sloppy things, seals, and she had experienced her share of them on Naturae. She sighed. Boring to watch and hard to hunt. As prey, they were likely to slide off their rocks and swim off under the water at the first sight of a fae, like many animals. Their blubber made calming them slow to take effect. If you could avoid it swimming away for long enough to land on it's back, it was harder still to keep a hold of it whilst you fed.

They also were very lazy with little playfulness about them, unlike dolphins, but there were none of those around at this time of year. More's the pity. She tentatively hopped another step forward. The Lifeforce from a dolphin pod would be very helpful and didn't taste as terrible or greasy as most marine creatures.

"Hey!"

She spun about. Tarl loped towards her. He bore a tight smile on his face, which she took to be a good sign. "I did as you suggested. Tied him up."

Oh goody. Finally, someone took her advice.

Aioffe turned back to face the sea and stepped forward again. "Ooow."

Stupid ankle. She balled her fingers and limped ahead.

"You're still hurt!" Tarl said, closer now. Almost behind her.

"Well, yes," Aioffe snapped. Another step.

"Let me help."

Another step.

"Please," he said, entirely unaware that his presence alone was an added complication. "Lean on me, if you like."

She glanced aside, noticing the brawny arm he proffered was covered in thin blond hair. He beckoned again with it, and she caught a whiff of his sweat. Earthy, with a note of fear still present. Rather alluring, in fact.

She shook her head; damp hair straggled around her chin. "I'm fine. I just need…" How could she tell him she needed a seal? Or needed him. What might he think of her then?

"Look, you are clearly not 'fine'. Neither am I," he said, somewhat stiffly. "We must leave this island quickly. Whatever you are, whatever those are," his eyes glanced behind to her wings, "it doesn't appear they work. I've secured Father McTavish in the Church, but I'm not sure for how long."

"Are you here to save me then?" Aioffe tried, and failed, to keep the sarcasm from her voice.

"Err…"

"Escort me home? Or perhaps drop me off at the nearest place where you can swap me for some coins?"

Economic systems mystified her. She thought they used coins, as a way to barter for goods, but wasn't sure. Humans did use slaves, though; her mother told her so. She hoped the thought hadn't occurred to him.

"Hang on there, lady. Look," Tarl said, with crossed eyebrows and tight lips, which suggested he had taken offence. "I don't make a habit of stealing, you know." He kept looking away from her, as if her nakedness offended him.

"So the Father was wrong then? Those pieces of silverware you made sure to bring with you are yours, are they?" Use of sarcasm as a way to get rid of him wasn't working, as he appeared to be oblivious to it.

Tarl looked down at the sack in his hand. "As we have to run away, selling this might give us a head start."

"Who said anything about running?"

"Well, limping in your case, I suppose."

Aioffe huffed then rolled her eyes. "Again, you don't understand. There is no 'we' in running. Only 'you' who should run. I fly." And she took another step forward. And another.

"Then you'll drop like a conker." He had the audacity to smirk - she caught it on the side of his mouth as he stared at the turn beneath. "Your wings are holier than my fishing net. There's no way off the island except by crossing the sea. Even if you could swim, you'd probably sink in the waves of the Sound. At which point, I, from my boat, will feel obliged to hook you out."

Aioffe glanced at him. He had a boat? Of course, how else could he have come to this island? She would have slapped her own face if it wouldn't have made it so obvious that she had been naïve.

"No-one else would pick out something as…" He paused,

staring at her face for a moment. "Peculiar... ly... pale, as you."

Aioffe burst out laughing. "Because my paleness is the odd thing about me, is it?"

Tarl flushed. "I meant.. What I meant to say was…" His eyes dropped, lingering just long enough on her legs for her to understand he didn't see many bare women.

"I'm pale, and should get some clothes on?" Aioffe teased. He was too easy to bait.

Tarl strode away. She smiled to herself, but limped a little faster behind him.

CHAPTER 8 – SEAL

Insufferable, that's what she was. Pale. Odd. Naked to boot. The sooner he reached Mark the Taff's boat, got away from here, the better. Perhaps the Father had been right - this Bishop of Norwich might know what to do with her, because he certainly didn't. He couldn't just let her wander around Wrye. Going back for her dress risked running into the priest again. Tarl wondered if there he could find an old blanket in Taff's boat. Something, anything, to wrap about her body to hide the nakedness. Her wings. And her nakedness. The strangeness of her.

Until today Tarl had never seen a girl unclothed before. His memory of fumbling two Christmas's past with 'Nancy from the mainland' reassured him that wings on shoulders were not normal in women. Nothing had been normal for a long time though, with the loss of his Da as a child, then his mother's troubles and death more recently. Most especially, the events of today would count as Not Normal.

His stride lengthened again. This fae-creature was going to cause him trouble. He could feel it in his bones.

"Wait!" She called, then he heard an ooph sound. He spun around, heart thumping. Had the vampire priest caught up with them already? He'd done everything he could to grant them a bit more time to escape.

His lips tightened as he looked through the thin mist and saw her white body sprawled. Head down on the turf. No-one behind her, or worse, on top of her. Her hair fell about her features as she pushed herself up. Why was she smiling? He frowned; how could a person so graceful in curves be so utterly clumsy as to face-plant on a flat field? He stomped back. "Honestly, for someone in a hurry to leave, you dawdle."

She giggled as he helped her upright. "I'm just not used to walking. Limping."

Goddammit, but her eyes were amazingly blue. A man could get lost in them. Bewitched. And her skin, it was so warm and soft.

She said, "It's not that I wanted to leave you particularly. Just… that situation."

Tarl rolled his eyes. The situation! As if he wished to stay here and lose his life as well. "The boat isn't far. Try not to damage yourself any further."

He took her elbow, but she jerked it away.

Fine. That was fine with him. The less he touched her, the less she could affect him.

His feet crunched the pebbles at the top of the wide bay, lapped by waves. The tide was coming in fast, about to turn. The seals which lounged on the larger rocks ahead brayed.

"Hurry up," he called impatiently over his shoulder.

Tarl guessed she was behind him as he heard her make a sort of mewing sound. Pain he presumed, as she walked barefoot over the shale whereas he was still appropriately dressed and shod. He set his mouth and ploughed on. He rounded the largest outcrop of boulders, ignoring the whiskered grey seal above the boats' hiding place, which snorted at him as he stomped. A pup, still growing out its white fur, glanced at him with doleful black eyes from the base of the seaweed covered stones.

Reaching the small sailing boat he had pushed up the beach this morning, he stepped into the hull and rummaged for a covering.

Finding a rough blanket stuffed underneath a bench seat, he shook it out over the side. Sand and shingle clouded around him as he snapped it back and forth. Brown and stained with god-knows-what, the cover would have to do until he could find her some clothes. The seal pup flopped down the beach, into the corner of his eye-line. Tarl sighed, hoping it would continue into the sea before he had to push the boat out. He didn't want to tangle with its mother; although grey seals were generally docile, this pup still looked just about young enough to need her protection.

A bray from the rocks behind made him spin around. The girl sat astride the mother seal.

"Get down!" Tarl ordered.

She ignored him, her wings fluttered half risen. Tarl dropped the blanket, jumped out of the boat and strode to the base of the stone. The seal brayed again, flapping its tail and jerking about its unwanted passenger. Tarl's heart sped. What on earth was she doing? The beast could flick her off at any moment.

He shouted as the animal's tail wriggled in the air, "Leave it alone! Come down!" Her leg, swollen with the injured ankle just by his head, squeezed the seal tighter.

"Quickly, before it bucks you off!"

She bent closer to the seal's neck. Her cheeks lay on its fur as her hands stroked its head. It seemed to calm as she hugged it. The tail flopped back down to the rock with a slap, and she smoothed her fingers in a caress down its side. Tarl's face screwed in confusion.

Her wings rose higher. He blinked, unsure if what he was seeing could be true. Beating increasingly faster, the down-draft pushed the hair from around his face back. The wings, before limp and shredded and no threat at all, were now fully extended. Like a butterfly's, they dwarfed her body. The translucent panes seemed to glisten before his eyes, their holes shrinking as his eyelids battled the draft. Tarl gasped. Even in the low dusk light, the girl and her luminescent wings transfixed him, as if she had some opalescent glow.

What kind of magic was this? So beautiful, yet, so strange.

Tarl shook his head, hoping the vision would disappear. Instead, a dreadful thought dropped into his mind - what if, like a butterfly, she could now fly away? Leaving him with an angry, injured Father McTavish, evidence of his crimes and his soul still to pay for.

He grabbed her knee and pulled.

CHAPTER 9 – SETTING SAIL

Tarl's fingers wrapping around her leg jolted Aioffe out of the feed. When he yanked, she was still too distracted by the seal's Lifeforce to resist him.

She squealed as she tumbled into his arms. Her wings instinctively fell flaccid to avoid further injury as he then stepped back. He neatly rolled her closer to his chest, side-stepping the falling seal which her legs dragged down with her. She glanced over as the animal bounced with a splat on the wet sand beneath. As it rolled onto its back, it barked. It raised its head at her, furry fins waved as it struggled to flip its blubber back over. They studied one another for a heartbeat, before her lips muttered, "Go with thanks" at it.

Tarl's arms tightened around her, then the seal jerked, twisting over onto its stomach. It flopped slowly, lazily almost, down the beach towards its pup without a backward glance. Aioffe's head dropped to the leather jerkin he wore, woozy from the Lifeforce still, but smiling.

She could hear his racing heartbeat, oddly mistimed with her own surging rhythm, yet somehow reassuring. His strong hands clasped her body, warm and firm against her skin. At this moment, when most vulnerable after feeding, she felt protected. His intervention, pulling her off the seal, should have triggered her into a frenzy, as it did when most fae were interrupted when feeding, but it was safe and warm here in his arms.

The sanctity of his embrace calmed her, and she

acknowledged there had been no need to keep taking. There were plenty of other seals to build herself back with. Leaving enough for the animal to live with still, and being happy with only that, was a sensation which was new to her. Besides, there had been no malice in Tarl's actions, only protection.

Just as her eyelids fell, a falling sensation jolted them back open. Her elbow banged on something as Tarl unceremoniously dropped her into cold seawater. She yelped as slimy wetness sloshed around her bare behind. Her skin prickled with revulsion, then her nose. The stink of rotten fish guts assaulted her, instantly turning her stomach and reminding Aioffe of where she was.

As she pushed herself up, Tarl's hand clamped her wrist. "Sorry about this," he said, as he wrapped a thin rope about her hand. "But I can't take any chances."

"What do you mean?" She blazed, and tried to take her hand back. "I'm not going to eat you."

Not now, anyway. Any lingering, warming effect of his embrace waned. She hadn't had quite enough Lifeforce to completely heal, but perhaps he wasn't to know that. Her ankle still throbbed and there were still holes in her wings, but time would cure those ills, if another feed didn't in the meantime.

He grabbed her other hand and pinned her wrists together. Not painfully, but firm enough to show her he believed he had no other choice. Perhaps he didn't, Aioffe thought, confused.

It was too late to protest further; in the blink of an eye, he had knotted the cord. Tarl stood, unravelling the hemp binding from its coil. He stepped over to the tall pole sticking up from the middle of the boat, and wrapped the other end of the rope around it. He crouched, knotting, and muttered, "Taffy, I caught a big one." After a deep sigh, he shook his head. "God, I wish you could see it. Maybe you'd know what to do."

"Who's Taffy?"

Tarl turned on his heel, grabbing a brown piece of fabric from the side of the boat as he did. "A friend," he said. "It's his boat. Cover yourself before you scare any more seals."

Although it smelled of many strange effluences, his offering would be warmer at least. With her hands restrained, Aioffe struggled as she took the blanket and tried to flap it suitably over herself. Pulling her knees up underneath, she asked, "Why have you restrained me?"

Tarl's mouth tightened. "So you don't fly off on the way." He stepped over the boat side.

"So you've taken someone else's boat, to take someone else's silver." Aioffe's brow furrowed. "And now you want to take me somewhere?"

"Yes," he answered as he walked to the pointed end of the boat.

"Why?" Aioffe raised an eyebrow. "What for?"

"Because." Then he leant into the prow and pushed.

"Why won't you tell me?"

He grunted, but the boat shifted down the sand a little. "Because," he panted.

The effort of pushing them down the beach was perhaps preventing him from elaborating. Still, at least she could rest awhile now, to allow her ankle and wings to heal completely. It wasn't like she could fly anyway. Or anywhere she wanted to fly to. No-one knew where she was, and no-one could find her here, hidden under a blanket. Despite everything that had happened today, she felt comparatively safe, and in need of recuperation. She nestled down, head on the side of the boat and waited for the rise and fall of the waves with a smile.

A boat! She was on an actual human boat!

*****

Aioffe awoke to the pitch black of night and the sound of retching. Somehow, in the deep meditative state which fae slipped into occasionally, she'd slid down into the bottom of the boat and ended up curled in the slop. She made to put her hands down to push herself clear, but the rope chafed on her wrist. She breathed in sharply, wincing as she bent her head to pull on the cord with her teeth.

Tarl's retching continued as she tugged, then, just as she released the knot, the boat pitched to one side. Goodness, had it been lurching like this all night? Aioffe brought her hands up to her head, disorientated for a moment as the vessel tipped the other way. On the mast, rope holds clinked against each other, and the sail, now high up the pole, flapped briefly and filled again.

From the back of the boat, she heard the thud of limbs knocking on wood. Her eyes shot over - catching sight of Tarl mid-stumble at the far end of the vessel. His hand, white fingered, clenched a pole sticking up. As the boat tipped once again, he reached with the other hand for the side. He gripped the rope attached to the sail as he bent over. That awful noise again as his stomach convulsed, then fluid leaked out from his mouth. His face was ashen in the faint glow of moonlight. She frowned as he pulled his sleeve across his face, then leant back into the wood.

Was this usual behaviour for humans at sea? It looked and sounded unpleasant.

"Are you ill?" Aioffe called over. The boat keeled sideways again, her legs tensed against the tilt.

He mumbled, "No," as he turned his back to her, splaying his legs for balance as he clung to the pole. She stood, wavering for a moment as her senses adjusted to the pitch and roll of the waves. A wind had risen, stronger than she would have been comfortable flying through, and more than enough to fill the light brown sail. The breeze brushed a chill over her skin as she scanned the empty rolling water. Aioffe remembered his avoidance, maybe a discomfort, at her nakedness, so pulled the blanket around herself before walking up the boat.

They must have travelled far thorough the night, as no landmarks were in sight. The expanse before them suggested there was much further to go with the boyman before they hit land again. She felt a flush of annoyance that she had missed some of the journey as she stepped over the benches, holding the boat side as it lurched again.

Tarl moaned. His head hung low, but still he clung to that rod.

She laid a hand on his shoulder. "Is there a problem with the boat?"

He jerked away from her. "No," he growled. He pulled on the sail rope and the sheet filled with the wind once more.

"Then what is it? Why were you making those noises? And that liquid spurting out from your mouth?"

His back stiffened but he didn't answer. His brows furrowed as he noticed her freedom of movement, yet it was clear he was in no state to restrain her again.

"Is there anything I can do to ease you?" Tentatively, her fingers touched his shoulder once more, trying to understand the complexities she saw in his Lifeforce.

She wasn't entirely sure why she bothered offering - her healing skills were hardly well developed compared to a witch's, for example, or so she'd been told. But, she was stuck here, with him, somewhere on the sea, so it seemed like a sensible thing to at least suggest, even if her chances of success in curing him were admittedly slim.

He cleared his throat, then provided a strangled sounding, "No thank you."

Aioffe nodded and removed her hand from his shoulder. She

had offered.

*****

Dawn broke and still Aioffe had no idea where they were heading. The foul liquid ceased from pouring from Tarl's mouth as the skies lightened. He remained stern faced by the pole, gazing out to the horizon and only occasionally glancing through tense brows at her. She lounged against the edge of the boat, enjoying the motion as it danced over the waves. Her skin tingled as the breeze brushed over her face while she watched the birds. She longed for their freedom to soar, but her own wings were still healing; more sustenance and time would be required before she could join their airborne acrobatics again. When she saw a flock of herring gulls circling ahead, she noticed Tarl tilted the rod. The boat's direction altered and before long, in the distance, a craggy land appeared on the horizon.

"Where do you take us?" She called out, watching a lighter cast spread across his face.

"England," he replied.

Aioffe's heart soared - England was part of the realm of Naturae and, until this experience, had been too far away for her to reach in one day's flight. A map of the Fae realm, scuffed and worn from many feet walking upon it, was inlaid on the floor of the Great Hall. When she had been allowed in to this heart of power in the citadel's palace, the faded shapes and tones of the wooden shapes had always intrigued her. The names of the areas and the Fae Elders who governed them were familiar, although she had yet to visit them. Regretably, for the last few centuries, the Elders appeared only infrequently at Court, and rarely spoke to her of their lands.

"Where exactly?" She asked.

"Never you mind," Tarl grunted. She had the sense that he

was also unsure of their precise location.

As they skirted the coastline for some hours, his lips crusted and dried with thirst. The skies overhead clouded then cleared, bathing Aioffe in cool sunlight. The wind kept their speed steady, progressing them south. She grew used to the adjustments he made with his ropes, innately understanding how he applied the wind and sail to push the vessel across the water, much like she coasted when high in the skies. Unlike flying, the closer to land they drew, the faster the boat's progress. The wind whipped her hair, reminding her of how strong the blusters could be at this time of year.

As the sun lowered over the seas behind them, Tarl's stoic stance seemed to tire. His back hunched and she realised his knees shook. Aioffe approached him.

"Why not let me have a go?"

His head turned to her with a vacant expression, as if he were somewhere else in his mind. She inhaled, tasting his tangible but weakened Lifeforce. "You should rest," she murmured. Humans needed to do that, and Tarl was exhausted.

His voice croaky as he rolled his shoulders back and shook his head. "Can't."

"Can't or won't?"

"Won't. What could you know about sailing?"

"I've watched you all day. It seems simple enough. You need to keep the wind in the sheet by holding it firm with that rope. You steer with that pole."

Tarl blinked.

"It's not so different from flying," she added. "And I've plenty of experience at that." She adjusted the blanket wrapped around her, securing the edge underneath her arms so it wouldn't fall off with movement. Her wings relaxed against her back inside the tube of fabric.

He must have been too tired to argue. His hand shook as he

proffered the sheet. "Show me first."

Aioffe turned and stood next to him, wrapping her fingers around the rope. The sail remained full but, as he let go, she realised just how fierce was the wind propelling them. Her arm muscles tensed and her slim frame leaned against the rear of the boat. She glanced down at his arms, wondering how he had managed to hold on for so long. Biceps far larger than she had ever seen on a fae answered her unspoken question. Tarl then shook his arm out, clenching and unclenching his fingers.

They stood in silence, watching the sail and her slight adjustments to keep it filled. A few miles later, he said, "Take the tiller."

Leaning across, she wrapped her fingers around the warmth of where his grip had been and stared straight ahead. He waited for a moment next to her as she leant on the rudder to turn the boat, then straightened its course again. He nodded, and her cheeks flushed with his approval. She turned her head so he wouldn't see her rapid blinking. It wasn't often she felt appreciated, or could be of use, so this moment was one to treasure.

Tarl then lumbered down the boat and collapsed onto the deck between a willow basket contraption and some netting. Closing his eyes, his head tipped against the side and within seconds, his breathing had relaxed. The strands of Lifeforce she saw around him slowed their dance and the greyness about him faded. She smiled and tilted her body back so the wind caught her hair. This was almost like flying, and she loved to fly.

CHAPTER 10 - A DISTANT, DIFFERENT LAND

Tarl awoke with a jolt. Heart thudding against his chest as his body accounted for the vessel's steep lean as it sped across the water. He scrambled to his feet, then grabbed the boat edge. At the tiller, the girl-thing grinned wildly, her face tilted skyward. Her long blonde hair streamed behind her, waving in the wind, and her expression was as close to ecstatic as he had ever seen anyone's. She wasn't even looking where she was going.

He jerked around, eyes frantically scanning the landscape they skirted. Entirely unfamiliar, he had absolutely no idea where they were, or how far they had travelled. He huffed away his annoyance at having slept for too long; another mistake he'd made on top of everything else. The sun hung low across the sea, blushing the sky a deep pink. His stomach lurched, empty. How long since he had eaten? Tarl's jaw clenched; there was nothing on this boat, not even fresh water. They would have to land to find something to eat; perhaps then he could figure out where they were as well.

"I'll take over," he said. He tried to walk as steadily up the timbers as he could, lurching despite his best efforts.

The girl opened her eyes. Disappointment sagged her shoulders as she silently passed him the mainsail line.

"We'll land soon," he offered as consolation. The prospect cheered him greatly until he cast his eyes over her attire. His lips pursed. "I'll have to find you something to wear." Clothes were valuable items. He hoped he could sell enough of the silver to cover the cost of suitable fabric but it was by no means a certainty, not to mention the tailoring. Even though she had said she could sew, creation of garments took time. He sighed. Perhaps he'd have to hunt down a washing line.

"I'm warm enough. I can walk in this covering." Leaving him with the tiller, she walked away as if she had been at sea her entire life.

She completely misunderstood his quandary. "No. You'll have to remain in the boat."

A half naked woman was bad enough, but what would happen if the blanket shifted and people saw those wings? The memory of holding her bare skin in his arms slipped into his mind. How soft it had been, how smooth. Tarl shook his head, hoping the recollection would dissipate before his heartbeat sped up too much. "And stay covered."

Her face fell.

"I'm sorry," slipped out of his mouth before he could stop it. Deliberately gruff, he said, "I'll have to secure you again."

Not that it would make much of a difference, he supposed. The girl could clearly manage knots and ropes, and he doubted Taffy kept manacles aboard.

"For your own safety," he added. "If they saw you, most people wouldn't know what to do with... someone like you."

Her eyes widened. "Peculiar people, you mean."

Tarl nodded, then glanced towards the land. "Here we wear clothes. Skirts. A bodice. A blanket is not clothing."

"I know. I tried to copy the style as best I could." She sighed. "It took me hours and hours. I should have grabbed my skirt back, at least, before I left you." She raised her eyes to his. "I'm sorry too. For leaving you with him."

Tarl's lips tightened. "The Father told me what to do with you."

"And what is that?" She laughed, almost mockingly, and the blanket slipped off her shoulder.

Her naked body, glowing, flashed into his mind. Protecting him.

Taunting him. Tempting him.

Repulsing him, Tarl reminded himself. He must get rid of her. "I'll take you to a higher authority than that 'thing' was."

Her eyebrows shot up her forehead as she pulled the covering back up. "You will?" Then she laughed. "I don't think so."

"And why not?"

"I don't want to go." She shrugged. "I'll just… fly home."

"If you could have, or had done, in the first place, then neither of us would be in this mess," Tarl said. He knew it wasn't fair to blame her, but anger and hunger rushed up. "But no, you had to get involved. Had to."

"I'm not the one who was doing anything wrong." Her gaze shot pointedly to the bag of silverware he had taken with her lips pursed. With a little cock of her chin, she turned to look away from him as if she were superior. Or a child.

Tarl breathed through his nose, gritting his teeth as he restrained a retort.

"Oh, look! A castle!" She pointed. "Which one is that?"

Tarl followed the direction of her finger, still huffing to himself. He shrugged, as it was pointless to pretend his geographical knowledge extended this far away from his home turf. He couldn't see anything, only the vaguest hint of a rise in the landscape ahead. Castles meant Lords. Soldiers.

"One with a gaol. Probably," he muttered. Which was where they would be headed if they got caught - him with stolen silver and her for, well, being odd.

"A gaol?"

"A dark hole where they lock away bad people."

She paled, shrinking into the boat side.

"Peculiar people?" The tremor in her voice told him, and he knew, in that moment, how to contain her. However much he didn't like it, or want to exploit her naivety, the threat might make her comply. He gave a slight nod but avoided her gaze.

Not knowing what she was, or what other secrets and skills she kept hidden, worried him. For all her innocent questions about how society functioned, he was the one who hadn't truly understood what he was dealing with. An unnatural priest who wanted them dead, with the strength of five men. A girl with wings who defied every convention. And himself, a mere, pathetic human, and ill equipped to wrestle with strange beings.

Perhaps, Tarl wondered, being human and with a knowledge of how the world worked was his advantage. He would be wise to try to encourage her compliance. Or, during the journey ahead, she might do something foolish and expose them both.

His threat was only meant to keep her safe until Bishop of Norwich could solve the problem. His problem. And the problem of her. Whatever she was. Immediately his chest tightened, for of course she was still a person. However odd she looked, she talked and felt. Even angels had names.

"What should I call you?"

She stared at him.

"Well? I'm Tarl."

"Smytheson. Yes, I know."

"And you are…"

She hesitated, her blue eyes holding his for a moment. Her name sang like a breath caught in the wind. "Aioffe," which sounded to him like, 'Eefa'.

He recognised the word; one of his father's far cousins had been promised to a girl called with the same name from Ireland long ago. The Irish lass hadn't been at all beautiful or radiant as the name suggested, turning out to be rather cumbersome and stout. Before the wedding the bridegroom boasted, and told tales of a brave warrior princess called Aife, after whom his soon-to-be beloved had been named. After seeing her in the church, other men from his village roared with laughter and joked about using said warrior-wife as a battering ram. The new bride sobbed behind her mousy-brown braids at their cruelty, demanding her new husband take her back to Ireland to settle instead, rather than standing up to the jeers. Tarl had decided then and there never to marry without first seeing his bride.

He glanced around, silently rolling the name in his mouth as he studied this Aioffe. Her face was undeniably pretty, and what did radiant mean if not to glow? She ignored him, statue-like a few feet from him, with her chin jutting towards the sea. With the appendages on her shoulders stilled and covered, she would pass as a normal lass, he thought. He wasn't losing his mind, after all, and hadn't been back on Wrye when he mistook her for an ordinary girl. The observation in the light of day gave him comfort.

Yet, the determination with which she stared at the faintly visible grey mass in the distance cautioned him. This Aioffe could be an altogether different kind of warrior, Tarl realised. She'd been strong enough to sail single-handedly through this wind. She was fierce enough to stand down that thing which threatened him. Threatened them both.

He moved the tiller so the boat headed towards land. His stomach grumbled appreciatively as his mind tossed around the options which a town might provide. A plan formed, finally.

CHAPTER 11 - BEAUMARIS LOOMS

A dark hole Tarl had warned, when he talked about a gaol. Like the Beneath in Naturae. An unforgiving, inescapable cell her mother had frequently threatened to throw her into. Over half a millennium, Aioffe had somehow managed to avoid Naturae's second harshest punishment. Even thinking about that buried darkness made her shiver, for the Beneath was what certainly awaited her after so many days' absence. Had she known the humans used such places as well, perhaps she wouldn't have strayed.

Yet, she would not go back home. Aioffe wrung her hands together. Not ever. Naturae was worse than whatever she would face here. A castle in the trees, hiding a deadly tomb. Living half a life, in perpetuity. She couldn't return. Anywhere was better than there.

The sea formed a bridge between her two worlds; this boat and the wind chasing her ever closer to a different path. Comforted by the expanse of empty air and water around her, Aioffe's eyes narrowed on the stone structure ahead. Far larger than any broch or building she had seen in the islands near to Naturae, circular towers crowned each corner as well as bulged from the middle of the high walls. Inside the outer barricades, yet more turrets rose, tall enough to overlook the sea and town beneath. The castle wasn't on a hill so much as being the hill. She wished she could fly above it to see the shape of the construction, and to wonder at it. Also, to identify where a gaol might be hidden. She shuddered; suddenly, the idea of approaching land seemed less appealing.

"I've had a thought about your clothes," Tarl called over.

She turned, her mind still preoccupied by the notion of being trapped.

Tarl unbuttoned his jacket; her eyes widened as he then whipped his beige undershirt over his head. Tossing it to her, he said, "Put that on, and tidy your hair somehow."

Bemused and made dumb by the sight of his naked, muscled chest, Aioffe picked up the garment. She longed to ask him to turn around, that she might see how smooth his back was, unadorned by wings, but then remembered his prudishness. Dragging her eyes down, she shook the linen then held it arms length. Even from that distance, the smell of old sweat, tinged with the acidity of the mouth-fluid, assaulted her. Her nose wrinkled, but he glared at her. "No clothes, no leaving the boat with me."

The prospect of being left alone, unable to explore and without protection from the gaol, emboldened her. As she pulled the shirt over her head, letting the blanket drop when the garment covered her, she realised it was, in essence, a dress. Much like those worn by worker fae, leather laces fastened at the neck to draw in the head-hole. The fabric, stiff with dried spray, fell shapelessly over her body. Looking over her shoulder, Aioffe was relieved to see the voluminous shift reasonably camouflaged the outline of her appendages. Tarl's height meant the garment reached her calves.

She glanced up to catch him nodding approval, then he pulled his jacket back on. "It's better than the blanket," he said. "You still look half naked, mind." He tutted, then muttered under his breath, "At least it hides the main problem."

Oh, for her needle and thread! She could turn this shapeless shirt into something altogether more flattering, if she had only been prepared. "It's… not quite like what other women wear, is it?" She beamed at him. "But, nothing that can't be fixed, I'm sure."

"Easy for you to say," Tarl grumbled, then jerked his head towards the approaching castle. "And, don't say another word. Let me do the talking."

"But..."

"You draw attention to us!"

Aioffe's mouth dropped at his harsh tone. How dare he! It wasn't as if she had asked to be in this position.

His lips clamped together, and they glared at each other. He blinked first.

"Attention risks capture," he said. "Neither of us wants that. You need to be careful or you'll end up in the castle keep." He jerked his head towards the ever approaching walls.

Aioffe breathed out through her nose, long and slow so he would know she was unhappy.

He continued, "I don't think you understand how peculiar what you are... have... is. Others might not be as forgiving, understanding, as I." He looked steadily at her. "I'm taking you to a place of safety. Where they know what to do with people like you." Then he busied himself with tacking the boat about.

How could she tell him there was no safe place for someone like her? That her life was destined to be a never ending battle of survival, wherever she was? Aioffe sagged against the mast.

"Mind your head! Look, I know you have no reason to trust me," he said grimly, as she ducked to avoid the swinging boom. "But it's obvious you aren't from England. Neither am I. We will both be noticeable, so let me take the lead. That's all I'm asking."

Aioffe nodded. Much as though she disliked it, what he claimed was probably true. She didn't know what she was doing in human society, so she resolved to try and do as he requested. At least until she could blend in more by herself.

CHAPTER 12 – OLD HABITS

Now that they were closer to the castle and the town low in its shadow, Tarl faced a decision. For once, it had nothing to do with Aioffe, and everything to do with his stomach, which ached with emptiness. The sun had already blushed the sky a rose pink, and he did not want to go to sleep on an empty belly. To fill it would require either stealth or coin, neither of which were readily accessible.

Not knowing where he was at the moment posed a problem: strangers in a small town were noticeable. Gossip-worthy. What he would prefer was someone who could use the cup themselves, for it was a shame to melt down such fine workmanship. Perhaps, Tarl considered, sell only the cup now, as metal to be melted down in return for coin. Then, hope the proceeds were enough to last them to a prosperous city where he could trade for the rest of it. Offloading the plunder as soon as possible would be wise, and preferably somewhere that was far from home, so fewer questions might be asked about providence. Acutely aware that he needed as much value from his crime as possible, for there was still a debt to be paid, it meant travelling with items that were obviously not the sort of property somebody lowly like him would own. It was a risk he had to take. In the meantime, he needed somewhere hot enough to melt the cup down into an ingot.

Most towns had forges, and certainly every castle, so there was ample opportunity here he could find one. They sailed past the high walls, with arrow slits dotted at various heights from sea level up all around the towers. The stones alternated in light and dark shades, lending the construction a chequerboard effect. These defences set behind an enclosing moat shouted their domination; within the thick enclosure, an even taller pair of gatehouse towers guarded the inner ward and main castle. It was a masterpiece of design, far more advanced than anything he had seen before - the interior buildings protected the entirety of the outer curtain wall, which in turn defended against attack from both ground and sea.

Rising out of bull-rushed marshes was a fortified tidal dock, which he steered to avoid. The entry point was guarded by a high wall jutting from the land out into the water, ending with a round barbican tower. Narrow windows along the stretch were encouragingly dark inside, and he spotted no soldiers patrolled the long stretches of curtain walls or the thick sea barrier.

As they sailed past, Tarl glanced through to the dockyard itself. A single ship, not much larger than this boat, leaned against a small jetty, half sunk. A huge wooden platform, tucked behind the tower and large enough to hold a catapult, listed in a state of disrepair. Next to the dock, a modest drawbridge ended with a rounded arch doorway. The gatehouse above it crumbled at the top, and the entire structure looked insecure. Although overall the fortifications were by far the largest defensive structures he'd ever seen, the lack of activity inside reassured him. Wherever this castle was, it had suffered an attack in recent years, but at the moment, it appeared to be without an occupying Lord or forces.

There must have been quite some army, he thought, to have defeated such a stronghold. The various skirmishes and wars outside of his local area were often only reported by word-of-mouth months later, if at all. Tarl's confidence waned; who was he, a lowly Orknean, to understand what happened in the far wider world?

The township, tucked in part behind a lower wall with ill-repaired wooden balustrades, which still bore the splinters of assault, was a relative hive of activity. Smoke drifted up into the evening sky, along with shouted orders and bouts of singing. Boats of all shapes and sizes clustered around the shallow port south of the castle, outside the town walls.

As they drew closer, Tarl's quandary resolved and his stomach growled. What better place to slip into and trade than where lots of people were already gathered? "Take the tiller," he said, failing to keep nerves from his voice.

As soon as Aioffe approached, fear widening her eyes, he darted down the boat to ready the drop anchor. "Head for beyond those merchant's vessels."

Mute, for once, she nodded. An incoming tide assisted them in as he dropped the sail, then grabbed an oar to propel the vessel into the shallows, keeping some distance from the other boats. Landing here meant they entered on the edge of town, instead of announcing their presence amid the busy docking area. The boat's hull drifted onto a sandbar and stilled once the anchor stone had splashed down. Tarl picked up his silverware and tossed the sack over his shoulder.

Aioffe's eyes darted towards the cobbled seafront where people busied themselves piling boxes and barrels. Carts were being loaded with sacks and bundles of fabric, followed by bales of hay lashed on top. Shouted orders reached their ears. Further down the stretch of waterside, a black clothed man wrestled with a pair of lithe dark brown horses. To his side, a long sword hung in a scabbard. Tarl noticed a battle between curiosity and fear dance across her face.

"Remember, follow my lead," he said gruffly as he stepped over the side. He held out his hand to help her down, but she hesitated. He added, "I mistook you for ordinary when I first saw you, so will others. As long as you keep your mouth shut and those 'things' still."

She nodded, meeting his eyes, her lips pinched closed. He felt a flash of guilt at appearing so confident when his own shoulders were tight.

They splashed up to the small beach, then headed towards the promenade. A cart barrelled down a muddied track to their left, flour and grain sacks bouncing as the horse stumbled on a dip in the tracks. It recovered as if it had been expecting such an obstacle in its well-trodden pathway. Aioffe shrank away as the wagon trundled past, her arms splayed to keep her balance. Perched on the front, the driver sniggered. "Act normal, will you?" Tarl grumbled. "It's only a miller."

"I'm not used to it, is all," she retorted. She jerked her head up and attempted to strut ahead of him. Then, her ankle twisted on an uneven cobble and she fell, face first and narrowly missing a pile of steaming fresh dung. With a grunt, he grabbed her wrist and hauled her back upright. He noticed, with some satisfaction, that her wing-lumps were barely visible and not twitching. She shook off his hand and pressed her lips together, not looking at him as she stepped forwards.

Passing a row of low thatched houses and a tavern doing a roaring trade, Tarl's mouth set. As they walked past, he caught a man letching at Aioffe's ankles. Tarl pressed nearer to her.

He should have left her in the boat. At least until he had done his business. "Stay close," he warned under his breath as they approached the hub of activity ahead.

As they drew closer to the throng, Tarl realised the dockyard was some sort of muster point. A semi-organised preparation for a battle, or perhaps a show of local strength. He groaned to himself; the last thing he wanted to do was get mixed up in a territorial dispute. What looked like a readying for departure but with no great number of ships meant further boat travel might be unavoidable for them to reach the Bishop of Norwich; his mission would be much harder if they were forced to explain themselves at a road block.

Piles of weapons - spears, swords, pole-axes and battered shields - were haphazardly being sorted through and assessed by a pair of officials in dark red jackets. Pitchforks, poles and poorly maintained bows littered the cobbles, as if found wanting. A few unstrung, longbows, as tall as Tarl and some longer, had been carefully placed on a rack with a padded base to keep them from harm.

Along the entire seafront, people milled about in various states of urgency and sobriety. Some wore high leather boots with smarter jerkins or furs, others clad in farming apparel. Numbering more than the men, clusters of wives gossiped in a language he didn't recognise; their heads shook, eyes following their menfolk whilst they still could. The noise reminded Tarl of his local market back home; food sellers circulated with their wares, and shouts of laughter from the several brew-houses close by punctuated the hubbub. A children's game of chase interrupted an earnest discussion between three fellows who watched their possessions being appraised, earning one boy a clip around the ear and a scolding for the other.

Tarl's eyes darted about, taking in the scene and hoping to be just another man arriving. He glanced at Aioffe. Her attire - his shirt - although better than nothing, was clearly unlike the bodices, warm skirts and other women's wear, and thus more obvious. With ankles and lower leg showing, it was only because she seemed so young and gauche which lent a plausible excuse for her appearance. As long as she didn't speak, he might be able to pass her off as a younger sibling; perhaps one who was too touched by the Devil to be seen in public. It was a half-truth, Tarl thought, given what she had on her shoulders.

Horses had been gathered in an area away from the water's edge; some left harnessed to small farm carts. Others stood already saddled, their reins tied to temporary wooden stands.

Rough furred, shaggy but strong ponies, much like the ones on Orkney, but stouter with long eyelashes. A few taller, riding horses, rolled their eyes with disdain at the barrel-chested drays, munching on a pile of hay.

Tarl's ears pricked at the sound of metal on metal. A young-looking farrier crouched in the middle of the herd. He bashed away with a hand hammer, closing a rein ring on a small, portable anvil. This kind of metalwork rarely required heating, but a farrier would frequent a nearby forge. So where was it?

He paused to peer over the crowd at the line of buildings stretching along the seafront. Thatched and slate roofs blocked his view of the town, but he noticed smoke drifting towards the castle. Charcoal grey puffs, pumped from a forge fire. A tightness he hadn't acknowledged around his chest released and he could breathe again.

"This way." He grabbed her hand so she would not baulk as he led her past the horses. She resisted with her nostrils flared, but he tugged her away. They rounded the end of a stone cottage and looked up the lane. The familiar smell of charcoal and metal being worked filled his nostrils before he saw what he sought opposite the town wall.

A dun horse and a yellow pony stood with their rears backed under the low overhang and heads held in the street. An angry shout burst into the lane. The young boy, stood close to their heads, jumped and dropped the reins. Freed, the pony darted forward, then limped on three legs down the flagstones, unable to put down its back foot. Tarl dropped Aioffe's hand and ran over to grab the straps. A shiny shoe dangled from the pony's raised hoof on a single nail.

Still holding the horse's head, he peered into the depths of the smithy. A rotund, red-faced man hopped around, from pillar to wooden pillar, clutching his foot. More expletives - presumably, as they were in an accent not very familiar to Tarl -

vented from his bushy brown beard. The shoeing hammer on the floor told him part of the story, a shaking, pudgy hand which accepted a flagon from the boy, told him the rest.

"I could finish that calkin shoe," Tarl offered, "if you want?"

"Fuck off," the blacksmith grumbled, more to himself. "Mangy cob needs a bar shoe, but I've run out." With cheeks blackened and raw with sweat, he took a swig before belching. "Bastard beast. It won't be my fault if he throws it before they're even in England." He took another gulp and cast his blurry eyes over Tarl.

"My Da used to call bar shoes the Devil's heart," Tarl shrugged. "But when the beast is burdened with closing hooves, you need one."

The blacksmith belched agreement and put the cup down. He stroked the back of his hand and winced. A cry of pain as he tried to form a fist, and failed. "Probably broken," he said mournfully into his beard, then picked the cup back up.

Tarl put down his sack by a stool, then walked over to the small shoeing hammer. He twirled it in his fingers as he hunted around the open fireplace, searching for the bucket of iron poles he knew every smith had close to hand. Finding a suitable length and width, he poked one end into the coals and pumped the bellows a few times to get them good and hot. He offered, "It wouldn't take long to weld a bar across it, if you've already got the shoe measured?"

The blacksmith glared at him through sooty eyebrows and rubbed his forehead with the flagon's side. He grunted and sagged against the pillar.

When the iron rod was red, Tarl plucked it out using the pincers, put it to the anvil and hammered, drawing the iron out until it was thinner and flat. He held it up and grinned, aware that he had demonstrated he clearly had the skill and know-how to solve the smith's problem.

The boy shot Tarl, then his master, a sceptical glance, but the smith said, "Best get the other horses back to the front, boy". With a dour face, the lad turned, pulled on the reins of the dun horse, and left.

Taking the removal of his apprentice as an invitation, Tarl strode over to the yellow pony, and picked up the offending hoof to have a look. Sure enough, the two ends of the hoof were closing together, pushing against the frog. Drunk though he might be, the blacksmith was right - a calkin shoe, often used on draught horses or for hilly terrains where the projection from the tips would provide grip, wouldn't do much to ease the burden for this beast. Inevitably, if the contracted heels of the hoof weren't supported properly, the horse would fall lame. The bone itself was not in the best of condition, but if the pony was about to undertake a long journey, a limping mount would quickly become a problem for the rider.

Tarl prised the dangling shoe off, then glanced over to Aioffe, who lurked outside the overhang. He gestured his head towards the stool, sometimes used when a blacksmith had to perform lengthier ministrations on a horse's foot than nailing a shoe on. "Have a seat," he muttered. "This won't take long."

She nodded and sat obediently; her eyes strayed around the street. He took the calkin shoe and clasped it between long-handled tongs to thrust it into the glowing embers. Ignoring a baleful stare from the smith, Tarl jiggled the iron and shoe until they were both the white-yellow needed to weld.

By the time he pulled them out, the blacksmith had sunk to the base of the pillar, his exhaustion and stupor rendering him asleep. Tarl used the sledgehammer to bash together the two pieces, forming a straight bar between the two ends of the horseshoe, and flattening the protrusions. Using pincers, he cut the remains of the pole off, then looped the shoe over the anvil point to shape and smooth it. He was so absorbed in hammering and tapping, re-firing, shaping some more, his mind cleared of all else but working the iron.

"Who the hell are you?" A voice interrupted, shouting over the clangs at his back.

Pursing his lips, Tarl continued to hammer the narrow punch to form the dip where the nail holes would be re-punched.

"Get up, Rhys, you tosser!"

Tarl raised his head.

A dark-haired man about his own age kicked the blacksmith on the thigh. Tarl recognised the man with the sword who had been struggling with the beasts on the embankment earlier, but now he realised the fellow was actually dressed to ride into battle, if he could control his mounts. He wore a black studded padded jerkin, with laced on sleeves which ended in fingerless gloves. In one hand, he held the reins of two dark, fine-headed horses. Their hooves clattered as they pranced, reluctant to enter the smokey recess.

Although he didn't want to further upset the horses, Tarl had no choice if the shoe was to be set and saved; he plunged the hot metal into the bucket, steam immediately hissing out as the heat transferred into the water.

The smith coughed, spitting up black phlegm into his beard. "Ap Tudor!" He grunted, then added sarcastically, "My *Lord*. This..." With his uninjured hand, he gesticulated around the smithy, then looked down at his swollen fingers, "is all your fault."

CHAPTER 13 - HEALING TOUCH

Dusk had fallen quickly, and the street outside echoed with the sounds of rousing songs and the ringing of Tarl's hammer.

Ap Tudor didn't even glance at Aioffe as he strode past. His horses reared as he dragged them in behind him, hooves scrabbling in the dirt and air. He yanked sharply on the straps around their heads, but their eyes rolled at her.

Aioffe's senses twitched, and not only from the proximity of prey. Something in the bearing of this arrival's chin, as he berated the fat man on the floor, reminded her of her brother, Lyrus. Entitled and arrogant. She froze. What to do with the sudden invasion of panicked animals and another human to the steamy forge?

When Ap Tudor started shouting, she peered over at Tarl, but he carried on clanging the hot metal as if the fight had no relevance. Her heart skipped a beat as she noticed the sack of silverware close to the dancing hooves. Tarl valued the items, so why wasn't he protecting them?

"It is not my fault you, yet again, cannot keep control of your drinking," Ap Tudor complained. "And now, we've slipped behind in preparations, and it's your lazy, drunken arse to blame."

"It's your family who lost this country to that English King Henry. This is how you make us all pay for it!" The local jeered. "Glendwr will find you, and all your stinking uncles, and dance on your father's grave for what you have committed the men of this town to now!"

Vitriol stirred the smith to his knees. With fingers splayed on the dirt floor for support, he lumbered almost into a stand. Ap Tudor flushed puce with anger and he kicked the steaming bucket from underneath the anvil.

The scalding contents splashed over the smith's hands and feet. He let out a screech, drawing his raw, red paws into his thighs and curled up on the ground once more.

But the noise panicked the horses even more. One reared so high, almost touching the overhead beams, its reins wrenched from the dark-haired man's fingers. As soon as its hooves touched the floor, the other wheeled around, dancing and flinging its head as it made a bid for freedom. Their legs and rears jostled in the cramped interior, banging into the supporting joists of the forge, then rebounding off with a whinny.

The yellow pony which Tarl was preparing a shoe for limped about on the edge of the overhang. As the blacksmith yelped again, the beast's nostrils flared. It flung its head up, yanking the knotted reins as it tried to avoid getting caught up in the tangle of kicking hooves and swishing tails. Unable to free itself, the beast then began to buck!

Aioffe shrank back, trying to put as much space between her and the hooves, but its wide girth blocked the finer mounts inside. The loose pair of dark horses circled each other, tossing their heads. Each sought to bolt, but found their exit thwarted by the restraints of the pony as much as its jerking legs, and her. In their desperation, their dangling leads caught on the hooks and nails running down the pillars and trapped them.

Closer to where the fire spat. Closer to her.

Tarl dropped his tools and shoehorned himself past the carnage, slapping the rump of the pony out of his way in between bucks. He grabbed an overturned bucket as he disappeared around the corner. Aioffe's heart raced - to follow him meant passing the powerful rear quarters of the pony, who now rolled its eyes at her. Hairy lips foamed as it chewed on the metal bit inside its mouth.

"My family paid their amercement in full, which is more than can be said for yours," screeched Ap Tudor. His haughty tone further reminded her of Lyrus's tantrums, which inevitably led to violence.

In the middle of the room, surrounded by chaos, Ap Tudor laughed. "No wonder your wife and children starve. You are the most useless 'smith I've ever had the displeasure of knowing. Even this boy can do a better job than you."

Tools and sacks tumbled to the ground as the highly strung pair tried to free themselves. And still the man stood ignorant of his mounts' growing panic and destruction.

She needed to get out of here before further injury happened.

"And you expect to regain your family honour by rallying for King Henry with Dafydd Gam, after betraying a true prince of Wales? You think that makes up for everything, do you?" The smith spat in the other man's face, cradling his hands in his lap. "You are a fool, like your father, and his father before, boy."

"Ap Tudor will once again become a respected name by this action. You should thank me for the business, not drink away the last chance you'll get to pay your debts. 'Tis a wonder you have escaped the Keep."

All Aioffe could smell and taste was the fear coursing through the horse's Lifeforce. A sourness which physically pained her to sense. As trapped as they, she changed tack. If she could show them she meant no harm, perhaps that avoided the situation worsening. The two arguing humans had ignored her thus far, so Aioffe reached her fingers out to the unsettled horses.

"Hush," she whispered. The beasts backed away, their heads turned sideways to study her with a mistrustful eye. "Hush now." She stepped forward, willing them to calm. Her fingertips twitched - not from wanting to take their Lifeforce, but with her own, ready and waiting. She understood their dread, for she was a predator and they had sensed it from the moment they had been pulled in. Yet all she wanted to do was ease them.

From behind, she heard the smack of flesh meeting flesh, bone upon bone cracking, followed by a yelp. She took another step closer to the horses. Then, more punches found a target. The mares' gaze remained warily on her, even though their master was clearly tussling and the iron tang of spilled blood sprayed into the air. With her fingers outstretched, she focused on reaching the warm fur before the animals inadvertently damaged themselves further.

Just as she touched the wide neck of one, Tarl's blond head re-appeared in her eye line. Their eyes briefly met over the horse's hindquarters. His face paled as they heard the clink of silver being disturbed. He blinked, lips tightened, then strode inside.

Since he hadn't intervened to stop her as she had half expected him to, Aioffe splayed her fingers, running them deep into the fur. She pushed a golden tendril of Lifeforce down. This was the way she subdued her prey before pulling Lifeforce from it, but she did not wish to feed this time, only still. She poured serene images, calm and reassuring, through her mind. Almost immediately, the beast's heartbeat slowed as it relaxed under her influence. Keeping one hand on its quarters for reassurance, she reached for the reins of the other.

Tarl shouted, "That's not yours!"

"Well, that much is obvious!" Ap Tudor sneered. "And it's certainly not his!"

Aioffe turned to see Tarl standing over the smith. Blood pooled in the dirt. Ap Tudor raised a dripping, bloodied fist.

But the smith lay silent. Tarl glared at Ap Tudor, the bucket of cold water redundant. "Stop! He's dead, you idiot."

CHAPTER 14 - BLACKMAIL

The smith certainly appeared as still and silent as if dead, but then, he spluttered and blood red spittle landed on his bushy beard.

"See," said Ap Tudor. "He's fine. Maybe learned a lesson." He rubbed his knuckles.

"And what have you learned?" Tarl snapped. He tipped the bucket of cold water slowly so it trickled over the smith's face and hands. Blood and dirt rinsed off, Tarl cast his eyes over his injuries. Recovery would be long, painful, and immobile, given the likely broken foot from the mare which had kicked him down in the first place. The smith flinched and moaned as his limbs shook under the cooling sensation.

"You've still horses to shoe, and now he's in no fit state to help you," Tarl glared at Ap Tudor. He knelt, grabbed the silverware, and slid them back into his sack while he tried to calm his anger. The smith was lucky to be alive after such a beating.

"If that's your silver… then I must be in the presence of royalty," Ap Tudor said, then kicked Tarl's crouched knee with his boot. As Tarl stumbled, Ap Tudor snatched the bag. He looked pointedly down his narrow nose at Tarl's worn jacket, taking in the absence of shirt and any other finery. "Because you don't look like any priest I've ever seen." His hand fell to the sword hilt, dangling from his belt.

"It's mine," Aioffe called over.

Tarl's head whipped around, his jaw clenched. The three horses stared at him from over her shoulder, their calm, dark eyes signalling a new alliance with the strange girl.

Ap Tudor held the sack close to his chest. "If that is true, my Lady," he said as his gaze fixated upon her bare calves, "then I am a sheep's arse. And believe me, there is no wool being pulled over my eyes. Don't mistake my youth for ignorance. This is stolen property. By whom and from whom, I do not yet know, but it is certainly not yours."

Her face fell, as if she were not used to being challenged about her status.

"It is hers, and she is under my care," Tarl insisted. He could only hope Aioffe wouldn't speak again, in case she somehow inflamed the situation further. Could he grab his sack back without having to hurt anyone, or getting hurt himself? He tested the water by reaching forwards. "And we are leaving with it now."

Ap Tudor grinned. "I don't think so. Either of you." His grip on the sack tightened as he drew it to his chest. His other hand gripped the sword hilt.

"You can't stop us!" Aioffe cried. She untangled the horse's reins from the nails they were caught on.

Tarl's heart thumped as he stood from his crouch.

A slow, assured grin spread across Ap Tudor's face. "Oh, I can, and I will, girl. You are a nobody." Teenage cockiness pasted authority into his stance.

"Who the hell do you think you are to order us about?" Tarl retorted, as he stepped closer to Ap Tudor, fists ready. Sometimes a man is left with little choice but to throw a punch. This may be one of those times.

"I am Lord Owain Ap Tudor," and put his hand on his hip. "Beaumaris, this whole area, is my town. My family's lands, and this," he kicked the smith, who groaned in response, "pillock is my tenant. Which you would know, if you knew anything about our country. But you don't do you, Scot?"

"I have no care," Tarl snarled, raising the only weapons he had. "You behave like a bully with a rotten temper. Hardly befitting the title."

The smith on the floor moaned and curled himself into a ball, as if concurring with Tarl's assessment.

Owain's lip curled. "You see, I know everyone in this town, and I've never seen a girl like that, or someone who isn't a priest, with silverware like this." He waggled the bag in the air. "So, one of you is a thief, possibly both of you. Just a shout from me, and all the men-at-arms gathered around the corner will charge in to my defence." He paused. "Then we'll see whose silver it really is, and who's the one learning a lesson." His eyes glittered with an implicit challenge.

Tarl forced himself to exhale. The young Lord Ap Tudor might be arrogant and violent, but he was not stupid. He wore armour and carried at least one weapon, whereas he was clad in a jacket with nothing but his bare hands. A poker or tongs wouldn't last against a half decent swordsman. His fist unfurled with the realisation of which player held the cards. Only days ago, he'd lost his temper and thought he'd killed a priest. The guilt of it still weighed upon him. If he threw a punch at a Lord, as he'd intended, not only would he have failed to learn his lesson, but more, he risked breaking his only way of making a living. He'd end up like the poor smith on the ground. He needed his hands to have any kind of future. Broken fingers rarely healed completely and true, and he would be consigned to the grunt work of blacksmithing, like his father had been.

Aioffe slapped the rumps of the horses so they ran clattering away and advanced on Ap Tudor. "I told you, it's mine!" She glared, then, snatched the sack so quickly he gasped. She nimbly stepped back, clutching the silver to her chest.

Her impudence inspired him. "Should I tell the men you cost them a blacksmith, or will you?"

"Ah, but I haven't, have I?" Ap Tudor retorted. "Because you'll come with us in his stead."

Tarl's eyes flared. "You jest. As if I would go anywhere with you."

"But you will," Owain said, carefully, as he dunked his bloodstained hands into the bucket of cold water Tarl had brought in. "Because I have just walked into here to find a pair of absolute strangers, violent thieves, have pummelled poor Rhys here near to death. Spooked my horses so they ran away. That's witchcraft. Not to mention, your actions have cost King Henry a blacksmith when he needs all the men he can get. Sabotage. Rhys can't go to war now."

"You beat him, not us!" Tarl shouted.

Aioffe's mouth fell open, and she frowned.

Ap Tudor shrugged. "Who do you think they will believe? Me, or some vagabonds?"

Tarl took a step towards the Lord, his fist shook but held by his side.

Ap Tudor continued, "Do you imagine you would get far when the entire town is already mobilised to move? To hunt down a killer and his strange-looking companion would be merely practise for hunting the French." He cocked his head to one side. "The punishment for murder, or theft from a church, is your life."

Tarl's blood roared, all he could hear in his ears with the pulse of it urging him.

Aioffe placed her hand on Tarl's arm, then leaned towards Ap Tudor. "But he's not dead! Surely…"

But Ap Tudor ignored her. His eyes narrowed on Tarl. "Or the price for my silence, and your survival, is your service."

"No!" She said.

"Do not speak for me!" Tarl shot her a cautionary glance. He looked Ap Tudor square in the face and lied. "The silver is mine.

I'm a silversmith and these items are a commission I'm delivering. She has nothing to do with it. Let her go. I will serve you if she goes free."

The words tripped from his lips before he considered the implications for himself. Aioffe did not deserve to die by this fool's lies, or get dragged into a war for his own mistakes. However strange she might be, she was innocent of the crimes listed, but her peculiarities would be exposed upon examination. And by association, he might lose the chance for absolution. Tarl shoved her towards the street. "Go! Take your freedom!"

The look on Ap Tudor's face suggested he would not have released her that easily.

CHAPTER 15 - THE PRICE OF FREEDOM

Why would he push her away? Aioffe faltered as she scurried out. She was still holding the sack! Her head spun back, hoping to catch his eyes, but he was in some kind of staring match with Ap Tudor. What was he expecting her to do with it? Or do now? Her lip wobbled as a peculiar and unfamiliar sensation of being rejected swept through her.

Immediately, she shoved the thought aside. Who needed him, anyway. She'd tried to help, offered to take the blame, but Tarl didn't want her assistance.

She stepped onto the track outside the forge and crossed to the wall. She wasn't sure why, but darkness had fallen and she sensed it was safer. Although she didn't need light to see her way by, her fingertips traced the rough crystals of the boundary as she walked.

She reached the corner. To her right, the noise of the quayside and harbour held the promise of company and the potential to learn more about how the humans lived. Or, she could follow the line of the wall left and around, towards the castle. A narrow track ran outside the town walls, quiet and offering hiding places. Possibly. And the probability of a gaol if she were discovered.

But, people, boats, and life, if she chose to turn right. She could taste the faint tendrils of their Lifeforce - from excited, to frightened, worried, frustration and reluctance. The range of emotions she sensed intrigued her. What could cause such a wide disparity? Was it this King Henry which Ap Tudor referred to?

There was no decision to make. Alone she may be, spurned even, at least she was free. That was what Tarl had wanted for her. That was what he said. Freedom was what she craved for herself all along - the chance to explore, to learn. Yet, his warnings about her being different lurked in her mind. But here, she had the opportunity. She ought to observe and learn, so that in time, she might appear less 'peculiar'.

She kept her head low enough to seem preoccupied, yet her watchful sideways gaze noticed everything as she crossed the cobbles, past the gathered horses, and walked onto the shore. Enjoying the gentle breeze about her ankles and the sand between her toes, she padded down to the shoreline. Bonfires lit the beach and people had moved from the pubs down to finish the day with more drinks and spend the night under the stars. They huddled in small groups around the driftwood fires, talking or simply gazing out over the moonlit sea. The tide lapped at her bare feet as she wandered along, mimicking out loud how they pronounced words with that soft rolling of sounds.

"I'll keep you company tonight, bach!"

The call interrupted her reverie. On the cobbles marking the edge of the quay, a man waved at her, slightly weaving. "We'll be gone in the morning, cariad, no-one need ever know..." He leered. As she stared, entirely uncertain as to what he meant, his eyebrows waggled at her. "Come on," he said. "Bea-u-tiful." The man stretched out the middle of the word in a lilting way. "I don't bite... unless you want me to!" Letting out a guffaw of laughter which shook the brown curls of his hair, he slapped his thigh at his own joke.

He didn't smell like a vampire, or danger at all, but his talk of biting confused her. The sweaty tang which carried on the breeze to her was distinctly yeasty, so she ignored him and continued walking.

"Come on bach," he called again. She glanced towards him, but her gaze fell instead upon Tarl, being half pushed, half dragging his feet around the edge of the still lingering crowd. She stopped, her heart pounding at the sight of him. His head was down, defeated. Ap Tudor strutted behind him, pulling the pair of now well behaved dark horses.

In the middle of the open seafront area sat a man clothed in a cassock, similar to the one the priest back on Wrye had worn. He hunched over a wooden box resting on his knees. A lone candle cast its flickering light from a corner of the portable desk and two goose quills poked from a recessed inkwell on the other side.

Ap Tudor gestured towards the line of men casually chatting to each other as they queued. Tarl was pushed forwards, to the head of the queue, where he, the man writing and Ap Tudor exchanged words.

Ignoring the lumbering idiot, who seemed to have taken her pause as an invitation to approach, Aioffe listened intently. She stepped up the beach a little, until she could hear what they were saying so far in the distance, but they discussion had ceased. The priest scrawled something on the papers curling over his lap desk.

"We can find us a cosy room, eh? I'll keep you warm enough."

Aioffe started. She wasn't cold in the slightest. The yeasty man grinned at her, foul breath puffing in the cool night air just a few feet off. She side-stepped away from him, and hoped he would get the hint as she focussed on the discussion on the quay.

"He's coming instead of Rhys the Smith," Ap Tudor said. "He'll cost us less in wine as well!"

"Name and rank?" The quill hovered.

Tarl's lips tightened. He glowered at Ap Tudor. From his terse expression, Aioffe had the impression that Tarl was reluctant to give his true name. Were she in the same position, she supposed, she certainly wouldn't give her name. A name had implications, a history. Hers carried an implicit meaning. To know it should cause a fear of retribution, if one only knew about Fae. Furthermore, Tarl Smytheson was, by now, likely to be a hunted man. When you were wanted for a crime on Naturae, the fae warriors found you. Perhaps it was the same for humans?

"Name?" The priest repeated.

"Just put Smith," Ap Tudor said, irritation in his voice. "Thomas, or Robert. Yes, Robert, as he's a Scot."

"Tarl Smith," Tarl's voice sounded hollow.

Aioffe realised the sweaty man stood behind her. She could almost feel his eyes linger on her back. She began to walk up the beach again, veering gently towards the cobbles as if she was meeting someone there, but all the while listening and watching Tarl's encounter from the corners of her eyes.

The priest scratched something on the manuscripts. He looked up and down Tarl's broad chest and arms. "Can you shoot a longbow?"

Tarl nodded, after which the priest scribbled again, then glanced up at Ap Tudor. "He'll have to be issued one, from your stock."

Ap Tudor's lip curled. "He'll be too busy making arrows for French heads and shoeing horses to need it."

The priest tipped his head as if he were weighing up options. "If he does both, then he'll be entitled to more wages?"

"I can shoot," Tarl interjected proudly. "And be paid as blacksmith and archer."

Aioffe's toes planted into the sand as she leaned forward to catch what Ap Tudor said into the priest's ear.

"Put both, and split the difference ourselves?"

Tarl shouted, "If I'm going to do two jobs, then you'll pay me, in full, for both! Or are you planning to take your cut from everyone here?" He looked around, gaging the support his outburst had stoked.

The men in the queue fell silent. The issue of money was apparently far more important than idle talk, and, judging from the stares the priest and Ap Tudor were subjected to, the entire reason for their being here.

Ap Tudor held up his hands, his dark eyes narrowing on Tarl as he proclaimed, "Every man shall be paid his worth. Do not fear, King Henry is more than fair with compensation for our service."

Aioffe noticed Tarl's fist remained balled.

Ap Tudor assured those in the queue, who had drawn closer and now shot anxious looks between themselves. "The King has promised to pay 40 marks for the year to all men at arms, and 20 for archers. More, and per day, if we sail to France, and the rewards there are greater still. By signing here tonight, you'll have a contract to be paid under the indenture, as agreed with his Highness, King Henry V."

Ap Tudor's announcement seemed to mollify the remaining conscripts, as they nodded to each other. One beckoned over his lady to impart the news of their forthcoming riches.

Tarl whispered something into the priest's ear, just as Aioffe felt a hand grab her shoulder. "He's not worth it, cariad. You need a proper man to look after you," slurred the man, who had followed her up the beach. "One who can afford to clothe you properly!"

"I can look after myself," Aioffe retorted, shaking his palm off, but it brushed over her wing-bumps. With her sudden movement, the silver clanked together in the bag. His eyes widened, and Aioffe knew then. She had to run.

Her feet pounded away across the shore, towards where they moored the boat, now beached by the retreating tide. Only when she had run past the little refuge and towards the end of the stretch of sand did she glance back... and stumbled again to the ground. She raised her head, spitting out the sand which had sprayed into her open mouth.

The man had remained shock still where she left him, weaving as if he couldn't quite make sense of what had just happened. Staring at his hands. Shaking his head at them, or at the recollection of what they had felt. He turned this way and that. Searching.

A shiver ran through Aioffe. She was not safe. It had been too easy for that man to get close enough to touch her. Tarl was right. Even without wanting to, even saying nothing, as a young woman on her own and flimsily clad, she drew attention.

Attention means capture.

Tarl's fawn-coloured smock was almost the same colour as the sand, and she had run far enough away from the beach bonfires for their light to cast no shadow and expose her. Lying low, Aioffe stilled herself and waited.

Later, when the night grew quiet and all movement on the waterfront had ceased, the last flames of the bonfires dwindled to glowing embers. The safety and shelter of their boat beckoned. Aioffe crawled back towards it, through the damp ripples left by the receding tide.

The hull lay fully exposed as it tilted, the mast pointed towards the town. Beached at such an angle on the wet sand, the vessel's interior offered her little protection or privacy. Instead, she walked behind the steering pole to sit and consider her options, tilting her head back to rest against the underbelly of the boat as she gazed out over the lapping waves in the distance. Unlike the beaches on Naturae, shrouded by the fog which hid her fae homeland, the sands here were fine, barely a pebble amongst them and she could enjoy the expanse of the water as it stretched into the horizon. The sea had retreated so far, the effort of pushing the boat across the bay to meet water seemed insurmountable. She suspected her ankle, although less painful after the seal, simply wouldn't manage the exertion. Her wings needed more time - possibly weeks - to heal. Until they did, she could not fly. She could not return home immediately, even if she wanted to. This much she knew, so she asked herself what else she knew, for certain.

That she was very different, possibly too different, to the humans was clear, and always had been. Yet, she had managed to fool that human who grabbed at her, and before him, Tarl. And that had been in daylight! If anything, flimsy though his shirt was, it re-enforced her opinion that with a better disguise, perhaps learning their language properly, she could pass for a human again. As long as they didn't get too close. The thought thrilled her as well as caused a tightness to her chest. Living a life which was also a lie - how was that different to home?

She looked out at the expanse before her. The limitless possibilities which travel afforded her - even without wings. The variety. What else was to be discovered?

She couldn't even plan to go back to Naturae when her wings healed. Tumultuous though the last few days had been, fraught with danger and unexpected encounters, she didn't want to return. All that awaited there was boredom. A half life, waiting for something to happen. Or worse, The Beneath. In her heart, Aioffe acknowledged that she would rather live just one more day with this freedom than remain in Naturae for the rest of her eternal life. No-one knew who she was here, and no-one would. Half a lie was better than half a life. No question.

Which left her with a dilemma. To survive here, she needed proper, appropriate clothes. Which, according to her pursuer, she needed a man to provide. Coming from Naturae, ruled over by a queen, with worker fae of all genders to serve, it seemed strange to think that a female would need a male. Yet, everything she had witnessed in this society suggested as much. The women fussed around the men in the town. The way Tarl had ordered her to follow his lead. Taken the decision about when and where to land. And, Ap Tudor, ostensibly of a senior rank, had ignored her entirely - much as she used to ignore the workers. This reversal of power, of male over female, made her stomach tight, but it was a small price to pay for the freedom to decide her own future.

Yes, to have her freedom, she would first need to be dressed more appropriately. Which apparently meant a man had to give her them. A man who knew of her particular requirement for privacy. To not be touched. Which meant…

She had to stick with Tarl. At least until he could provide her with the information and attire she needed to survive on her own. Only he had not wanted to touch her. Only he had protected her, defended her, and offered freedom. And only he made her skin tingle and heart race whenever she was around him.

Making her decision was easy. But convincing Tarl she should accompany him after he had told her to go was another matter. Aioffe gathered the sack to her chest, wrapping her arms about it. He'd want her to keep it safe. But would he want her? She closed her eyes, dropped her head onto her knees, and sighed.

CHAPTER 16 - CONSEQUENCES

The grey-haired clerk had answered Tarl's whispered request of whether the Bishop of Norwich could be contacted with a firm, "We leave at dawn, and muster in Southampton." But then a guarded look had appeared in his eyes. "I understand many senior members of the clergy will accompany the King, but, I cannot be expected to know whom precisely."

Tarl's face fell.

The clerk's lips tightened. "But, given the Bishop is a close personal friend of the King, I would, however, expect him to come."

Tarl's stomach clenched. He suddenly worried if, by asking about the Bishop of Norwich, the clerk-priest also knew something of these other creatures who lived amongst humans. Had he put Aioffe in greater danger by alerting a local to his need to see this specific Bishop? How much might a low-ranking clergyman know about what Norwich dealt with? These other kinds of beings?

Somehow, in the shock of finding himself conscripted and about to travel to France to war, he had forgotten about the need for secrecy impressed upon him by Father McTavish. He chewed his lip as he cast around Beaumaris's seafront.

And where had Aioffe gone after he dismissed her? She left with the evidence of his crime. The shame and guilt, not to mention the debt he was supposed to repay with it, remained with him. Tarl recalled how she had tried to take the blame for the obviously stolen silverware, then shook his head. He now had too much to consider without the added complication of her. At least he would be legitimately earning, and for a war which presumably was just, so that might salve his conscience and solve his financial woes. It was better for everyone that Aioffe, and the silver, were not under foot any more. All she did, all she was, created more problems for him.

But, what was the point of leaving to see the Bishop of Norwich without her? Why should he play the charade of going to war, apart from the wages for just turning up, if not to hand her over to the ecclesiastical authorities? Tarl wondered if he had made the wrong choice. Travelling in a large, well supplied retinue might not bring him the salvation and answers he sought, but he had little other option if he was to avoid being hunted down himself. The decision had been forced upon him. And him alone.

He had told Aioffe to go. Be free. Leave him. He had only wanted to protect her from the killer he suspected Ap Tudor was, but he could have suggested she wait outside for him. Instead, he had offered her the freedom he thought she craved.

Why had he done that? She was the reason he was here at all, and now look what had happened! He was about to leave for a war he never even knew was about to happen. His mind circled around the issues, with no resolution.

Dismissed with a grunt by the priest and told to move along, Tarl's stomach churned as Ap Tudor dragged him past piles of weapons and armour neatly piled or packed in carts which filled the seafront. They stopped at an alehouse overlooking the sea, which was doing a roaring trade as the dusk fell and anxious men numbed their nerves.

His new commander pressed into his hands as if the purchase could absolve him of the blackmail, and Tarl downed it. Bile rose still in his throat. As they stood, surveying the preparations and awkward with the uneasy secrets which bound them in the cooling evening air, Ap Tudor gave him a hard stare. "Remember, Smith, I can always find you. Don't think about disappearing. You won't get far. I know what you truly are, thief, and you are under my command now." His eyes narrowed.

Tarl quashed his impulse to punch him, but it was growing harder to restrain himself when this young upstart kept poking, reminding him of his guilt and obligation. He shook off his anger and concentrated on containing his emotions before they landed him in further trouble. Through his nostrils he huffed, and said, "And I see you for what you are as well."

He slammed the empty cup down before stomping off.

He found himself back at the forge. After being frog-marched out earlier, the smith's fate sat on his conscience. He swallowed, and was honest with himself - he also wanted to check he was still alive and could, if necessary, swear to the fact that Tarl hadn't been the one to beat him. Tarl's impression Ap Tudor was untrustworthy had not in any way been salved by the small ale.

Rhys had crawled closer to the fire to nurse his broken fingers and foot when Tarl arrived. He glanced up at him, then burst into heaving and unmanly sobs. His swollen hand lay in his lap, and he'd pulled off a boot to wrap his foot in a rag. A small keg by his side and an empty cup suggested how he medicated his pain. In a strange way, there was relief that an injury remained, given what he had experienced with Father McTavish.

"No need to ask how you are feeling," Tarl said as he patted Rhys's shoulder. "Is there anything I can do to help?"

"He's a bastard," Rhys spat out, referring to their mutual enemy, Ap Tudor. He heaved another sob. "I've a family to feed, for God's sake."

"And I've to go to war in your stead."

They shared a look of mutual disgruntlement.

"You'll need tools," Rhys' sniffed and hiccuped. "There's a

travel bag somewhere." With his eyes, he indicated the far corner of the room.

Tarl rummaged around in the dark recess. His father had used a specialist leather satchel when operating outside of the forge, which Tarl had inherited but left behind.

"Got it. Thanks." Tarl found an unused looking bag hanging alongside a tatty lap apron. He flipped it open to see a basic selection of chisels, awls, swages and punches of varying sizes tucked behind a strap at the back, their sharp ends kept neatly in a flap at the bottom. There was plenty of room left to pack hammers, pliers, and tongs. "I'm sorry to take these." He shrugged. "I'll send you some money for them as soon as I've earned it."

Rhys said, "I should thank you for stoppin' him. The tools seem a fair recompense. I'll borrow replacements, so make sure you have what you need, lad. I won't be needin' them for a long time."

"You'll heal, eventually." They both glanced at his swollen hand and understood Tarl was saying this from kindness only. It was unlikely shattered bones would ever regain full movement. A livelihood equally smashed, which made the Welshman's kindness all the more generous. If only he had the silver, he could leave it for Rhys and his family, but he was empty-handed. Tarl scrubbed his hand over his face and sighed. Neither of them believed he would be back.

Wandering over to the fire, he chose the shoeing hammer and a pair of short-handled tongs. As he packed them, his empty stomach gurgled. "Do you have anything to eat?"

Rhys nodded towards a doorway at the back of the open space. "The wife will've left a meal out," he mumbled. "She usually does."

"Perhaps she could bandage you up? Make you more comfortable?"

Shaking his head, the blacksmith then snorted. "She's her own woman, really. Wasn't bothered about me having to go off in the first place, an' now she'll be pissed I'm not bringing home the shillings if I survive. Or, the pension if I don't." He took swig of ale. "No pleasin' her whether I'm here or not."

Tarl poked his head through the narrow door to their living quarters, then hunched his broad shoulders to enter the gloom. On a low table, with stools askew underneath, a clay pot sat on a piece of slate. At the far end of the room, gentle snores sounded from the three lumps on a bed, huddled together. The stuffy room held the lingering smell of ale. Rhys was clearly not the only one who had quenched his thirst a little too much with the pressures of the day.

He lifted the pan lid and sniffed - mutton and spring greens, and probably not a lot of actual meat. Using the blackened spoon leaning against the side, Tarl served a portion for Rhys, then ate the cold remains.

At least with his belly partially full, his mind cleared a little. With a croaked, "Good luck," from Rhys as he left, Tarl set out into the night. Before long, he stood by Taffy's boat as it listed towards the town, peering into its depths.

He frowned, his eyes not seeing any covered girl shaped lumps. Nothing out of the ordinary at all, although by only moonlight it was difficult to be sure. Disappointment pulled at him and his hands dropped to his sides. He had half-convinced himself on the walk back , that Aioffe would return to the boat. He sat on the rim and leaned back against the hull inside. Ahead of him, the bonfires on the beach had burned out, families huddled asleep together under a full moon. His soul yearned for the comfort of another person, someone who would miss him when he was gone, but there was no-one. No-one at home, nor here. Not even the Lord above would look kindly upon such a sinner.

After a few moments, lulled by the crash of waves in the distance, his eyelids had just dropped when he heard a small squelch. His head jerked. Awake and alert as his heart thumped. Another squelch, then a bump which reverberated through the wood of the boat. His hand fell to the tool satchel, fingers grasping at the buckle.

"When do we leave for war?" Aioffe asked.

Tarl pulled the knapsack to his chest instead. "I go at dawn," he growled.

She approached, bare feet sinking into the wet sand. With the low winter moon behind, her shadow cast him in shade, but he lifted his face. The light shone through her white hair, her skin luminous and pale. His heartbeat refused to calm as he couldn't shake the image of an angel from his mind.

"I will come with you," she whispered.

Tarl's mouth gaped. He wanted to say she didn't have to. She couldn't. That it was too dangerous for a woman. That she should take the freedom he had offered and leave him, for he was not worthy. But he was weak, and longed more than he could bear for something, someone familiar, who would side with him. "As you wish," he croaked.

She leaned into the boat, reaching towards him with her slim fingers. He froze, lost. As her fingertips touched his hair, pushing a strand from his face, he met her eyes. How could they be lit as if from within? At her light touch, his fear seemed to lift. He stared into her eyes. His heart calmed, yet somehow swelled at the same time. Tarl could not pull away, could not move, not even to breathe. He sensed she was mutely asking for something, but what he did not know.

Instead, she stepped backwards. A gentle smile played on her lips as if she were rewarding him. His skin tingled as she withdrew, yearning for her touch to return. With a great gulp, Tarl drew in a breath, expelling it slowly and with it, a panic he hadn't realised was there subsided.

She pointed at the satchel. "That looks like a safer place," Aioffe lent behind the stern of the boat, "for these." Her grin widened as she presented his sack.

His lips tightened, but he took the silverware from her. As he undid the buckle, he stared at her, then frowned. "Why didn't you leave when I told you to?"

She shrugged. "I need clothes."

Her simple answer caught him off guard, and he let out a snort of laughter. With this amount of silver, she could have bought dresses fit for a Lady. Traded for a passage anywhere.

Yet, when he raised his head to glance at her again, she stared at him with an expectant expression on her face.

His hand stopped mid-buckle. She was expecting him to provide the clothes! He blinked. It seemed like a reasonable ask, he decided. He had already given her his shirt. Why wouldn't she expect him to give her more clothing? The realisation that he didn't mind this very ordinary and practical responsibility made him collapse back into the boat. Trouble though she may be, and peculiar in almost every way, ordinary she was definitely not.

After a wry smile, at himself more than her request, Tarl said, "We will probably travel through towns. I'm sure we can get something more suitable for you to wear."

He was rewarded with a grin so wide it showed almost all her white teeth. His heart leapt briefly, then he muttered, "I need to rest. Dawn will come soon enough."

She plonked herself down in the sand next to the boat. "I'll wait," she said, then turned her head out towards the sea.

At least she wasn't planning on staring at him whilst he slept. He leaned his head back and half closed his eyelids. She remained motionless for as long as he kept his gaze on her. Somehow comforted by her silent presence, he fell asleep.

CHAPTER 17 – DISGUISE

Dawn streaked the sky with bright pink and orange hues. Aioffe stretched her legs out and circled her ankles. Mercifully they didn't hurt any more.

A few fishing boats had left with the tide and horses nickered on the quayside as hay was strewn in front of them. Already, she had watched the beach empty of families, their faces splashed in the seawater to freshen themselves for the journey ahead. She deemed it was probably time to wake Tarl, yet he looked so peaceful she was reluctant to disturb him. That humans needed to sleep was not a revelation to her, but the depths to which they lost consciousness was. Fae required only a few hours of rest a day, entering into a more trance-like state than such an absolute loss of awareness of one's surroundings.

The shouts became more militant, with barked orders to mount up and make ready. The waves lapped the hull, chasing the boat to buoyancy. They could delay no longer, so she shook Tarl's shoulder. When he mumbled, she said, "Dawn! Time to go!"

He jerked awake, shrugging her hand off and staring at her with confusion.

"You said dawn," Aioffe reiterated, despite his frown.

His shoulders slumped and he groaned, then clutched his satchel. "I hoped it was just a dream. A nightmare."

She bit back a smile. There was something endearing about his grumpiness which she couldn't determine was because of their imminent departure, or finding himself faced with her upon awakening.

His eyes blinked against the rising sun as he sat up and peered out of the boat. "Holy Mother! Why didn't you wake me sooner?"

She glanced over her shoulder. On the quayside, Owain Ap Tudor trotted up and down the cobbles, a deep furrow on his forehead. He raised his hand against the glare of the sun and squinted down the expanse of the beach.

Tarl shuffled out of the boat and unfurled his tall frame. He spotted Ap Tudor kicking his black horse into a canter. As the young Lord covered the sand at speed, staring at him, he turned to her. "Sister or wife?"

"What?"

"Which would you prefer to pretend to be?"

Before she could answer, Ap Tudor pulled his steed to a halt a few feet away. "Get a move on, smith. Say goodbye to your wench and stop holding the convoy up."

"She's coming with us," Tarl said, grabbing her hand.

Aioffe started at the touch of his roughened fingers as they tightened over hers. "I'm his... wife?"

She was already a sister to Lyrus, and that was an uncomfortable enough a relationship. Ap Tudor's gaze swept over her as he moistened his lips. With a note of defiance, she added, "Where he goes, so do I."

"Another mouth to feed? Well, it's coming out of your wages." Ap Tudor yanked the reins to trim his ride's head. "And I've no spare horses for womenfolk."

Aioffe's face dropped.

"She won't be any trouble," Tarl said. His squeeze on her hand tightened. Comply.

Ap Tudor sneered, "Trouble will find her if she doesn't get dressed properly!"

Tarl grimaced. "I know."

After throwing her a leer which made her skin crawl, Ap Tudor nudged his spurs into the horses's flank. A cloud of sand sprayed from the hooves as he cantered away. Tarl dropped Aioffe's hand, picked up his satchel and set off after him. She scuttled after, finding the sun-dried beach less forgiving than last night. She held her arms wide of her body to try and balance, but still tripped and fell her way up the beach behind him.

On the quayside, Tarl had been handed the reins to a light brown mare. Her broad hooves clattered on the stones as Tarl struggled to adjust a strap running from a leather seat on her back underneath her rotund belly.

The majority of other horses had riders perched on top. Saddlebags, bundles of blankets, and cloth were strapped over hind quarters and most people wore their clothing layered over them with pots, pans and weapons strung over their shoulders or dangling from the saddle. Now that she saw everyone weighted down with their daily essentials, it occurred to her that riding, not walking, was expected for a long journey. Her heart sank.

It looked precarious.

As she approached, the horse pranced, tossing its head in alarm. Tarl yanked on the straps leading from the mare's mouth and snapped a warning to behave. When this didn't work, he stroked the shaggy neck and murmured softly for it to stand still. The horse rolled her eyes at Aioffe. The animal was as frightened of her as she was of it!

She reached out her fingers to the hinge of its jaw, softly stroking the fur while Tarl tightened the girth. The horse and Aioffe stared at each other for a moment before it stopped jiggling around, just as the other horses at the forge had calmed after her reassurance.

"I don't know what you are doing, but it's working. Thank you," Tarl begrudged. He jerked his head towards a wagon.

"Probably best if you hitch a ride on that, though."

She stood on tiptoes to peer over the horse's hind. The cart was stacked high with barrels with bundles of hay lashed haphazardly on top. Peering around it, she saw on the bench seat at the front, two people sat wedged together by brown sacks on either side of them. A grey-haired woman held the long reins, berating something or someone behind them on the wagon. Her loud scald was ignored by the dark-haired man next to her, who appeared to be asleep cuddling a chicken. Where Aioffe was supposed to have sat on the overloaded cart confounded her until she saw a skinny boy, half the height of Tarl, poke out his head up from the middle of the hay bales. A human child! She stared in fascination as he shook loose stalks from his head.

The youngster giggled, then wriggled his arms out. "Just be sure to steer around the pot-holes this time!" He clambered out and jumped off the cart. "When are we going to move off? I can't wait to see a King."

"You're not," the woman said. "I told you, you're too young. Now get on home to your Ma. And there's sheep to feed back on our land, which I'm paying you to take care of. So you'd better hop to."

The boy's face wrinkled into a scowl. "But I want to skewer someone. With one of these!" His hand reached into the back of the wagon and pulled out a bundle of spears tied together.

"There'll be no stabbing or skewering from you this year. You've plenty of time for fighting when you're older. Now get on with you." The woman appeared around the side of the wagon and grabbed the spears back. After shoving them back in place, she folded him in her arms, then dropped a kiss on his head as he pouted. "And tell yer Ma we'll be back for the harvest! She should have sufficient ale brewed to last her until then." After ruffling his hair, she pushed him away and clambered onto the wagon.

The boy's lower lip trembled until she picked up the reins and relented. "If we have enough lambs, I'll let you try to skewer one of them for Easter next year. I'm trusting you with my herd, so you'd best take good care of them for us."

Satisfied, the lad waved, then sloped off into the town.

"I'll walk," Aioffe said to Tarl. The opportunity to encounter a child would have to wait.

His eyes roamed over the shirt she wore and his jaw tightened. "As you wish."

Before she had time to regret her decision, the convoy started trundling away from the quay. Leading them, Ap Tudor and a priest each dragged a pair of horses behind them. Tarl put his foot in the stirrup and swung his leg over the mare's rear. He shuffled his bottom in the saddle and tightened the reins. His heels nudged the mare forward.

Aioffe rolled her shoulders back and stepped alongside him. Thanks to the seal, her ankle had healed and, although she had no idea how far the journey might be, she was optimistic her legs could manage it. The walk would be good practise for life on the ground, so the quicker she got the hang of it, the better.

As they left Beaumaris on a well maintained coastal route, she managed to keep pace by the side of Tarl. Chatter between riders quietened, replaced by a grim determination to avoid the worst of the puddles and bumps as the level flagstones petered out and turned into a deeply furrowed and narrow track.

But the uneven route exposed her ineptitude. Each time she stumbled, usually pre-occupied by looking longingly at the sea birds which swirled above, Tarl exhaled loudly through his nostrils or tutted. The mare shied away, tossing its head so he had to wrestle to regain control of it. After several miles, when her lurches drew derisive laughter from the riders behind and the gap between them and the convoy widened, he said, "You ride, I'll walk." He leaned back on the reins and the horse slowed.

Aioffe shook her head and soldiered on. There was no way she wanted to perch up on the mare. Although she had never tried riding, the lumbering gait looked uncomfortable. Besides, to sit astride like he did invited exposure of her wings. Tarl kneed his mare to catch up.

When he reached her, he unbuckled the looped reins, then tossed over the nearest leather strap. "Hold this to stop you from falling so often. You'll end up under her hooves otherwise."

She held the strap and felt like one of the other horses being led. He was right though. Annoyingly. Having something to hang on to helped her balance.

When the sun was high in the sky, she was all the same relieved when the convey ahead slowed. The track widened on both sides and the carts pulled up by the side. People dismounted, stretched, then wandered down a short pathway to a pebbled beach. After catching them up, Aioffe and Tarl stopped by a stream which trickled alongside the lane, where the horse could have a drink. Like their mount, Aioffe's legs were muddied halfway up her calves and there seemed little point in washing them, but the soles of her feet throbbed. Standing in shallow water helped ease them but she dared not leave and hunt for true relief. The horse snatched a mouthful of grass before Ap Tudor shouted at the group to mount up again.

The convoy reassembled, stuffing half loaves of bread back into bags and taking last swigs from canteens. Tarl's face was pale and drawn as he glanced at the food. With a look of grim determination, he held his arm down and beckoned her closer. "You walking slows us all down. I could do without any more strange looks."

"I cannot," she said, then glanced over at her shoulders, then down at his baggy shirt.

His lips tightened as he scowled with understanding of her fear. He bent and, before she could object, hooked his hands under her arms and hoisted her up. Her bottom was deposited, sideways, in front of him on the withers. As she looked around in confusion, he gathered the reins and squeezed the horse's belly.

Pitched into his chest by the rolling gait, she grabbed onto Tarl's jerkin and squealed.

"Just relax. You'll get used to it," Tarl said in a low voice.

The horse plodded on, and after a few steps, Aioffe's torso flexed with its rhythm. Her wings softened, still covered by his billowing undergarment, and hung down the horse's shoulder. There was no escaping the warmth of his skin or the scent of his sweat, which made her insides clench. Encircled by his arms, Aioffe attempted to sit up, before the temptation to pull from his weakened Lifeforce grew unbearable. She tried not to be offended by how upright he held himself, with his shoulders rolled back as if he couldn't bear to have her touch him. His tight jaw told her their proximity was as uncomfortable to him as it was for her, so she inched her bottom around until one leg kinked over the lump of the mares' flank. By twisting her torso, she looked forwards rather than out to the sea. Her feet, without weight upon them, throbbed their thanks.

Her new view, between the mare's ears, was of two-thirds of the convoy ahead. She counted some forty heads riding or on wagons. Without her walking, or stumbling rather, the pace quickened. She hadn't understood how much she had been slowing progress down - no wonder Tarl had been so frustrated.

As the hours passed, Aioffe studied their surroundings, memorising copses and woodlands en route for when night fell and she could hunt. As the horse jogged onwards, she stopped resisting its gait and began to enjoy the ride. Until the ground seemed to give way beneath them.

CHAPTER 18 – LAME

The two ruts of the lane tilted towards the sea as it wound around the hillside and down. When the cart in front rounded a tight bend, its rear wheel broke the compacted soil on the cliff edge, and stuck. The wood creaked under the strain and crashed on to the axle joint. The wagon jerked to a halt.

Trailing behind, and its way suddenly blocked, their mount balked. Aioffe pitched onto the mare's neck, just as a precariously balanced and sloppy hay bale fell out of the ropes which lashed it atop the barrels. As the sheaf plummeted down the cliff spraying loose stalks into the air, both horses spooked.

His arms tightened around Aioffe's waist as he pulled the reins, but that didn't prevent the mare's panic. Rearing up, the horse's front feet stumbled on the lopsided ground when she landed. Aioffe, having nothing to grip onto with her legs, was thrown off balance again. Before he could pull her body back into his, the back hooves slid on the mud.

She gasped and seized his lapels as soil and stones tumbled over the cliff and rattled down into the sea.

"Whoa!" Tarl said, in as calm a voice as he could manage. The horse struggled to get a purchase on the slope. He loosened the reins, hoping that if the mare's back legs dug in, an imminent tumble off the edge might be averted.

The sturdy mount gave a great lurch forward onto the middle of the track. But the damage was done. As Aioffe tried to right herself between his arms, the mare stopped next to the off-kilter wagon and dropped her head. Instinct made his clutch on her tighten as he leant over the saddle. The horse's front left leg was not bearing any weight.

"Oh!" Aioffe cried, her fingers gripped the mane. "The poor creature!" She wriggled. "Let me down."

He forced his arms to release her. She slid down, then crouched, wrapping her hands around the lame fetlock. Her face screwed with concentration for a moment. She looked up at Tarl, bewildered. "I can't do anything right now." She blinked rapidly, her fingers gently stroking the injury.

He breathed out hard through his nose. What on earth could she do about their predicament anyway? He joined her on the ground. After handing her the reins, he ran his hand down the mare's leg, noting the rising warmth of the strained muscle. "I know, old girl. I'll make a wrap and poultice and hope that some rest will help." Their mare nickered in response to his crooning tone. He straightened, shaking his head as he patted her mud splattered neck.

Aioffe said, "There's some woodland further back. I could…"

She tailed off as Ap Tudor cantered towards the stranded cart. He shouted, "A hundred miles to go and you can't even keep your nag on course right where you live? Idiots."

"The crossing is at the bottom, Lord," the dark-haired man on the wagon said. "It's just a wheel off. Nothing broken."

"I can see that, you dolt!"

"We'll still catch the tide, don't you worry, my Lord," said the woman. "Send over some help to lift, and we'll get back on course."

Her companion jumped off the wagon and walked around to check and unhitch their horse.

Ap Tudor harrumphed and beckoned some of the mounted archers and men at arms to return. While he waited, he shot a glare at Tarl. "And what's a face like that doing on your head, Smith?"

"My mare is lame." Tarl's lips tightened together. "I'll need to poultice her joint before I can tell you if she's fit to go on."

"That was my uncle's palfrey. She never puts a foot wrong." His eyebrows furrowed. "It must be that wench of yours. Yesterday, I thought she knew what she was doing with horses, but now I see she can't even ride. Is she a witch or something?"

Tarl gasped. "Of course she isn't." He looked down at the mare's knee before his face gave away the untruth.

"I am no witch," Aioffe said. Tarl shot her a cautionary look, which she ignored. "And the horse will be well by tomorrow, I assure you. We'll be fine to travel."

Ap Tudor sniffed, expression unconvinced. He pointed up the road. "Half a furlong around, we'll stop anyway to let the tide fall over the evening. We wade across overnight. If you miss the low tide," he snapped, "then you cross with the pigs on the morrow. You'll have to ride hard to catch up, or pay the consequences." Dark, hooded eyes narrowed, flitting between Tarl, Aioffe, and the mare.

She frowned at him, but it was not the time for Tarl to explain what Ap Tudor meant with his threat.

"We will keep up," he said, although he had his doubts.

Aioffe concurred, patting the horse's neck as well. Ap Tudor's eyes narrowed before he wheeled around and stomped back to the head of the convoy.

Within minutes, the cart horse had been freed and a team of able-bodied men encircled the wagon. The bossy wife coordinated, lifting their transport back onto the track while Tarl led the mare out of their way.

He moved out of earshot as the men heaved and tugged the wagon away from the edge.

"I need to gather some healing herbs and clay for a poultice," he said to Aioffe in a low voice. His mother had taught him a proven method for easing lameness from a young age, but ideally, the horse should be rested until it took effect. The potion was so potent, the villagers back home proclaimed it miraculous, until the trial, when it became evidence of witchcraft. "I won't be long. Can you lead her down the track, slowly mind, and I'll meet you at the crossing point?"

She whispered, "Will it really cure her?"

Tarl nodded, pleased she was keeping their discussion in quiet tones, and even more pleased she was cooperating. "Maybe."

"I can heal her," Aioffe said. "And then we'll be able to continue tonight."

The confidence in her voice, coupled with the memory of how she had calmed the horses in the forge last night, gave him cause to reconsider.

Wagon wheel freed and hitched up once again, the wife clicked her tongue to urge their cart horse on. He waited for them to trundle out of sight before he asked, "How can you?"

Aioffe gestured back towards the bend. "I need to hunt. A woodland is best. My... energy is low. But once I've ingested, I'll be able to help her."

Tarl snorted. "A little low on specifics. No seals nearby either." He looked sideways at her, daring her to deny her peculiar behaviour of a few days ago.

"You don't believe me?"

"It's not a question of belief," he said. But it was, at the heart of it, and they both knew it. "My way is more usual. Practised. Proven."

More human.

"And mine isn't?" She raised an eyebrow.

"What you do isn't right. Isn't normal. If anyone saw, they'd call it magic and that could get us both killed."

She frowned. "It's instinctive. I'm no witch, though."

He sighed. "I know." Then he shrugged. "I knew a woman they called witch once." He looked out to sea. "And she died for trying to heal others. I've seen what you are. In part." He glanced at her shoulders. "But magic, or whatever you use, isn't the cure for everything."

"At least this witch you knew before tried. Aren't you at least willing to let me try?"

His mother always did say 'there's no harm in trying.' He chewed his bottom lip and thought. It was clear Ap Tudor would not wait for them. The mare was lame. An injury such as this would usually take days, or weeks, of rest to heal entirely. If it didn't mend, the horse was virtually useless and would likely be culled. He didn't want to get further into debt, especially not to Ap Tudor.

There were few options available, and he was backed into a corner by the problem. He studied her young, eager face and wondered. As long as she was careful, he could not see any good reason not to let Aioffe attempt her magic, even if the hypocrisy of it stung. There were more factors to account for than she understood, and a working horse was essential to progress. "Do you know what? Let's try both methods."

Aioffe beamed at him.

"I need to collect some ingredients," he said. "Whatever you have to do is best done under cover of darkness, anyway."

They split, her crooning softly as she led the mare away. He stalked up the trail, veering inland as soon as he was around the bend. Dandelion and coltsfoot were easy to find in the field. A patch of comfrey or another borage to help bring down swelling took him longer. Venturing further across the rolling countryside, he found a copse of beech and oak. He dug down with his heels and fingers to expose wild garlic bulbs and then, in the shaded edge of a meadow, he spotted the purple flowers and wide leaves of a symphytum plant. Unfortunately, the peaty mud underfoot was not at all clay-like and would not suit his purpose.

Dusk had fallen by the time he jogged back down the track. His mind was so preoccupied by the problem of how to keep the herbs he would mash together pressed to the mare's fetlock, he had all but forgotten Aioffe. As he descended, he looked across the beach and remembered.

The sand stretched as far as the eye could see, with a fast-flowing strait visible between this island and the steep mainland opposite. As the tide retreated from the strait, leaving water filled dips and low knolls topped with grass, a fordable area was revealed. But, during his absence, the convoy had scattered and pandemonium greeted him. He swallowed a snort of laughter as he approached.

The more space exposed, the greater opportunity for two dozen early arriving pigs to charge about. Huge, hairy, black-spotted pink beasts trotted and snorted their way between carts and bags, horse and soldier. The carts to had to keep moving to avoid the wheels sinking in the wet sand. Some riders from the convoy galloped around, trying to chase or encircle the miscreant animals together. Tarl wasn't sure if their efforts were helping or hindering. Those not galloping about remained on their wagons and guffawed as the beasts squealed, swerved and splashed to evade capture.

In the middle of the carnage, Ap Tudor stood in his stirrups and berated the pig-master. In response, the farmer leant on his stick with a defeated air, occasionally shaking his head as if words failed to adequately explain the disarrayed drove.

As Tarl sloshed through the puddles towards the travellers, his mouth grew dry. The squeals and shouts turned louder. He couldn't see where she was. Was she the cause of porcine distress? His heart pounded as he berated himself for leaving her alone.

From behind, he heard the soft thud of cantering hooves approach. Tarl's head whipped around. His mare thundered to a stop several feet away and nickered. Her hands gripped the mane as she sat upright on the horses's back. Her face flushed with that strange glow he recognised. Vivid blue eyes burned into his. After a moment of staring at each other, her mouth split into a grin. She glanced at the herbs wilting by his side.

"No need for those," she said, sliding to the ground as if she had been riding all her life.

Tarl frowned, his gaze fell to the mare's legs. He felt down the musculature. All swelling had subsided and despite the recent movement, the fetlock was cool to touch. "How did you make her better?"

Aioffe's eyes sparkled at him. "I told you. Instinct." Then she oinked.

Tarl's lips pressed together. "And that chaos is the result?" He jerked his head towards the ongoing commotion.

She laughed, the sound annoyingly sweet. "Oh no, that was after and nothing to do with me. One of the pigs was trailing, so I had the opportunity to ingest what I needed. No-one saw me, they were all down here on the sand. It's joined its family now." She pointed at the only pig who seemed calm, stood by the farmer. "Except down here, on the beach, someone else is upsetting them. Not me."

Tarl looked sceptical.

"Truly!" She twirled her fingers in the air. "Perhaps it's a daemon."

"A daemon?" He shrank back in horror.

She nodded. "Yes, I've heard of them, but never met one. They smell different. Apparently. That's how you know."

Tarl's nose wrinkled. All he could smell was the usual scent of unwashed human, stale drink and, now he sniffed, the faint cabbagy odour of pig shit. As if it wasn't enough to discover there were people with wings, or fangs, but stinking daemons too? Tarl crossed himself and looked across the group of travellers in horror.

CHAPTER 19 – CROSSING THE SWELLIES

"Get moving! Leave the Porthaethwy pigs alone. You can rest when we are across."

Ap Tudor's shout across the beach was ignored by the evasive hogs, but Tarl started as if he'd been prodded. "Is it him?" His dark blond eyebrow arched as he whispered. "I wouldn't be surprised."

Aioffe bit back a giggle. "No, he just carries a foul stench of superiority about him." There was definitely something of her bossy and cruel brother in their expedition leader.

His shoulders dropped. "I really thought perhaps, if anyone was in league with the Devil, it would be him."

"I don't think it's got anything to do with your religion. Daemons are a different kind of creature, like witches or fae."

"Or… Father McTavish's." His eyes flared, and she nodded.

As the convoy drifted back together despite the pigs' best efforts at disruption, Ap Tudor cantered over the sand towards them. "Are you coming, Smith, or staying overnight with the rest of the swine?"

"We are crossing with you, my Lord," Tarl replied. His voice clipped and the lump in his neck bobbed up and down as he swallowed.

Aioffe glanced over at the dark, swirling sea water in the centre of the vast sands. Ap Tudor said, "Be sure my horse is fit enough. I don't want her losing her footing midway through the Swellies. The pigs usually have to rest on Ynys y Moch. That island," he pointed to a small mound, barely visible in the midst of the waterway. "Then you have to poke them off!" He barked a laugh, which made Aioffe's blood run cold.

Gathering the reins, Tarl turned his back to Ap Tudor and mounted. "I've forded worse with plenty of horses. Don't worry about us." He lent his arm down to her. His eyes cautioned her to obey his unspoken offer. She noticed Ap Tudor had not left, but was staring at her loose shift. Self-conscious under his roaming gaze, she grabbed Tarl's hand and allowed him to swing her up in front of him.

Tarl squared his shoulders and turned their horse towards the channel. "Let's hope it's not so deep that we have to wade so the horse can swim." He nudged the mare into a faster walk.

"Swim?" Aioffe shivered against his warmth. "That might be a problem."

"A wet gown will cling," he growled as soon as they were away from Ap Tudor.

Ahead, horses were being guided into the dark water, encouraged by clicks, kicks and prods to keep their steady pace through the current. Her eyes widened as he urged their mount into the eddies of the serpent-like stretch of seawater. Although she could see perfectly at night, daylight had all but disappeared and a palpable tension fell as the convoy began to cross in near darkness. A few people carried flaming torches, but as the group entered the Swellies, the line spaced out. The flickering light was only useful to those who held them.

The channel was deceptively deep between the island and mainland, swirling on the surface and dragging underneath. In the low tide, even smaller horses could keep their heads and haunches dry if they followed a set route through. By the time the water deepened to a ripple over the mare's knees, the first wagon stuck in the sand ahead of them.

"Ropes," Ap Tudor ordered, and two men at arms, primed for

such an eventuality on large destriers, splashed back to assist. Aioffe watched as they threw the lengths over, which were then secured to the axle and sides. The huge hooves of the fearless war horses dug in as their riders urged them forward. The cables strained across the horse's chests to drag the wheels free.

The convoy line adjusted course to avoid the dangerous depths and snaked through the eddies in tense silence. Tarl's chin was set with determination. Quite secure clutched in his arms, she gazed ahead to the village on the other side of the channel. Low stone houses stared out from the wooded rise, the grey slate roofs faintly lit by the rising moonlight. Aside from the sloshing of water as the group traversed the pass, the quietness of the night surprised her.

"What happens when we reach the other side?" she asked.

"I suppose we stop," he replied. "People need to sleep. And eat."

His surely tone put her off trying to make further conversation. Her toes dipped in the water, and before long, her calves were washed clean as the horse plodded deeper and deeper.

Cold sea splashed over her knees and onto Tarl's thigh, but their brave mare kept steady and true. She patted her neck before glancing back. The pigs, left on the beach until the more favourable dawn tides, had clustered around their master for comfort. Being smaller in stature than a horse, a perilous journey awaited them on the 'morrow. No wonder they wanted to cavort a little before they dragged their low bellies through the shifting sea.

Much to her relief, they soon entered shallower water and the threat of having to swim receded. Ap Tudor led the dripping, shivering group away from the causeway, and up a winding track through a deep forest. When he reached the top of the incline, he held his torch high and shouted, "We make camp here for the night and continue at dawn."

The convoy trundled into a clearing by the side of the trail. Aioffe slid off the haunches and waited. White of face and shivering, Tarl tied the reins to a wagon and gave the horse a brisk rub down with his sleeve. Colour returned to his cheeks as he stomped over to the base of a tree at the edge of the open space. He dropped his knapsack and collapsed into a nook between the roots. Leaning his head back against the trunk, he closed his eyes and his breathing steadied. All around, people unpacked blankets and followed suit. The carts and horses were left in the middle, secured to each other and a hay bale distributed for the animals to feed upon. Within minutes, the group settled on the leaf-strewn earth and fell quiet.

But not Aioffe. The crossing had left her jittery. As the moon rose, the bare, overhanging branches around the edges of the clearing laced like prison bars over the ground. Her wings fluttered against her back, asking for their freedom. She glanced over the sleeping bodies. Surely no-one would notice if she snuck away? Her eyes fell again on Tarl.

He stared directly at her, his expression unreadable. As their eyes met, he shifted as if to get comfortable against the tree trunk. His eyelids dropped as he feigned sleep once again. Aioffe padded over and leaned against the trunk on the opposite side of him. She stood motionless and silent as the blanket of night fell.

After a last peek around at him, the strands of his blond hair rising and falling with his breath, she surmised he slept at last. Satisfied that Tarl, or anyone else, was unlikely to follow her, she crept away. she stalked between the trees, watching out for trip hazards with every pace.

Once deep in the forest, she found a space between branches wide enough for her to slip through. she checked behind once again, before stripping Tarl's shirt off with one smooth motion. Naked, her wings rose and fluttered in the moonlight. She examined their edges, the translucent panes shimmering as they wafted. Even though she had felt them healing after the pig's life force, to take flight too soon risked a longer set back, or worse, mid-air failure of their integrity.

She shivered, noticing the eyes of forest creatures appraising her, the intruder. The urge to feed again declined as her need for freedom overwhelmed her. A tentative downward flap held promise. Her wing joints smooth and responsive as they fluttered. She jumped, whooshing straight up like an arrow released from the confines of a bow. The night air brushed cool over her skin as she flew, higher and higher, climbing with each mighty beat. Stars twinkled, beckoning and encouraging as she ascended.

Absolutely alone in the sky and high above the forest, Aioffe's breath puffed out in milky clouds. She hovered, glancing down. From below, the densely wooded landscape could be anywhere on these isles, but with the same height advantage as a kestrel on the hunt, she recognised where she was from the shape of the coastline. The bulges were familiar to her from the Great Hall floor map. Aioffe twisted in the air, studying the landmasses and calculating until she understood the scale of the journeys ahead of her. To either reach home, or the distance to travel with Tarl to war with King Henry V in France.

On a horse, by foot, or over sea, remaining with him to discover more about humankind was undoubtedly a great challenge. Flying North, to return to her life in Naturae, equally possible.

And entirely unwanted.

Aioffe beamed at the moon, then twirled around, pointing her toes and stretching her arms high. There wasn't really a decision to be decided; she'd already made it before in her heart. Even as the opportunity to change her mind presented itself, she was still certain. She had discovered how to alleviate her need to fly and recaptured the freedom of the sky. Everything felt possible.

CHAPTER 20 - CONWAY AND CLOTHES

His cheek itched. Tarl's fingers moved to scratch it. His other cheek tickled. Again, his nails raked his face; relief was replaced with a twitch to his other cheek and a soft giggle. His eyes shot open, swatting away the hand holding a leaf in front of them.

"What are you doing?" He mumbled.

Aioffe snorted, quite inelegantly. "Time to wake," she said. "Dawn is nearly upon us." The mare nickered over her shoulder. The sun had yet to appear above the treetops and the ground was still hazy with early mist.

Tarl pushed himself up from the tree trunk and scanned around. A few people roused, but most lay still enough to be mistaken for logs.

"Why do you wake me so early," he paused, recalling the charade he had instigated in order to keep her safe. "Wife."

Her expression fell. "You say that as if I'm supposed to do something when you address me."

For a moment, Tarl gazed at her. Her face blank, meeting his eyes as an equal, understanding dawned on Tarl. "A wife would be considerate of her husband's needs. Prepare him something to drink and eat upon awakening?"

Aioffe's eyebrows shot into her forehead. "Are you unable to fetch it yourself? What ails you?"

Tarl bit his lip. "It's what's expected of a wife. To do as her husband commands. To service him. Me," he added, just in case she had forgotten. With his eyes, he bade her look around at the camp, where the womenfolk were the ones up and about, doing precisely what he had suggested.

After a brief glance at their industry, she shrugged. "What are you in need of?"

"A drink of water would be nice." He glanced at his shirt, which looked suspiciously clean yet damp and clinging to her curves. And bumps. Perhaps having her wander around camp would not be wise. Drawing a deep breath in, he said, "But I think you'd better just point me in the direction of the stream."

"It's just yonder," she tipped her head towards the tree line. "Is there anything else I'm supposed to do?"

"Dry out," he grumbled, then pushed himself up from the trunk. "I'll see if I can find something to eat as well. That's also what you should be sorting out. We'll be off before long, I'm sure, and hopefully through a town. You still need better clothes."

"That's your job. I'll do what I want," she said, a note of pride in her voice. "Husband."

Hearing her call him that made his heart race. It must be the exertion of standing after sleeping on the ground, he reasoned. Her wing bumps rustled underneath the linen shirt she had borrowed as their eyes met.

As if anyone would want to marry an abomination like her. He muttered, "Did I mention obedience?"

She stiffened, then picked up the mare's reins and led her away to a grassy patch, without the retort he expected.

*****

Mounted once again, Aioffe and Tarl rode in silence. He could sense the tension in her by the way she held herself rigid and away from him on the mare's haunches. The convoy ambled along the track at a steady lick, skirting mountains, fields dotted with fluffy sheep, and dense fir copses, before rejoining the coastline. Grateful for the peace, he turned his mind to practicalities. It seemed unlikely he would be paid wages any time soon, so he would have to barter his silver quickly if he was to purchase fabric to cover Aioffe. Given how entirely without shame and convention she was, the sooner that could happen, the easier he would feel about being around her. And having her around other menfolk.

Ap Tudor called a brief halt for lunch when the sun reached its apex several hours later. As he loitered for a hunk of yesterday's bread, Tarl took the opportunity to question the grey-haired cleric, now in charge of food distribution, about the intended route.

"Chester, then down to Shrewsbury," the elder said. "If the weather holds, should take us no more than four weeks to reach Southampton." His lips pursed, and he glanced at the sky. "If the weather holds."

Tarl nodded, as if travelling long distances was commonplace for him. "Seems reasonable."

Four weeks riding at close quarters with Aioffe wasn't so reasonable, but his hunt for the Bishop of Norwich must continue. His soul was at stake, and his mother's soul, which was worth travelling any distance for. Relinquishing Aioffe was the price. This pilgrimage, the pain he would suffer for penance.

"I've cheese too, if you want some?" The priest glanced over Tarl's shoulder. "Your wife looks to have taken a chill. Maybe she ought to wear a few more layers?"

"I would know your name, Father?" Tarl accepted the crusts and a knob of cheese.

The priest studied him with hooded eyes. "Father Thomas. I'm always available for those in need of enlightenment." His smile revealed no unnaturally long incisors, and he didn't smell any different to anyone else. In the daylight, the elder looked as human as he, thank the Lord. Tarl ignored a sudden urge to unburden his sins and offered the Father his thanks instead.

As he loped over to where he left their horse towards the end of the line, Aioffe glanced at him. She nudged herself close to the mare and bent her forehead to its neck.

"What's wrong?"

She muttered into the fur, "Four weeks. Everyone looking at me." She shivered and her eyes flicked to the right in explanation. Three soldiers loitered, muttering between themselves. He hadn't noticed them before, but he knew what being gawked at was like.

Beneath his shirt, her wings quivered. Unable to help himself, he reached out and touched the bump near her shoulder. She flinched as his fingers made contact and he retracted with an automatic apology.

When she said nothing further, he unbuttoned his jerkin. "Wear this." He dropped the thick linen over her shoulders.

She glanced at his bare chest. "Is that your order, husband?"

Tarl tore off a piece of crust and chewed. "Yes, I suppose it is," he said after swallowing. "But I didn't mean for it to offend. Only to cover the obvious."

"I could just fly away," she whispered.

"I know."

She turned her head to face him. "I'm not sure what's keeping me here."

The violet-blue of her gaze drew him in. He found he struggled to draw breath when she looked at him like that. In their depths, a vulnerability reminded Tarl of the look his mother shot him when they took her to the village stocks for delivering a stillborn. The accusation was the first of many which led to her eventual disgrace. But this creature was far stranger, more dangerous and more obscene than any of the charges levied against his mother. Yet There was no mistaking the fear he saw in Aioffe's eyes.

Before he could reason why she ought to remain under his care, she rallied. Blinked his stare away as her chin jutted out. "Tis only because it suits me to."

Tarl's lips tightened, if only to prevent them from rising. Her impudence he expected, like a sign that she was returned to the feisty girl he took her for. "As you wish, my lady. And I'll want my jacket back later. You don't seem to feel the cold, even at night."

This raised a small smile and her jaw relaxed. "I suppose it would hardly do for both of us to be inappropriately dressed."

To fill the awkward silence which followed, he offered her a piece of the bread.

She shook her head. "I have no need."

"Suits me." He took a bite and chewed thoughtfully. "Four weeks." He raised an eyebrow. "Where did you hear that?"

"Father Thomas just told you?"

His forehead wrinkled. That conversation had taken place some distance ahead. "What else did you learn?"

"Apart from something about tupping from the men over there," she tipped her head to the right at the soldiers.

Aioffe continued, "The sheep farmers in the wagon travelling two before us are worried about their horse casting a shoe, and the girl dressed in the green cape wonders if Ap Tudor will lift her skirts tonight." She raised an eyebrow at him. "What's tupping, and why would she need someone to lift her skirts? Can she not do that herself?"

Tarl tried, unsuccessfully, to keep the smirk from his face. "Does she indeed."

"I assumed we would stop for the night again. For rest." She shook her head. "Was I wrong? Should there be something more?"

He snorted, after which she said, "People - humans - are so

confusing."

Because fae-girls weren't? Tarl stuffed the last of the bread into his mouth and chewed vigorously.

*****

Two days later, on the approach to the walled town the farmers in the wagon ahead called Conway, Ap Tudor bade the men at arms lead the procession. He dropped back and lurked in the middle of the line, his head low and covered by a cap. When Tarl grumbled about his proximity, Aioffe relayed a rumour she had overheard. The huge castle had been taken over by his kinsmen during the uprising with Owain Glyndŵr only a few years before.

"Probably shares the same brutish features," Tarl speculated. "Doesn't want to be recognised."

"Humans look so different to each other," she replied. "Why is that?"

As she turned to him, his cheeks flushed. "People's likeness mixes within families."

When they neared the walled town, Ap Tudor ordered an early overnight stop in a nearby field. Shopping was permitted to replenish bread and other fresh foodstuffs. By late afternoon, many of the menfolk had left their women stirring pots of stew over camp fires to visit the town's alehouses.

Tarl argued with Aioffe about whether she should accompany him into the township or remain here, with the other wives and servants.

"I've nothing to do here," she maintained.

That much was true. He'd taken to scrounging himself leftovers as she showed no inclination to cook, nor did they have any equipment for it. Their travelling companions were wary of them both as foreign newcomers and mostly spoke in Welsh, so friendships were slow to form.

"I can be there and back faster if you stay," he snapped. Ap Tudor wandered over to their mare.

"That leg seems to be holding up well," he said, running his hand down the previously swollen fetlock.

"Aye." Tarl closed the straps of his satchel, hoping the silverware inside wouldn't clank too much as he made to leave.

"What's your secret?" Ap Tudor dropped the hoof and turned to them. His gaze lingered on Aioffe's hem. Her bare calves.

"No secret," Tarl replied, grabbing her hand. "Just an old Scottish remedy."

Ap Tudor's eyes narrowed. "Remarkable how quickly it worked."

"A blessing," she offered. Tarl's mind flashed back to her face flushed with pig, leaving him with the impression the word meant something different to her than it did to good Catholics.

"A prayer," Tarl corrected. Her eyes flitted to his and he squeezed her fingers. Hard. "We won't be long in town. I need some more ingredients for it, in case it happens again. Dried herbs from an apothecary are sometimes more powerful. Some cloth, if they have it."

Ap Tudor straightened. "Be back before sundown. We leave at the break of dawn. There had better not be any repercussions from your trip into Conway. No questions." He glared at Tarl and his lumpy bag, then at Aioffe. "They're more English than Welsh here, and don't take to strangers. Or Scots. And no-one likes a witch."

Tarl's lips tightened. "There won't be any upset, I assure you. If there were to be, you would find yourself short a blacksmith. I'm sure a Lord as well known as yourself wouldn't want to raise an alarm…"

Without saying anything to counter the implied threat, Ap Tudor clenched his jaw, then spun on his heel and stomped away.

"Don't think he isn't serious," Tarl said to her. "He's looking for a reason to be rid of you. Me, he needs, but that kind of man only has one use for a woman, and you wouldn't like it."

"My skirt may be short now," Aioffe said, and the side of her mouth lifted a little. "But he would be the last person I'd want to lift it when I get a longer one."

His heart thumped, against his wishes. He dropped her hand like a pair of hot tongs. "I hope you can sew fast."

*****

Their stroll into the town was punctuated by Aioffe stumbling. "Tis only because I have spent so long in the saddle," she reasoned to him the fifth time he caught her elbow. "Fae are meant to fly."

"Hush!"

"Well, it's true," she continued. "What's the point in having wings if you aren't to use them. And you have boots on, whereas I have none."

How her feet weren't blue with cold he couldn't fathom. Underneath the cake of mud, they were annoyingly pink and pretty. "Please stop talking about it." He nodded to a man staggering past, laden down with baskets and bundles.

She huffed. After a moment, she murmured, "This journey would take half the time if we could fly."

Tarl held his silence, reluctant to admit that maybe she was right. Unnatural though they may be, there were clearly advantages to flight.

"Couldn't we have travelled by boat?" She said.

"Do you ever hold your tongue?"

Aioffe's lips clamped together as Tarl took her arm so they could stride faster. Why did the track look so short from the vantage point of their camp, yet stretch before him now?

Ahead, the entrance to the town was announced by a pair of

gigantic, linked towers accessed by a drawbridge. High limestone walls, thick enough for soldiers wearing embroidered tabards walking atop, loomed above the road leading towards the gatehouse. Tarl swallowed as he scanned the stretch of defences on either side of the gatehouse - every one hundred and fifty paces along, stood a large crenellated tower of fifteen feet in width. A merlon with cross shaped slits punctuated various heights every three feet of wall. Below, a deep ditch, a killing zone, trapped its victims in mud at the base of the stone fortifications.

This was by far the largest, most well-defended town Tarl had been in. Surely they had several blacksmiths here?

After crossing the drawbridge, he felt her shiver as they entered the darkness between the vast, heavy doors of the gatehouse. Steadying her as she stumbled into him again, her head bowed as if she would be recognised. In truth, the scale of the walled township made him apprehensive, not that he would let her know he hadn't travelled outside of the wide open spaces of Orkney before.

He pulled her through the dim entrance towards the street. Sequestered and protected inside, a variety of houses and merchants lined the cobbles, all clustered higgldy-piggldy together in a colourful stretch. Despite being several stories high, they were dwarfed by the castle itself. The shops were doing a roaring trade, the alehouses spilled customers into the road and the hubbub swelled.

Aioffe's hesitation to progress from the shadows concerned him, so he glanced down at her. Her eyes fixed on the many turrets of the castle ahead.

"Is there a gaol there too?" She whispered.

He frowned, staring through the busy main street to the enormous fortification.

Then his arm was yanked away from hers and she screamed.

CHAPTER 21 ~ A DAEMONIC INFLUENCE

As her scream died on her lips, Aioffe's fingers tingled with her captor's Lifeforce. It invaded her very being as his rough hands tightened around her arm. In the shadows of the gatehouse, the guard's helmet loomed too close to her face as he stared at her. Her nose identified a peculiar stench emitting from the man, reminiscent of wild garlic, but with something confusing and... tasty about it.

Physical proximity was a mistake, for both of them.

Aioffe's heart raced as his quizzical gaze roamed her face. He looked like an ordinary human but was most definitely different.

"Where are you from, then?" The soldier asked, not unkindly but with genuine curiosity. His eyes dropped down her body, as if only just noticing her strange attire.

"She's done nothing wrong," Tarl interjected. "Get your hands off her."

The guard kept hold of Aioffe's arm, and she breathed in, tasting him further. The rush as his Lifeforce hit her nostrils was so powerful her head span. She could not stop pulling. The tendrils glowed faintly, mesmerising as they entered her fingertips. Alluring and delicious.

Daemon.

The stories were true. They did smell different. Taste different.

Their eyes locked together, and she leaned in to narrow the

gap between their bodies. She wanted more…

Tarl's hand slapped down on the soldier's arm, breaking the physical contact between them. "I said, get off her!"

As if in a daze, the soldier turned to look at him. His mouth moved wordless, gaping then closing as he stepped back. His hand rose to his helmet as if it pained him, then dropped to grip the red tabard he wore.

Aioffe wrenched herself away from the pull of his Lifeforce. Something that divine seemed implicitly dangerous. Forbidden. The jumble she felt inside as the energy entered ignited sensations unlike anything she had ever tasted, inviting exploration and unravelling. That she craved more after just one taste alarmed her more than she could ever have explained.

Without consideration of why, one abiding thought appeared in her mind. Flee.

Her head swivelled about in panic as she became aware of all the eyes watching them. No direction on the ground was safe. Too many people. The earth too uneven. But neither could she fly! Not here, not now.

Her wings objected, rustling against her back, until she felt Tarl's arm slide over her shoulders. As it dropped to her waist, pinning her appendages down underneath the linen shirt as he pulled her nearer to his chest, he said, "Unless you have a good reason for touching my wife, I'll thank you for your enquiry and inform you we are travelling to Southampton. To fight in the name of King Henry."

The soldier recovered himself and cast his eyes low. "I meant no harm. The town is full of strangers today. This one," he shrugged, "seemed especially peculiar."

Tarl's eyes widened. "This one?" He glowered at the man. "Is that any way to address a lady?"

Her skin burned with a blaze of shame. She was different; there was no hiding it when she had almost lost herself in the guard's Lifeforce. And now Tarl had been forced to intervene on her behalf. Again. She hung her head, Uncovered hair fell over her face, hands flat to her thighs. She looked at her bare feet and exposed calves. Her lack of clothes in public was, no wonder, the reason everyone was staring at her. Why she had been targeted by the soldier in the first place. Aioffe breathed a fraction easier. Singled out not because she had wings, but because she didn't fit in to a spring evening, in an affluent town in Wales.

"I just need some new clothes," she said, keeping her head subservient, as that seemed to be the obedient way wives were supposed to behave in the company of their superiors, or any man of power. "My garments were..." She searched for a reasonable explanation.

"Stolen, just the other night," Tarl said. "You'd be better off hunting down thieves than accosting victims." He swept his arm around the expanse of the town. "Perhaps it was someone local? You would be doing us a great service if you could find her gowns. Haven't you noticed anyone wearing an unusual amount of finery?"

Aioffe's lips twitched in admiration at Tarl's misleading suggestion.

The soldier's lip curled. "This is a well-ordered town. We tolerate no crime here." Then his eyes roved over Tarl's buttoned and muddy jerkin. "Finery. Fie! Neither of you looks able to afford the fine clothes of a knight. Who are you anyway?"

Before Tarl could proffer another lie, Aioffe took his arm. "Come now, husband, this man judges by what he sees, but not what he knows." She threw a fiery glance of superiority at the daemon, who had the decency to recoil. Her mother would be proud. She patted Tarl with her fingers and began to lead him out of the shadows. "I know you to be an honourable and courageous warrior, who has no need to prove himself to the likes of an ordinary guard just trying to do his job of protecting this good town."

She dipped her head to the soldier as she and Tarl stepped away. The lingering effect of the daemon's eyes on her tingled as they walked over the cobbled street ahead of the gatehouse. Only when they had turned into another road, where the buildings ran into each other to form a solid barrier, did Aioffe let out her breath.

Tarl's jaw remained clenched, though. His face was impassive whilst his gaze roamed the traders and houses to either side of the street. His hand lay almost possessively on top of her own as they passed butchers, candle-makers and inns. He paused as they reached a shop which, above its black and white frontage, had an ornate wrought iron sign hanging over the door. A pair of scissors. Open, glass-less windows afforded a view of a few rolls of fabric propped against whitewashed side walls. In the centre of the shop floor, a slim man bent over a large square table, laying out cut pieces of dark woollen cloth.

"When I've sorted out my business," Tarl said, "then we come back here and get what you need." His abrupt tone left no room for questions, so, after a lingering glance, Aioffe accompanied him onward. Her mind whirred with combinations of fabrics which she could fashion into suitable garments for them both.

Further towards the sea end of town, close to the castle, Tarl dropped her arm. His jaw clenched so hard it distorted the fine oval shape of his face. Ahead, thick castle walls absorbed any hint of activity inside as they faced the closed doors of a no less substantial inner gatehouse, even to Aioffe's hearing. Her chest relaxed as her fears lifted. Perhaps they had other ways of dealing with peculiar people than a gaol.

Aioffe followed Tarl's gaze to where smoke drifted around the tower corner. He sighed and she couldn't tell whether from relief or apprehension until the corners of his mouth lifted.

Heat from the forge fire warmed the cooling sea air in the late afternoon. As they approached, from deep inside, high chinks rather than clangs sounded, along with off key singing.

"Wait here," Tarl ordered, pointing to the side of the open fronted establishment. "I'll not be long."

Aioffe raised her eyes to meet the blue-grey steel of his. He was expecting her to rebel, run perhaps, she realised. So she curtseyed and simply said, "Yes."

"Try not to get into any trouble."

She nodded. His lips tightened as he disappeared inside. His absence afforded her the chance to study passers by and mentally design garments as she lurked underneath the timber overhang. After a while, she stopped listening in to Tarl's whispered negotiations. His haggling over price held little relevance to her as she had no concept of value and prices in this land. Instead, her toe ran absently over a raised cobblestone outside as she considered how quickly she would be able to stitch through the night.

A few minutes later, Tarl emerged with a broad smile plastered across this face and a chink of coins in his pocket.

"Nothing like as much as it was worth, of course, but, he at least didn't ask about the cup's providence." He looked mighty pleased with himself, taller somehow, as he took her elbow and steered her back towards the fabric shop.

Once inside the drapers, they fell into a husband and wife pretense with surprising ease, examining and discussing the materials as if they had been partners for years. Although the stock was limited, Aioffe chose a light brown linen to fashion both of them upper garments: a jerkin for Tarl and a bodice for her. A heavier tan wool for a skirt, then a lighter material to sew them both new undershirts was added to the pile.

Running her fingers over the rolls, Aioffe tried to contain her amusement that their clothing would co-ordinate like soldier or worker fae. Then she chided herself. The more they appeared like an ordinary couple, the greater the chances of her blending in. He caught her expression and frowned. She added a further stretch of mid-weight fabric, just because she liked the feel of it, without explanation of its purpose, although she fancied it would make a nice scarf for her head. One fine and one thicker needle, two reels of thread and a pair of shears turned up on the table before she nodded her satisfaction.

His eyebrows raised when the shop keeper totalled the price. Tarl winced, but handed over most of the coins he had in his pocket without complaint.

With a heart lighter than it had been in days, Aioffe skipped out of the door clutching one of the bundles. And promptly tripped over a raised cobble, flat on her face.

Behind her, Tarl sighed. "You fall even without a skirt to trip over." He rolled his eyes and proffered his hand.

Aioffe ignored it and proceeded to stomp ahead of him the entire route back to camp. She did not fall over again.

CHAPTER 22 - BUTTS

The retinue's numbers swelled after they left Chester. Daily archery practise for the men was added to the routine as the trail snaked South. Yet every evening, Tarl was called upon to assist with a cast shoe, to repair a broken cooking pot, or find a local forge for an hour. Under orders from Ap Tudor, any spare time he had was allocated to increase their arrowhead supplies.

When Aioffe questioned why he looked so longingly at the hay bale butts arranged for practice, he avoided answering with the shameful truth. Instead, he talked about the arrow-tips, the process of making them, and the necessity for variety. He tried to put it in terms she might relate to. "It's not just drawing a bow and firing. To pick which arrowhead will be needed means knowing what your target wears. How far away they are. Only then can you pick the right weapon for the job." Then he shrugged. "That's why I'm making broadheads, bodkin points and the stubby ones for crossbow bolts."

"But everyone needs to practise," she said.

His biceps pulsed with tense irritation, and he huffed. "It's been made clear what my job is."

Aioffe looked confused but didn't press; his surly mood only lifted when they rode into the next town where he could beat it out on yet another borrowed anvil.

One sunny but otherwise unremarkable evening, in a field some miles south of Gloucester, just as the butts were being positioned and targets pinned, Tarl plonked himself cross-legged on the grass. They sat in silence for a moment outside their waxed fabric sheet of a makeshift tent which they had been loaned. He sighed, then pulled out his whetstone from the satchel. He peered at Aioffe, expecting her to trot off and scrounge some food for him as she had taken to doing each day, but instead, she rummaged in their growing sack. His eyebrows knitted together as she presented him with a material parcel.

"I spoke to Nancy - the girl who's skirts Ap Tudor is lifting at present," Aioffe said, with a proud look. "She told me that the longbow men wear a padded jerkin, for ease of the draw movement in battle." She leaned in, "Our Lord needed his letting out at the sides, so I copied the design and made one for you."

He glanced at her, not knowing what to say. No woman had ever sewn him protective garments before. No-one had cared enough about his survival, he supposed. Equally, he'd never been to war before, either. Untying the neat bow which held it together, he shook out the light armour. His fingers then smoothed over the stuffed puffs, stiff with feathers underneath the thick linen. The stitching was, as he already had experienced with his new jerkin and trousers, exquisite. Seams stitched so tight, the clothes withstood the daily eight or more hours in the saddle without a tear. Testament also to her skill, was the fit. He pulled on the sleeveless jacket to find the same care had been given to mould the garment to his broad chest, and wider than usual arm holes to accommodate his biceps.

He grinned, then stood. After lacing the front, he pretended to draw and release in quick succession, just to test if the jacket strained with the exertion. Tarl was delighted to find his unexpected gift gave him all the flexibility his broad shoulders needed to pull back. "This should keep me warm even if I end up waiting for hours for the moment to arrive," he said after a few minutes before unlacing it with a sorrowful look on his face.

"Aren't you going to use it now?" Aioffe asked.

Tarl shook his head. "I have to sharpen these broadheads." The deep-tanged steel arrowheads took more work than the simpler thinner points, as they were designed to pierce plate armour.

"I can do that for you?"

Tarl looked at the cloth bundle of roughly hammered tips, the whetstone, then at her. There was nothing particularly technical or skilled about the job, he supposed. He'd been doing it for his father since he was a child, after all. "If you are sure? I'll show you how."

"I've seen it done before," she replied, looking at the yellowed grass. He saw her smirk, then she arranged herself on the ground next to him and took the leather lap cloth and whetstone from him.

She seemed competent, he had to admit, as he observed her slim fingers gliding the rough edges up and down the stone. Finishing one side of what was, admittedly, a not terribly flat curved broadhead, after only a little advice on pressure from him, she held it up for approval and beamed.

Her smile almost melted his gruffness, lighting up her pale skin and her blue eyes danced with pride. He took the arrowhead and twirled it, using the excuse of a close examination to hide his own relief.

"That's lovely work," he said, placing it next to the pile of fifty-odd other roughened shapes.

"Go and practise," she urged. "Before the sun dips." She picked up the next, then paused as he dithered. "Go!"

He bowed his head in gratitude and retied his jerkin as he strode off. As he made a bow with the thin leather strips, he glanced back at her. Catching his eye, she shooed him on with a vaguely threatening mime of throwing the next arrowhead at him, followed by a giggle which lingered in his ears after she disappeared from sight.

*****

The lone bowstave left in the barrel which they were transported in was old. As he unwrapped pole, the ash's heartwood at the front was cool and stiff from disuse. Years of layers of wax and tallow paint had darkened the flexible sapwood behind it. When he leaned down on the shaft, it still had a suppleness to its spring as the wood yielded. He ran his fingers over the swell, the belly where his hand would grip, noting a few knots had been left by the bowyer to keep the strength in the pole rather than weaken it by removal. Tarl rubbed the stave with a leather rag, hoping the warmth of friction would smooth out the cracks on the surface so the whole bow might appear less ancient.

After a few minutes with no difference, for a moment he considered asking someone for another, perhaps newer, or a yew bow, but, as he burnished, he changed his mind. There was something in the shape of the stave - the elegant curvature peppered with raised knots - which grew on him. Written off, consigned to the back of the barrel. This longbow had once been cared for. Well used, possibly victoriously, by someone who knew what they were doing. Tarl stroked the length of the stave and muttered a prayer, for himself and for the bow's former master.

The wood seemed to warm to his touch thereafter. He held it at arm's length, then balanced it on the edge of his hand, lightly gripping it between thumb and forefinger. Whatever else this bow had seen over the years, wherever it had battled, it still kept its level and integrity. That suited him and would serve him well, Tarl decided.

Pulling a stretch of cord out, he tied a loop knot in the hoof glue coated hemp and hooked it over the notched horn-tip. He pushed down on the stave's top, assessing the length required before he cut the string to size. Then he adjusted and knotted the loops at either end so that the middle of the cord, where the hemp had been thickened for strength when notching into the arrows, was correct for his long arms.

With a sense of the bow's history weighing on him, Tarl picked out a new-looking bracer from the sack next to the barrel, and tied it to his left forearm. A slip of horn positioned on the inside of the wrist would protect his skin from the lash of the powerful release. Grabbing a bag of arrows, he walked down the field to the make-shift range. As he passed the long line of archers shooting arrow after arrow into the bale targets, he studied their form through lowered lashes. Some received instruction from older, experienced soldiers, on grip adjustment or stance. Others simply worked on their speed of draw without wasting missiles, just mimicking the movement as he had earlier.

When he reached the end of the row, Tarl pulled out the arrows from his bag and stuck the tips into the earth in a line to his side. He limbered his legs and flexed his arms in the manner his father had taught him to as a boy, before repeating the draw and release to warm the bow. His heart thudded when he noticed that several of the archers alongside him had downed bows to watch his exercise. In their expectant eyes, he understood that they too were appraising his skills, and awaited his performance. The weight of expectation and competition bore down on him as he nocked his first feathered arrow.

'Test with one. Try with two. Fly with three.' The words of his father echoed in his mind as he half drew. Holding his breath, he tilted his head to look down the straight ash shaft briefly, as he would were he trying to aim.

The cord twanged, vibration shuddering through the bowstave as he let loose. The arrow landed a few feet off and skidded to a halt, flat on the ground.

He set another, ignoring the laughter to his right. This time, he stretched the string back slowly, as far as his muscles allowed. The jeers died down as he raised the bow up just a few inches from the ground and froze in his stance. His right arm jittered with tension. Held just behind his ear, the smell of the fresh hoof-glue binding on the fledgling feathers reached his nose and grounded him. Although he had not made arrows in many a year, the scent took him back. To happier times. To home, where his father's stinking glue pot would simmer for hours next to the forge fire. He stayed his grip and breathed out through his nostrils.

Counting back from three and returning to the present, he released the string. The arrow veered to the left, entirely missing the target some hundred feet away and overshooting by miles. Tarl smiled to himself. Someone gave a slow clap as he reached for a third arrow.

Tarl focused on a bale a greater distance off. Pivoting on his heels, the goose feather fletching brushed past his cheek as his fingers tucked the tiny groove at the end onto the hemp. His legs flexed as he drew back the cord and smoothly pushed the bowstave forwards. The fluid movement as his back arched, chest stretched and arms lengthened washed over him, wiping away any doubts. He pulled the string to his ear to give it the fullest power, the arrow almost flush to his cheek. Tarl again eyed the target, then let the arrow fly.

A dull thud announced his success, followed by a youthful whoop from his neighbour. The arrowhead had buried through to the feathers in the centre of the painted linen circle. Tarl grinned as he lowered the bow.

"You've done this before," the young archer stood next to him said. His round face suggested he was of a similar age to Tarl, but his clothing was grubby and untended. Tarl fancied he was only a few years older than the youngster.

"Can you do it again?" Ap Tudor shouted as he advanced,

limping somewhat, down the hill towards him. "Once is just luck, but if you're to stand with my line, I want to see speed and accuracy."

"Aye," Tarl said, bending down to grab another arrow. In brisk succession, he let loose five more arrows, all hitting the further target in less time than it took for Ap Tudor to step ten strides closer.

His face reddened from exertion, Tarl's arm dropped so the bow hung by his knees. Their commander nodded once, with a tight jaw. Then he snapped at the youngster next to them. "If a blacksmith can do it, then it can't be that hard."

Tarl noticed that Ap Tudor did not hold a bow in his hand, or any other weapon, for that matter. "I've arrows left if you want to show him?" He said, proffering his bowstave.

Ap Tudor's lips tightened. "A knight does not need to pull a string," he muttered. He rubbed a bruise on his cheekbone, then spat. "Just as a blacksmith does not need a wife to follow him to war."

Tarl bit his lip and turned back to face the butts.

"He's no knight," the lad murmured when Ap Tudor half stomped, half lurched away. "Just some jumped up Welshman trying to regain the King's favour."

Notching up another arrow, Tarl said, "As long as he pays my wages, I don't care why he's here."

"And your wife is pretty to look at," the lad continued. "I'd be happy if she followed me to deepest France. To tend my wounds and rub my muscles at night." He leered.

Tarl's chest tightened. He flashed his eyes at the boy and cautioned, politely but firmly, him to keep his distance from both himself and Aioffe in the future, if he wanted to make it as far as France. He shot another arrow off, which veered way past the hay bales and missed the targets, before un-hooking the cord. Practise was over, he concluded. The sooner he found the Bishop of Norwich in Southampton, the quicker he could cease pretending Aioffe was his wife and responsibility. Still fuming, although he wasn't sure why, he slung the bow over his shoulder and stalked back to camp.

CHAPTER 23 – UNWANTED ATTENTION

Aioffe crouched in the edge of the woodland, watching for Tarl's return. Her hand, still clutching the sharpened arrowhead in her palm. Blood dripped from it, dark and thick into the earth. The pain of the metal digging in kept her alert. She dared not release the weapon. Not yet. Perhaps not ever.

Her skin prickled as the memory of what had just happened replayed through her mind. She'd managed to escape Ap Tudor's clumsy touches whilst Tarl was at archery practise, by swinging a glancing blow about his face, then dropping the whetstone on his toe. Cussed shouts followed her as she stumbled away, into the woods, so now the whole camp knew of her mistake.

As if Ap Tudor's rants hadn't announced it, his nails had marked a deep scratch down her neck and across her collarbone which would be hard to conceal.

Her lips pinched together, only for a moment. Gritting her teeth, she hissed a curse of her own in faelore, just a minor one, but still one which her worker fae minders would not have approved of. She thought she'd been playing the part of a dutiful wife quite well. Until today. However, she had learned enough to know a woman striking a blow to their leader would not go unpunished. In Naturae or England, aggression to superiors wasn't tolerated.

And Tarl would not likely leave her alone to sharpen blades again when he found out. Her freedom would be curtailed at the very least.

But Ap Tudor hadn't followed her stumbling escape. Instead, she watched him disappear from her leaf-hidden sight down the hill, towards the make-shift range. He would be Tarl's problem now, she suspected. She might ascertain how much of an issue when she saw the expression upon Tarl's face on his return. Would he look for her? Whose version of events would he believe?

She wished she could dart up a tree, perch there for a while, but a dry summer already curled the leaves so camouflage was better in the bushes. After a while, when no-one searched for her, or even passed the treeline, she forced her mind to relax. Her toes, clad in leather soled boots, which were far too big for her but had been leant by Nancy, dug into the earth beneath for balance. The quiet rustles of the trees surrounding her soothed and her breathing came easier.

She was so still, when a squirrel dropped next to her and stood on its haunches as it nibbled on a green hazelnut, it made the mistake of thinking she wasn't a threat. Her mind snapped out of its semi-meditative state. A snack was needed to heal the cut to her hand. Her eyes slid sideways to study it. This time, the squirrel wouldn't escape!

Her arm shot out, grasping the rodent by its neck and she picked it up. Bringing it closer to her face, she smiled at it, even though its little feet churned in panic. Crooning as she cradled the beast, the soft red fur flattened as it relaxed. She rubbed it's white belly with her thumb, her mouth watering as she waited for the lull when it would be ready to surrender to her. The threads of the squirrel's Lifeforce, orange and faintly oaky, swirled into her nostrils. Her eyelids dipped.

Then, she delicately bit into it's neck and drank. Thin bright blood rolled around her tongue and she moaned. Having not eaten for many nights as she sewed Tarl's jacket, the refreshment bathed her body with a warm, vibrant embrace. Closing her eyes, she pulled on the little animal until there was no more to take. The husk, a floppy sack of fur and bones, she kept hold of as she sat on her haunches in the bush.

"What in heaven's name are you doing there?"

Aioffe's eyes flew open, her fingers dropped the squirrel.

But Tarl had seen. Stood a few feet from her, his lips tightened as she met his glare.

His eyes widened when he noticed her exposed collarbone. Then his voice hardened. "Disgusting behaviour."

"I'm not the brute," she said, pushing the hand clutching the arrowhead behind her back. With the other, her fingers brushed over the neck wound. Thanks to the squirrel, it had healed, so what he saw could only be the remnants of where nails had raked the skin, leaving dried blood as evidence. "That's Ap Tudor."

He glowered as his eyes darted over her person. Still warm from the direct infusion of Lifeforce, Aioffe's mind raced. To deny what she had done with the animal made little sense. Feeding always flushed her cheeks.

Tarl's head shook when he looked again at the squirrel's body.

Aioffe stiffened. Humans needed sustenance as well. She didn't eat the food she brought for him. What did he think she ate? Yet, his opinion mattered as the only person who knew how different she was. The only one who could instruct her in how to behave in human society. And now, his fists clenched. He obviously reviled her.

"Whatever you did to Ap Tudor to piss him off, he probably deserved," Tarl said in a calm voice. His eyes returned to the scratch, and he stretched out a hand. "But there's no need to hide in the bushes. You should have come and found me."

His gaze lowered to the ground. "I shouldn't have left you alone."

"I... I'm sorry." Lost for words, Aioffe stood on her own.

"As my wife, you are supposed to be under my protection, even when I'm not there."

To expect Tarl to shield her from the repercussions of her actions seemed odd to her. She had delivered the blow, in the full knowledge that her assailant was their designated leader. She had not behaved as a woman ought, and had challenged a man's authority. In doing so, she risked blowing her disguise as well as jeopardising their place in the safety of the convoy. Now, it was clear, the journey ahead would be all the more unsafe.

She frowned. "I don't need protecting." She thrust out the arrowhead in her hand, the point jabbing into the air between them. "See. I can take care of myself. I should have plunged this into his dark heart when I had the chance." The cuts to her palm had healed, but the deep red stain of her blood tarnished her pale skin and the metal.

His expression softened when he saw. "You're twice wounded." With two strides, he was by her side to take her fingers in his. His eyebrows knitted as his eyes scanned her body, blinking when he noticed the rip on the shoulder of her bodice. "Where else did he hurt you?"

Aioffe pulled her hand away, turning her head to stare at the earth. Once again, her skin prickled as she replayed how Ap Tudor had bent over her as she sat, muttering about how he liked her better before, when she wore fewer layers.

How much more comfortable it must be walking around so close to a natural state.

How much easier it was for a man to lift a shirt than a skirt.

Then Ap Tudor's hand had plunged.

Her face flushed with shame as she recalled how his fingers had so easily hooked themselves between fabric and skin, worming their way down below her collarbone, before she whipped around and thumped his face. She didn't understand what his intention was beyond trying to grab her chest, but it felt wrong to have a man so close, so intimate with her body without asking.

All of a sudden, the urge to run again coursed through her limbs.

Tarl's hand touched her shoulder, covering the tear in her chemise, stilling her. Her lips trembled as she raised her head to look at him.

"Did he force you? Uncover you?" Tarl asked. There was a catch in his voice she didn't understand.

"No!"

He exhaled. "Then what you are is still…"

She nodded, but her shoulder blades shook with vibrations from her pinned down wings.

"Good," he said gruffly. "He shouldn't have laid his filthy hands on you at all." He glanced down at the squirrel's limp body. His hand retracted as revulsion flashed again over his face. "Was that enough to heal?" His head rose and so did his eyebrow. "Or do we need to find something larger?" He turned to scout the woodland.

Aioffe blinked. His concern for her well-being was unexpected. Her behaviour, her entire persona, revolted him, so why did he show care? "I'm fine," she insisted.

He swivelled back to study her again. "You don't look fine."

Her eyes blazed. "I said, I'm fine." She stepped out of the bush and away from the evidence of her feeding.

"Then why are your shoulders shaking?"

She huffed a breath out.

He leaned closer. "And your knees."

She glanced down. The woollen fabric of her skirt waved, brushing her ankles and she realised her entire body quivered with tension. A too familiar desire to escape whirled into her mind, for there was no more pressing time than now to leave this situation.

Then she saw his stoic stance. The bow strung over his shoulder, which she had barely noticed before. The wrinkle of genuine concern at the corner of his eyes. And she reconsidered.

A soldier does not flee from battle. And this was a battle, she realised. A fight to survive against the odds in a society which was alien to her; its ways needed exploitation for her to succeed. And a warrior has allies. Tarl was her only ally. Any concept of returning home already discounted.

He reached out his hand, palm up. "I will protect you," he said in a gentle voice.

She pushed her chin out. "I don't need protection," she repeated.

"Maybe you don't," he replied. "But whatever occurred with Ap Tudor might happen again, if you are on your own." He stepped closer and took her elbow, as he had in Chester. "From now on, we do things together."

His tone left little room for doubt, and her heart thumped.

"Come back with me," he said. One side of his lips lifted. "Those arrows won't sharpen themselves, and I blunted more than enough today."

"What about Ap Tudor?" The mere thought of facing him started her quivering afresh.

"Leave him to me." Tarl reached over and took the arrowhead from her fingers. He squeezed her arm. "You won't be exposed. Attacked in any way, by anyone. You have to trust me on that. If he thinks a good blacksmith can only make weapons rather than use them, he can think again."

Mollified by the glower on his face as Tarl glanced at the campsite, Aioffe's heartbeat calmed. She, too, could wield a sword, but an ally, especially a man, couldn't hurt. As he led the way out of the woods and across the wide open space of the field, she leaned into him as she had seen other wives do.

CHAPTER 24 – ON THE SHORES OF SOUTHAMPTON

By the time the convoy progressed towards Winchester, midsummer had passed. The long days of travelling, punctuated by restless, humid nights, left Tarl weary. Aioffe, by comparison, seemed invigorated with each new town or hamlets en route. Charmed by the differing landscapes, she chattered away with an energy only tempered when they camped on the edge of cities, such as Marlborough and Gloucester.

Deep in the countryside, though, she thrived - positively glowed - when afforded the freedom of dark skies. Although tired himself, when the camp fell silent with sleep, he often lay awake with his eyes closed as she slipped out from their tent and away. After she left, he stuck his head out from under the canvas and stared, knowing that if he gazed at the sky just above the tree line for long enough, he would glimpse an angel ascend. One night, rapt at the moonlit sight, he noticed she had adapted her nightshirt with well-hidden slits at the back. Her enormous wings could slide out on such excursions, and he presumed it also made flying and landing all the easier. Whenever he managed to stay vigilant and watch her soar, his heart yearned to join her.

Try as he might to avoid feeling envious, as the trek continued, exhausted and with the prospect of battle looming, he understood her desire for liberation. And felt at war with himself even more. Was he doing the right thing? Should he sacrifice her innocent joy and freedom for his own salvation?

His recourse was to push her aside, shun contact where possible. But, she was persistently attentive, picking through his defences with charm and chatter on a daily basis.

By morning she would return, to wake him with a steaming cup of tea. She learned which berries to forage, although all of her attempts at cooking verged on inedible. Raw even. He swallowed down what she provided, hiding his grimace out of politeness. Her wifely behaviour served to remind him that she was making a constant effort to behave in an appropriate manner, which made his decision all the worse.

As the weeks wore on, he became a little less grumpy upon waking to her smile, but still he couldn't voice the question which ran daily through his mind: why she stayed, when they both knew she could so easily leave? Half of him wished she would, for her absence might ease of the burden of what would transpire if she were discovered, or, what her pale skin would feel like next to his.

As they drew nearer to Southampton, where Henry V mustered his troops, the convoy's pace hastened. The tens of travellers ahead and behind them in the long train now numbered some two hundred people. Conversation, which had become a sort of schooling for Aioffe as Tarl explained various blacksmithing techniques to her to pass the hours, grew stilted as they listened to the excitement build in their comrades, mile after mile.

Tarl's shoulders tensed with apprehension and his head lowered. In his prayers each morning and night, he asked for the Lord's forgiveness for his unnatural, growing feelings about his peculiar passenger. Every step brought him closer to the Bishop of Norwich. To salvation for his soul. To handing over Aioffe to a higher authority. Tarl knew he ought to feel relief at the prospect, but as Southampton appeared, the lump in his throat grew.

When no order to halt and make camp was given at the usual late morning-time, Aioffe, riding behind him on the saddle, tapped his shoulder. When he turned his head, her eyelids flared and she pointed. His gaze followed down the slight dip to the horizon, where the grey-blue of the sea lay. The gateway to war. Or, where he would find the Bishop.

If it was possible for his spirit to sink any further into his boots, it did. She must have sensed his dread, for an arm sneaked around his waist and she rested her cheek on his back. Tarl's eyes filled as he stared straight ahead. How could she know this meant goodbye? Did she sense the conflict within which caused his heart to thump?

He blinked rapidly, then cleared his throat. They were not even on the outskirts of the town, still several miles away, but the road snaked past fields covered in tents, equipment, wagons, and horses. His eyes widened as he tried to calculate how many people awaited the order to sail off to a foreign country to fight for their King.

"So this is what an English army looks like," he said, his chest tightening. How would he ever find the Bishop amongst the thousands here?

Tarl stiffened as a rider thundered past, shouting, "Clear the route! The King, the King!" He held a pennant aloft, with three golden lions on a red background, split in half by blue with some sort of swirling insignia in silver.

He tugged the reins to the side and urged their mare up, onto a narrow embankment. Ahead, men jumped off their wagons and tried to haul their carthorses over tighter to the hedgerow. "Get down," Tarl muttered to Aioffe, who gazed ahead, curiosity wrinkling her brow.

Sliding off their mount, he followed her stare. All he could see in the distance was a cloud of dust thrown up by galloping hooves. "Please," he urged. "For the love of God and King, dismount." He dropped to his knee and bowed his head. All along the track, others were doing the same, but she remained, mesmerised, on the hind of their horse.

"Wife!" Tarl grew desperate as he heard the thunder of approaching hooves. He reached up and tugged on her ankle. "To show disrespect is to announce how different you are."

She nudged his hand away, so he glanced up. Her mouth pinched as if she were restraining herself from blurting out a response, but before he could press her further, a troop of four armoured guards cantered past. Tarl's head whipped about, catching sight of three more people approaching on horseback. In the middle, rode a young man with a star-like scar to his cheek and a thin circle of gold atop his jaw length brown hair. He was flanked by two older men with dark robes flowing behind them. All were grim of face as they urged their mounts along the haphazard queue.

Tarl's heart hammered, and he dropped his head again. In the presence of royalty for the first time in his eighteen years, when the King's horse kicked dirt up as he passed, Tarl's sense of expectation dissipated. He chided himself, blinking away the dust from his eyes. What had he expected? A golden aura? A man larger than life itself?

No, this King Henry was but a man. Little older than himself perhaps, and already battle scarred. For all that a king was divinely blessed with power, there was no visible statement of his position other than a thin ring of gold upon his head and the proclamations. If it hadn't been for the fore-rider's calls and banner, Henry could be mistaken for any other well born, young Lord.

Still, he was a royal, a King no less, and thus required respect. This had been drummed into him his whole life. Respect the Church and respect the Ruler. Henry might not be his King, but he was the King of England. Yet disappointment prickled as

Tarl stood.

One person hadn't afforded the ruler any sign of respect. Still sat on the horse, Aioffe's head turned to keep Henry's retreating back in her vision. Had she seen something different, he wondered?

Tarl scowled as he put his foot in the stirrup.

She raised an eyebrow. "He looked so… ordinary," she said. "But then, I've never seen a King before."

Perturbed that he had just been thinking the very same thing he grunted. "In this country, show some respect." Tarl swung his leg over the saddle, then reached for the reins.

She bristled. "What does he do, then, to afford him that respect? What powers does he have?"

"Powers?" Tarl scoffed. "He's the one who makes the laws, dictates the tithes and leads the country."

"Into war? For what purpose?"

"It's a righteous war, I'm sure."

"Right for whom?"

The scepticism in her voice hushed him, but she continued. "I just wondered what would happen if people didn't follow his lead. What powers of enforcement he has to make them do his bidding."

Tarl shrugged. "For honour. To avoid punishment, I suppose. He is God's anointed ruler."

"What does anointed mean?"

Tarl shook his head. "It's complicated."

He didn't exactly know. "There's a ceremony where God approves and bestows his wisdom and powers upon the King."

Aioffe sniffed. "A King is a God?"

"No, there is only one God."

"Who gives the King his powers?"

"Yes. No. When he is made King, he gets the power officially. Until then, it's kind of taken on trust, I assume."

Sort of. Tarl's lips pinched together. He hoped she wasn't going to ask how the transfer of sovereignty and godly authority worked. "Until he has a coronation, and then it's official."

"But you can't see the powers?"

"No. I suppose not. Other than in the wearing of a crown."

He could sense her frowning as the convoy set off again. They progressed a few paces before they turned through a gate. Across the meadow, tents, fireplaces and makeshift washing lines dotted around the dried grass. Marching down a slight gradient, the line dispersed. The Ap Tudor contingent assembled on the far side of the field. As they dribbled over, instructions were issued to secure their belongings and horses in the area between a hedgerow and to the edge of another Lord's encampment. All men were ordered to gather their arms, so they could present for inspection by the King's clerks.

Returning to her after collecting his weapons and trying not to show his nerves, Tarl slung his arrow sheaf over one shoulder and his satchel over the other. Aioffe was unusually quiet as she unstrapped their remaining bags and bedding from the mare. He stood in front of her, fingers curled around the old bow. "I'm not sure how long this will take."

His mind was less on the muster, and more on his personal quest. Given the sheer scale of the army they had already passed, finding the Bishop of Norwich required time. He might be quartered in one of the outlying abbeys, friaries or country estates, if he was in the area at all. This realisation dictated his immediate decision. Looking at her now, Tarl decided he needed more information on the official's whereabouts before he brought Aioffe before him.

"I know I said we would stay together, but as long as you remain with the other women, and Ap Tudor comes with us, you'll be fine. Will you wait here until I return?" He studied her slim figure, motionless as she gazed towards the horizon. He wondered for a moment if the sight of the army would prompt her to take her freedom while she still could, while another part of him couldn't bear the consequence.

She nodded, not meeting his enquiring eyes as her focus remained behind him.

Tarl hesitated, then mumbled, "There's always more arrows to sharpen? If you have the time."

She chewed her lip, then said, "If we are to go to war in another country, had you truly considered getting there?"

Tarl turned to see where she looked. In the distance, the countryside sloped gently to the coast. Beyond the town walls. The towers of a castle. His stomach lurched. Entirely filling the river mouth and sea, the view was dark with hundreds, maybe a thousand, ships. Just the sight of them sent his heart pounding. If he was to escape that watery doom, he had to move fast.

"Smith!" Ap Tudor cantered, clanking with armour, across the field. He shouted, "No time for gawking. The King's inspector awaits." His lip curled as he reined up a few feet from them. "Let's see if a puny Scot can impress him enough to justify a wage." His eyes narrowed on Aioffe, then he jerked his horse around with a face like thunder.

Tarl's grip on his bow tightened. With a last glance and a gentle, reassuring smile at her, he strode towards the line of men marching across the field.

CHAPTER 25 – JUSTICE SERVED

The land had been stripped of woodland for miles around, which gave Aioffe some cause to worry. It didn't look like the encampment was moving any time soon as the women and pages busied themselves unpacking the horses and wagons. The prospect of travelling on one of the many vast ships which jostled in the Solent excited her, but, without any sense of when that might happen, it looked like they were staying put for now. With a sigh, she reined in her disappointment and steeled herself for frustration at the curtailment of her liberty. Once she had pitched their accommodation, she sat cross-legged and began to sharpen arrowheads whilst keeping a watch around her surroundings.

She started to form an idea of how the English humans fought as she watched twenty men manoeuvre a large wooden device down the track. Although disassembled, it looked as though the wheeled triangular shaped frame was designed to support the long arm, the length of a tall tree, to toss something held in a leather bucket. The prospect of seeing how hurtling objects would work in a battle intrigued her. Aerial combat, fae on fae, was all she was used to. Her brother and the Naturae army practised it all day, every day. She, on the other hand, had spent her centuries perfecting needlework. As a result, her perfect and swift stitching was all she had to offer the camp, and soon in demand. It hardly seemed a fair exchange with the prospect of war looming, and now, more than ever, she wished she'd done more to learn one end of a sword from another. The aerial acrobatics, though, that she could do, but that wasn't much use to the humans.

Tarl returned early in the evening, by which point Aioffe had finished her task and found a stream to wash their dusty travelling clothes in a few fields away. He dropped a bundle of white and red fabric down inside the awning and sighed. With a regretful glance at their damp shirts hanging on the line, he pulled off his padded jerkin and swapped it for the jacket she had made him.

"Let's go back into Southampton," he announced.

"Have you just come from there?"

He nodded, rummaging for the small bag of coins in their travel sack. He tipped some more coins into the retrieved purse, then buried it in his tool satchel. Only one item of the church silverware remained in its depths - the ornate silver cross. Everything else had been melted down and exchanged for money, which they had spent on food and material on the way. "I've passed inspection and paid as a smith and an archer. Come on, we're leaving."

Tarl wasn't looking at her at all, she realised. A nervous tension in his aura caught in her mouth and she swallowed the lump in her throat.

Aioffe blinked. "Do we set sail already? I've only just got unpacked." She glanced around the closest tents, where there was a distinct lack of activity. She bundled the arrowheads back into their bag, then reached for the material he had left. "What's this fabric for?"

"Identification. All Englishmen are to sew a red cross onto a white jupon. So you don't shoot one of your own. Or, so they know which side of the battlefield to bury the bodies. I doubt they would ship us home."

His answer sent a shiver down her spine. She would recover

from a mortal wound, Tarl would not. Many husbands, fathers and brothers would fall in battle, irrespective of which side they fought for. This, Aioffe realised for the first time, was the problem with human warfare: their fragility, on top of their shorter lifespan. Fae and vampire could heal themselves, given enough Lifeforce or blood, whereas mortals simply died. No wonder Tarl was afeared.

"Come on," he urged, plucking her cloak from the tent pole. He tossed it to her. "This will all be over soon."

"The war?"

"No, that's very much still to come."

She bit her lip. There was something very ominous about his tone, and his anxiety still soured the back of her throat.

"Have I done something wrong?" She asked.

He shook his head, then held out his hand even though he didn't meet her eyes. "Just… there's someone I have to see before it gets too late." He looked at her then, through veiled eyelashes. "And I'm not leaving you here on your own." His lips pursed. "With Ap Tudor wandering around all inflated with how many men he's brought to serve, it's not safe for you."

Aioffe threw her cloak over her shoulders, although her chill was not from the air. Her fingers uncharacteristically fumbled with the clasp. "I'm ready."

But she wasn't. As he took her elbow to walk across the field, it seemed more as a way to improve their speed than for support. His quick march past other travellers, carts, construction yards and bustling hostelries kept her quiet as she concentrated on keeping up with him, without falling over.

He kept his grip light but firm all the way into Southampton, not even releasing her when they approached the impressive Bargate entrance to the walled town. Five archways of varying size lead through the stone walls, its gleaming white edging which spoke of recent renovation. Red and blue embroidered pennants hanging down from the four arched and glazed windows above left no doubt that the town was under royal occupation. Poking between the crenellations, next to the bell on the top of the wall, rested three black mouthed metal tubes, facing the coast. When she pointed at them with a query in her eyes, Tarl snapped, "Cannon," and urged her on.

He hustled her past merchants houses, candle-makers, bakers and butchers with huge fitches of bacon hanging in their open windows, and even more inns. Tarl resolutely ignored cries from shop-keepers still selling their wares on the warm summers' evening. Any attempt at conversation between them was drowned out by the volume of their entreaties and the hubbub of drinking games. It was so busy that, for once, Aioffe felt insignificant. Unnoticed amongst the throng of people which filled the wide avenues.

Something about the massive numbers of humans congregated in one place sent her senses on alert, which was an unsettling sensation. Wisps of Lifeforce emanating from the humans almost overwhelmed her at first, and she was glad of Tarl's arm guiding her until she grew used the kaleidoscope of colours and sounds.

They dodged clusters of guards, then down a narrower road to the right. The flagstone street which led to the base of the castle hillock clattered with equine activity, and must have required constant sweeping to remove the dung from countless deliveries and mounted guards.

By the time they reached a smaller gatehouse in the walls circling the base of steep hillock, Aioffe's skin crawled, her senses overloaded by differing smells and Lifeforces. The undercurrent of excitement made her head spin; her fingers twitched on Tarl's arm but she resisted pulling even just a strand, for fear she would lose concentration and fall. Or, be noticed.

While Tarl discussed entry through the gates with a soldier, she glanced up at their destination. Accessible only by steps winding around the mound, the round pimple of a castle overlooked the town and coastline. Although it was smaller than many they had journeyed past, her ears pricked at shouted orders from inside its thick walls.

Refused admittance, Tarl strode back, scratching his neck and scowling. "There's some sort of trial going on."

She detected a camouflaged note of desperation in his tone. "A trial?"

"A plot to overthrow and kill the King has been discovered. A trial is where they determine who is responsible for a crime and what punishment they should face."

In Naturae, such matters would require only the Queen to pass judgement, and it was usually swift and brutal. Aioffe thought of the tense yet determined look upon King Henry's face when he rode past them earlier. "Is there some question about it, or who's to blame?"

"There's always a question," Tarl said. "The extent of the plan might not be as elaborate as reported, of course, but it's to be brought before learned peers and any witnesses called upon to determine the facts." He sighed. "Such proceedings usually would take many months to complete. The guard said, those involved had only just been outed."

Intrigued, Aioffe mused, "What about the war? Would that wait for a verdict?"

Tarl lifted his eyebrow. "His life has been threatened. Who knows which Henry would decide is more important? A war at home, or a war in France." He let out a huff then cast his eyes up the tall tower.

Aioffe understood the King's dilemma. A threat to a ruler must be taken seriously, but the timing of a lengthy trial could be catastrophic if it led to a delay. "It's costing the King to keep men standing around here. Every day brings us closer to winter," she said, "and fighting on the ground will be harder in poor weather."

Confusion replaced the frustration on his face, then he frowned at her with eyes which questioned. She quickly shook her head. "Of course, what would I know of such matters." She followed with a titter, and his shoulders relaxed. But, she was intrigued by what might happen in such proceedings in this land. "Did you say witnesses? I could be a witness. I've seen lots of things."

He snorted. "A witness to plots and subterfuge?" His expression cast doubt upon her assertion.

"I know more than you think about betrayal," she said, her eyes wide as she stared at him. As for deception, having first escaped Naturae in disguise, she accepted her new life was one of constant hiding who she was, just to survive. What better experience of deceit? More than that, Aioffe knew about lying to authority, and was well practised at saying what someone wanted to hear, and dealing with the pangs of guilt afterwards.

Tarl's stance shifted, and he studied the ground. In the slope of his shoulders she could see his despondency. Whatever he wanted inside the castle meant a lot to him. He'd been twitchy for days, as they neared Southampton. His essence, the dancing orange strands in his Lifeforce, told her this was of such significance to Tarl that he could think of nothing else but resolving the issue. She glanced at the soldier. Could any man fight effectively if so distracted by another matter? She doubted it. Lyrus, although he'd never fought in an actual war, constantly disciplined the fae soldiers to 'Focus, focus, focus to fight.' Her mind resolved. For the sake of preserving Tarl's life, she had to help so that he could go into battle with a clear conscience.

"Having come this far, we could at least try?" She offered, "Let me speak to him. I know something which might work."

After swallowing hard, he then gazed at her for the first time all afternoon. In his eyes, she saw a conflict. A fear.

"Please, trust me," she said.

Then, his mouth set and he took her hand.

She had never tried to lull a human before, but it seemed like now might be the time to try. She led Tarl to the gatehouse and stood as close to the guard as was respectable. "Kind sir," she started, touching his bare forearm with her fingertips. "My husband tells me he neglected to inform you I am needed for the King's trial."

The guard's eyes lifted from her hand to meet her gaze. His mouth dropped as she pushed her will down through her fingers into his body. Just a little, but enough that he would become suggestible rather than soporific.

"I'm a witness, you see, and must make my testimony before the…"

She was unsure of the right words or who would be there to judge, but as she let her explanation hang, Tarl intervened, "Court."

Aioffe tasted the guard's Lifeforce, sweaty and stale, tinged with cabbage, before insisting, "So, if you permit us entry, we can find our own way. We mean nothing you need to concern yourself about."

The solider nodded, dazed as she pushed a little more of her entreaty through her fingertips. Tarl entered the low doorway first, dragging her after him. "Thank you so much," she called back.

Her head span with the effort and her focus blurred as Tarl stepped through the passage, and into a small courtyard. In the distance, she heard a hammer banging on wood, and the scrape of chairs being moved. While she recovered her wits, Tarl stopped, sizing up the narrow doorways which offered access to the towers at the corners of the main building. Before he could decide which to head for, the double doors flung open and a stream of well-dressed people poured out. Removing their official but warm capes as the trapped heat of the late afternoon assaulted them, the crowd barely paused their discussion as they dispersed across the cobbles.

The grip Tarl had on her hand tightened as he froze for a moment. Aioffe's nose twitched. More than one of those present in the yard were vampire and daemon. Her heart thudded a warning.

Tarl dropped his grip as eyes darted around, searching the courtiers as if he would recognise one. He glanced quickly down at her and she smiled at him, expecting this to reassure her husband. His lips tightened with resolve.

"Are you looking for someone in particular?" She ventured.

Saying nothing, he strode towards an old man wearing a long, gold chain of office and a floppy black hat. In his arms, the official clutched a heavy-looking stack of papers to his chest.

"Where can I find the Bishop of Norwich?" he asked, without polite preamble.

The man started, then wafted his hand towards the round tower of light grey stone. "In the new tower, I presume. Why?"

Without answering, Tarl grabbed Aioffe's arm again and propelled her towards the sturdy double doors. Her heart fluttered. Why was he being so rough with her?

"Don't I know you?" The man asked, scurrying after them. Behind him, a boy page hastened across the yard carrying a portable desk.

"I have business with the Bishop, my Lord," Tarl said over his shoulder. But the man's arm shot out to stop them. The action jostled the paperwork he clutched, tilting the sheets awkwardly out of their neat pile.

"I recognise you! You were one of that Welshman's men, Ap Tudor was it, from this afternoon. Although, I recall upon inspection, you intimated uncertainty as to whether that would be a permanent arrangement when you were demonstrating you abilities as both archer and... smith wasn't it? Yes, Tarl the Smith, I remember now. With the Welsh, but from Scotland. An unusual combination of celtishness."

The official looked Tarl up and down, ignoring her completely. Tarl shuffled his weight between his feet and kept his head low. "I remind you that you have been bound to serve at least one quarter year under his command for the wages Ap Tudor has drawn on your behalf." Wise eyes narrowed on Tarl's broad chest and strong biceps, and the man's thin lips pursed together for a moment.

"Of course, if you were to reconsider whose banner you fell under, I could, perhaps, adjust the paperwork. For the same compensation. A fine young man like you might be better placed with someone more... experienced." A grey eyebrow waggled up. "Sir John Cornwaile for example, would know where best to place another longbow, although he has fulfilled his indenture for archers." He shuffled the bundle of papers in the crook of his arm, and a few sheets slipped out. "Or perhaps the Duke of Gloucester. The King's younger brother."

Tarl bent down to assist the page with picking up the paperwork. Aioffe coughed delicately to distract the man as she noticed Tarl sliding a slip into his satchel.

After returning her smile as he rearranged the bundle so it was more secure in his arms, the official continued, "Although the Duke lacks experience, he is certainly well educated, and politically, you couldn't be better placed for loyalty to be repaid when this is all over. Lord knows, the boy needs some good shots to command, for he cannot keep his head out of his books. What do you think, Paget?" He accepted the final lost papers and turned to question the page, who rolled his eyes. "Perhaps you're right," the official chuckled. "A little late in the day to be making changes to the rolls."

The young page looked relieved, then ventured, "The recess has almost passed, Sire."

The official seemed to remember where he was, and his beady eyes narrowed on Aioffe. "But, what business could you both have with the Keeper of the King's Jewels?"

"He's an old friend of my family, and I have a message I need to pass on." Tarl patted his satchel.

"I can make sure he gets it," the page volunteered.

The official's eyes slid to Aioffe, after which Tarl hastily added, "And I need to introduce my wife to him and ask him to bless our union. We thank you, however, this is a family matter."

"Well, think about what I've suggested." The official nodded. "The Bishop has much on his mind, Mistress, and I doubt has time to hear entreaties for her husband's safe keeping." His eyes snapped to Tarl. "Although, I don't recall you mentioning her at the muster?"

"I stated I travelled with an apprentice?" Tarl's jaw clenched.

"Well, every place on board has to be accounted for." The official's fingers rifled the paperwork as if the answer lay within. "You did not specify your apprentice was a woman, much less your wife." He shook his head.

Paget piped up, "And you didn't declare for certain if she was coming with you."

Aioffe switched on her most beguiling smile, hoping the man would soften. "I require no payment or food," she offered. "Only the experience of supporting my husband serving your King and this country."

By her side, Tarl stiffened. In his aura, the wavering strands of Lifeforce betrayed an indecisiveness.

The elder sniffed. "It is an honour to serve. That is true." His gaze bore into her. "But, 'tis a rare apprentice who does not seek payment, especially during such a time as this."

Tarl put his hand on her arm. The wisps slowed in their

vibrations as he said, "She shares in my rations and my wages will more than support her. Without her, I could not be both bowman and blacksmith."

"Very well then." The official waved a finger at Paget. "Mark down Mistress Smith at the bottom of the roll when you get a moment, boy. She is still a body which takes up boat space, even if she apparently requires no sustenance or payment."

Still looking sceptical, the official nodded at them both and left.

"Why wouldn't you have said I was accompanying you?" Aioffe asked as soon as the pair were out of earshot.

His lips tightened together. Once again, she sensed that indecision in him.

She hung her head. "I know, I'm a risk. But I won't betray you, or what you have in the bag."

"I… I just didn't know if you cared to come to war," Tarl replied, his voice quiet.

He led them through the double doors into a large vaulted chamber. At the far end, a long table stood in front of five high-backed chairs. Stools and lower backed seats were being shuffled into place by servants, and the candles replaced as if preparing for an audience to arrive. The vast room smelled of fresh chalk whitewash, obscured by heavy tapestries rich with images of people and quotes on every wall. Above them and running around the hall, narrow wooden walkways provided access to cross-shaped window slits in the stone.

Tarl peeled to the right, where lighter coloured stonework marked out a more recent construction. In front of a curtained doorway, a soldier picked at his nails.

"I have business with the Bishop," Tarl announced.

The guard's eyes stared balefully at them.

"Treasury business," Tarl jutted out his chin as he withdrew the slip of paper secreted in his satchel. "Under orders from the

King's Inspector." He waved the note in front of the soldier, who scanned the neatly written ink all too fast.

Perhaps to hide his illiteracy, or because Aioffe leaned over and gently touched his wrist with a smile, the guard relented. As held the curtain to one side for them to enter, Aioffe rolled hers shoulders back and pasted on her most demure expression in readiness. This time, the effort of calm persuasion cost her less.

But when Tarl opened the door behind the drape, a stench she recognised wafted out. Her heart thumped against her ribs.

Vampire.

CHAPTER 26 – COUNTING THE COST

Tarl's throat was dry. Aioffe's talk of knowing about betrayal outside the castle reminded him that he was a thief, and worse, a liar and deceiver himself. But what choice did he have? His stomach knotted when he saw the robed figure sat behind an enormous desk. For the last few months, he had committed himself to handing her over to someone in higher authority. Absolve himself of the burden of his own guilt and the burden of responsibility for her.

Now, when it came to the time to fulfil his task, and with her small hand warm in his, he again wavered.

The Bishop's head, abundant with curls, didn't even rise as he said, "Fae. Who brings me a fae?"

Tarl's tongue lay thick in his mouth. He could not answer, or swallow. Just stood there like the village idiot. Without explanation, the Bishop knew what she was.

What had he done?

The quill stopped scratching, and the Bishop looked up. Tarl could only stare at the cross which hung from a heavy braid of gold around the middle-aged man's neck. Taunting him. His head reeled at the betrayal and he almost crumpled as he stood.

"Well?" The Bishop's gaze slid to Aioffe and his lips pulled back.

Bared incisors. Unnaturally long. Tarl's heart raced. How could he have been so foolish? His faith and naivety had blinded him to the obvious, for who else but the Church was going to take care of the oddity which was Aioffe? Who else but another freak of nature. Why had he not thought of this probability? How had he been so selfish? All he had considered was salving his own pain. This was only repeating his mistakes.

She squeezed his hand, and he felt a tingle spread up his arm. He wondered if she was doing the same mesmerising, calming thing he had seen her do with animals and the soldier at the gate. It was pleasant, like being stroked with a summer breeze on a hot, dusty day.

"I come to see who we sail with," Aioffe said. Her voice seemed distant, and yet at the same time, so close it was an intimate whisper.

Aioffe! Tarl's head swivelled to look down at her profile, his heartbeat pounding in his ears.

The silence between the Bishop and Aioffe yawned between them as Tarl's mind struggled to plot a course. His plan dissipated like grey clouds parting. Through the window slit behind the desk, bright white sunlight peeked through, bathing her in its warm embrace. Her skin shone silver and he yearned to stroke its softness.

With every fibre of his body, Tarl realised he could not bear to be parted from her. The tension clamped his chest like a vice, forcing a separation between his head and his heart.

He, Tarl Smythson, a thief, almost a killer of priests, and son of an accused witch, had brought an innocent into the lion's den. Looking at the Bishop's teeth, he recalled the story of Daniel. But unlike Daniel, no-one else would take his place in this pit.

And yet, there was no peace to be found for his conscience without the Bishop's help. God would surely not have accepted a vampire as an ordained priest if he didn't want them to be a vessel for forgiveness? Despite the danger, perhaps this vampire was different?

"My Lord Bishop," he said, "I came to ask... to offer...."

"Ask?" The Bishop's head cocked to one side. "One does not bring me a fae and try to bargain." His eyes narrowed on Aioffe. "She would know that." The Bishop's nose wrinkled with obvious disgust.

"The Sation wars have been over for centuries," she said. "Our peoples are at peace."

The Bishop's lips parted. "When you live for long enough, there can never be sufficient time to forget what has passed."

Tarl frowned. The Sation wars? Centuries? What were they talking about?

Aioffe hung her head. "There was much loss on both sides, and you were the victors. I hoped you would show some graciousness to my kind."

"That all rather depends on what you want, doesn't it?" The Bishop tipped his finger towards Tarl and continued staring at Aioffe. "Here you are, with a… mortal. Is this not breaking the agreement between our kind?"

"We were permitted the freedom of Naturae's realm, as long as we did not interfere. I have not."

"Then why are you here? As a spy, perhaps?" The Bishop's lips curled.

"No!" Aioffe whispered. Her hand wriggled, clammy within his, but he would not loosen his grip on her.

This was his doing. He had to take responsibility. Save her life. "She is no threat to you," Tarl said. "She is my wife, and we came for your blessing to travel with the army," he improvised.

She deserved better. She needed better. His eyes darted around the room. Locked chests were stacked up against the walls. On display, a variety of ornaments, shining with jewels. The wealth of a Kingdom. Before him, a person who obviously valued responsibility for such trinkets. Why else had they been left unpacked if not to proclaim ownership over these riches?

Despite what the Bishop had said, about trying to bargain, at least there was a discourse. The vampire was a politician as well. Striking a deal was how things were done. Bargaining was their only way out. However much he disliked what he had to offer, it was necessary to keep them both alive. First, her freedom.

"But more than that, your Excellency, we want to be of value to the King. This will be a difficult war, and my wife's particular abilities could be of use." Tarl's eyes dropped to the bumps behind Aioffe's shoulders. "You need aerial assistance to win."

At least she might fly away then. Far away.

Aioffe pulled her hand from Tarl's and glanced up at him. Disgust spread across her features and Tarl felt instantly ashamed. He was no better than a whore-master offering her up in service, but getting them both out of here alive was more important than what she thought of him. Any thought he had of absolution already hung in tatters. This Bishop was no more holy than he was. Above all, after everything they had been through and irrespective of his feelings, her loyalty to him and her steadfast protection meant he could not be parted from her without a fight. Without knowing she would live another day.

The chair creaked as the Bishop sat back. Dark, beady eyes roamed over Aioffe as his lips pressed together. "And how, precisely, am I to trust the word of a fae? For all I know, she could feed us falsehoods."

"I never lie!" Aioffe exclaimed.

He knew this wasn't entirely true, but Tarl wasn't about to dispute it now. The Bishop tapped his fingers on the desk. Tarl sent a silent entreaty to the Lord for guidance as his heart thudded. All they needed was time.

As if by divine intervention, the Bishop then splayed his hands on the desktop and spoke formally, as if reciting an oft cited piece of legislation. "Any such deal is bound by an exchange of items or services. That is the custom between our kinds. I would require some surety." He glared at Aioffe. "A guarantee of truth. Without that, I cannot overlook how this activity would violate the long established agreement between our kind. You do not interfere, only report."

She frowned. "I have nothing. Only my word. And why would I trust you to keep to your word?"

"I have something to offer, as surety" he blurted out. As his hand reached into his satchel, he wondered whether he was about to make a bargain, after all - with the Devil.

"An artefact. A relic which stood over a pair of shoes made and blessed by St Crispin," he said with all the gravitas he could muster, "has been held in my family vault for more generations that I can say." He pulled himself tall, gaining confidence in his lie as the Bishop sat up. "I offer it to you, as a talisman, that you might know the saint is with us for this righteous cause. After the war has ended, it will be yours to keep. It will stay with us until then." Tarl withdrew the cross from his bag and kept it clutched tight to his thudding chest.

The Bishop's eyes glittered. "St Crispin? His cross!" He licked his lips. "Did any shoes also survive?" He craned his neck forward, his hands reaching for the cross, but Tarl held firm. The balance shifted, and if there was one thing Tarl understood, it was negotiation.

"Oh yes," Tarl nodded with solemnity. "The leather has deteriorated, but, a blessed pair remain safely in my ancestral lands. Far, far away."

With narrowed eyes, the Bishop sized Tarl up and down, his gaze returning to the partly obscured cross. "You don't look like a Lord. Where did you say you were from?"

"Alas, my family fell on hard times." That much was true at least. "And we are not originally from these shores, or Scotland's." Also true. He found the lies slipped from his lips easier when there was an element of truth within.

"And you would be willing to give me the shoes as well?"

"After the war is won," Tarl replied after pretending to consider. "I will bring you shoes."

Whose shoes hardly mattered at this point. He would give up his own if it got them both out of this office. He held out the cross to distract from his slip.

"Wars can go on for a hundred years, boy. Exchange the cross or we do not have an accord." The Bishop's eyes glittered as he reached for the shiny talisman. "I would see its providence. Give it to me now, so I can assess its worth." He licked his lips, beckoning Tarl with outstretched fingers.

Tarl's grip tightened. "What guarantee do we have that you will keep her secret and safe if I give it to you?"

"My word." The Bishop's eyes narrowed as Tarl held the cross just out of his reach. "My word as Keeper of the King's Jewels is never in doubt."

He needed something more to seal the bargain, Tarl realised. Something now, something held back for after. What he needed was a threat of what could come if the deal wasn't seen through.

A word could be doubted. The timing of this meeting suddenly seemed prophetic. "I would have thought the same of any of the King's advisers, but for the betrayal which preoccupies this court right now," Tarl said. "Does the King know the 'blood-thirsty' truth about who he goes to war with?"

Slumping back in his chair, the Bishop fell silent for a moment. "Sad times indeed when a man's word of loyalty is questioned, that is true." His expression darkened. "The King does not know, nor need to know. He needs only to believe that his cause is blessed by the Church."

Tarl glanced sideways at Aioffe, who was staring stonily at the floor, and he thought about betrayal. All that was left was betrayal. It was just a question of who, and how it could be leveraged to get them out of this room in one piece. Everything was a bargain, he told himself, and the price was his soul.

"I know a man's word alone is insufficient," he said, deciding. He placed the cross on the desk in front of the vampire. "Everything I believed about the Church and the nature of those who run it is also in doubt. I was sent to you by another so-called priest. One like yourself." Keeping his fingers curled around the base of the cross, he pointed to the paper on the Bishop's desk. "So I will sign a deed here and now, giving you ownership of my precious and holy artifacts. But, you should also know," Tarl set his jaw. "Before we came here, I signed a statement naming those priests who cannot be trusted to act solely for the good of the realm and Church. Those like you who serve other masters. Have other priorities and other loyalties. This statement includes their names and everything I know about the immoral activities of those like you."

He bared his top teeth at the vampire in illustration, then took Aioffe's hand again. The Bishop glowered as his lips pinched together.

Tarl glanced at Aioffe, then said, "If we fail to return, today or from the battlefield, then a copy will be delivered into the King's hands. More copies spread around all the men who camp outside the city walls. Given the upsetting plot the King has just learned of, I'm sure his justice would be swiftly dealt, if any more of those he trusted were to fall under suspicion. Be sure, Lord Bishop, even high ranking names will land in the hands of our star-scarred ruler if we do not receive your protection."

Aioffe blinked. Her hand tensed in his, but he held his nerve. She turned to the Bishop. "All that would be needed is for Henry to look closer. Ask questions about your behaviour and feeding habits, and your secrets would unravel," she said. "That kind of attention and exposure to the humans would break the agreement between fae and vampire."

The Bishop's head swivelled to stare at Aioffe. "You told him about our kinds?"

Tarl continued, "She didn't need to. I've already experienced it. Documented it. I know what you are, you see. I also understand how easily fear that this is not a righteous cause, but a cursed one, can scatter an army. Costing you and the King a war and wealth. And you are someone to be feared, not revered."

Stepping forwards to the desk, Aioffe whispered, "Do you think King Henry would still trust you if he knew how old you are? Of the battles you have already survived eight hundred or more years ago?"

The Bishop started to rise from his chair and snarled.

"We both have things we wish to hide," she said to the Bishop, then she glanced at Tarl. Her eyelids flared. "And ways to make people forget what they have witnessed."

The Bishop raised his eyebrow. Tarl met his eyes. Although he didn't really understand what Aioffe was talking about, he heard a warning in her voice. As if he would forget this day!

"But I will not let you do that unless you agree to his offer," Aioffe said, moving in front of Tarl and into the Bishop's eye-line. She jutted her jaw out. "And I, too, have already written names for my people. A kestrel is standing by for release if we do not return, so you had better decide fast who you want to trust with your secrets. A fae and a mortal?"

She waved her hand at the chests which lined the walls. "Or will you risk your position and good favour with the King, and all that wealth you have collected?"

CHAPTER 27 – AGLOW

She held her breath. An ultimatum was always risky, but to protect Tarl, she had no other choice. He seemed to have forgotten how quickly a vampire could move, but she had not. This one was uninjured, in the prime of his life.

Her stomach knotted while the Bishop, or whatever name he claimed now, glared at her. What was Tarl thinking when he threatened a vampire with exposure? And here he was, trying to bargain his way out by offering her services! Besides, there was no point now in telling Tarl how long it had taken faekind to reach a peace agreement with the vampires, of the decades of negotiations before the Treaty was signed.

He had placed them both in an intolerable position. She still didn't know why they were both here, for her 'husband' was still not telling the full truth. She could tell from the prickles in his aura. Now, she was forced to go along with the lies as well.

The only saving grace was, in all this talk of naming names, that Tarl hadn't spoken her name, so far. It seemed the vampire didn't recognise her, which was fortunate. She knew well of him, though. His profile adorned the walls of the training room murals of Naturae, detailing him as one of the many who had conquered her kind during the Sation wars. Knowing her given name would put an entirely different complexion on the situation. The danger in exposing creature-kind to humans was bad enough and broke the Treaty, but if anyone had the slightest inkling of her presence in the matter, then little would stop another war from starting.

The vampire tried to peer around Aioffe and catch Tarl's eye to mesmerise him. Tarl continued in a firm, yet placatory manner, "Once Henry is satisfied, and his claim settled, then we can complete our business and all forget about what we have seen." He pushed forward the cross but kept hold of it. As if he were the one in command of the situation, he stared at the Bishop. "Draw up the paperwork."

Aioffe groaned. Tarl really had no idea of the danger he had opened himself up to. She yanked on his arm and kicked his leg so he was forced to wince. Anything to reduce eye contact. If Tarl were to forget who he was, perhaps even who she was, then everything she had done to protect him would have been in vain. He would be little use to her as a provider. Worse, the very thought that he wouldn't recognise her made her chest feel tight.

With his jaw clenched, the Bishop rose fully to his feet. "My surety first," he said, and snatched the cross from Tarl's fingers. Running his hands over it, he said, "When we have returned, the shoes of St Crispin will be brought to me." His gaze darted between both Aioffe and Tarl for a moment, then dropped to his desk. "Along with the written list of names so that I can deal with them myself."

Tarl gaped as the vampire stepped around the table and pointed at her. "In the meantime, aerial observation will be required during the time we are away, which I will take on trust to be accurate. Then it all will be forgotten about. The matter will be closed."

Their eyes met. The number of times the vampire used the word 'will' made the knot in her stomach tighten. Even if they went along with the bargain, it was clear the vampire intended to obliterate all mention of the arrangement at some point in the future. When he had what he wanted, no doubt. Whilst she was grateful for a pair of shoes herself, the lengths the Bishop was going to for this St Crispinian's pair was... peculiar. Perhaps it was a Church thing. Or a vampire thing.

"Are we agreed?" Tarl said.

"In as much as one can agree to trust a fae. Yes," the Bishop replied, still staring at her. "I will draw up the agreement."

Aioffe bit her tongue. "Let's go," she said to Tarl.

With a last glance at the cross, Tarl dropped her hand to open the door. She followed, only turning back when the Bishop asked, "I would know the name of the fae I am to place such faith for our victory in?"

"Mistress Smith," Aioffe replied. Behind her back and unseen, she crossed her fingers.

"Your real name. There will be hundreds of Mistress Smith's."

"And I take comfort in that, for I am one of many. Do not forget that," she warned. "Just as there are many of your kind. Waiting. Watching. Do not give cause to rally into another kind of war when you have one pressing upon you now. Fae also have long memories, and far less to lose."

Still feeling his eyes on her back, she walked past Tarl and out into the main room before she let out a long breath.

Tarl's fingers curled around her upper arm as she paused, and he pulled her towards the double doors out. She was glad of his support, for if ever she was likely to stumble and fall, it was while she still reeled from the exchange. As soon as the fresh air caressed her face, she felt calmer. She hadn't realised how toxic it was for her to be in such close, and closed, proximity to a vampire. Any further encounters with her new master would have to be outside. Preferably, there wouldn't be any future encounters at all, but, given the task which lay ahead for them both, that might be unavoidable.

"What did I just agree to?" Tarl muttered as he hustled her across the courtyard. "And what was all that Sation war stuff?"

Aioffe put her hand on his forearm. "The less you know, the

better protected you are. Please, do not ask to know more. I beg you." She suppressed the shudder which threatened to ripple through her. Even though the Sation wars had ended long before her birth, Tarl should never know how close he had become to being another casualty, or stoking the embers of a protracted and bitter war back to life.

Barely pausing his stride to glance at her, Tarl said, "If it involves your kind and his, I don't want to know. It's bad enough I have made you his spy. Exposed you when I should have protected you. I'm so sorry." He hung his head. "The Church should be a sanctuary, respected by everyone under any circumstance. But I was wrong. They can't offer you, or I, protection." He sighed, and with that, she understood how difficult it had been to admit his Church failed.

"That's not the issue," she said, tripping on a raised cobble and falling into him somewhat. He paused so she could recover her balance. Her eyes met his and something between them shifted. She glanced at his flat satchel and murmured, "It is you who has given away everything you have."

"Not everything," he mumbled. "Just a thing. Not all." They passed through the archway, then he stopped abruptly and leaned against the castle wall. His face was pale as he stared at the flagstones.

Aioffe could taste the despair emanating from him. Her hand reached to touch his. "Tarl?"

He bit his lip.

"It's over now," she consoled. "We are fine. We will be fine."

A blond lock of hair fell over his face as he shook his head. "No, I nearly...."

"Nearly what?"

"I almost lost you to him."

"No you didn't. There was never any danger of that." Not

really. She hoped.

He raised his blue eyes to hers. "Yes. There was. I was about to betray you."

Aioffe's eyebrows drew together. "He knew what I was anyway. You didn't need to tell him. Creatures smell different to each other, remember?"

"You misunderstand. I was going to trade you for salvation. For masses to be said."

"Masses?"

He nodded and his head fell again. "For what I have done. For my mother. And my soul."

"You're right. I don't understand," Aioffe said.

"You can't. You are.... Different. We believe different things." He glanced at her shoulders and she knew then what he meant.

She looked across the street, emptier now daylight had fallen into dusk. Although people still milled about in the streets, no-one was close enough to hear their conversation at that moment. "That we are different is true. I don't know what to believe myself. I never learned of faith like yours. But you said you doubted the Church. Does that mean you doubt what you believe now, or do you still believe you need these Masses?"

Was it her? Had she caused him to lose his faith?

"I don't know," Tarl said. He blinked his eyes. "I just don't know what I believe any more. Or what I'm doing here."

Still in a quiet voice, Aioffe said, "And now we have committed to going to war for a King I do not know, for a cause I do not understand. With a human who wants rid of me."

And she risked breaking a peace treaty if she failed. A tingle of fear crept over her. All she wanted was to be ordinary. Free of responsibility. Now the burden of responsibility beckoned, no matter her reluctance to bear it.

"But I couldn't do it, don't you see?" Tarl said. "I couldn't let him take you."

She frowned. "Why did you change your mind?"

He let out a snort. "If I knew that…" His gaze moved up the street.

He did know. "Why, Tarl?"

Still looking ahead, he pushed himself from the wall. "I don't know, I told you. I just don't know anything any more."

"Well, I think you do," she said. She walked a few paces up the street, then stopped as he wasn't following. When she turned to him, he stared at her with wide, tear-filled eyes.

"I'm sorry," he said.

"I know."

A few feet apart, they gazed into each other's souls. Aioffe felt a shiver run up her arms. The hairs on her skin stood proud, but it wasn't a warning. More of an enticement. In her belly, butterflies fluttered and the lump in his neck bobbed as he swallowed.

"Please forgive me?" His voice sounded strangled. Tarl's hand shook as it stretched forwards, reaching for hers. She dropped her eyes, staring at the shaking fingers while her heartbeat clamoured. Then her hand appeared in her view, touching his. A jolt shot through her as if she had been struck when their skin collided. The warmth of his hand eased the ripples which threatened to engulf her, spreading from her arms through her tight chest and down through her entire being.

Inside, she experienced a yearning unlike anything she had ever wanted before. To be held. To be touched. To be… with him. Aioffe blinked, not comprehending what the sensations meant.

He pulled her close to his chest, cradling her the back of her head in his hand. She heard the rush of his blood as it pulsed like a boom of the thunder from his heart. Within his arms, she felt secure, protected, but at the same time, thrilled.

"Aioffe," his voice was gruff in her ear.

His arm snaked around her waist. Without thinking about it, she reached up to splay her fingers against his broad back. It felt peculiar to run her hands over smooth shoulders, to hold a person such. Yet, she could not help but press her the entire length of her body into his. Thighs touching through the fabric of their garments, holding him was familiar, yet alien. It wasn't like riding next to him. This was more. Right. Fitted. And new.

She had never been at such close quarters with a human, or anyone. Not like this.

His arms tightened around her, and she realised he was embracing her with not just his body, but his soul, his aura as well. Aioffe felt as if she were glowing with heat from the mingling of their Life-forces. In a trance, she brought an arm forward, then traced her fingertips from the back of his head and down his neck.

His head lowered towards hers. She could hardly breathe for craving. To be closer to his body. His fingers caught hers and he brought them towards his lips.

Only then did she glimpse that her skin was sparkling.

"No!" She gasped, and pulled her head back.

He was gazing down at her, his red lips slightly parted, and a misty sort of expression in his blue eyes. Her fingers tingled, yet she knew she was not pulling from him. Rather, he was pushing his aura around her. Did he know? The effect was both delicious and, unfortunately for her, highly visible.

Her chin wobbled as she said, "This is dangerous."

"What is dangerous?" His voice was thick and deep. "Us?"

With a wrench, she dragged her arm away from him and levered them apart. "Look at me," she whispered.

His eyes roamed hers. "I am looking, and I can't believe I didn't see it before."

Taking a step back, she held out her pale hand, still glittering from their encounter. "This!"

His mouth formed a silent Oh.

"Whatever that was, we cannot do it again. I'm too obvious."

His gaze dropped to the pavement and a flush rose to his cheeks. "I… I see now. Yes." He sucked in a breath. His hands fell to rest on his hips as he surveyed her. "You're right. Obvious. Beautiful. But obvious."

For a moment, they stood awkward and apart. Gradually, sounds of the townsfolk going about their business diffused the tension. Just to be sure, Aioffe stepped back and leaned against the wall, hoping that the shadow would hide the few exposed parts of her skin until the glowing stopped. But he kept staring at her as if seeing her for the first time. Only this time, the revulsion in his face was absent, replaced by glitter in his eyes.

"What happened?" Tarl asked, sounding more normal. "I've only seen your skin do that when you have been flying, or feeding."

She shook her head, then glanced up at him from under her eyebrows. "You've been watching me fly?"

Tarl cleared his throat. "Yes. At night. You glow a little in the darkness. It's a bit like watching an angel."

Aioffe snorted. "I don't think you should look at me again, like that. Or touch me. Like that."

There was no denying to herself that she very much wanted him to. Her skin, fingers and a warm ball in the pit of her stomach disagreed with her statement. She had to study the ground intently to resist throwing herself back into his arms just to feel that way again.

"Perhaps you are right," Tarl said, sounding like he was being strangled. His cheeks flushed even redder. "Some distance would be… appropriate."

Aioffe moistened her lips then pushed herself away from her lean on the wall. "Yes. Distance. Good job we don't have to ride anywhere for a while."

Tarl started up the street. "Right. Just the intimacy of a voyage instead." He sighed. "I can't wait."

CHAPTER 28 - GOOD SHOT

Tarl could not remember when he had last felt as physically tortured. Having held Aioffe, and held her in a very different way to touching her before, it was as if all he could think of was repeating the embrace. Every fibre of his being wanted to, and the constant battle of head over heart grew wearisome. His forehead ached with the effort of keeping his distance, for fear of exposing her again when there were so many people about.

As they were no longer riding together, physical proximity was not required. In the few days before they set sail across the Channel, it had been easier to manufacture reasons to absent himself from her side, yet keep her in sight for safety. She never seemed to stop looking at him though, with rosebud lips parted a touch as if waiting for him to crush his onto them, before glancing demurely away.

Had it been anyone else, he would have put it down to coquettish flirtation, but not Aioffe. She was too naïve in the ways of enticement to play games. Without wanting to, his heart flustered with panic if she fell out of his sight even for one moment. Several awkward verbal exchanges between them as the troops packed up and prepared to embark only made his guilt and confusion worse. Each night, he lay fitful and awake under their canvas, whilst she busied herself, or disappeared to fly again. Yet still, she returned each morning. And then the preparations were complete, and the order given to board one of the hundred of vessels which would transfer them to France.

Once they boarded, staying distant was entirely impractical. Low in the water, in a matter of days, the ship was rammed, loaded with livestock, food, ale and weapons, alongside scores of men. There was no privacy for anyone and almost every inch of floor was taken up by barrels, sacks and bodies. As the final passengers, the horses neighing and kicking their displeasure, were lifted by sling onto the deck, the reality of confinement gnawed at his mind. What if they brushed skin and she glowed?

Through the awful seasickness he experienced in the stinking bowels of the Lady of Falmouth, Tarl could not purge himself of either the desire to hold her again nor the memory of what she felt like in his arms. Any thoughts of how different, how much he regretted his earlier revulsion of her lessened as, like a good wife, she checked on him regularly and offered to fetch anything he might need. He could not bring himself to ask for what he really needed. Her.

Most people who initially sickened at sea as they left Southampton found their sea legs after a day or so, but not Tarl. When the sickness had first hit, Aioffe tried helping him up to the deck, in the hope that a view of the horizon would calm his gut, but leaning against her slight frame only made his stomach clench more. At least in the belly of the boat, he could see her lumpy body, hear her breathing in the next door hammock, but not have to touch her. By the third day, he reserved his energy for nodding weakly at the cup of water she offered. He moistened his mouth, then fell back into the linen cocoon, away from her fresh pine scent. Anything more than a sip would be regurgitated, although the seas were, according to the other men who intermittently jeered at him, tranquil for the time of year.

Her fingers shook as she sponged his brow and he grazed them with his own and an apology. "I wish I could ease your suffering," he was sure she whispered, but he was drifting in and out of consciousness. "We sailed past white cliffs taller than the mast at the close of yesterday, so they say we will land soon." He could muster no energy to respond to her enthusiasm.

Later that day, they slowed to a stop. The sails dropped and the anchor rattled down. Knowing the confinement would soon be over, he breathed a little easier. Orders were given to dress, arm themselves with whatever they could carry, and wait until darkness before they would disembark. After loading themselves with belongings, they waited on deck in silence, listening to the excited banter from their shipmates. Woollen clad arms and thighs touched, warm against each other with the motion of the bobbing ship.

Only then did the churning in his stomach settle. Strangely, her presence eased him, and thankfully, her skin remained its usual clear pink. The promise of dry land beckoned and Tarl succumbed to the comfort of her proximity. He even managed to keep down the dry ship's biscuits which passed amongst the crew.

He was still a little light headed and faint with insufficient energy as they scrambled down rope ladders into a waiting row boat. The whispered chaos in the depths of night soon clenched his stomach again. Ahead, large boulders sat turtle-like in the shallows. A three-quarter moon's hazy brightness enough to cast ominous shadows onto the dark water. Hundreds of rowed crafts ferried people from ships to shore, depositing them inside a small cove. The narrow beach swarmed with men, horses, bundles, and chests, lit by only a few flaming torches propped in the sand.

Rising in the distance, wisps of milky-grey smoke streaked through the black sky. A signal fire. There was no chance the French could miss the English approach. Even if they hadn't spotted the white sails approaching, they would have heard the hundreds of horses screaming their displeasure. Swine, oxen, and war horses were all unceremoniously dropped over the side into the dark, cold water via a hastily tied sling. Shouts and whacks to their rears herded them to swim ashore. Aioffe's wide, tear-filled eyes betrayed her yearning to assist the animals, and frustration at being unable to do so.

"Get moving up shore, and roll a barrel over while you're at it," Tarl and Aioffe were told as soon as they splashed their way through the shallows. The fellow muttered, "Stay low. The Frenchies just felled a man with a lucky shot."

Together with the eight other occupants of their boat, Aioffe gasped as the air suddenly whistled with a volley of arrows. One landed with a clatter on the stones, right by her foot. Her lips tightened, as if insulted, then she kicked a stubby, now shattered, thick shaft away. Tarl grimaced. If the French were using crossbows, which had a shorter range than the longbow, the enemy was closer than was ideal and the small beach was about to become a death trap. His heartbeat quickened.

They tipped over a tall barrel painted with a white arrow icon on the side and shoved it, crunching in front of them, as they trudged up the shore. Spread across the shingles on the brow of the beach, a line of archers pulled out unstrung bow staves from a leather bundle. Tarl felt around his belt with numb fingers, finding the pouch which held a spare coiled bowstring and the leather brace he'd tied on.

While he was distracted, Aioffe flattened herself against the ridgeline then crawled up, ahead of where a few other men were lying. Before he could stop her, she raised her head to peek over the brow.

"Four to the north-west, in some woodland," she whispered over her shoulder. "And a cluster more, maybe eight, to the east."

Tarl glowered at her. "Get back!"

"Are you sure, Mistress Smith?" Another man also heard her - a farmer they knew from the journey. A good shot, but he was prone to ending the day half conscious with ale, Tarl remembered. "I was hoping it was jus' one of them getting lucky."

"How can you see them?" A clipped English voice Tarl didn't recognise snapped from behind.

"What distance?" Tarl asked. His stiff fingers fumbled to loop the string over the horn nock.

Aioffe looked again, the top of her head outlined too much for Tarl's liking. After a few seconds, she turned to face him. "A hundred feet to the four, and perhaps the same for the eight. There's a fence and tower three hundred feet beyond that."

"Waiting for us then. Should have just unloaded in daylight," the unfamiliar Englishman groaned, hearing her precise report.

He trusted Aioffe's night-vision, but then, he had seen it in action before. Tarl frowned and wondered whether the Bishop had already instructed the commanders to take heed of whatever she had said. When they had returned to the castle the day after their negotiations, the Bishop hadn't been there, but the deed had been drawn up. He had signed it as Tarl Smith, the same as on the paperwork for the muster roll. His true name could only leave a trail for the Bishop to chase down if things went wrong and there seemed little point in risking the lives of his extended family back on Rousay.

He had to stand, awkwardly balancing on the shifting sandbank, to bend the bowstave. One end on his boot between toes, he flexed the wood so he had a greater length of cord to loop into position at the top. This bow was newly fashioned, barely used, but its youth would afford it a great range, if stretched to its fullest extent. His fingers caressed the grip, then he tested the draw a few times to get the feel of the ash. He preferred yew, but in such a pinch, this bow would suffice. Having not eaten or drank for days, it was an effort, and his muscles shook with the sudden exertion.

Satisfied he had the string tension correct, he pulled off the leather covering on the barrel which they had pushed up the beach and hauled out a bundle. Noticing the five men who spaced out a foot below the ridge with their bows already strung shared only one stave of arrows, he tossed more wrapped parcels over to each. Further down the beach, more archers jumped off the boats and readied themselves in small companies. Behind them, clusters of men at arms withdrew their swords and stood ready to charge.

A lone crossbow arrow catapulted over the ridge. It clattered harmlessly onto the shale, having flown over the bowman's heads but not quite reaching the men at arms further down. But it was too close, nonetheless. The archers's heads rotated to see the English commander nodding to himself. "Right, eye your targets," the Englishman ordered. "You heard Mistress Smith."

Tarl took two paces forward, motioning with his head and a flick of his fingers to indicate Aioffe should come down. His shot would fly true, but he couldn't vouch for the other archers thrust into combat without warning. Her eyes widened, and she scrambled down the slope towards him. Once by his side, she reached out to brush his drawn bow with her hand. In the moonlight, her slim fingers seemed almost luminous as she stroked the shaft. Somehow, the wood warmed in his grip. He tilted it away from her touch, and the bow cooled just as quickly. He took another pace up the ridge.

Setting an arrow onto the string, Tarl drew back. When his hand reached his ear, his head tipped a fraction to look down the length of the dart balanced, and beyond. He breathed in and out through his nose and steadied himself.

He adjusted the angle on his bow so the curvature of the arrow's flight would reach Aioffe's distance measurement. In the distance, he spotted movement and his stance swivelled to bring the arrowhead in line with where he thought the body might be.

The English commander let out a peep signal, and Tarl let loose. Without looking to see if he had hit a target, he bent down and pulled out another arrow, notching it and drawing in one practised motion whilst all around the air hummed with the low whistle of goose feathers flying. When the volley landed, everyone listened in the silence for groans. Movement on the beach ceased and the army seemed to collectively hold its breath. He waited, watching down the shaft for any further movement.

After a few minutes of focus through the darkness, Tarl jumped when a voice called "Advance!"

The order came from behind. Tarl remained posed and ready as men at arms nudged between the line of archers and stomped over the ridge. Their helmets gleamed in the moonlight as they marched ahead. Aioffe pushed herself up on her arms and watched their progress. Tarl crouched beside her, holding his tongue between his teeth as he observed.

The troop slowed a hundred feet in - their march impeded by boggy land. All the archers tensed, their breaths held as they listened for the sounds of steel and screams. No pot-shots from the walls came to hit the floundering troops so the soldiers persevered, regrouping on a track beyond the marshland.

"Keep your bow's strung," the Englishman ordered, as he stepped forwards himself. "We follow when given the order."

Aioffe let out her breath, warm against his knee. "Some welcome to Normandy," she said and smiled weakly at him.

CHAPTER 29 – A SPY IN THE SKY

The chaos of the beach landing cleared and calmed within days. Few lives were lost, and all haste was made to establish camps, grouped by commander, in nearby fields and woodland. Tarl, like most of the archers who seemed to make up the majority of the army, had been deployed first to move equipment, then to dig midden trenches. Although he said he was reluctant to leave her, especially for such a grim and dirty task, Aioffe was far from being left alone. It was hard to be when there were so many people clustered in one small area. Aioffe soon felt quite nostalgic about the comparative freedoms she had enjoyed during the journey to Southampton.

While Tarl was absent, she kept busy sewing. At all costs, he had suggested, she should avoid anything which required walking, and thus stumbling. Or, handling hot pans, which required actually having to know how to prepare human food. As 'not human', her inability to make even the most basic of pottage would mark her out as odd. He was probably right. Her needlework skills were much in demand as one of the comparatively few women who accompanied the vast army, and word soon spread of her neat and speedy stitches. The other wives and servants were assigned similar menial jobs, like cooking, gathering of firewood and generally running around after the menfolk whilst they awaited the next command.

Aioffe's fingers ached from stitching red crosses onto white jupons, repairing tears and punching buckle holes into belts and straps. In relative terms, she was quite happy with the arrangement. Sewing was the one activity where she would cause the least damage, and have the least exposure. But her growing reputation was most likely to blame for the ease of her discovery within the ever-expanding camp.

Only four days days after the excitement of landing in France, Aioffe began to wonder whether the three week-old spying deal had been forgotten about, when the Bishop of Norfolk appeared before her. So much had changed in the intervening period - from their location and circumstance, to her friends and, most significantly, her relationship with Tarl. As the vampire stench grew stronger, Aioffe's senses tingled a warning. Another shift was coming, just when she had settled into their current state of existence.

The Bishop found her amongst Ap Tudor's party, who had been corralled onto the edges of an area otherwise occupied by Sir John Cornwaile's men. Within hours of setting up their tents in the misty morning after they landed, those who journeyed from Beaumaris with were informed they would now take their orders from the senior commander and leader of Henry V's army. This development displeased Ap Tudor, who then spent the next day glowering and stomping around the fields instead of helping, complaining he hadn't travelled such a distance to be ignored to anyone who would listen.

A small monastery close by was claimed as a temporary base for the King, yet Ap Tudor was repeatedly not permitted entry to make his objections known to the monarch, despite visiting it several times wearing in ever-increasing amounts of armour. As a relatively low level landowner, and son of a Welsh traitor to the crown to boot, Ap Tudor's infantile behaviour was soon ridiculed by the women Aioffe had become friends with. The King was not even there, they crowed! Indeed, Henry cantered around on a white horse during the daylight hours, personally overseeing the disembarkation arrangements. Highly visible and never in one place for long, he established himself from the start as someone in control of every aspect of his plans for invasion. Ap Tudor was merely one man amongst thousands.

Besides, the women laughed, until the ships were empty, the army wouldn't be going anywhere. Aioffe considered the ship they voyaged upon was busy, but as the ever swelling ranks of men, horses, carts, barrels, more horses, more men, and eventually siege weapons and cannon cluttered the field, the extent and result of the King's plan was more obvious. The more she saw, the more she marvelled at how many elements Henry needed to co-ordinate, and upon hostile shores. Even though she had flown over the gathered troops at Southampton under cover of darkness, in the daylight and contained in a smaller place, the army's true size was also evidenced by the growing pile of clothing she repaired.

The Bishop's smell bothered her before his presence did. Aioffe kept her head low as she stitched. There were few other vampires and daemons in camp, as well as a few witches, but the Bishop had a particular aroma she now associated with threat. Perhaps he was not seeking her, she hoped, as her nose wrinkled. She could feel his eyes on her as they roamed over the camp-fire around which the womenfolk sat sewing. Unobtrusively, she straightened her spine and rolled her shoulders back so her wing bumps were even less apparent beneath the blousy shirt she wore. Next to her, Agnes and Charis muttered, "Your Excellency," with a dip of their heads in acknowledgement of their robed visitor. Aioffe plunged her needle into the broadcloth on her lap instead and assumed he would not single her out.

"Mistress Smith," the Bishop snapped. "I would speak with you in private."

His boots tapped his impatience on the sun-baked earth, so she raised her eyes to meet his. He was so tense it caused a tick in his jaw, then his gaze slid about the women. Defiance now would make matters worse. Aioffe put aside her sewing and stood, gesturing that he should lead the way. Charis raised an eyebrow but said naught.

He led her some distance from the fireside and away from the ears of her friends before he paused. In a low voice, he said, "Tonight, you begin your real work."

Aioffe nodded, her palms clammy in the light summer breeze. With tents as far as the eye could see, anyone could hear their discourse through the fabric.

He continued, "A scout has spotted an advance rider, possibly ahead of a re-enforcing army, approaching the town of Harfleur. It is likely they come to defend that which is rightfully England's. We want to know numbers and in what direction they travel, to be sure." He peered at her with dark eyes. "I don't need to impress upon you that this information will determine how much faith we place in your judgement."

"Haven't I already proved myself to you upon our landing?" Aioffe asked.

The Bishop's lip curls unattractively to reveal his incisors. "That was mere co-incidence," he said. "I shall expect your report at dawn. Meet me there," he inclined his head towards a small rise to the west, topped with a copse of trees. "And remember, at any time, I can sniff out where your husband is. Oh yes, your stench lingers around him like a cloak. It takes but a moment for him to be persuaded to forget he ever set eyes upon you. Upon us."

Aioffe shivered beneath her dress, even though the sun shone down brightly. So this was how the Bishop planned to keep her in line. She glanced across the field, to where she had last seen Tarl at first light this morning, but of course, he was not there now.

"And I still know where my kestrel is," she said. "And from

the air, the King is doubtless quite obvious on his white charger. I heard he dispatched the heads of the traitors with almost unseemly haste before we left England. I would so hate for any questions to be asked of you."

As she turned and walked away from him, a smile played on her lips. It was surprisingly liberating to not have a care for rank and position. However, a bargain had been made back in Southampton, and she intended to stand by her word.

*****

When dusk fell, and with Tarl not returned, Aioffe found herself with a dilemma which could only solved by trusting her new friends. Given the awkwardness between herself and Tarl with the state of their relationship unresolved and unspoken of, she did not want him to worry about her absence. Her absence so early in the evening would doubtless give him cause for concern.

Part of her felt as if she had been given permission to fly, an opportunity for freedom for which she so yearned. She did not want to waste a moment of the night. Also, it would take time for her to walk, or stumble, far enough away for her to be unobserved when ascending. Using the narrow thoroughfares between fields invited trouble from lonely men. The only way was to circumvent the more populous areas was to weave through the plentiful trip hazards of the accommodations. Just the thought of navigating the ropes holding up the pitched tents, packed tightly together, made her reconsider leaving alone. But she could not wait any longer for Tarl to escort her a more direct route. Slowly and surely was the only way to move clear of all human sight by the time darkness fell.

Her mind resolved, she wrapped her long cloak around herself to hide her freed wings, and padded over to Agnes's tent.

"Agnes, it's Aioffe. If you see Tarl, could you let him know

I've been sent on an errand?" She whispered through the tied-closed opening.

"'Tis late, bach. Surely you should be accompanied?" Agnes pushed up the bottom flap of her tent, stuck her head through, then pulled dishevelled clothing across her hefty bosun. As she passed her hand over the straggles of grey hair which poked from her mobcap, her lips twitched with worry. "Hang on, I'll grab my coat and come with yer. It's not like I've got bairns to take care of, more's the pity."

Aioffe's arm shot out to stop her. "I'll be fine, don't worry. Honestly, I can look after myself."

Agnes's face pitched up towards her, querying the wisdom in Aioffe's assertion, unconvinced. From inside the tent, her husband's voice drifted out.

"He won't be long. The midden he was working on was close to dug deep enough. Besides, I'm sure Mistress Smith will be back as soon as she is able, woman."

"The master has spake," Agnes said, jokingly. "How kind of him to be so concerned about another wife's safety, eh?" She called over her shoulder, "Would you be so quick to let me walk amongst thousands of lonely men in the dead of night, eh?"

Her eyes flicked back to Aioffe's as her husband's voice grumbled, "No-one else would want yer cold toes under their covers."

"He doesn't mean it," Agnes said, as an indulgent grin spread across the shadows of her features.

Aioffe smiled. "If you hear Tarl return, I'd appreciate it if you could pass on the message."

She was still thinking about how Agnes and John, brewers and sheep farmers in Wales, interacted so easily and whether it was because they had been together for so long, when she first stubbed her toe on a wooden tent peg. Lurching with arms out for balance, she put their easy rapport from her mind and focused on the uneven ground beneath her. By the time she crossed several fields, made her way up a hillock and waited in the copse's darkness to be sure no-one was on guard there, the stars had filled the sky.

Once airborne, with every beat of her wings her soul soared higher. Truly, there was nothing else to compare to this sensation! The chill of the night air brushed her skin, and she pulled the cap from her head to free her hair. Reaching a height where she could safely hover, she began to search the ground for signs of an approaching army. Silent in the sky, Aioffe scoured the countryside. Off the shoreline and in deeper waters, the flotilla of English ships lingered. Flying further down the coast, a bird's-eye view of a large walled town made her pause.

Harfleur.

At first glance, it appeared like many other walled towns she had flown over in England and Scotland. If this was target Henry intended to reclaim with only ground troops, it would take monumental effort and much time. Twenty four towers studded high walls circling the settlement, but that was not the real problem. A river, which would have run directly through the wall to empty into a well defended port, had been dammed before it reached the town. Its waters spread in a great lake to the west and north so that Harfleur itself appeared an island.

Wooded hills dropped into a valley of doom, so dense as to make it very difficult for large numbers of troops to engage in hand to hand combat outside of the walls. Wisps of smoke from blackened timbers were all that remained of any outlying buildings, and within the lake, only rooftops remained. Henry's scouts had already been busy clearing the way for his forces to advance to the marshy edge of the new lagoon.

Aioffe clenched her teeth together, confused as to how the natural and unnatural obstacles could be overcome on foot. With an airborne fae army, the landscape would give them the advantage, but for humans, the water and stone defences appeared insurmountable. Without getting closer, there was no way of knowing how many troops were inside those high walls, and only a few boats bobbed in the harbour.

After she had flown miles along the coast, then looped inland and back to Harfleur's northern edge, she travelled further up the course of the river. No sign of an army could be seen, but she wanted to be thorough in her assessment of the situation before returning. To contradict a human scout's word, she had to be certain there.

It must be past midnight by now, she estimated, and dawn would be only hours on its heels. Her wings, unused for weeks, tired, so she searched for a suitable gap in the trees in which to set down for a rest. Flying lower, she skirted the treetops. Dense oaks, ashes and maple formed a canopy which offered protection for her to hunt for the first time in a month as well.

Her feet touched down on a jutting stone outcrop, the perfect entry to the woodland. A steep drop lead almost to the river, and a thick rope, knotted at intervals for ease of climbing, was tied to a trunk. Glancing down the ridge, she decided that the outcrop must also be a lookout spot, as a path led through the trees and along it. Her nose picked out a smell - a familiar tang which caught in the back of her throat.

Charcoal. Every village and town, almost everywhere, would have need of the high temperature fuel needed for metalwork, but it was universally a slow process. Aioffe knew the age old method of production had changed little, even in her seven hundred year lifetime. The powdery black stubs resulted from gradual pyrolysis, often burned deep in the woodland. A collier piled billets of wood on their ends, creating a tall conical pile. At the underside of the heap, an opening lets in air while a central shaft allows the wispy grey smoke to escape. The wood pile is then covered with moistened clay or soil. Firing begins at the bottom and gradually spreads outwards and upwards, and had to be observed for many days with vigilance in case the stack should collapse incorrectly and the fire spread. Her people balanced on wooden stools which missed a leg, so if their attention should waver, the observer literally fell off.

Why had she not seen wisps of grey smoke from the burner, though? Aioffe hesitated, listening. A small human's cry wailed thin into the air, followed by a cloud billowing up through the trees. Immediately, Aioffe took flight, darting over to the source of the smoke deep in the woods, then dropped into a clearing.

She coughed as her feet touched earth. The pile had tumbled midway through firing! Attention had not been paid to the top, and a smouldering branch had fallen. It must have rolled down, catching in its path other sun-dried fuel which now filled the expanse with dense, earthy-tasting smoke! Spotting a stool, three legs upturned a few feet from the stack, Aioffe understood what had happened, but, where was the child now?

Aioffe began to stamp on the flame tendrils, in a vain attempt to stomp out the spreading danger. Her eyes blinked as she spun around, looking through the mist for the child. Where had he gone? And why hadn't he even attempted to remedy the disaster caused by his own negligence? Pulling her cloak tightly around herself to protect her wings from stray sparks, she stamped and stamped.

A rustle came from the bushes and she whirled about, ready to berate the boy. Unintelligible words poured vengeance from a bearded man's mouth. Another stood behind him, a pitchfork in hand. The points dropped to jab at her! She screamed and jumped back.

Still, the shouts continued in a language she did not understand. Aioffe sank to her knees, hoping that the subservient gesture would indicate to the colliers that this was not of her doing. But there was no-one to defend her, no-one to speak for her innocence and intention to help. Her hand fell to her pocket, where she kept her sheathed dagger for safe keeping. Not that she wanted to fight, but…

The bearded man saw her movement and guessed. With a growl, he hustled her to the ground. Shocked by such rough treatment, she pulled out her little knife. Before she could unsheathe the blade, he kicked her fist. In pain, her fingers flew open. The dagger, her only memento from home, was thrown across the clearing and landed near the treeline. The man bent over, shouted something in her ear, then wagged his finger in front of her eyes. A steely look told her he would take no more chances.

Without any other weapons to hand, Aioffe had no choice. She did not dare wrestle with them, for fear that her cape would expose her unbound wings and make matters worse. Her heart pounded. She knew not the words to explain herself, her presence here, nor had she the strength to overpower the stocky pair. Her lips tightened, but she stayed on the ground.

Then, they bound her hands in front of her.

With a face dark with fury, one of the colliers set about dousing the fire with a bucket of water which he pulled from behind a bush; the other muttered, grumbling from his tone, while keeping Aioffe within reach of his pitchfork. As the smouldering flames were dampened, the men argued between themselves. When the water ran out, they began to stomp. Sparks filled the air as dry twigs, flickering into yellow-orange life, were flattened.

A spark found a home in the beard, the cloying smell of burnt hair alerting the man who yelped, then slapped his hands about his chin. Singed and with soot-blackened faces, the pair frowned at Aioffe as they methodically stamped and bickered their way around the earth, clearly undecided about what to do with her.

Until they did decide. She knew when as they both nodded,

clasped hands and put their disagreement behind them with a grim smile at each other. But what had they agreed?

She glanced over to her knife, lying beside exposed tree roots. The damp moss glinted with tiny beads of dew before the last flames were stamped out. Aioffe's heart hammered as the men performed a visual sweep of the clearing.

Then they approached her, determination tightening their faces. She dug her fingertips into the earth and, looking at the blade, pushed a message down. With her mind, she touched the spores intertwined with the tree, nudging buried seeds to her will and hoped.

Dragged to her feet, Aioffe wiped the earth on her dress and looked at the pair with as much meekness as she could manage. The bearded man scowled, his thick lips pressed together in disapproval.

Then the men led their prisoner, stumbling yet silent, out of the forest.

CHAPTER 30 – BLINDLY BUSY

Tarl's biceps ached. If he had to dig one more midden trench, he thought, he'd end up curled at the bottom of it and probably wouldn't even notice excretions raining down on him. He was that tired, but he was not alone.

"Master Tarl Smith?" A voice called from above the lip of the ditch. "Are you down there?"

His co-digger, Alfred, took the opportunity to pause throwing the earth and rested on his spades. The hole was already as deep as Tarl was tall, but still required extension if it was to cater for this field's occupants.

"Aye," he shouted back up. "What of it?"

"You're needed. Get out."

Anything to leave this shit hole. As Tarl clambered out, dirt splattered down from the steep sides in great clumps. Next to the pile of excavated earth, Tom-the-carp had already constructed a rudimentary bench in readiness, which would be lifted over the midden when dug. There wasn't time to smooth away the splinters. The army needed sanitation points quickly, and the hope was that they would be moving deeper into France soon. The professional diggers were tasked elsewhere, so the order for hollowing out ditches had fallen to the archers and men at arms. With a nod to the others still digging along the hedge line, Tarl rammed his spade's blade into the field, then flexed his sore fingers.

'Lucky bastard,' Alf grumbled from below. Short of stature

and arm, he flung the loose earth back up with annoyance.

'Watch it!' Tarl shouted as the clumps narrowly missed his boots. A pageboy stood, self-important with a torch, a few feet away. So focused on the exhausting labour, Tarl hadn't noticed dusk had darkened into night. 'What am I needed for?'

"Follow me."

The page trotted off, jaunty as he held the beacon aloft above his clean white tabard. With a groan, Tarl rolled his shoulders back, cricked his neck, and followed.

As they walked up the embankment, the smell of stews and soups cooking over camp fires made Tarl's mouth water. His rumbling stomach would have to wait, though, as the page beckoned him onward. They crossed field after field, and Tarl wondered what Aioffe might have scrounged for him to eat later, or, if she even thought of him. He shook his head - that was his tiredness and hunger talking. Since landing in France, she had somehow managed to find him food whenever he had returned to their tent to rest. He could not fault her constant graft, and her ability to ignore the mental pressure, not to mention the threat of exposure, which the deal he had struck must have heaped upon her. Somehow, she balanced taking care of him with all the work clothing this enormous army. Despite her ministrations on his behalf, the awkwardness between them since they had kissed bothered him.

That kiss… A pang clenched his stomach and he pushed the memory of it from his mind.

Days had passed since he last talked properly to her. He gazed across the field, at the men gathered around fireplaces, or snoring in their tents dreaming of back home and the ache within intensified.

It dawned on him, as he ambled behind the page trying not to think about Aioffe's soft lips, that what irked him the most, was the lack of resolution. Was what he felt real or just an extension, a continuation, of the pretence which he himself had suggested? Now they were both here, in imminent danger, and it was all his doing. The further away from the army camps they walked, the more he resolved to return to her this starlit night and discuss it with her - before the campaign commenced in earnest. He surprised himself by this desire to actually want to examine emotions with another. New territory for Tarl. A little unsettling as well.

A path through the woodland towards the monastery had been cleared. The remains of felled trees lay by the track side, ready to be stripped and used for repairs, weapons, and firewood as needed. Deep ruts now criss-crossed the lane, forging alternative routes through. Carts and heavy cannon had been dragged or rolled across the landscape as Henry prepared to besiege the nearest town of Harfleur.

The page was waved through weathered wooden gates without being stopped, even though several men at arms kept watchful eyes on the surroundings. Once inside the fenced boundary, Tarl glanced around. The monastic building sat square and simple in the middle of the enclosure, with stone walls for the first floor, and timber constructs above. A high angled roof reminded him of home, where community buildings were modelled upon the great halls of Viking forefathers. This hall was half church, half makeshift miniature palace with a partial conversion into royal sleeping and meeting accommodation. The entire building was swathed in colourful pennants so there was no mistaking who ruled now. This was Henry's main command centre, his first small foothold in this part of France.

Tarl dusted his hands on his trousers, then rubbed at his gritty face. The mud barely shifted, but there was nothing he could do to smarten his appearance. A quick wipe would have to suffice. At least that last trench hadn't been in use yet.

To Tarl's right, a stretch of stone outbuildings thrummed

with activity, including a forge, a bake house, and storage areas. On the other side, makeshift stabling had been built. Concentrated in one small space, the noise of people, animals and industry assaulted his ears.

'Your fires await,' the page said, pointing to the anvil in the forge's aperture. Now that they weren't walking, Tarl noticed the boy hopped from side to side as he stood with a curious energy. When he spoke, the words seemed to babble out with a haste which verged upon unintelligible. "Sir John asked for a smith to be on duty at all times, and someone called Ap Tudor volunteered you to take the night shift."

Tarl's eyebrows knitted together. "I've not had rest or anything to eat for hours, and you want me to man a forge? For what?"

The page shrugged. "Everyone else is busy tonight, or sleeping before tomorrow." His eyes swept over the busy yard.

"What happens tomorrow?"

"You'll see."

Tarl glanced over at the forge. At least the fire would keep him warm, and he smelled bread in the yard ovens already. His stomach gurgled at the prospect.

Then he saw the queue of people waiting, various parts and pieces chinking in their hands. Horse bits, broken links, warped cannon bands and bent tools. From squat, bearded men to willowy serving maids, everyone who broke something made of metal in the course of their day's work had come here, his way, to be fixed overnight. Already, he could hear their grumbled complaints about waiting in the coolness of the air, when they should be bedding down or eating.

The page flashed a tight grin. "Try and get them to keep the noise down. Our King rests in readiness." He jerked a thumb towards the back of the hall then trotted away.

Tarl sighed. It was going to be a long night.

CHAPTER 31 – ON THE OTHER SIDE

A slightly singed, small lad had appeared through the trees and trailed behind them, silent and fearful. Or perhaps guilt was the reason why he cast such guarded looks at her from dark eyes whenever she glanced back. The edges of his smock were brown and burnt, his muddy feet blistered and sore, yet he did not complain on the long walk.

After stumbling through the forest at the end of a rope, Aioffe, her two captors and the boy emerged into a peach-streaked dawn by the edge of the lake which surrounded Harfleur. The slate and thatched roofs of the submerged houses outlying the town had been claimed by flocks of magpies and seagulls perched on the ridges, squawking in the morning sun. Around the edges of the valley, any buildings not flooded by the dammed river still smouldered. Once more, Aioffe wondered how a ground assault could overcome the extended moat around Harfleur.

The men dragged her towards the water. Resisting and stumbling with more deliberation to slow their pace, Aioffe shot glances around the hillside, desperately hoping to see the flash of a red cross against a pure white background peeking through the trees.

But there was no-one. No-one to rescue her. No-one who even knew where she was. Trapped far outside the English camp, and here on a vampire's instruction, which was eminently deniable. With a heart which sank further with every step towards the water, Aioffe realised she was expendable.

She had never felt more ordinary, which on one hand pleased her immensely, but on the other, caused her pulse to quicken with fear. Were she someone special to the English, perhaps more effort would be made to find her. Her absence noted, and a search begun. Try to stay positive. Aioffe forced herself to smile. She had achieved her ambition of blending into the human world outside of the world of the fae. This was no small feat! It was certain that by now, her absence from Naturae had been noted, but the trail any fae might use to recover her was most definitely cold.

She ought to take comfort in this, she told herself, then pinched her lips. Hiding within human society had been such a success that her disappearance was likely to only be noticed by a few inconsequential people. The Bishop for one, and he would not care a jot as she had failed on her first mission.

And Tarl. He would notice her absence, surely. Eventually. Where was he now? Did he even know she was gone? If he did, how long would it be before he searched?

She caught a glimpse of the lopsided, burnt beard of the collier, as he pulled her through the marsh towards the water's edge. Tarl kept his facial hair short, the reason why clearer to her as she thought about the risk of working with fire. His chin was firmer than this man's, and he had no need to hide it either. He needed to hide nothing, she realised. Except her. Would he miss having to keep her true self a secret? Inside, her stomach clenched. Would he prefer to be free of her? He had so many burdens, she feared she was just another. But he was different. She ran from her troubles, been happy to cast them aside, but Tarl... Tarl's concerns, aside from her, she considered to be more internal. One cannot fly away from those.

She was still wrestling about whether Tarl would look for her when they reached a river boat. More of a canoe than a sturdy trade vessel, with a pair of slim oars resting across narrow plank seats. The boy scrambled to the far tip and sat, staring intently into the distance at the pale walls of the town as he dangled his feet in the water. As if he sensed her mounting despair, the older collier grasped her sleeve to steady her as she stepped inside, splashing through the shallows as he guided her over the first seating plank, then pointed for her to sit on the second. He then lashed the end of her rope around the bench.

As the men pushed the craft off the shore with barely a grunt, Aioffe considered her narrowing choices. The colliers talked between themselves as soon as both were aboard, but she could not understand them. As such, what they planned to do with her remained a mystery. There was little doubt that the French knew the English were close. And no doubt the colliers thought she was English.

Huddled low in the boat, Aioffe's heartbeat fluttered as each dip of the oars brought the vessel closer to Harfleur. The fortifications were even more substantial close to - the lake created by the dammed river stopped shy of a deep ditch, then hastily constructed wooden balustrades had been erected between the moat and the high stone walls. From the windows of the pale towers which punctuated the looming barrier hung pennants, bright blue with the gold symbol like a leaf embroidered upon. The statement announced the town's intention to defy Henry's claim and remain under French dominion. Patrols protecting the kill zone created by the bastion, moat and lake. She spotted glimpses of their hats and the points of pole-axes slung on a shoulder between the crenellations.

Aioffe considered fleeing before they rowed within range of the weaponry on the walls. Open air was vastly preferable to entrapment. Her wings were lay flaccid against her back, covered by her cape, but the chafing rope restraint prevented her from simply flying up. If she did dare to defy her natural instinct to keep her true nature hidden without first escaping her constraints, the most likely consequence of attempting flight was capsizing them all. Although an attractive opportunity to be rid of her captors, she calculated that even emptied, a dangling boat was too much of a weight for her to fly with. Land was still close but not near enough.

As she pondered escape scenarios, the dip and splash of the oars competed with the sounds of Harfleur awakening. She doubted the humans could hear it, but to Aioffe, the calls and clops from inside the stone walls grew in volume as the sun rose. Wriggling her hands in her lap in an effort to loosen the rope, her mind turned to what torture awaited her in the town. Try as she might, her fear of a gaol loomed to the fore of her consciousness, and she shivered. Cold. Dark.

Forgotten.

She squeezed her eyes shut, trying to push the crushing vision aside. A low moan escaped her lips, startling the boy. He cried out, jolting her out of her reverie, and she noticed he pointed at her. Pausing mid row, men's conversation ceased, and they all stared at her. The boat continued to drift along its course.

In the sudden silence, Aioffe realised that they too were frightened. Of her? Had they seen her wings? Was it her 'otherness' which they identified? She glanced down at her hands, still bound in her lap, and hunched over. Instinct told her to make herself as small and as non-threatening as possible. Perhaps they would take pity on her then?

She hadn't tried that yet. Pity. Anything to play for leniency, she justified herself.

Raising her head a fraction, she blinked away the tears in her eyes and allowed her lip to wobble. Dropping her eyelids with deliberation, she attempted to catch the men's attention with a pleading look. Then she blinked again, and stretched out her slim ankle so it peeped from beneath her skirts.

But the Frenchmen were not deceived. The boy, impervious to a female's wily charms, laughed, then spat over the side of the boat. In a heartbeat, the tension broke.

"Les Anglais!" A collier said, then joined the boy in showing his contempt. He suggested something to the bearded one, then made a gesture as if he were cupping his own breasts. Aioffe had the distinct impression they were mocking her for being female!

She ducked her head again, furious at herself for even trying to use helplessness or her gender to better her situation. Or, had she done it wrong, she wondered? She tried to emulate the demure eyelid batting methods she'd witnessed used by other women to attract, but gave up as their guffaws and jeers continued. To be reliant upon the attention of a man was, at best, a poor reflection on womankind. At worst, it was completely contrary to her independent nature. It was frustrating enough in human society that she had to depend on Tarl, a kind person at heart, for clothing and cover. She huffed and retracted her legs, then stared ahead to Harfleur instead.

The colliers directed the boat around towards the long stretch of wall with a tower on the end, facing out to sea. This was the entrance to the harbour Aioffe had seen last night. A strong, inbound tide pushed against the light craft though, and, as they drew closer, navigation without crashing into the craggy rocks at the base of the embankment proved tricky. Eventually, the bearded one gestured to a narrow muddy tract of land outside the main town walls instead.

With Aioffe still tied to the seat, the other man grunted something to the boy in a firm, admonishing tone. Both men then stepped out of the boat to approach the walls, behind massive wooden barricades, by foot. The child brandished the pitchfork tangs at her with unwavering focus, as if trying to make up for his earlier lack of attention. They stared at each other as his elders squelched away through the mud.

An enormous splash broke her tiny captor's concentration. Aioffe ducked as a curtain of water rose from the shallows, drenching her and the lad. The boy spluttered, then resumed his guard. His skinny frame shook with fear as more missiles landed in the lake.

After a few minutes, the rain of stone ceased. Aioffe's heartbeat returned to its normal pace and the boy remembered his duty. Then, he paled, his shoulders hunching as he curled over.

Silently, with no announcement, more great lumps of rock splashed all around! Closer and closer, until finally one hit. A crack sounded from above and she wheeled about on her seat. Stone chips clattered down. From the walls, screams and shouts reached their ears.

A loud bang echoed through the valley. Deep and ominous.

Henry had began his siege. Aioffe suddenly understood what all those strange and huge contraptions were. And how the wide lake was of little consequence to cannon and catapult.

CHAPTER 32 – UNDER SIEGE

Aioffe crouched low in the boat, too frightened to move or look. An unexpected sense of helplessness gave her goosebumps. There was nothing to do but wait and hope the assault would stop. But the bangs continued to echo around the valley.

Amidst the terrifying noise, she was not alone in feeling exposed. Yet she would not leave the child to suffer this trauma by himself. Held from his perch on the stern's tip, the pitchfork shook in the boy's hands but remained pointed at her. Aioffe beckoned for him to come down, join her, but he shook his head. Wide eyes betrayed his fear and Aioffe had to admire his courage.

The rope lashing her to the bench had been drenched and the knot was swollen and tight. The boy saw her attempts to release her binding, but was apparently too paralysed by fear to poke her into submission. Try as she might, her fingers could not loosen it for escape. To distract herself from the noise, she considered other means of leaving this exposed position.

If she used the oars to push the vessel back out into the lake, they became a target for the guards above. It was a mercy they hadn't yet been spotted beached below.

Even if she could leave the boat, where could they both go anyway? Nowhere along the wall offered sanctuary, not even the wooden barricades in front of the stone - for they splintered or collapsed under the barrage.

As more stones left their noisy mark on the walls, one landed on the walkway above. A guard tumbled from his post to his death a few feet away. His screams cut off by landing with a squelch in the mud.

The lad's face paled as he glanced at the body, then back, to over her shoulder. His mouth fell open.

Aioffe looked around across the lake then up, just in time to see another rock hurtling towards them!

Its trajectory meant the missile would hit the boat's tip - right where the boy perched! With no time to evacuate, the best she could do was protect him from its impact. The boat listed in the mud as Aioffe half-stood. Her tied hands shot out to grab the pitchfork. She yanked and the youngster tumbled towards her as she jerked backwards. Her fingers grasped the front of his shirt, twisting them both as they fell. His slight torso landed on top of her as they hit the boat's floor.

With a tremendous crack, wood splintered up into the air as the missile hit. The lad screeched as the hull smashed behind him. Judders ran through the timbers beneath them.

As she tried to pull them both up the boat, away from the damage, the boy screamed again. Aioffe glanced down his legs; his foot was contorted at an odd angle. Twisted and caught by the spikes of what remained of the stern. Blood welled from splinters which had embedded themselves into his exposed skin, but, he was alive at least. His little frame quaked with shock and he looked up at her with tear-filled eyes.

'I'm sorry,' she said, trying to offer him comfort even though he couldn't understand her language. The boy burst into tears. She stroked his shoulder, but the action felt ineffective. He was only a child, caught up in an adult's war. Alone and hurt with a stranger.

Her heart ached for his pain. Aioffe pulled him closer, gathering him onto her lap. Her body would do little to protect him should a missile actually land on them, but there was some comfort in clutching one another. As they huddled together in the hull, her fingers smoothed his ankle, plucking out the splinters. His sobs eased as she pushed tendrils of her Lifeforce into his swollen limb until he relaxed into her embrace. Close to, his essence smelled like ripening apples and cut grass, pure and innocent.

Throughout the morning, the English catapulted Harfleur with boulders and cannonballs. Now Henry's gunners had the distance gauged correctly, the pale walls were subjected to a battering unlike any they had endured before.

She listened to the boy muttering to himself every time a boulder whistled through the air, his voice muffled as he cuddled into her shoulder. After a while, Aioffe was able to identify certain words within his language as being similar to English, and some in Latin. Fervent prayers perhaps? The more she heard, the more the cadence of the phrases sounded familiar, and she recalled the blessings offered by various priests on the ships. If nothing else, listening to the boy's babble distracted her from the smacks of stone on stone, of rubble falling and beams cracking, and the screams from inside the walls. She held his head buried into her stomach, cupping her hands over his ears so he would not hear the sounds of destruction and death.

As darkness fell, the firing continued for a while then abruptly ceased. The boy, shivering from hunger and exhaustion, sank asleep in her arms. Aioffe watched on, waiting for her moment to move. Only minutes after the bombardment stopped, her eyes made out flickering torchlight on the opposite shore.

Some figures approached the water's edge - English scouts, she thought. Come to assess the damage. With a whistle, darts fired over Aioffe's head, followed by the ratcheting of crossbows being reloaded. The arrows landed harmlessly in the shallows, but their message was clear. Any attempt to approach the wall would be taken as aggression and met with swift retribution.

Aioffe sighed, the English were too far away to see her in the darkness. Not that she was wearing anything which identified her, of course, nor was she able to bring herself close enough to shout to them. The boat was no longer capable of floating, and even if she could free herself to fly, the bowmen above would doubtless spot her before she got out of their range.

Then there was the boy... she refused leave him here, injured. Not in the dark. And alone.

Her head whipped around at the squelch of footsteps. Squelch, slap, squelch across the muddy embankment. In the still of the night, they might as well have announced themselves with trumpets to Aioffe. She shifted the slumbering child so she could tug on the knots again.

Her fingers worked frantically against the thick, still damp rope. Digging into the twist, it remained steadfast around her wrists. She bent her head and gnawed at the twine, pulling the strands until they broke. Tearing through for her freedom became a race against the approaching footsteps.

Then, from the walls above, wood creaked and snapped. Hammers tapped. Clods of something hit the mud with a splat.

Harfleur was repairing its defences.

Low voices found the body of the guard at the base of the wall, disturbing the boy's slumber. He pushed himself up, away from her and peered over the boat side. Aioffe gnawed on, but he had spotted the rescuers. Before she could stop him, he shouted, "*Ici! Je suis ici!*"

Then, just as she pulled to break the last strands of the rope, he turned his head back to her as he waved to the soldiers. His face fell, as if realising a mistake.

A soldier approached, consternation upon his brow. He grabbed the boy's arm and hauled him up, berating him. The boy jabbered something, pointing at Aioffe and the splintered end of the boat. Despite all of her listening and learning, she only caught one familiar word - '*ange*,' which sounded a little like the Latin term, '*angelus*.'

Aioffe kept her head down, confused as the youngster continued to argue. Had the child seen her in the air last night? Angels were to be feared as well as revered, Tarl had mentioned. Was she the reason the boy had run away? Left the charcoal fire just as it was about to cause a disaster? With a sickening lurch in her stomach, Aioffe understood the child's frightened glances, and his prayers. She felt like a fraud, and to blame for everything which had happened since.

It was clear that the soldier didn't believe the boy anyway, as rough fingers lifted her chin and he glared into her eyes. His gaze flicked between her and the child, undecided. Aioffe held her breath. All it took was some curiosity, a flick of her cloak, and he would discover her wings! She raised her fingers to touch the back of the guard's hand, then pushed in the soothing acceptance which she had successfully used on a human in Southampton. Acceptance of what, she didn't know, but it seemed important that he believed what he saw before him as being the truth, so that was the thought she tried to encourage. Aioffe did not dare speak her wishes though, for that would identify her immediately as being English.

The guard blinked, then retracted both his hands. For a moment he looked, bewildered, at his fingers.

Before the man could decide what had happened, the boy tugged on the soldier's arm, scrambling to his knees in the boat. He babbled more words, which Aioffe didn't catch. Only the universal note of pleading in his tone.

But something had changed. Another of the men who accompanied the search party shouted over, a muddy corpse half upright in his arms. The soldier glanced over, then back to them. "*Allez*," he said, motioning with his arm towards the town. "*Va vite*."

The boy obviously understood the command. His shoulders sagged with relief as he shot Aioffe a sly, triumphant look. Then his lips rose at the corners and she understood. The boy had spoken for her, with a story so ridiculous it was unbelievable. Perhaps, his tale came at a time when there were other priorities than indulging a childish fantasy.

"*Un ange! Mon cul.*" The soldier rolled his eyes and chuckled as he wheeled his legs around in the mud. Whatever the lad had said, it appeared they were now free to leave. To all intents and purposes, they were just a mute woman and a talkative child, caught outside the barricades when the siege had started.

As the guard squelched away, Aioffe let out a long breath. Her new young friend bore weight upon his ankle as he unfurled himself from the soggy boat floor. He winced, then turned to her with pleading eyes.

She stood, smiled at him, and offered her hand. It hadn't been so many months ago that she had limped. Humbled by the unspoken yet growing kinship with the boy, they set off through the mud. Their progress might be slow, but at least they had each other.

CHAPTER 33 – DISCOVERY

Tarl felt a boot nudge him. Then again. Bleary-eyed, he raised his head from his arms. Having previously not slept for two days and nights, he blinked to gage the brightness level, to give him some indication of the time. It was night. Torches had been lit and the smell of gunpowder lingered in the air.

"Have you seen your wife?"

It was one of Aioffe's friends, the older farmer's wife they had travelled from Anglesey with. Her husband was a passable bowman and a better brewer. In his confusion, he couldn't bring to mind the wife's name. He shook his head at her instead.

How long had it been? Digging, then all night at the forge, then dragged off to somewhere else to fortify the wooden barricades in front of the trebuchet. Then hours and hours of lifting the panel to one side, letting the siege weapon fire, then moving it back into place. After a while, he hadn't liked to look too often at the damage inflicted, because the French hung the bodies of captured English scouts from the walls. The stones could not help but bash their own countrymen to death. Bloodstains decorated the pale fortifications of Harfleur in a grisly reminder of the human cost of war.

The last thing he remembered, as dusk fell, was being sent to a field on the far side of the camp by Ap Tudor to fix his horse's shoe. He'd sat down for a moment, leant against the fence, and the next thing he knew, this woman placed a boot on his bottom!

He drew in a ragged breath, then the stench of dung hit his

nose and his stomach turned.

"Well, she's not returned." The woman shook her mop cap. "I thought maybe she'd come to find you."

Tarl stiffened.

"But you're over 'ere, and she's not."

"When did you last see her?" His heart raced. "I thought she was sewing with you?"

She glanced down, then shook her head.

Oh God, where was she? He hadn't set eyes on Aioffe in days. A crawling sensation crept up his arms. There were some twenty thousand men here - most of them bemoaning their lack of feminine comfort, especially now the battle had begun and the reality of war and mortality bit. All of yesterday, from dawn to dusk, the siege weapons had pummelled Harfleur, not that he'd seen much of the damage from behind the movable wooden shields. How could he protect her from there? It only took one person to discover her secret and everything was lost.

"Ap Tudor!" Tarl blurted out. "Where is he?"

The woman shrugged. "Probably bossing everyone about. As usual." She sniffed.

Tarl jumped to his feet and his satchel thumped to the earth. He gawked around, hands raising to his forehead as if that would pummel some sense into it. The sudden movement to upright made his head spin, so he grabbed hold of the fence. He looked hard at the woman. In the shadows on her face, the way she hesitated in front of him, Tarl knew there was more she hadn't told. "Please, where did she go?"

"All she said, two days past, was she had to go on an errand." Her face creased with concern. "I was supposed to tell you this, but I haven't seen you until now. You didn't return to the tent." Her arms crossed and she pouted. "I only happened upon you here, as I wanted to check on my Bess." She pointed to a pony resting its fetlock on the far side of the enclosure.

"I know. I've been busy." Tarl said, then swallowed, but it didn't ease the sudden dryness in his throat. Had he been deliberately kept away? He wouldn't put it past that bastard Ap Tudor to take advantage of the chaos. "Who sent her on this errand?"

"Well…" The woman smoothed her skirts. "I don't think it can be Ap Tudor, for he came by yesterday and said nothing. No-one else of seniority was around much, what with all the blasting. All the men went off, waiting with the cannons and the like." Under Tarl's withering stare, she thought, then added, "We did see that priest, though."

"A Bishop?"

"I suppose. I don't really know who he was. Only that he wore a robe with a jewelled cross. Very fine it was, too."

"Did he speak to Aioffe?"

The woman nodded. "Oh yes. Took her off, then they spoke for a while, then she carried on sewing. If anyone wanted stitching of finer things, she'd be the person they'd come to, I'm sure."

That was enough for Tarl. A starting point, at least. He would place money on where to find the Bishop - wherever the money was. "I thank you for letting me know…?"

"Agnes." The woman frowned. "I do hope you find her. Pretty little thing like that. She'd be a temptation for many a lonely soldier, I'm sure." With her lips tightly pressed together in disapproval, her expression suggested Tarl ought to have kept a closer eye on his wife. How he was supposed to do that, Tarl couldn't fathom. He juggled two masters. But, factoring in a curious and attractive wife should have been more of a priority.

Swallowing back a retort, for it was not Agnes's fault he had been so remiss, Tarl lifted his hand in farewell and strode off.

*****

One couldn't just barge in and demand an audience with a Bishop, Tarl realised, when the guard at the monastery gates laughed at him. Poking from under his helmet, the soldier's nose then wrinkled. "He's far too busy for the likes of you."

Tarl had to admit, he probably looked, and smelt, worse than the lowest of cattle herders.

"Besides," the soldier went on. "He's not here."

"Well, where is he?"

"How should I know? Do you think the high and mighty tell me their every movement?"

Tarl supposed not. "Does he at least rest here?"

"Again, I don't know."

"Can I wait? I'm Tarl Smith. I was working at the forge, just the other day."

The guard paused, sizing Tarl up. "No."

Tarl dithered. The chances of finding where else the Bishop could be amongst the camp fields, in the dark, without someone ordering him somewhere else, were slim.

"Please. I can keep an eye out for him from the forge."

The guard shrugged. "No. No admittance. No-one in or out. Those are my orders."

"Am I allowed to wait here, then?"

"Don't know."

"You don't know much, do you?"

"Shouldn't you be somewhere else?"

"I don't know," said Tarl.

The soldier rolled his eyes. "Begone with you. I've better things to do than stand around."

Tarl's frustration boiled over. "That's exactly what you are doing."

"Because that's what I'm being paid to do. If you are challenging me, one call and all hell will break loose." The guard brought a horn to his lips and made ready to blow.

Scooting about on his heels, for the last thing he needed right now was to be detained for causing a disturbance, Tarl plodded away. The guard's chuckle followed him down the track.

*****

Although a few beacons and intermittent camp fires lit the way, navigating the maze of tents in near darkness made Tarl's weary head ache. When he reached Sir John Cornwaile's field, he picked up his pace. By the time he jogged to the far side of the encampment, he had convinced himself that he'd acted too rashly. Maybe the last few hours, since he'd woken, were just an over-reaction to an awful miscommunication.

Surely, Agnes had been wrong. Maybe Aioffe had simply been reassigned duties elsewhere. Or, did he dare to hope she had been searching for him? Through no fault of his own, he hadn't been with the rest of Ap Tudor's troops for most of the day, and didn't know who had ordered him to work the forge fires the night before. He'd followed the page's orders on the assumption that they came from someone senior.

And yes, he'd welcomed the chance to be away from their awkward exchanges. At the time. It also made sense to him she would also want to avoid his presence. And yet…

A part of him worried he was fooling himself with delusions, while another part of him prayed that the Welsh woman had been mistaken. Even if Aioffe had been sent on an errand by the Bishop, perhaps beginning her role as spy, she ought to have returned by now. A night, a day and night had passed since she'd been seen speaking to the Bishop. More than enough time for Aioffe to have flown back, surely? With the army here, he couldn't see why the vampire would send her too far away when the siege was here.

Dodging a guide rope, Tarl shook his head and muttered to himself, "She will be there, she will." Aioffe would be waiting for him in their tent, a meal set aside for him, and a comfortable bed to finally rest upon. His absence was the reason why he'd not seen her, not because she had disappeared. The more he said it, the more it would be true. "Holy Mary, please let her be home."

He flung open the tent flap. Even though it was pitch black, he sensed the absence of another body inside. Disappointment forced him to his knees. His hands padded about the ground, knocking over a bowl of cold pottage in the narrow space between their sleeping rolls. Lips wobbled then tensed against each other, as he tried to hold on to vain hope, but it was futile.

She was gone.

"Gone," he whispered into the darkness.

His head hammered, reeling with regret. Earlier, as each booming cannon had brought the prospect of his own survival into question, he'd resolved to bridge the barrier between them. Too late. Tarl clutched his hands to his head. He wouldn't get to tell her. Could never say that she, after so long, had made him feel again. The change in his feelings about her wouldn't be acknowledged. So much left unsaid. Unresolved.

Around his ribs, the crush of remorse and fear tightened until he was breathless. He dropped to the rough blankets, still rolled and tidy. The cool wool rasped against his cheek, yet still, tears would not come.

He was too late to fix this. Too late for plans to be made. Without meaning to let it escape, a low howl of pain came from the depths of his soul. His fingers splayed against the rough weave, and he buried his head into it to silence his own mouth.

Her scent tickled in his nose, sweet like fresh fir. How she loved trees, any woodland. How the solid trunks were as home to her as this tent was now to him. To them. It was she who had made it a home from home with her warmth. His fingers clung to her blanket.

Her blanket.

Tarl lifted his head. The constrictions of sorrow binding his chest suddenly eased as the realisation hit. In the dim, his hands felt around again. Her belongings were still here! There was the sack she used for clothes, and the sewing bag with all the needles and threads she kept with her. He dragged the pouch towards him, checking inside. Her attire neatly folded, clean and ready for her to change into. She had so few possessions, so what she had was much prized and cared for.

He rummaged, tallying the clothing until he could determine what was missing - her cape, the dark blue skirt, and a smock. Her belt and knife, which she always wore. All of her headscarves were here, though, which struck him as odd. If she were to walk around in daylight, a lack of covering her distinctive hair would make her stand out.

Then he pulled out the wrapped leather bundle of arrowheads she had been sharpening for him. He opened it and count the batch. All but one had been cleaned and sharpened. A curved broad-head - the tip she had half sharpened when she first started assisting him. This one he vaguely remembered shaping - its barbs were wider than usual as he'd been in a hurry and the outline was more heart-shaped than flat and triangular. Despite the irregularity, when sharp, the head would pierce a hide or leather adequately, but she had left one side's edges dull. Perhaps she hadn't got around to finishing it?

The head fitted snug and smooth in his palm. Only one half of it deadly. For a moment, the warming metal felt as if he held her heart within his hand. With a deep breath, he drew the next conclusion.

Aioffe would not, he was sure, have left her clothes behind if she had meant to leave for good.

Unless... unless she meant to leave him. As the provider of

these items, was this her way of rejecting him?

The flicker of hope wavered inside him. He blinked, unwilling to let the wish extinguish. His mind weighed up the evidence versus his heartfelt fear. His fingers rubbed the soft fabric, reminding him of her affection, her care. That kiss….

A lock of hair fell over his forehead as he shook his head. Facts only, he told himself. Consider at what he knew, not what he felt.

Aioffe, from the very moment he met her, needed clothes to blend in. It had been so important to her to look the part of a human, to be seen as ordinary. His heart thudded. If she had left him, would the fact that he had provided the means for the purchase of the clothing be reason enough to leave them here? They were of no use to him. Meant nothing to him, but everything to her. He tapped the broadhead to his lips and looked around again.

She'd placed a bowl of pottage just inside the tent flap, in anticipation of his return. Why would she have done that if she didn't care for him? Even though so much remained unspoken, unresolved, between them, their awkwardness hadn't stopped her consideration for his needs, in these small ways.

She wouldn't. If you are leaving because you are unhappy, Tarl thought, you don't plan for that person's comfort in your absence. That made no sense.

Something must have happened to keep her away. Ap Tudor? No, Agnes had said he was behaving normally. The lout would crow of his conquest. Would have sought him out to be sure, Tarl knew, just to cause him pain.

Tarl's pulse steadied. He'd been right to seek out the vampire Bishop. He must be responsible for Aioffe's disappearance, or at very least, be able to explain what they had discussed. Only by finding the vampire would he know where to begin looking for his wife.

CHAPTER 34 – ULTIMATUM

Despite his exhaustion, Tarl slept fitfully. Having decided there was little point in wandering the fields when everyone was asleep in an attempt to locate the Bishop, as soon as dawn broke, he dressed for battle and headed towards the monastery. After retrieving his bow and a quiver of arrows, he strung the weapon and swung them, and the satchel, over his shoulders and set out. His stomach tight with anxiety, he vowed would not be waylaid today. Orders be damned. If he wasn't at the command centre, then he would to search the entire front line. He would find the Bishop of Norwich.

Although the hour was early, camp fires were stoked back into life. Last night's leftovers scooped into hungry bellies before armour was fastened around anxious chests. Tarl kept his head low as he trotted past tents emptying themselves of yawning soldiers, and skirted away from the larger ones which housed nobles and commanders. The latrine trenches were already in use. Everyone, irrespective of rank or role, needed to relieve themselves, especially those soon to be laced into armour. From the groans though, some were suffering more than others. The effect of nerves on one's stomach was something Tarl had also witnessed yesterday.

As Tarl strode down the track, a battalion of men at arms marched towards him. To let them pass, and provide some distance between himself and their commander, he dodged to the side. As they progressed, he crossed himself and muttered a prayer, ostensibly, for their good fortune in battle.

Once the sound of boots receded, he spotted a knight cantering behind. Tarl stepped out into plain view in the centre of the path, and stared. On the horse's flanks, a blanket with the Norwich heraldry flapped with every hoof fall. Tarl's hands tightened around his bow stave as he questioned why a man of the cloth would wear armour. The visor remained up, but was too far away for him to confirm it was the vampiric face he sought.

Silver barding glinted in the sunlight, as the horse gathered pace and thundered towards Tarl. Within seconds, Tarl notched an arrow and drew his bow. He stood his ground, trusting that either the rider would swerve to avoid him, or pull up. If it was not the Bishop, then perhaps the knight would know where Norwich was. Confident that he had correctly identified the colours, it became a question of nerve.

The rider yanked on the reins, mud splattering from the horses' hooves as it skidded to a halt. The huge black destrier tossed its head at Tarl as the vampire himself glared down.

"Where's my wife?" Tarl said.

Black eyes narrowed on him through the open visor, obscuring the Bishop's mouth. "She has failed."

"What do you mean? Where is she?"

A slight rise and fall of the shoulder plates suggested a shrug. The Bishop tugged the reins to the side, but Tarl caught them. "Where did you send her?"

"She was supposed to scout for reinforcements we suspected were heading towards Harfleur. She did not return."

Tarl's mouth dropped along with his bow. So the Bishop had sent her away, but the confirmation did little to ease the knot in his stomach.

"So," the Bishop continued in an imperious tone, "we have neither information about numbers, nor, apparently, do you still have a wife."

"But… have you sent out a search party?"

The Bishop leaned down towards him. "And what do you suppose I would instruct them to look for? A girl with wings? Anyone English?" He sat back in the saddle. "If you think the French will take pity on such a creature, then you are more stupid than I took you for. Best you forget all about her."

The vampire was staring at him in a peculiar way, his face indecipherable but his eyes dark and unwavering as they focussed on Tarl. "I can help you forget her, if we can conclude our business."

He didn't want to forget Aioffe, not now. Not ever. Tarl's hands dropped the reins and he bowed his head, avoiding that unnerving stare as his mind whirled. Irrespective of his feelings, Aioffe had survived so much, travelled so far. It was simply unacceptable that her adventure ended here. In a fight she had no stake in. A dispute over land, not even one which had the weight of a holy war behind it. Not really.

Tarl shook his head. "Until I see her body, I won't accept she has failed. You're responsible for her disappearance. If you want my affidavit naming names back, and the blessed shoes, then it's in your best interests to find her."

"I don't think you are in a position to be making such demands," was the Bishop's sardonic reply.

"If she is alive, she would return." Tarl's certainty and loyalty could not waiver now. He remembered the bloodied walls of Harfleur. "And if she is dead, then the French would surely be very keen to announce their victory by displaying her body." The very thought of it made his stomach sick.

The vampire's lips pursed as he said, "And what if she was captured? Tortured? How much does she know of our battle capabilities?"

Tarl's belly wrenched. Why had he jumped to either alive or dead conclusions, for there was something far worse in between.

"She knows nothing of how large the army is, or even what siege weapons we brought. She's just been sewing, for God's sake."

"She's a spy. I said it all along. The question remains, for which side?"

Tarl exploded. "It was you who sent her away!"

"At your suggestion and with your blessing, if I recall," the Bishop laughed cruelly.

Tarl gritted his teeth. Never had he regretted anything more than offering her up, an innocent, in the vague hope of making a deal for himself. He had to make amends. "You should be the one to find her. Find out what happened to her."

The Bishop snorted. "If you think I'm going to expose myself by asking questions about a missing commoner's wife, you are mistaken. The French would presume that we brought women to fight a man's war." He barked a laugh again. "Besides," the Bishop glanced down at his gleaming protection with pride. "I would be a high value target for the French, so I'm not going anywhere near them."

Tarl looked at the shiny armour and wished he had brought a dagger with him instead of the dulled arrowhead he had stashed in his pocket. A blade like the neat, sharp one Aioffe always carried. A slim knife would slip through the armour pieces like butter, no matter how polished and clean it was. He grunted, and recalled how he had thought he had killed a vampire back on Wrye, only for the Father McTavish to rally despite his extensive injuries. A knife alone wouldn't work, nor did he need another death on his conscience.

He nodded with affected resignation. "So, I will send out my letters, and hers. Expose you for the coward you are. King Henry doesn't seem in a forgiving mood right now. Your betrayal of his trust when he most needs unity isn't going to end well. For you." For illustration, he pointed the tip of his bow at the Bishop.

"Tsk." The vampire waved away the threat. "You imagine

you know a king's mind, Smith."

Tarl raised an eyebrow. "I don't need to know his mind. Just a man's paranoia when he feels vulnerable."

"The King is no ordinary man. He is a king."

"But still a man who pisses and shits like the rest of us. He may be king, but he still feels the stab of betrayal. For all that he is a decisive ruler, a trusting one, his actions in Southampton demonstrated just how quickly he deals with those who betray him and his cause."

The Bishop recoiled. "I have not betrayed his cause, nor will I, you impudent son of a whore."

"The discovery that his money man is not who he purports to be, but something else, not human or holy, is as close to a betrayal as I can imagine is necessary."

"I have no need to fear death, mortal. I have lived for far longer of your years than you can possibly imagine."

"Then you are a coward who fears injury. Like every other man here. I'm assuming you bleed and shit the same as we do?"

The Bishop looked down his nose at Tarl. "A little blood being spilt won't harm me in the slightest."

Underneath his sardonic tone, Tarl detected an unspoken 'But'.

Before he could work out precisely what the Bishop was afraid of, the vampire dragged his horses' reins to the side. As the destrier turned, the Bishop dropped his visor. Although muffled, Tarl could still hear him take the last word.

"Time will tell if your wife is true. She has failed in her mission, that much is obvious, for we have begun our attack. Blind." He snorted and kicked his horse on. "Better start praying, for I know where to find you if she has not resurfaced by the time Harfleur falls. Her kind always survive." The Bishop shouted as he trotted away, "By then, we'll know which side she flies for."

Rather than feel threatened by the taunt, Tarl's heart leapt at the Bishop's word choice. That she had flown somewhere was a given, but 'her kind always survive,' implied that she could, despite everything, be alive. Perhaps in hiding. Unwilling, or unable, to return. Although the thought of her captured wrenched his innards, it was certainly a possibility.

What was it the Bishop had said when he saw Aioffe? 'Here you are, with a... mortal.' He paid no attention to the remark at the time, being too caught up with his damned emotions, but now, the implication of it resurfaced for examination in a logical manner. He was the mortal, which suggested they were not. It then occurred to him that Aioffe might also have lived for a very long time.

Was she, in fact, immortal?

That would explain why she had no fear of accompanying him into a war zone. Little regard for sharp weapons. Could she even be killed? Injured, certainly, but he'd witnessed her remarkable way of restoring strength and healing herself.

He stood, stroking the soft and short hair on his chin for a moment as the destrier cantered away. A cranking, creaking noise of ratchets reached his ears as the army prepared to fire again.

Until he saw Aioffe's body on the ramparts, he would not believe she was dead. He could not.

Which left the question of where was she?

CHAPTER 35 – UNAVOIDABLE DEATH

Aioffe followed the boy, winding through darkened but noisy alleyways. Deep inside the town, the houses jostled for space, their roofs overhanging the cobbles. Far from being subdued, Harfleur's residents rallied to restore order during the night hours. Wounds were tended, meals shared as roof holes patched. Neighbour helped neighbour. Yet Aioffe heard the notes of fear in the muttered undertones of conversation on the debris strewn pavements. She smelled their sweat, their terror and panic, in the tendrils of the townsfolk's Lifeforce.

They passed a church, its shattered stained glass windows still glowing with flickering candlelight, offering fervently whispered absolution. Aioffe paused, struck by how in the midst of carnage, human's faith in their god endured. As she listened to the sobs and the salves proffered wafting through the broken panes, she suspected Henry's forces were equally praying, but for a swift victory. Salvation for either side seemed optimistic to her as she considered the chaos of last night.

Then, bells began to toll from high above her; the clangs echoed between the buildings, swelling in the night air as more bells joined the solemn dirge.

The boy halted, sensing perhaps that the peeling marked something significant. He turned to look at her, the shadow in his eyes lifting when saw her solemn expression. As if her pause at this spot proved something to him. His head cocked to one side, eyes flicking to the church with an enquiry. Aioffe shook her head. She did not want to intrude on a ritual she didn't understand. Besides, she had come from the invading party, which caused the pain which hung like a pall over town.

His face still wary, the boy nodded, then reached for her hand. Cold fingers clutched at hers as he pulled her on. Aioffe couldn't help but feel claimed somehow, and it warmed her heart. The bongs ceased, and the lad began twittering away to her as he limped by her side. His previous fierceness with the pitchfork replaced by an eagerness to bring her with him, wherever he was taking her.

The road opened onto a square, as yet unharmed by the English missiles. Amassed in the centre stood a motley selection of soldiers and citizens. Various liveries over rag-tag pieces of leather and steel armour adorned the men. Some carried huge, cumbersome crossbows, as wide as a longbow was tall, but heavy and unwieldy-looking. Having watched the English archers firing both elegant longbow and small crossbow at the butts, this combination of weapon seemed to offer no advantage, for the string could only be wound back a short distance, reducing both its power and range, and not reloaded or easily aimed with any great speed.

A knight corralled the troops on horseback, gesturing to individuals with a thick longsword and barking what she presumed were orders. Instinctively, Aioffe ducked her head.

By her side, the boy froze. The commander's glare swept around the square; it would surely not be long before it alighted upon them. Several roads led away from the gathering point, any one of which offered less exposure.

Had she been too quick to trust the boy? Her wings fluttered in readiness beneath her cape. She tugged him along, but the child resisted. His feet planted on the cobbles.

"Come on," she whispered, yanking his arm. The horse's hooves clopped closer as the commander corralled his troops. She dared not raise her head. "It's not safe here."

Almost imperceptibly, the boy leaned into her, then lifted his arm to point. Her gaze followed his wavering finger. On the far side of the square, a young priest hunched over a line of bundles, crossing himself. As he bent down to anoint the forehead of one of the corpses, she noticed the bundle next to it. Peeking through the blanket which covered the body was a soot-blackened face and half a beard.

Aioffe's hand tightened around the boy's small fingers. He blinked and stared at the half hidden form intently, his loss still too recent for words, and their friendship too new for her to offer much solace.

"Do you want to go to him?" Aioffe said in a soft voice. She gestured with her finger and a raised eyebrow.

He turned his shadowed eyes up to hers, glistening with tears, and shook his head. His gaze moved briefly to behind her shoulders, then back to her face.

There was no mistaking the pleading tone in his voice. "Est-il avec les anges? Comme toi?"

That word again, but she understood what he meant. Angel. The child's conclusion, or confusion, about what she was, seemed to hold some comfort to him. She remembered Tarl's reaction to her wings, to seeing her fly, and how he had found something otherworldly in them. He had told her she looked like an angel when she flew, but she hadn't questioned further what an angel exactly was. She'd been a little affronted at the time, if she was honest. She was a fae, she thought he knew that.

The child's eyes searched hers, though, in such a manner that she hated to disappoint him. Perhaps an angel had something to do with human death rituals, she wondered, so she nodded.

At this, his lips tightened and he blinked furiously again. She watched as he swallowed, then rolled his shoulders back. He motioned the sign of a cross on his chest, as she had seen many men do in the presence of a priest, or when they felt the need to summon the support of their god. His gaze flicked to her, and, with her head bowed, she copied the movement.

Seemingly satisfied by her response, the boy led them into the shadows and away.

*****

The building which the boy led her to was at the far end of town. Entry was via the narrowest of alleyways, then into a small yard. Up some rickety stairs to the side of a high storehouse, all the way to a loft. A tiny balcony, barely wide enough for two to stand upon, jutted out, higher than many of the rooftops. A wooden door, paint peeling from its rough surface, swung ajar.

The boy's expectant face dropped as he peeked inside. After flicking his gaze back to hers, he then hung his head. She took his little hand and urged him in.

In darkness, the hovel was defined more by the stench of charcoal and stale ale, which wafted over like an invisible cloud, than the lack of home comforts. Aioffe didn't need the candle stub which the boy hastened to light, to notice the sparse furniture - a table with two stools and a low, wide pallet for a bed. A fetid straw mattress, flattened by the weight of previous occupants, had only a threadbare blanket bundled on the top. Dotted across dusty, bare floorboards, a variety of pots and bowls were full of dank rainwater. A more miserable existence Aioffe had never encountered.

The boy stared at the bed. In his hand, the candle spluttered. The cheap wax cast only a dim light against the absence of anyone else who lived here. She tasted the grey grief in his Lifeforce, unavoidable to her as the boy seemed frozen, tears rolled silently down his cheeks. For a moment, she considered trying to ease the pain with her own touch, but something held her back. There had been an occasion when Tarl's Lifeforce was tinged with the same musty sorrow, especially when he referred to his mother. Indeed, there had been wisps of it emanating from several individuals they had passed on the walk here.

Aioffe swallowed. The unpleasant tang was just another aspect of the human world which she would have to get used to, she supposed. Perhaps, someday, she would learn what to do to ease it because there was no avoiding death for humans - it was part of their short, natural life cycle. For now, maybe the best she could do was make sure the youngster felt less alone.

But they weren't alone for long. A bang on the door made them both start. "Benediet? Benediet? C'est toi?" A female voice called through, thumping on the planks again.

The boy rushed over and flung open the door. Outside, leaning against the wonky stair-rail, an old woman reached for him. She bundled the lad into her arms, whispering in his ear.

Benediet pulled back, his face stricken. "Où est-il?"

The woman gestured behind, over the rooftops with her hand, then down into the yard. She gabbled with urgency in her voice. All the while, she shook her head.

Benediet's eyes spilled over with tears as he rapidly explained something to her. Only then did she peer over the boy's head to see Aioffe. Her face paled, and she pushed Benediet back out of her arms and glared at him full in the face. An angry tone led to another argument.

Aioffe stayed motionless as once again, the child defended her presence and she caught the word angel. He pointed to his ankle, then at Aioffe. The woman frowned but said nothing more.

He looked back at Aioffe with eyes wide and teary, then pushed past the old woman and clattered down the stairs. After a wary glance in her direction, the old lady clumped and limped down the stairs after him.

Aioffe went to the doorway but lingered, uncertain as to if she should go with them, or stay. The night sky beckoned her;

how easy it might be to fly away. Find Tarl. Go back.

But the boy's wail from below reached her ears. The pain in it etched upon her heart, and she knew she could not abandon him now. She checked her cape still covered her wings, then, gripping the rail, she followed the sound.

Across the courtyard, his cries drifted out from another dwelling. The iron tang of blood assaulted her as soon as she entered. A few candles along a shelf lit a sorrowful sight. Face up on a table lay the other collier who had brought her to Harfleur. Benediet clasped his hand and wept over the thick chest. In the corner, the old woman poured water into a small wooden cup. She didn't acknowledge Aioffe as she bent over and tried to dribble some into the man's mouth. Then Aioffe noticed his injuries. His arm, or what was left of it, dripped blood onto the floor through a cloth wrapped around the elbow. Below that, there was nothing. Aioffe advanced toward the table. Her hands reached out to touch the collier's distended stomach. His heartbeat too slow and arrhythmic. In his faint Lifeforce she tasted pain, and the grey cloud of impending death.

It would not be long.

Aioffe recognised there was nothing she could do. She understood the peculiar pallor of both the human and his Lifeforce, just as she knew when an animal was in its final throes of life. Usually, she would calm a beast as it passed. Aid by drawing out the Lifeforce in the full knowledge that it would sustain her, and she in turn would gift it to the earth in the form of growth. Such was her cycle of life.

But this was a human. A father, she suspected, given the facial likeness she now saw between the child and man. She could not 'take' this life, however compassionate her motives were.

Helplessness and an unexpected heartache swept over her, and, through her fingers, a tingle. But she was not touching skin, so there was no release. Aioffe studied the boy, who stroked the man's dirty hair. His fear and grief emanated with a force that was repugnant to her, yet, she still could not bring herself to escape it.

The woman crooned softly as the drink dripped down his slack cheek. Her futile actions perhaps about occupying her hands. Aioffe sensed the neighbour's care thus far had been driven by duty than emotion. Their eyes met and the woman shook her head a little. Her lips clamped together as they silently acknowledged their mutual inability to save the collier's life. A world-weary sorrow crept into the creased face as she glanced at the boy. The neighbour held no love for this man. Her sadness was for the child.

A rattle in the collier's breath signalled his passing was close. The wheeze frightened the boy. "Papa, papa!"

Benediet's hands grasped the colliers clothing, white knuckled and shaking. Aioffe reached across the man's chest and touched her fingers to Benediet's. This pain, at least, she might ease. There was little point in wasting her own Lifeforce to make the inevitable passing faster, it was already close, but the boy's pain she could numb.

As the rattle faded, she pushed the golden warmth of her tendrils into Benediet. The boy heaved a sob. His grip loosened on the collar. The man's pale face fell slack as the last wisps of his Lifeforce disappeared.

Aioffe took the boy's hand fully in hers and bowed her head. In the silence which followed, she tried to push something, anything of comfort into him, but he pulled his fingers away.

"Papa...?"

The woman bustled over and drew him into her chest, muttering over his head towards the body.

In her arms, the boy began to thrash, pushing against her embrace. She held him firm, even though his thin arms lashed out, pounding into her bulk. Aioffe frowned. The child needed something, but she didn't know what. She glanced at the corpse, half expecting it to disperse like her kind did, but the human's skin simply greyed.

The boy threw himself over the table, sobbing and shaking. Despite the old woman trying to pull him off, he gripped tighter and screamed. The screech pierced and Aioffe clapped her hands over her ears, shaking her head. His anguish washed over her, making her skin feel shivery and her wings fluttered beneath her cape.

The woman snapped at her, then motioned a cross over her chest then glared at Aioffe. But this time, Aioffe could not bring herself to make this gesture of comfort at this moment, because she did not believe it meant anything. Simply doing it for the sake of it was hollow and meaningless. It would not provide the relief the boy needed, nothing could she saw now.

She stared at the child whose pain froze her to the spot although she felt nothing herself. Stared at the still chest of the man who had brought her to this nightmare. Then she stared at her hands, useless to do anything to help. Her wings rustled against her skirt, as if reminding her that escape was always an option.

Yet, her feet seemed rooted to the floorboards. All of her life, she had run, flown, away. Even now, her presence in Harfleur was because she so desperately wanted to fly. And look what it had led her to. Capture. Pain. Death. Her escaping would not stop this from happening. Turning aside, and leaving, was simply hiding in a different way. A pretence which would not alter that fact that it was happening.

Was it better, then, to stay and face this as humans did? Loss was a part of the human experience, and if she was to remain in their society, wouldn't it be beneficial to learn to understand their emotions and remain?

Besides, as she looked at the boy, she was already indebted to him. Like Tarl, he had saved her. Kept her secret. In a sense, now he needed her and she owed him something by return.

CHAPTER 36 – BOOM AND BELLS

"That's the only sack left." John, a farrier working alongside Tarl panted as he dragged the charcoal over. "I dunno what we're supposed to do when it runs out. Them gunners," he shook his head. "Theirs won't last forever neither."

Gunpowder was a finely balanced mix of saltpetre, sulphur and charcoal, blended by experts who guarded their ingredients vigilantly. The stalled campaign had already surpassed everyone's expectations for duration and supplies brought over from England were finite.

Tarl shovelled a scoop into the forge fire. "Where did the monastery get their coals from?"

"I asked a monk, but he said the townsfolk contributed it. Or, I think that's what he said." John rolled his eyes. Language barriers were the least of the problems in the only place set up to handle metalworking in the army's vicinity. John rubbed his stomach as he leaned against the workbench. "And nothing's coming in or out of Harfleur these days."

"I'm surprised we lasted this long," Tarl replied. August was already half passed, and still Harfleur would not capitulate. Much to everyone's frustration, and in spite of the near constant battering of those pale walls, the army could not advance. Re-damming the river so it flowed away from the town had been partially successful, although the flood waters had not entirely receded. Boggy land bridges appeared, but they were almost impassable. Bringing the siege weapons closer, or traipsing men across such narrow paths, made them too vulnerable to the archers and small guns atop the remaining stretches of walls.

"Well, if the King wants to keep firing those cannons, he's going to have to find more fuel." John picked up the barrel band Tarl had been working on and inspected it. "We can't carry out repairs if there's no heat. This is for the King's Daughter, right?"

As the largest of the mortars brought over from England, she was rumoured to have taken two wagons to move to her heavily defended dug out position. She was slow to make ready to fire, but boy, did she boom! With a mouth was so wide a barrel of ale could be fitted into it, the rattle of firing boulders, used when the cannon balls had run out, meant the structural integrity of the gun was a constant worry.

Tarl chewed on his lip. "If we can't find more charcoal, then we'll have to make it." He understood the principle of its creation, but it was possible someone here was more skilled at the process of building the pyre than he. Besides, between shifts in the forge and manning the barricades in front of the catapults, there was no time for him to spend watching charcoal burn. Most charcoal making was done inside a large woodland to save labour, and it was not the sort of job done close to habitation as the burnt stench lingered. The forests outlying the camp were already depleted, the oaks in particular felled and used in defences to protect their siege weapons.

"I'd enjoy the peace of sitting and watching," John said. "But I've seen the fever strike so sudden once the gripes start, I'm not the man for it right now." He grimaced and doubled over. "Sorry."

As John waddled off to relieve himself again, Tarl poked at the embers, then stuck the band back inside for reheating. They were down to two smiths manning the forge. Others lay a-bed in the grips of the illness which had swept through the army these last few days. The midden trenches overflowed with groans and the stench of fear and sickness. Some were struck down so quickly, so violently, the priests barely had time for last rites.

The malady knew no boundaries - all ranks, gender, and jobs fell to the curse of watery bowels, levelling them all. Tarl had heard the cannons were blamed - the rotting egg-like stench from the gunpowder hung over the valley, and everyone thought the air had become toxic. Yet they kept firing.

Cleaning heat was Tarl's protection. Ever since the sickness began, he had only drunk fresh stream water, boiled on the forge's fire before decanting into his flask - like his mother had taught him. So far, he had not succumbed to the bloody flux and keeping the fires burning a pressing concern to his superstitious mind. He jiggled the cannon band about in the embers, waiting for it to glow to the right colour, and thought about who he could go to for a solution.

Tarl did not much consider Owain Ap Tudor as someone who would be able to solve this, or any other, logistical or practical issue. Easy to find, he only had to turn around to spot the Welshman lurking, watching him with suspicious eyes and ready with an order. Tarl was certain there had not been a collier amongst his men from Wales. Archers, miners, and men at arms, during the long journey, Tarl had socialised with them all, and not one mentioned charcoal-making as their usual trade. No-one he had thus far encountered carried that particular, pungent odour about them either.

Sir John Cornwaile, Ap Tudor's superior and in overall charge of the archers, attended the monastery early each morning, for a war council. Often found astride his brown mare, Sir John covered as much ground as the King every day, as, organising teams to scout, dig or fell trees to construct more barricades.

The barrel band glowed the right shade of white orange, so Tarl pulled it out for hammering. Yes, Sir John might know of a charcoal maker amongst his ranks, or where to find that official who had taken down names in Southampton. The problem was where to locate him at this time of day.

Tarl flattened the joint again, tapping until it was smooth on the weld, then set the band into a pail of water. A quick glance at the fire showed there wasn't enough heat for another piece to go in and he was loath to use what little fuel they had on anything unnecessary. Since charcoal took days to make, time was of the essence. They could not afford to wait until tomorrow morning for him to catch Sir John.

He grabbed his satchel, slung the white-tipped tube of arrows around his neck and gripped the ash longbow. Every time he held it, he thought of how Aioffe had caressed it when they found themselves under fire upon landing. The unnatural heat from the wood, which had reached his fingers, scared him at the time, but now he longed for that comfort. He still didn't understand what she had done, but he had claimed the bow as his from that point on, even though most archers returned their weapons at the end of each stint on duty. Since she had disappeared, he slept with it by his side, but the bow was no replacement for his wife.

There had been no news. His hopes of her safe return were stretched thin by vivid nightmares of her hung on those pale walls every time he closed his eyes. Work was the only thing which distracted him, nothing else. And if he couldn't keep the forge fires burning, and if the army didn't break the defences soon, then he didn't like to think of the consequences. The Bishops' threat to help him forget her loomed into his mind. Laying down the burden of his worry tempted, as much as it revolted him. His fingers tightened around the shaft. He did not want to forget Aioffe, not ever. He needed to make amends for how stupid he had been. Hope was all he clung to as the days passed without news of her.

"Back soon," he said to the guard on the gate, who knew him better by now but was still an arse. Ignoring the grunted reply, Tarl set off towards the frontline before the day slipped into night, and more time was lost.

*****

Sir John stomped out of the tunnel with a stony look upon his grey face. The entrance was guarded by half a dozen men at arms, poised with their pole-axes. They lowered them a fraction on recognising their dusty haired leader. A page dashed over, skirting around the piles of timber already sawn to size to bolster the shaft walls. Sir John's mare lifted her head from the grass as the lad proffered a rag at their master.

Tarl waited until Sir John had wiped his brow before approaching. "Sir, I'm afraid I need to raise a potential problem with you." His fingers gripped the satchel straps.

As if Tarl wasn't there, the commander scowled, walked to his horse, put his foot in the stirrup and jumped up. "Find someone else. I've got enough on my plate." He gathered the reins and turned his mount about.

"I would Sir, but I don't know whom else to ask." But Tarl's word's were lost in a loud 'whump' noise from behind him. The enormous sow, a wooden shoe-shaped structure which protected the tunnel opening, then echoed with shouts from inside. He spun around, alarmed by the urgent tone.

"Bloody French are about to break through with their counter tunnel," Sir John sighed. "Finch! Get your men down there!"

The soldiers trotted into the hole. Sir John glanced down at Tarl's bow stave. "Archers are supposed to be scouting. Do you have sight of something I should know about?"

Tarl shook his head. "I'm also a smith, Sir. And we've nearly run out of charcoal for the forge."

Sir John huffed, then as he thought through the implications, the corners of his lips turned down in a grimace. "Henry won't like that. Won't like that at all." He tutted. "But then, we hadn't planned on this taking so long either."

"I wanted to ask if you knew of any specialists in the ranks who could fire some more?"

"Running low on gunpowder too." Sir John raised his hand to stroke his beard. Then he frowned. "There's wood enough still up on the ridge." He pointed west. "I'll warrant that's the best place, easy access to the river as well." Wheeling the horse around a pile of timber, he nudged it into a brisk walk.

Tarl half ran, abreast of the mare. "Have the scouts found a site used before?"

"I can find out tomorrow morning. Assuming we don't have some sort of break through by then and advance. "

"Is that likely?"

Sir John shook his head. "I don't know how much more that town can take. There can't be many people left alive. They send men to discuss capitulation but have no intention of committing to it. All the while, the residents suffer. Fools."

"The bells haven't tolled for days," Tarl said. Silent bell-towers meant no kills. No French deaths to mark.

Sir John's head dipped and Tarl saw his exhaustion in the lines of his brow. "And yet they still don't surrender? Still fire at us from what remains of the walls. There's no prisoner exchange; they have no mercy, unlike us. And now they dig like us."

Prisoners. Tarl's mind was frustrated once again by thoughts of Aioffe. Was she captured? Tortured as the Bishop had suggested?

"We're so close with the tunnel," Sir John went on, his voice tight. "It would only take a few men to round up whomever's left, if we can only get inside those cursed walls."

Tarl suggested, "If they are tunnelling towards us, that's a help though. Isn't it? We can use their way out as our way in?"

"They have sabotage in mind, man. Sabotage!" He gritted his teeth. "I'll flatten that damned town to the ground, or sink it.

Blow them up from underneath. There's to be no mercy now. Every resident in Harfleur will die, if not by our stones and swords, then from hunger. Then we can move on with this blessed campaign whilst we still have men to fight it."

Lost for words, Tarl stopped dead in his tracks and stared at his bow. Could she realistically be alive after all this time? He struggled to draw breath as his chest clamped with the effort of holding his emotions inside.

Sir John pulled up the reins and twisted around in the saddle. "Don't stand around wasting time. You dither here, smith-bowman. Scout that ridge upriver. We need charcoal. There's no two ways about it. I'll see to it we find a collier tomorrow, so you make sure we have somewhere suitable for them to work. Unless you'd rather dig?"

Tarl's head shook, but it did not dispel his fears.

"Thought not." Without waiting for further response, Sir John trotted off.

CHAPTER 37 – KNIFE IN A CROSS

Walking through the forest provided Tarl with some relief. Here at least he could be undisturbed with his thoughts, however miserable they soon turned. He found a track which wound up river, occasionally skirting the edge of a cliff to head west as directed. It wasn't peaceful, as the echoes of the cannons reverberated around the valley, followed by the crash of falling stonework. When he reached the highest point, where the precipice edge crumbled, he paused and scanned down towards the town. A cloud of smoke hung over Harfleur, enveloping the devastation. Walls and towers which once glowed under the sunlight were now streaked dark with ash and blood.

His heart thudded, not just from the exertion of climbing, but also with fear.

The wreckage below him struck a chord deep inside him, as if he were looking down at an impression of his life. He stood, toes on the edge, struck by how alike this town and he were. How he too had made himself an island for protection. The cloud of misconception and superstition had cloaked the reality underneath. The pain, the blindness to the truth of the hopeless situation. No-one was coming to save Harfleur. No-one came to save him when he was alone and driven to desperation.

Except Aioffe. Bombarding him with kindness, her curiosity and compassion, she had broken through his walls. She was different from other people, and not in the way he had initially thought. A force terrifying and determined. Although she was unlike anything he had ever known, her view of this world offered a change. A way to live again, to feel. And now, just when he longed to capitulate and let her in, as surely the people of Harfleur did, she was gone.

But where? Was she down there? Or taken somewhere else? His new awareness of other dangers, other immortal creatures with their own interests to serve, muddled matters. Aioffe could be anywhere - alive or dead - and here he was, wandering around a wood, trying to find a place to make charcoal! Not knowing what happened to her weighed as much upon his mind as mourning. He sighed, wishing he could return to the numbness he had lived with for so long since his mother's death. Aioffe had awakened emotions in him which, in her absence, he could hardly bear to live with.

Tarl looked up the river, to where it disappeared into the hills. Once Harfleur fell, for fall it surely must soon, Henry would press on with his campaign whilst the season's weather held. He realised he would have to either abscond, to search the ruins for her in the unlikely event she survived the English assault, or, pack up his broken heart with his belongings and follow.

Duty or clarity. Absolution or answers.

An urge to leap over the cliff edge swept over him, to avoid the decision. Was it better to step off, into the abyss? Both choices held the likelihood of a terrible outcome, and neither offered salvation for either Aioffe or his own soul. What would it feel like to be free of this burden, even for just a moment?

As his head bent to look down the drop, his satchel nudged his knees. The tools of his trade inside poked at his conscience. The absence of the stolen altar goods lightened the bag, but, at that moment, it weighed heavy with duty and conscience. Other people relied upon him now, had need of his skills and his bow. If he jumped or fell, others might suffer when he could have saved them. Whether or not he liked it, he was now a part of something bigger than himself and his own troubled life.

Tarl jerked. Stumbling backwards, his bow-arm instinctively flung out for balance. The tip of the bowstave found purchase in the ground and he steadied. Suicide was a sin. Of all people, he knew the perils of making that choice, and the shame of those who were left behind.

With a low moan, Tarl fell to his knees and prayed. For guidance. For forgiveness. In penance. His eyes squeezed closed as he muttered his entreaty over and over with the passion of one who had forgotten his strength and sought it. Of one who was lost. More than ever, he wanted to trust in the Lord to show him the way.

"May I join you? It seems a worthy spot to seek instruction."

Tarl's eyes shot open as his head whipped around.

Behind him, on the path from the forest, was a face he recognised.

Tarl dropped his eyes as a flush rose to his cheeks. King Henry approached and put his helmet down next to Tarl's knees. The red-ridged, star-shaped scar marred the King's cheek, somehow lending a rakish air to his ruddy complexion. From behind the straggles of tousled brown hair, the monarch ran his gaze over Tarl. "And, I confess," he said, as if he were just another soldier, "after that climb, I am in sore need of a rest."

He knelt, crossing himself and stared out over the valley. After a weary sigh, Henry closed his eyes. "Lord, in your wisdom, I pray you bestow your guidance and blessings upon your subjects." He then paused for a long moment.

Tarl realised he was holding his breath and wondered whether his King was silently praying or just searching for the right words for his own entreaty. He kept his head bowed but couldn't help but peep at his King. Knelt side by side thus, they were the same height. Neither wore nor carried armour, save for the shiny helmet with a thin circle of gold embellishment around the crown between them. A sheathed longsword nestled abreast of Tarl's unstrung bow on the dusty earth. Not much older than himself, Henry's young, battle hardened shoulders drooped.

The king caught Tarl looking at him from the corners of his eyes. The edge of his lips rose and his expression softened. "Do you ever think, is he's really listening, or if I'm just praying into thin air. Especially outside. Somehow, being inside a holy building lends gravitas."

"I used to feel the same way, Sire. Perhaps it's all the incense," Tarl said and Henry nodded. "But there is greater peace to be found outside. One can listen easier."

"You have a point. In the midst of all the noise, it can be hard to hear God's will."

They knelt in silence for a moment, then Henry put his hand down and levered himself to standing. "Perhaps it is best that I don't listen today. I might not like what He says." He brought his hands to his hips and surveyed Harfleur. A cloud passed over his face as his fingers curled around the knob of his sword handle. "I came here for inspiration."

Tarl met his eyes briefly, then looked out over the valley. A boom echoed, so loud it almost muffled the crash as the target was reached. Henry's eyelids fell as his lips muttered silently. He crossed himself as he finished and turned to face Tarl. "I have to believe it's right, you see. Even if the pain is great, the end justifies the means."

"It does?"

Henry nodded. "This battle is about more than conquest." He swept his arm towards the path leading into the woods. "Let me show you something I found the other day, the reason I come up here. Tell me if it's a sign of my just cause, or if I am fanciful."

Tarl nodded and followed. The narrow track wound through dense woodland, away from the ridge, then opened out into a clearing. A pile of charred wood and soil sat in the middle, with a wisp of smoke rising. "Charcoal!" Tarl exclaimed. "Exactly what we need!" He spun on his heel to look for Henry with wide eyes.

But the king had passed him and stood on the far side of the space, gazing down. Tarl loped towards him, grinning. He stopped in his tracks when he saw what Henry was so absorbed in.

At the root of the tree in the shadows and bright against the dark soil, a bed of forget-me-nots had grown. Their presence was unnatural so late in the summer, Tarl realised. His heart leapt. Aioffe had left a flush of the same flowers on his mother's grave! It was as if her essence had seeded itself into the soil, sprouting the delicate flora to leave her mark after tussling with Father McTavish.

"Look," Henry pointed, his gloved hands tracing the shape the plants created - a cross of tiny sky blue blooms. "If this is not a symbol of how peace can follow the pain of a righteous war, I don't know what is."

Tarl bent closer, frowning until he saw what the king meant. At the centre of the cross, in the join between the two lines, a glint of silver, the length of his finger, caught his eye. He knelt, reaching with shaking hands for the carved bone handle he knew well. Aioffe's knife.

"Don't! Leave it," Henry ordered.

"But..." Tarl tipped his head up. "The knife belongs to my wife."

Henry frowned. "Why would she leave it here, then?"

"She was sent on a secret mission before the attack began. For you. I have not since seen her."

"I don't understand. Women are supposed to stay in the camp."

Tarl's hair fell over his forehead as his head dipped. "My liege, my wife is not ordinary. She is extraordinary, you could say."

"Who sent her? When?"

He could not lie and no other name sprang to mind other than Ap Tudor, the least likely person to have influence with Henry. "The Bishop of Norwich, Sire. And she disappeared just before the siege began." Tarl blinked as a wave of sorrow washed over him. "I don't know what happened to her."

The warm weight of Henry's gloved hand rested upon Tarl's shoulder. "My friend would not let harm come to her, of this I am sure."

Tarl wasn't. At all. But he bit his lip - any hope he had of the Bishop working with him relied upon being selective with the truths he told. Even to a King.

Henry's voice was surprisingly sympathetic. "Is it possible she is still here? In the woods but not returned to you? Many are frightened by war. Those with delicate sensibilities in particular."

"I don't think so. She never struck me as someone who was afraid of a fight." He shrugged. "She always carries that knife. If she were still here, in the forest, I'm certain it would be on her person. Not lying... here. The cross - it's deliberate. I'm sure, somehow, she made it."

Tarl could not explain and prayed Henry wouldn't ask.

The King studied the flowers, tapping his finger to his lips. "If that is so, perhaps it's a message, then?" He raised his eyebrows at Tarl. "I certainly took it as such when I first came across this place a few weeks ago. And still it blooms."

Henry's lips pushed together. He recoiled suddenly, glancing up to the sky. "Was I wrong?" His hand dropped to the handle of his longsword.

"I do not know, Sire, but I think you are correct. This is a message of sorts." Tarl reached into his pocket, curling his fingers around the half sharpened arrowhead he carried there.

The King stepped backwards, his face paling. "Perhaps I was

not the intended recipient. You were." He pulled in a shuddering breath. "Have I kept us here...?" Henry's gaze dropped as he shook his head to himself.

Tarl let his bow fall to the ground and reached his hand out. "My liege! If this is a symbol, a message of some kind, there is nothing to say that it wasn't meant for us both."

Henry froze. "Both a king and an... archer? What would a woman have to say of war or of faith?"

Wetting his lips, Tarl said, "As I told you, my wife is extraordinary. Wild. Knowing. Wise and yet naïve."

The King stared at him as if he were speaking another language.

Flustered, Tarl said, "She is not from around here. Or England. I'd say she was heaven sent."

Oh God, what was he saying?

Henry's eyebrows lowered together, darkening his face.

Tarl's tongue felt thick in his mouth as he tried to tread carefully around an issue he knew so little about. "She made this message, I've no doubt. The shape, a cross, has a relevance to me. That's not to say it has no relevance to you. I know it does. And I know you to be a godly King, for why else would you seek his blessing?"

"Then what does it mean?" Henry growled, his arm shooting out to point at the knife..

Tarl's fingers tightened around his bow. "It means whatever you take it to, Sire. You needed a sign that your cause was just, and there it was. Here it is still, growing even though the season for those flowers has passed. They are forget-me-nots - a delicate flower, easily trampled upon, yet will loyally grow year after year if left in peace. If the shape they have grown into is not a true sign from God, then I don't know what is."

Henry's fingers relaxed on the sword handle. He nodded once. "It is a question of faith, then."

255

Tarl noticed the scar on Henry's cheek seemed less prominent as colour returned to the King's skin. Keeping his head bowed, Tarl said, "I have struggled with what to believe for a long time, Sire. Some days, even a failing faith is all which keeps me fighting on. But I have never doubted there is a higher purpose to everything we do."

His confession had the opposite effect to the reassurance Tarl intended. Henry's face fell and his voice sounded hollow. "Do the other men believe our cause is just?"

"I have heard naught to suggest otherwise," Tarl replied. "Even in the grip of fever, no-one regrets coming. Tis only the staying, and the length of time it has taken which concerns the men. Not the siege or righteousness of your claim itself."

Henry turned to leave. Tarl's fingers wrapped around the arrowhead. "Sire, I need to acknowledge the message. In case she returns. May I replace the knife with another item?"

The King's head swivelled to stare at Tarl. His solemn look prompted Tarl to show the arrowhead. Henry's lips stretched into a smile, and he nodded. "Perhaps victory will be ours, not by the blade, but from the bow."

Tarl stood and walked to the flower cross. As he pulled Aioffe's knife from its leafy entanglement, he heard the soft crunch of footsteps as the King disappeared into the forest. Tarl kissed the heart of the arrowhead, then nestled it into the hole left by the blade. He closed his eyes and sent up a silent prayer of gratitude for faith restored.

Alone and with bow in hand, Tarl strolled over to the woodpile and examined it. The fire had lingered, spread judging from the charred earth. Perhaps there was some workable charcoal underneath, and the site was perfect for raking over and making more.

After a last glance at the flower cross, he strode back to camp with spring to his step. The evening drew in and the blasts echoed still, but, with Aioffe's knife in his belt, his mood was lighter than it had been in weeks.

CHAPTER 38 - GRIEF AND GROWTH

Since Benediet's father died, Aioffe had taken care of the child. The woman downstairs must have dealt with the body because she troubled them no further, except to leave a pair of tatty boots outside the door. Church bells peeled that night, and for many nights after.

For the first few days, Benediet suffered terribly. It was beyond him to interact with Aioffe, and he curled up on the pallet, sobbing until he shuddered into sleep. Even in his slumber, he clutched the boots, which stank of charcoal and earth, and refused to be parted from them. Through sultry nights, feverish nightmares wracked his thin body, in which he called out 'Papa, Papa' in a pitiful voice. Aioffe thought perhaps he was re-living the moment his father passed. Nothing she said or could do would change the fact he was gone, and she was helpless to do anything other than hold the child until the dream broke.

Eventually, the grief settled, like a stone sinks to the bottom of a pool. In the way his shoulders sagged, and his lack of energy, she observed her charge had moved into another phase of coping with his loss. He showed little interest in the bombardment of his home, staring away the hours wrapped in a world of his own sorrow, which blanketed the sounds of destruction. At least the constant sobs ceased. Then, intermittently, he babbled, thumping himself and shaking his head. Often he collapsed to his knees with his hands together. He berated his god with his face turned up, his anger pivoting to a plea when it met with no response from either his Lord or Aioffe. The prayer went unanswered, even though he would glance at her through long eyelashes in hope.

Weakened after such outbursts, she thought he too would die. But, gradually, his sleep became calmer, less broken. And then began his aches. His tummy, his head, Benediet cried out, doubled over in pain. Aioffe saw the pale orange hunger in his Lifeforce. The boy needed sustenance to survive, but finding food proved to be problematic. Unable to ask for help and with no ready supply of morsels to tempt him with to hand, one night she resorted to slipping out while he slept and stealing what she could. With little remorse, for to her mind food should be shared with those who required it, she pulled carrot plants from pots, plucked blackberries from bushes and foraged whatever she could. The boy awoke when she returned, wolfed down her findings, and promptly fell back asleep.

Mindful that her grief-stricken human needed regular meals, the next morning she laced Benediet into the boots, took his hand in hers and they walked the streets in the hope of finding discarded scraps of food. A bare, routine existence emerged thereafter. From when he awoke glassy eyed after a disturbed night's sleep, it revolved, for Aioffe, around keeping Benediet alive. In this way, she repaid her debt to him - he had freed her, and, since his father's death, which she considered herself responsible for somehow, protecting the son's life was the payment.

Keeping him safe wasn't easy. From two sides of the town, the English catapults besieged Harfleur, until a backdrop of thuds and clattering stonework seemed normal. As they wound through the narrow passages, past half demolished buildings in their quest, she glanced up with almost every step, mindful that, at any moment, something could rain down on them. Smoky air lingered above the town, making them both cough, but experience had taught her that even a few seconds' notice was enough to dive away from a missile's path.

Going out to seek food was better than staying in the hovel, where the likelihood of an unseen stone dropping through the roof tiles was ever present. Yet inside, Benediet's flagging energy levels compounded his grief, like a boulder he carried with him always. Sometimes, if she moved something in the house or sat on the larger stool, he would simply burst into tears. There was no right choice, Aioffe decided, and time spent in the home where he had lived with his family upset him, not to mention the danger.

He could not bear to be alone, though. When he was tired from a lack of food or from bearing his sorrow, and she tried to indicate he should stay in the hovel and rest, he wept pitifully until she conceded. Oftentimes, she ended up carrying him through the streets like a babe, perched on her hip with his arms clung about her neck. His weight didn't seem to lessen even though he starved, for she herself weakened with the effort of survival.

After some weeks, her constant exposure to the French tongue seeped in. At night, she practised rolling the words around her mouth, and, eventually, Benediet picked up on the game and corrected her. They settled upon his pronunciation of her name as Eva, as he was unable to wrap his tongue around her the 'f' sound properly. She found he was particularly receptive to teaching her after food. It didn't seem to matter what he ate, it was never enough. The only advantage of living street-scrap to mouth was that Aioffe's cooking skills, or lack thereof, were not needed.

The ongoing siege, however, began to wear on the residents of Harfleur. Scrapings, fresh vegetables and cast-offs were harder to find. Even though the townsfolk rallied with their support, Aioffe noticed fewer and fewer people came out during the daytime as the days slipped into weeks. The town was a prison of sorts, and all liberties distilled to survival only.

There was no opportunity for her to fly away unseen, and simply walking out was impossible. No-one entered or exited the town, except the heralds taking refusals to capitulate to King Henry. The walls were constantly manned, where the walkways survived, with cross-bowmen and gunners firing off the little cannon as English trenches encroached.

At night, the townsfolk were more active and organised, shoring up the barricades, or making repairs to defences and strategically important trade centres. When darkness fell and as soon as the shelling stopped, buildings damaged by stones or fire were assessed by members of the council and the dwindling garrison commanders. Increasingly, certain parts of the town were closed off by the officials. Declared out of bounds, entire streets were cleared and people were commandeered to dig tunnels under the walls and out. They left only a pile of earth, all nearby buildings stripped of masonry and timber to shore up the passages.

Aioffe and Benediet learned when a tunnel was getting close to its target because a troop of soldiers would be pulled from their watch and readied to run down. The prospect of being buried alive in a collapsed hole sent shivers through Aioffe every time they came across such an entrance, and she would lead Benediet away, making a mental note to avoid it for the next few days - lest she be petitioned to dig. No particular skill was needed to scrape with a shovel and many women and children were thus kept busy.

Of an evening, from the top of the stairs, the pair watched teams of neighbours cart away rubble to shore up a collapsed part of the wall, or re-purpose beams to restore integrity to the barricades. Their recycling made her think of Tarl, and how he would keep every scrap of metal ore he cut off, to fashion into something new under his hammer. In those moments, when all they could hear was the tapping of hammers, and the dragging of wood, her heart ached. Each night, she looked to the stars and wondered if he thought of her. Whether he still fought, or forged. If the arrows they made would be used. If he would ever break through the walls, and of what they would say to each other if he did. Could two such different people ever share a life? Aioffe glanced then at Benediet, and took heart in his acceptance of her. But could a man? Would Tarl ever see her and accept her in entirety?

Gradually, the town centre, the churches, and homes disappeared, leaving great pockmarks in the sea of rooftops. It was in these gaps that Aioffe found another purpose. One day, they encountered a sorrowful man of the cloth, staring mutely as pews were removed from his church. The long stretches of wood were to be used for repairs, and no-one had the time to sit and pray these days.

Benediet asked him for food, but he shook his head and bemoaned the dwindling edible supplies as well. The priest glared at the freshly dug grave mounds before he muttered, 'God will provide.'

"The roll tastes of sawdust," Benediet complained that evening, tearing off another piece and chewing it with his mouth open in disgust. He had long ago stopped asking why she didn't eat, and had not noticed the rat problem was less of an issue. "Do you think God will send something more flour-y if *you* asked him?"

Aioffe giggled and shook her head. "I don't think so." But it made her consider. It had taken them all day to find this stub of bread, and the boy hadn't had any vegetables at all for days. If it was at all possible, he was even skinnier, and his pink skin held a grey pallor which concerned her.

She reached for the bowl of rainwater. Placing a piece of linen over a cup, she poured the water over so it filtered the ash out before passing it to him.

"Papa used to take me to the forest through the fields outside the walls," he said, wistfully. "I liked to watch the sheep. All big and fluffy. I was smaller, then, and the grain stalks were taller than I. But I think they must be under water still, or trampled over, now." He shrugged. "Perhaps that means the stalks will grow back taller next year, now the seeds are so deeply buried." His eyes flicked to hers. "Do they have fields in heaven? They must do, to feed all the souls up there."

She mused, "You would think so." She thought of the graveyards, filling up with graves. "How long would grass and grain take to grow?"

"They plant it in spring, then wait until it turns from green to golden," he replied. "Last late-summer, everyone had to help bring in the harvest. Papa said it paid better than charcoal, for a few weeks."

But the economics of harvesting were not what interested her. Aioffe thought about the ripening of crops and the passage of time. A tingle ran through her arms, a reminder of her own abilities. "Do you think there would be some grain left over?"

The boy's shoulders lifted and held around his ears in a long shrug. "Maybe, but the windmill is outside the walls." His shoulders dropped and he shook his head. "We tried the town storehouse, remember, but it was empty. The rats will have eaten every last grain on the floor by now."

Aioffe tapped her finger to her lips. The lack of food affected everyone in Harfleur, not just Benediet. King Henry would not move on until the town conceded or fell. Surely the army lacked supplies as well? Yet, while they remained, Tarl would still be close. Then again, the more time the residents survived, the longer the siege might continue. There were no signs or rumours that they would negotiate a peace.

She chewed on her lip as Benediet leaned against her for warmth. She would not leave him until his future was secure, under whichever ruler. Taking care of one person, that was what her life had become. If anything, she reasoned, he was reason enough to solve the problem of food.

"But it just takes one person, like it takes one seed...." She gathered her skirt and stood. "Come on, let's see what we can find."

CHAPTER 39 – STALEMATE BREAKS

Tarl jolted awake at the cry from outside his canvas. "Armour up! Gathering!"

The sides of his tent flapped as a hand banged against the fabric. All around, he heard the grumbles of tired men unexpectedly awoken in the middle of the night. Sound sleep was an aspiration for most, plagued as they were by the illness, boredom, and ever decreasing rations. Exhaustion, loneliness and fear were now Tarl's usual bedfellows, and his stomach churned as they tortured him for awaking too soon.

He reached to the end of the sleeping roll and pulled over his haubergeon. The metal plates sewn over the padded bodice clinked together as he laced the sides by feel. Some archers wore chain mail underneath, but he preferred to take his chances and have the flexibility a lighter armour afforded. Also, he never knew when he'd be called to fix something - hammering with the weight of steel over him tired him out more than the meagre rations could compensate for.

He strapped on his belt, then pulled on his muddy boots. Between leather and trouser leg, he poked Aioffe's knife, snug and sheathed in her headscarf. As he adjusted the bundle so the blade lay in line with his shin, he muttered a prayer that the boots wouldn't disintegrate and that the weapon would be soon reunited with its owner. With bow in hand and satchel slung over his shoulder, Tarl crawled out to meet the chaos in the dark.

He jogged over to join the steam of people pouring from tents towards the gather field. Ap Tudor found him within seconds of arrival. His eyes glinted by the light of the braziers as he grabbed

Tarl's arm. In a frenzied voice, he whispered, "They must be attacking!"

Tarl wrenched his arm back and glowered at the overexcited Welshman. "Why else would we be woken at such an hour?" He started to walk off, but the young Lord tugged on his jacket.

"This is it! Action at last!" Ap Tudor slapped his hand on his sword hilt and grinned weakly.

He stared at him, silent. It didn't surprise him that Ap Tudor needed to bolster himself before battle, but Tarl was disinclined to offer encouragement when he was unable to predict the odds of success himself.

Ap Tudor apparently wasn't satisfied with his lack of response. "Time for you to prove yourself as well, Smith. Would be a terrible shame to leave your wife a widow, but I'd be happy to take her under my wing if you fail to return, don't you worry."

Tarl's chin set as he glanced at the gleaming armour. "You'd better fasten your breastplate properly then, or you'll end up flying into my fist." He indicated with the tip of his bow to the flapping leather strap on the left of Ap Tudor's ribs. When he had reached for his sword, the cumbersome protection had misaligned, exposing a wide chink wide enough for a punch to enter. The Welshman's lips tightened as he turned away and fiddled to right the wonky plate.

Tarl ambled away with his teeth clenched. He had little enough energy. Better to conserve what he had for a worthier adversary. It served no purpose to enlighten Ap Tudor about his missing wife, and to think of her now would be a distraction he dared not indulge. All the same, as the field filled with whomever could stand, his heartbeat thumped beneath the bulky fabric armour Aioffe had sewn.

For weeks, the French stayed hidden behind their increasingly demolished walls. The English had made little headway into the drying moat, save a few trenches. Worse, the rumour was a few days ago, a French ship had slipped past the English fleet. Fresh supplies for the besieged town had re-invigorated their defence. A surprise assault by the Harfleurian garrison, when Henry's army was laid so low with sickness, was a move Tarl had been concerned about ever since hearing the gossip. Nothing else would tip the stalemate which both sides found themselves in. Would today be when the course of this siege changed?

As he crossed the field, he prayed for a sign. He passed someone handing out more protection and weapons from a wagon. Tarl found himself laden with a battered helmet, three arrow-bags, a spike tipped war axe and his trusty longbow. He stuffed a spare bow string under his helmet. It never hurt to keep a dry one handy.

Sir John thundered into the crowd which had amassed at the edge of his field, wheeling his destrier to a halt and spinning around as he shouted. "They're making for the gun pits. Find your ventenar, archers, and arm yourselves to the teeth. I want each centenar and his forces to cover a station, clear it, and hold it." He glared about, beady eyes glared at the still half asleep troops. "Show no mercy. They dare to attack our soil, our sovereign ground. Centenars, to me for your assigned position. Men at arms, gunners, you are to report to your commanders. Go!"

As the knights and foot soldiers clanked away to a different field or the trenches, Tarl removed his helmet and stood on his tiptoes. Archers had been organised into what was originally groups of twenty or so under a ventenar, and ten such units were commanded by a centenar. Tarl's vent had shrunk to just six men through sickness with the bloody flux or injury. As of yesterday, Tarl had been told to assume the position of ventenar after John-the-brew took a crossbow bolt to his thigh on a brief foray into the frontline trench. He had served only three days as their leader. His wife Agnes had cried all night as the wound rapidly festered with infection and his moans grew loud with fever.

Until this night, an air of dogged stoicism had pervaded the camp, until rallied without notice in the middle of the night. All around, an anxious energy made men jiggle and fuss in the darkness. Tarl cast his eyes around, seeking the remaining four men who now fell under his command. One by one, Alf, William Ap Greffuth, Jones-Jones, and Tom-the-carp found his light blond head amongst the crowd of steel-capped confusion and moved to join him. After a reassuring smile and a quick check of their readiness, he left them stood in a clump so he could gather with the other vents for instruction. His stomach tight with tension, he rubbed his face and took a sip from his flagon as he waited for their cent, Sir Thomas Rempston, himself under the command of Sir Thomas Erpingham.

Although they were some distance from the gun pits, the clink of steel on steel echoed over in the nervous silence of the field. "They make for the trenches first," Tarl guessed, as he studied the gathering of cents around Sir John.

The other vents nodded their agreement and muttered between themselves. A priest lurked on the edges of the group, offering blessings to any man who wanted absolution or courage. Before Tarl could fortify his spirits, Sir Thomas Rempston glanced back to his men, unsheathed his sword, stuck it in the air and jabbed to the east. The vents hurried back to their units and urged their archers over to the far side of the field.

As he walked across to the corner of the hedgerow where Sir Thomas's men headed, the battle axe in his hand weighed unfamiliar and heavy, so he looped it through his belt. While he waited for the others to catch up, he fastened a horn bracer to his forearm. "String your bow while we wait for details of the route and target we're covering," he suggested to Jones, who was young and often dithered, irrespective of clear orders being given. He also stammered which many found frustrating to hear. Tarl unravelled a fresh cord from his pouch and passed it to him before hooking his own.

Alf stared into the distance, his face pale and his hand rubbing the base of his torso. The stench of flux drifted across the fields, turning any stomach which wasn't already suffering. Tarl couldn't spot where Ap Tudor had disappeared to amongst the throng, but he was relieved the Welshman wasn't close by to stoke anxiety amongst his countrymen or irritate Tarl with his bravado. The task ahead was daunting enough and his mouth was dry with apprehension as it was.

"We have a hike ahead of us," Sir Thomas said, as he trotted over to them. "Our orders are to defend the catapults and trebs toward the coastline, ideally before they reach them. So make ready." He wheeled about, checking his page had arrived with the pennant. "Keep it low, boy. So far, they don't know we're onto their game. We must protect that flank or they'll have us surrounded by dawn."

Alf bent over and vomited. Tarl's heart sank. "Go back to camp. You can defend there," he whispered.

"Nah," Alf replied, wiping his mouth with his sleeve. "I'll be fine. It's the smell."

No-one believed him, but since half the army were stricken, or dead, there was a solidarity in pushing forwards and hoping their victory would be swift. At least something was happening, even if it was the French advancing instead of Henry and England's assault.

Sir Thomas set them at a quick pace out of the gather field then looped down towards the sea. Tarl's squad were the last to follow because they waited for Alf to empty his bowels once more. The troops skirted hedgerows on a path that was well trodden, leading to the trenches and gun pits south of Harfleur. The further away from the braziers they walked, the more their eyes adjusted to the moonlit landscape. After a quarter of an hour or so of walking uphill, he saw the glinting choppiness of water. The tide was already coming in. To his right, across the swamp, the darkness was punctuated by the glow of abandoned torches. A low harvest moon illuminated the moving shadows of the French as they swarmed silently through the valley.

Tarl gripped his bow as the line slowed, then stopped. Ahead, Sir Thomas jumped down from his horse and marched back up the pathway whispering directions. Vents ahead dispersed, peeling off to narrow tracks down to the gun pits. "Take the ridge," Sir Thomas said when he reached him, "and pick them off before they reach it. The others take the low route across to the pit."

Tarl glanced back to Alf, Will and Jones. They nodded, grim of face, then followed him, making quick, quiet progress along the ridge track. As they neared their designated pit, housing a mid-sized trebuchet known as Bess, Tarl held up his arm and stopped. Scanning the ground beyond the screens of the hollow, he spotted a group of perhaps ten soldiers picking their way through the drying swamp. Their helmets reflected the dull sheen of the moon as they crouched to move stealthily closer.

Tarl squatted, trusting the others would follow suit. He reached behind to the quiver and pulled out an arrow, then checked either side of him. Tom the carp stood to his right, Jones to the left. Tarl jerked his head towards their quarry, then rose.

With the arrow balanced between his knuckle and the stave, he pulled the string back, past his cheek and held. His knees flexed until he felt the harmony between himself and the bow balance. After eyeing his target several hundred yards away, he let loose. With a quiet whoosh, the white fletching darted towards the soldier in the lead. Without waiting to see him fall, Tarl reached for another arrow and slapped it into place. To either side, his archers released their darts.

After a few more shots, Tarl stopped and assessed again. The ten were down to six. Bodies were left writhing, gurgling in the mud. However, more soldiers appeared on their tail.

A cry from just below their position rent the air, then a thud. Tarl peered down, but with the darkness and distance, he couldn't see what was going on in the gun pit.

Thuds and gurgles, cries and screams told him the French had reached the trebuchet beneath. The French which Tarl's squad had dropped were not the first to reach the gun pit. The overnight guards and the rest of Sir Thomas's cent arriving by the lower pathway must have been taken by surprise.

Will whispered, "We need to be closer."

Tarl nodded, heart hammering against his chest. Alf dropped his trousers and bent his knees. As he groaned, Tarl said, "Stay here and cover us," to him. The ailing archer groaned his agreement as he gripped his belly.

Tom led the way, slinging his bow over his shoulder and drawing out his hammer. Tarl glanced back at Alf before bringing up the rear as they trooped down the slope. Walking with a strung bow and notched arrow in his hand at the ready wasn't easy, but he felt more confident he could head off anyone who might pop up in front of them with his weapon prepared.

As they approached the pit, he saw the trebuchet arm stuck straight up with the bucket dangling empty. Ordinarily when it was too dark to see clearly for firing, there was little need to keep it locked down and under pressure so this did not strike him as unusual. He presumed the structure had been left lightly guarded overnight, on the assumption that the next day would be like the previous forty-odd.

When not in the forge, or digging trenches in on the front line as the army tried to make advances on the town, Tarl had spent many hours hefting a gun pit's defences back and forth. Tall screens fashioned from tree trunks protected both weapon and gunners whilst the bucket was cranked down and loaded, which sometimes took several hours. Because the panels in front and to the sides of the huge contraption were thick and heavy, they required co-ordinated manpower to roll them aside for firing. For some of the smaller cannons, like those worked by the Dutch, the panels had a mechanism to flip them up just before fire, akin to the gun ports of a ship, but a trebuchet was too large and cumbersome for such sophisticated protection. Its size meant it was also an easy target so as much of it as possible needed screening from sight.

Tarl surmised the problem - because the trebuchet was set into the cut out slope, anyone hidden down in the pit was vulnerable to an on foot attack. Blind to what was coming across the swampland, he suspected they were too few in number to move the screens to see the French approaching. Any soldiers already inside the dug out would be trapped there because of the steep, unclimbable wall of earth behind them.

"Tom!" Tarl whispered ahead. "Hold up!"

But he was too late. Tom the carp had disappeared from sight.

CHAPTER 40 – CONSTERNATION AND CONSTELLATIONS

The town had seemed unusually full of energy earlier that day. Expectant wisps which had reached her fingertips and promptly been passed down into the vegetable beds in the graveyard. Aioffe had been so pleased with the rush of growth, and, as Benediet had awoken early from a dream, she persuaded him into an excursion to check on their precious crop, although it was the dead of night.

As Aioffe and Benediet walked through the alley in the dark, "Tis happening then," the neighbour downstairs called out. "Finally." Her door cracked open.

"What is?" Aioffe asked. They hadn't seen the woman in weeks, although, since the gardening produced results, Aioffe had shared what she could amongst those still living in the area. She noticed the gift of vegetables they had placed on the doorstep earlier had disappeared.

"An attack." Gnarled fingers clutched the wood and the elderly woman wobbled on the stone ledge, with only in a shawl wrapped over her nightshirt. Frailty did not diminish the pride in her voice.

Benediet's hand tightened in hers. "The English?" His eyes widened in the darkness.

"No. Us! The English," the old woman sneered. Her accusative gaze narrowed on Aioffe. "They could not beat us, so we take the fight to them!"

Aioffe's heart flopped over inside her chest. Tarl. She wondered if he fought, and where he was.

"I saw our soldiers, you know," the old woman continued. "Any man who could hold a weapon gathered at the marketplace this afternoon."

As they stood in the alleyway, her ears tuned to pick up distant noises. Battle. Cries and groans as men fell. A clash of steel and shouts echoed across the valley. Her stomach fluttered in response.

She had to get closer, see what was going on. To see Tarl. Could this be her moment to find him, whilst everyone was distracted? Tied, as usual, underneath her bodice and skirt, her wings rustled against the fabric.

Aioffe glanced at the old woman and hoped she hadn't noticed the quiver of wings underneath her cloak. "Can you keep Benediet safe here?"

Before the neighbour could answer, the boy cried, "No! I want to see!" He pulled himself behind her skirts. "And I don't want to go in there."

"You've done a good job of keeping him, thus far..." A beady look appeared in the woman's hooded eyes. "Very tasty, those carrots you left were. Especially out of season. What's your secret?"

Aioffe took a step back, into the shadows of the alley. "No secret," she said, waving her hand. "Just good soil."

The woman looked down her nose and held her gaze. "I sold some to the parish, and even the priest said they tasted flavoursome. Funny thing though," her eyes dipped to Benediet, and continued in all seriousness. "He had some last week, he said, which tasted similar. Found them growing in a graveyard with some parsnips. Just popped up one day. The most unusual blessing the Lord ever gave, I told him. Hadn't we all been praying for some relief? And the lad looks well fed now. Perhaps you can enlighten us all as to your source? I've customers would pay handsomely. For any food really, but especially such freshly harvested vegetables."

Her expression reminded Aioffe of the way a hawk sizes up its prey.

Benediet piped up, "Eva says it's the golden threads which only she sees."

"Does she now." The woman's back straightened and her lips pursed as her eyes ran over Aioffe.

The neighbour knew there was something peculiar then. She took Benediet's hand before he started up about angels again and made matters worse. "Let's see if we can reach the walls," she said, tugging him away.

"Which side will claim your heart, I wonder." The old woman called after them. "For sure, it's a bad night to be English. But then again," she muttered, retreating into the doorway. "It's been a bad summer for France."

No matter how well she spoke their language, she was not French. Or English, for that matter. A change was coming, and Aioffe didn't know whether to fear it or embrace it. But Benediet was already dragging her towards the defences to see. Whether she liked it or not, their fate marched inescapably forward.

*****

Quick as a rat, Benediet scampered through the alleyways, pulling Aioffe behind him. He barely stopped when she stumbled, just spun his head around and shot her a look of frustration. The sounds of attack didn't grow closer, which she took as a good sign. By the time they reached the walls, the reason became apparent.

The boy scrambled up the earth and stone bank which propped up the Leure gate. Several other women already lay down, peeking over the top. Unafraid, Benediet stood, his small outline a dark shadow as Aioffe slowly picked her way up the incline.

"Get down," she hissed.

"Fires! They set fires!"

Aioffe crawled up the remaining few feet and peered over, across the lowland. The men from Harfleur must have slunk silently across the swampy barrier, hidden by the night. Snuck through the English defences like humankind had crept into her heart. And now, they fought for their very lives.

The moon hung low in the sky, casting enough light on the ground for human observers to join its yellow face in watching the skirmishes beneath. The soldiers swarmed towards the English trenches, ant-like with their helmets faintly glowing in the moonlight. From this elevated vantage point, disappointment in mankind's short-sightedness coloured her vision. To fight over land or borders only marked upon a map had always seemed futile to Aioffe, whichever realm she considered. Even though she had come to understand that the French fought not for their King, who was rumoured to be mad, but for their homes, any war was a waste. Henry's claim to rule over France, he considered his by right. As she surveyed the destruction and listened to the anguish of violent death, a ball of anger at the futility and human cost of asserting the claim grew in the pit of her stomach. Their short life was hard enough for the humans. To waste time arguing over who ruled a patch of earth and costing lives in the process seemed ridiculous.

On the far side of the valley, Benediet was correct about fire setting. Siege engines burned orange as they caught aflame. Without the stone wall to dampen the sound, man-to-man combat announced the furtive fighting to her ears. Axes hacked at timber, and men oohed and groaned towards death. Her eyes narrowed, focusing on the pockets of resistance. But, through the haze of smoke which lingered over the ground, she could not identify individuals, even with her fae night-sight.

Her skin chilled as she scanned the shadows, seeing for the first time the maze of trenches the English had dug to claim the ground as their own. Tarl must be out there somewhere. Or was he already dead? She shook her head. Above all else, she must cling onto the hope that he survived.

Benediet gazed out, rapt at the scene.

"There!" He jabbed his arm out. "The Fleur-de-Lys!"

Following his finger, she saw the blue French flag hanging from a spear. Golden tri-pointed petals glinted, reflected in the firelight of a captured gun pit. She reached up and yanked him down beside her. "It's not safe! Don't make yourself a target!"

After everything she had done to keep him alive, a stray arrow would render her efforts meaningless.

She blinked, lips tightened as an inexplicable heat flooded her body. A fear of losing him, as she had lost her other beloved, paralysed her as the neighbour's words echoed in her mind. Who did she want to win the night? The English or the French? Having spent weeks with Benediet, over that short a time, he accepted her in a way that no-one else ever had. Even if he didn't understand entirely what, or who, she was. Once he had got over his initial fear of her, the child had brought her into his home, opened his grieving heart to her without once blaming her, even though she held herself accountable for his loss.

Tarl had been frightened of her, too. But he, the man who made her glow, was someplace close by, with the English. Despite his initial revulsion, he was kind, cared for her, she thought, and provided for her in spite of his distaste and mistrust. In his presence, she craved his acceptance of her as a woman. Her chest tightened as she pictured the firm cast of his face. That gentle smile which more readily curled into laughter with her. She closed her eyes and admitted it to herself. She craved more time with him. What they had experienced together so far was not enough. He made her seem ordinary, when she was, without wanting to be, extraordinary. More than that, he had defended her.

She glanced up at the human child and her lips softened. Both these humans who knew what she was and still stood by her. No-one else, over the centuries, had ever done that. All her experience with humankind told her these two humans were unusual. Most would shun or revile her if they knew, or try to use her gifts for their own benefit, like the old neighbour or the Bishop.

She peeked out at the valley again and sighed. Here she was definitely one person amongst the many. Lining the walls were the last few hundred townsfolk, equally powerless to do anything to change the outcome of what happened beyond. There was a comfort in their company. No-one conferred, just held their tongues and watched. Hands were wrung, occasional prayers whispered. For bravery. Courage. Success, even though the odds were surely against them. Aioffe stared at Benediet's head and breathed in. She tasted the anticipation in his Lifeforce, but it was bitter, soured by fear despite his boyish fascination with the macabre scene below.

The bitterness pervaded her tongue and she could no longer watch. Did it matter who won the night, she asked herself. Turning onto her back, she gazed up at the stars and tried to block out the noises, the tang of blood, and fire in the air. The twinkling pinpricks in the black soothed her, eternally there to guide her. But the stars did not map out what happened on earth. Nor could they divine or determine the future, as some humans believed.

Destiny had brought her to this point, Aioffe considered, and swallowed back the bitter taste of Benediet's fear. Destiny alone would influence what would transpire tonight. One person could not transform the course of battle. One fae alone, like one prayer, could not alter what will be. Even if she escaped, or flew away as she had done from many of her problems before, the outcome for the two sides would be the same.

For all of her abilities, she was powerless. There was no other option right now but to wait and see what the result was. And no need to make a decision between the two humans until she knew.

Aioffe smiled to herself. In this strangest of circumstances, committing the next few hours, or days, of her existence to destiny, awaiting it even, was a curious relief. In Naturae, and for all her life to date, she had known what her future was supposed to be. The very reason she had run away. Here, far away from that ominous duty, the powerlessness of being unable to change the outcome, only accept it and make the best of it, was curiously liberating. Thrilling even. Perhaps this was the appeal of faith to the humans? She had always believed in the power of destiny, but choosing to accept fate in this way lessened its fearful hold over her. She would survive, she always had, and would defend those who defended her until she could no more. This much Aioffe could control - who she chose as worthy of her protection and love.

Shuffling down the slope and stopping beside her, a pale-faced Benediet moved his hands together and bowed his head. Silently he prayed, although she knew not what for. It didn't matter. She understood that now. If she ever returned to face the Bishop, she would make that clear, because the events of the human world were not hers, or the vampires, to affect. By choosing to live here, amongst them, in whichever country, they must embrace what destiny herself intended for their kind.

Her breath came easier with acceptance. She had to hope, rather than know. If she was destined to be with Tarl, he would find her. If her home was to be with Benediet, then that too would come to pass. She gazed upwards to the place the humans assumed was heaven. For once, the expanse didn't tempt her to explore its great stretch. Instead, a warm child who nestled close to her side, grounded her in the present. She pointed up. "Tell me what shapes you see in the sky. There's the great bow." She traced the contour between the pinpricks of light and smiled at him.

"I see a blade!" Benediet responded, with shining eyes and his finger outstretched.

Given the circumstances, perhaps it would be better to avoid alluding to weapons. "It could be a pot handle," she said and laughed softly. "What else can you spot?"

"There's a dog! He can keep you safe when you go back home, like you keep me. But don't go yet, will you?"

She cuddled him in her arms. Naming the stars might keep his mind off what was happening below, at least. Constellations were ever changing but somehow always the same, like the warm sun welcomed each day with a different dawn, yet it rose without fail. She needed to be his constancy in the darkness of battle.

"Where you go, I go," she said. "Until you are safe and happy."

CHAPTER 41 - A BATTLE FOR BESS

Tarl heard Tom's yelp of pain. Common sense told him it was better to have the strategic advantage of height and sight over the screens, but Tom had blundered down regardless of Tarl's orders to wait. He drew his bow and stalked down the slope towards the gun pit. The grunts of a fight rose from a few yards away.

Tarl stepped closer to the edge and glanced down. An English guard sat, bloodied with his head askew against the counterweight. Another lay battered and motionless on the ground. A third, still clutching his pole-axe, clawed his way over the ground to the relative safety of the shadow. His groans were swiftly silenced by a sword slash to his throat. The Frenchman responsible turned and cast his gaze towards the hollowed out rear of the pit, where the earth had been dug out to accommodate the timber base frame and the length of the arm for loading.

In the hollow, Tom jabbed at a swarthy soldier with his bow. He stood awkwardly, balancing more on one leg as if the other could not bear weight.

Appearing beside Tarl, Will swore under his breath.

Tarl's bow stave warmed in his grip, as if it were an extension of his arm. He let loose his arrow, barely needing to aim as his target was so close. The broadhead embedded itself in the armour-plated chest, killing Tom's attacker instantly. He whipped another from his string, felling the man at arms by the screen. That soldier dropped silent to the ground, but, with battle-cries fit to wake the dead, three more Frenchmen rushed from behind the screens.

Tom shouted, "Curs!" He swung his hammer around on the leather strap as two lightly armoured soldiers slapped through the mud towards him.

As one ran towards the weapon, the others swung their swords at Tom, pinned against the muddy wall. There was no room for him to retreat. As quickly as they could, Tarl and Will shot off two more arrows.

The men fell by Tom's feet. Without hesitation, he leaned over and bashed their foreheads with his hammer.

Tarl gasped but, before he could question his friends' new found blood lust, the third soldier leapt over the trebuchet's foot. Tarl's fingers sought another arrow. The hook on the broadhead caught on the quiver edge. Wrestling to free it, the shaft slipped through his fingertips and dropped to the ground. As Tarl cursed and reached for another arrow, from the corner of his eye, he saw Will grab the lost arrow.

With a wild screech, the assailant barrelled towards the lone defender in the pit. Spinning on his heel, Tom swung his hammer around. The pair beneath fell to the ground, toppled by the collision and motion.

Setting arrows onto strings, Tarl and Will drew, then paused. Tom and the soldier tussled below, rolling around taking swings and throwing punches at each other so fast, a misplaced shot could accidentally kill them both.

"Sh-sh-sh. Shoot, g-g-g-goddammit!" Jones's voice wavered as he slunk up next to them.

Then, without saying anything, Will's bow clattered to the ground and he jumped down. He landed well, although the drop was six or seven feet. He grabbed the long shaft of a discarded pole-axe from the ground and charged the Frenchman on top of Tom.

Tarl's eyes widened in horror. As Will's wide blade

skewered the soldier, more guards swarmed around either side of the panel. Armed with swords, spike-tipped pole-axes of their own, and wearing chain mail, the new arrivals became Tarl's fresh targets.

Arrow after arrow spun from his bow. The growing pile of bodies were trampled over as a stream of soldiers poured around the screens. Will and Tom swore as they danced a deadly dual beneath Tarl and Jones, punching, stabbing and swinging for their lives.

Until, Tarl reached behind, and there were no more shafts in the bag. His arm dropped, just as Will's roar abruptly cut short.

Tarl's heart faltered. In his frenzy of shooting, the sobering thought that he hadn't heard a swear from Tom either for the last few minutes then pounded into his consciousness. He cast around the ground near him, hoping to spot Will's discarded arrow bag.

Jones, stood a few feet from Tarl, shot his last into the killing pit then froze. He met Tarl's eyes, panic rolling off him as he lowered his bow. No arrows, no more advantage. Jones's bow arm shook.

With the low moon shining behind the lad, Tarl realised how exposed they were. How alone. The mound of bodies below evidenced the fate of others in their cent. The rest had been sent to different locations along the long front line, no doubt to face the same foe. To call out for help might alert the enemy to their lofty, vulnerable position.

Yet, Bess must be defended, and who knew how many more soldiers would come? His mind reeled. The moon's yellow light dimmed as a dark cloud passed across. In the valley below, he smelled the fires the French had set in other gun pits.

He had to decide, fast. Fight or flight.

For almost certain, Tom and Will were gone. Dead already or mortally injured. Alf was shitting himself to death, literally, way back up the field. Jones next to him was a quivering wreck, and could not be relied upon. What hope had they of holding the pit?

But failure - quitting - was not an option. If the French broke through, many more lives would be at risk. Thousands of men still lay abed in camp, too sick to fight tonight. Their slaughter would mean the end of Henry's insurgence, and possibly his rule.

It was Tarl's duty to follow the orders of his commanding officer. His heart pounded as he glanced to the sky for guidance.

Above, the stars twinkled reassuringly. He remembered the journey here, when he would watch for his angel as she flew through the night. Aioffe's face drifted into his mind as a cloud passed clear of the moon, bathing him in light once more. Oh god, how he longed to have wings like she! For flight to be an option, rather than fighting on the ground.

His throat tightened. With every breath he had left, he had to find her. She could only be in Harfleur, for all other outlying villages had long since been pillaged and destroyed. His belief that she was inside the town, somewhere, had sustained him through this protracted siege. His only hope of redemption, of feeling whole and loved.

And the only way to reach her was through those blood stained, mud stained walls. Rubble in places, but still a barrier to his love, his future. They couldn't be destroyed without this mighty hurler! He swallowed and refocused on the mission.

Having reconciled duty with desire, Tarl hastened to take stock of what he had, and, what he knew. There were no more arrows, thus, the tactical advantage of height and bow was lost. Tarl's hand reached up to unhook the bowstring from the nock. He wrapped two-thirds of the greased cord around his wrist, and left the rest dangling and to hand. A garotte was always useful.

Next, a main weapon to attack with. Close fighting, man to man, might now be needed. His teeth ground together as he wished he had thought to bring a small sword. As Tom had demonstrated, an unstrung, straight bow could be used as a spear, but it wouldn't penetrate armour very well. Strong enough to wield as a staff, but the tapered shaft was vulnerable to a direct blow by sword or hammer. Tarl had no experience with a pole-axe as swung by the men at arms, not that he had one up here. A longsword was more familiar, but he hadn't been given one. Most blacksmiths could slash and stab, if only to test the balance of their creations. In this army, such expensive weapons were reserved for those most likely to see hand to hand combat.

Aioffe's slim knife was still wrapped and nestled securely next to his ankle, but he didn't intend to be so near to a soldier as to have to use it like a dagger. That manner of killing he had always considered too personal in nature, and been loathe to make such blades for people he knew in case they were used for ill in a drunken tavern fight or suchlike. Although he had no intention of getting caught in a tussle, wearing her knife was a small comfort. A last ditch protection from her if he should find himself face to face with the enemy. With a sigh he acknowledged it was not a good enough weapon to protect the pit with, and his bow was woefully insufficient.

As he stepped back, his right hand brushed his hip and he felt a nudge on his thigh. He groaned at his own foolishness for not having remembered the hammer axe dangling from his belt. His fingers fumbled, slippery with sweat as he pulled the weapon out. Although the shaft handle was short, about the length of his calf, it boasted a vicious spike to the top, a curved beak of a blade on one side, and a head with spikes on the other. It looked similar to the basic maul most archers carried, a multi-purpose lead hammer and spike which could be used for both battering and stabbing. This lethal weapon, received without much thought of the likelihood of its use at the gather field, was fancier, fashioned from steel with pointed knobbles on the hammerhead.

"You find Will's arrows, and cover me," he whispered to Jones as he swung it around a few times to get a feel for the weight.

The lad nodded, mute with fear.

Tarl crouched and crept along the side of the gun pit. He glanced over the edge. Not even the moonlight lit the dark hollow. From this angle, it was hard to differentiate who or how many remained alive down in the mud.

Shadowy figures moved towards the trebuchet. Tarl eased his breath in and out as he watched the screens and listened. In the distance, shouts and clinks told him the English were still ·battling to defend their weapons and trenches. There was little to gain by launching an attack if he was clearly outnumbered. He had to make the most of the element of surprise.

While he waited for the right time to enact his plan, he studied the siege weapon and assessed the damage done to it so far. A trebuchet was both simple in construction and complex in physics. Inbetween two upright triangular structures, a wheel twice the height of a man was spun to bring down the long arm and raise the counterweight. Once the ash throwing arm was lowered, the axle was bound and locked into place. A lengthy rope was drawn beneath the counterweight, through a V-shaped groove, measured to cross the distance the load needed to reach the walls. At the end of the slinging rope, the bucket pouch was loaded with rocks, or sometimes bound pitch-soaked twine and set alight before being flung over. On occasion, the missiles were swapped for rotting animal carcasses, although these were unpopular to with the soldiers responsible for loading because of the stench.

Three men below started hacking at ropes and beams. As he breathed, biding his time, a calmness flowed over Tarl. His objectives crystallised. To him, the moments spent observing his quarry felt like he was monitoring metal heat in a forge. Take it out too early, strike it too soon and the piece would warp under his hammer. Harmless slag might splinter off, and the metal would remain misshapen until re-heated. He needed the soldiers to flatten, and die, swiftly with the first strike.

The French busied themselves destroying the siege engine without consultation between them. Watching them, Tarl figured that their basic instruction must be: destroy. Whack it and hope bits will fall off. If all else fails, they might resort to setting fire to it, but that took time or gunpowder to catch.

As far as he could tell, the three soldiers were trying to dismantle the base, possibly in the hopes that the trebuchet would collapse. The thick trunks of the frame, however, had taken men many days to fell before being crafted to withstand all the pressures of firing by expert joiners. Tarl's lips tightened as they hacked through the lashing which gave extra support to the A-frame, but was replaceable. He had to stop them before they took it into their minds to destroy the wheel, axle and the cog mechanisms which were at the heart of the siege engine.

After a final glance past the screens, and hearing no sounds of reinforcements, Tarl took a deep breath and jumped into darkness down the side of the embankment. Silent as he landed, he ran over the bare earth, fleet and still shadowed by the pit edge. Balanced with the bow gripped in one hand, his hammer arm raised to strike…

Just then, a trumpet sounded, startling the soldiers engrossed in their demolition. Their heads turned towards the screens.

The nearest soldier thus missed seeing Tarl swooping his hammer in a wide, upward arc. Blood sprayed as his jaw shattered. Neck flipped backwards, it slid back off the curved point of the battle axe. His body briefly lifted through the air then dropped in a heap.

Not stopping, Tarl pivoted his body around following the hammer's swung momentum. His bow arm shot out for balance as he bent his knees. The battle axe ploughed into the next soldier's knee, toppling him. Damp bloodied hair whipped the side of Tarl's face, as he swooped the weapon high, ready to crash down as he completed the spin.

The floored soldier grunted. His leg had taken the brunt of Tarl's thrust and he writhed on his back. His injured knee bent with blood spurting from it. In one hand, he still clenched a maul. His sword, fallen from fingertips when Tarl attacked, lay close to his other arm. Aside from a leather jerkin, so heavily stained it was black, the man wore little armour.

Tarl glanced down mid swing and realised: the soldier wasn't even holding the maul correctly, .

This was no trained soldier. No more than an ordinary villager like himself, Tarl thought, as he made to drop his hammer - and froze. Killing him was unnecessary. The man was only doing his duty, like he was. This conflict made monsters out of simple men, but he could choose mercy. Here and now, the choice of life over death was his to make. He lowered his arm and straightened. "Mercy," he whispered, catching the man's terrified eye. The soldier nodded and whimpered.

Then Tarl glimpsed a movement from the other side of the trebuchet frame. The last soldier had seen him!

Before Tarl could react or step away from the villager, the soldier clambered over the frame with a snarl. Distracted, a sudden pain shot up Tarl's shin as Aioffe's knife tip jabbed his ankle. Although prone and on the ground, the villager had swept his maul onto Tarl's boot. Because of the steel blade hidden inside, the blow's force dispersed through the metal instead of smashing through his leg. The maul's swipe may have been insufficient to shatter his calf bone, but it was enough to throw Tarl's balanced stance out. His knee buckled and he toppled. His arm flung up and the heavy battle axe flew out of his fingers. It landed several yards away with a splat. Tarl glared down at the Frenchman as he righted himself.

The villager's second chance at survival disappeared. The

unspoken bargain made man to man had been betrayed. There could be no further mercy. It was kill or be killed, and Tarl had no intention of dying with so much left unsaid. Almost of its own accord, Tarl's powerful bow arm smashed down. The horn tip slid between jerkin front and sleeve. With a sickening crack, the ash pierced flesh and bone, stopping only when it had spliced the joint and reached ground. The villager let out a bellow of pain, but they both knew he was pinned down and likely to bleed to death.

Tarl's head whipped around. Ignoring a second trumpet call to retreat, the third soldier advanced over the timbers towards him. Dark, glinting eyes focused on Tarl, sizing him up as if calculating how best to bring him down. Stout and face scarred, he moved across the pit with controlled purpose and wore heavier amour - a dented steel chest-plate over a chain mail neck hood. This man, Tarl understood in the heartbeat it took to assess his foe, had already experienced close combat, and survived.

His hammer now several feet away, and Aioffe's knife lodged in his boot, he only had one weapon left to keep the warrior at a distance. Tarl tried to pull his bow out from its fleshy hold, but it was wedged between bones. The horn nock embedded, caught like a harpoon.

The guard flew at him with a yell and an axe. Tarl ducked his body to one side, dodging the charge. As the soldier jerked to a halt, Tarl grabbed the hanging length of bowstring with one hand, and unwound the rest from his wrist. He launched himself onto the exposed back, hoping the thrust of his bodyweight would bring him down.

The soldier staggered as Tarl's knees squeezed his fat belly in a deadly piggy-back. Almost riding the soldier, Tarl plunged his forearms over the helmet and looped the bow string around the chain-mailed neck. He slid off, landed on the balls of his feet, then yanked the cord up as he stepped backwards.

The soldier dropped his axe and brought his hands towards his throat. He staggered and reeled.

Tarl twisted the garotte tighter around the soldier's neck. As he tugged the stout warrior backwards by the cord, the man wheezed. An arm flailed behind in a vain attempt to grasp for release.

Unable to see where he stepped, Tarl stumbled over the prone, still bow-pinned villager. The soldier's head jerked up. As he found his footing again, the villager screamed. The villager's cry was smothered as his heavy, armoured colleague fell on top of him.

Tarl winced as the cord ripped from his fingers. His knee twisted on the uneven earth. He cursed as he staggered to right himself, then limped a step away from the heap of bodies. He glanced back, hoping he'd done enough.

Unbeaten by the garotte or fall, the soldier rolled then flipped like a beetle righting itself. Still rasping for breath, he twisted himself onto all fours. With blazing eyes, he snarled at Tarl as he pushed his helmet straight. He half stood, lurching forward with his empty hands outstretched. Beneath him, the mud slick with blood and gore, his feet scrabbled for purchase. He rasped and wheezed, then slipped, landing on his arse.

But he did not stop. With a laboured grunt of annoyance, again he twisted to a crouch and crawled towards his dead compatriot in search of a weapon.

Out of nearby heavy weaponry himself, Tarl reached into the side of his boot. Keeping his gaze on the soldier, his fingers found Aioffe's knife. He whipped it out and lumbered across the ground.

The helmet turned towards him, and a gloved hand rose.

Tarl slammed the sharp, short blade into a dark eye. When it was buried to the hilt, his fingers released. He stepped back.

As blood and gloop spurted from the wound, the

Frenchman's mouth dropped open. With his one remaining eye fixed on Tarl, his lips quivered. A gurgle rattled from his throat. Then, he collapsed on top of the villager.

Tarl scrambled away. Unable to take his eyes off the soldiers' pale face, as soon as there was a man's body length between them, he stopped and panted.

A trumpet sounded, echoing eerily through the darkness. But nobody from Bess's pit answered its call. Tarl limped over to his last victim and retrieved Aioffe's knife. He wiped the blade and handle on his jerkin before replacing it, unsheathed and clean, in his boot. His knee couldn't bear weight without pain, so he bound it with the knife wrap, Aioffe's headscarf, for support. It would heal long before the memories of the night could.

Jones-Jones appeared through the darkness, mute and shaken. Together, they knelt next to Tom and Will's bodies and bowed their heads in grateful prayer until the sun rose and reinforcements arrived.

CHAPTER 42 – RETALIATION

They watched stars and fires until the trumpets sounded for a third time. Aioffe's heart raced as men answered the call to retreat. As they streamed back across the valley, chased by soldiers wearing white tabards with a red cross, Aioffe still couldn't determine who had won.

Benediet's face turned to hers, fear widening his eyes as the English picked off Frenchmen as they ran. "Will they reach us?"

Aioffe glanced along the wall. Some of the women had already scrambled down, others stood, shouting, pointing and looking bewildered.

An aged, rotund man, spingolt in hand, hustled up the embankment. "Get away, get away," he shouted, brandishing the weapon. He peered over the edge.

Aioffe's mouth set as she scanned the no-man's-land again. Amongst the English staggering across the swamp wielding swords, no-one seemed to have the stature, or bright blond hair, which she sought.

Benediet tugged on her hand. "Eva?"

The old archer put the springolt down and frantically began to wind the string back. The weapon was larger than a crossbow and took a few minutes to ready. Aioffe stood.

"Where should we go?" Benediet asked, but she didn't know. It was impossible to know.

Below them, a horse clattered up to the gate. "Open for your heroes!" The rider proclaimed.

A smile lit up Benediet's face. He slid down the slope, half on his bottom, half on boot-heels. Aioffe's chest tightened. Her reluctance to leave was noticed, though.

"Go, woman, go!" The archer hefted the bow up and reached behind him for an arrow. He grimaced at carrying the weight of it above his belly, then set it down on the ground to fix the arrow in. A long winded and slightly breathless cuss followed, as the fiddly contraption refused to hold the shaft in the correct place. Panic had over cranked it.

To her right, the huge plank which held the gate closed clattered to the cobbles.

"Eva!" Benediet's pleading voice reached through her reverie.

"I'm coming," Aioffe called back. After snatching a last look, she scrabbled down the earth mound. The gates were being heaved open, and fighters started to pool in. Benediet cheered and clapped, but Aioffe's senses were assaulted by the smell of blood. The irony tang almost hid the stench of daemon and witch, but not quite. She grabbed Benediet's hand and yanked him away.

"The soldiers will need feeding," she offered by way of consolation. "Let's go and pick some vegetables for them?"

He turned shining eyes up to her. "They deserve a feast!"

"I'm sure the troops will be very hungry."

"Tomorrow, I want to get a bow. One of those ones you wind up so I can fight too!" He punched the air as he skipped.

She didn't have the heart to point out that the crossbows and springolts of the French were bigger than he was. Her mind was still on the crazed daemon Lifeforce. Bloodlust was a known problem for their kind, and she hoped the calming influence of witches would steady those soldiers, or violence and chaos could break out in the streets of Harfleur. All the more reason to get her charge to safety.

"Let's see how quickly we can pull those carrots, shall we?" She tugged him towards the graveyard. "Then we'll get them ready for tomorrow morning. You need a rest after all that excitement."

By the time they had gathered an armful each of carrots, turnips and parsnips, Benediet was yawning. Dawn was almost upon them, but Aioffe could not relax.

*****

Tarl's head had barely hit his sleeping rolls before he was roused again. "Gather field. Arm up, any man who can stand," a weary voice shouted, far too loud through the thin fabric of his tent. He rubbed his hand over his face, rinsed his mouth and swallowed from his canteen, and dressed. His calf ached, a purple bruise already risen and tender. He withdrew Aioffe's knife from under the pillow and made to stick it safe inside his boot. Then he collapsed back down again, lost in a fug of tiredness. With the knife in his fingers, images of its last use flooded across his vision.

The slight resistance of an eyeball before the blade punctured.

A spurt of liquid and then blood pulsing out, covering the shining silver before splashing onto the brown soil.

The horror and disbelief on his victim's face.

A dark remaining eye gazing upward, staring into the sky.

How quickly the soldier had fallen. Dead. By his hand.

Tarl lent over and vomited. His eyes screwed shut, as if that would protect him from seeing the truth of what he had done.

Killing a man, face to face...

He gagged again as the knife dropped from his fingers. He retched and retched silently until there was no more. The images kept passing in front of his closed eyes, as if he were back there, in the gun pit. So vivid, he could almost smell the stink of their sweat. Of fear. Of crazed determination as the last soldier ran at him…

"Tarl? Tarl, are you still in there?" The tent flap whipped open and Agnes's white haired head appeared.

But he was lost, gazing at the knife as his mind replayed last night. His reverie was only broken when she shook his shoulder.

"Are you ill? Is the fever upon you?" Her nose wrinkled as she gawked at the pools of vomit on the grass, then shook her head. "My poor John's been taken bad. Up all night with an ague, and his leg's all swollen. He's not long for this world, I think. Barely knows who I am."

Tarl stared up at her. "I'm sorry."

She sniffed and wiped a tear. "An' I hear poor Alf is down with it too. What happened to Tom, Jones-Jones, and Will?"

Tarl shook his head. "Tom and Will fell defending the pit last night. Jones and I are the only ones left in the unit."

A lump just wouldn't shift from his throat, and his stomach constricted again. He bent, thinking he was about to void further, but the knot remained.

Agnes's fingers tightened on his shoulder. "I heard the call to arms. Are you too sick to fight?"

Tarl said nothing, just stared at the knife on the ground. The handle was dark with mud and blood. He rocked his head. "Sick of heart, maybe, but I can stand, draw a bow, or," his voice caught, "stab."

Her lips pursed. "You don't look right at all."

For a minute, they fell silent. Tarl's hands trembled, and the knot in his stomach sank further. How could he go? Could he kill again? An arrow was impersonal. Shot from such a distance, his victims were faceless. But this war had turned personal, and now he had tainted Aioffe's blade with the blood of the enemy. But it was not his enemy. Now he had seen the faces of his foe, felt the kinship of ordinary people called to battle in a war not of their own creation, he worried the next time, he might instead be tempted to fall to his knees and beg for forgiveness.

Jones's face appeared next to Agnes's shoulder. His thin lips but a red slash in a pale face. "Come on. We're supposed to be in the gather field."

His voice sounded as miserable as Tarl felt. There was little choice though. They were here to fight, and fight he had to. At least it was a better way to die than lying sick. Tarl nodded to Jones, then pulled on his boots.

*****

Benediet woke with a moan at the sounds of footsteps outside, thumping up their stairs in an uneven limp. Aioffe, absorbed in scrubbing and cutting the carrots with the only, blunt, knife in the loft, threw her cape over her back to cover her exposed wings and hurried to open the door.

"They rally what remains of the garrison again," their neighbour hissed from the balcony. "Something's happening. Can I stay here with you?" There was deceit, a mistrust perhaps, cloaked in the old woman's defensive stance. She kept her face low and wouldn't meet Aioffe's eyes.

The boy sat bolt upright. "Another attack?"

Barely concealed glee rang through his question and Aioffe's heart flopped over. There was bound to be a reaction to the forays into the English camp last night, but what that entailed for Harfleur remained to be seen. "I don't think that's wise," Aioffe said to the neighbour. "The roof tiles are so thin, as is the door. You'd be safer in your own home." She anticipated a renewed fervour to destroy the walls, but if the garrison rallied again during daylight, perhaps something more was planned.

The neighbour's eyes wandered to the pile of carrots. "Another crop already? It would be a shame if someone were to ask too many questions about how you came by such food.

Stealing is a hanging matter. Like they hang traitors."

Her blood had turned to ice, but she ignored the implied threat. "Do you want some?" Aioffe offered up a carrot. "We were going to take the rest over to the garrison."

The old woman's lips curved up on one side. "Oh my dear, I don't think you should be going anywhere. I've spoken to Captain Raoal De Gaucourt. You just don't know who you can trust these days." Her fingers gripped the door frame and her eyes finally met Aioffe's with a steady stare. "I'll stay here with you."

Aioffe knew then. The neighbour had been suspicious of her from their first, fateful meeting. Most likely wondered if she was English at the very least, but, she must have voiced her concerns to the garrison commander. Now, in a thinly veiled attempt to keep her here, Aioffe suspected she was about to be apprehended. Perhaps used some way to punish the English? If she was not to be detained, then why else would the old woman want to keep an eye on her?

The dark confinement of a gaol entered her mind, causing another chilly rush to sweep over her skin. Hanging wasn't such an issue, she could not die by rope alone. An accusation of treachery she could argue against, having done nothing to aid the English cause, and provided what she could in support of the French. But when they discovered her wings... there was no doubt they would call in the Church for advice, and imprison her while they passed judgement.

"I know who I can trust," Aioffe said, looking at Benediet. A smile spread across his face. She held up the basin of carrots. "And those brave soldiers need feeding before a fight."

"Yes!" Benediet punched a fist in the air.

"So let's go quickly then," Aioffe said as she stood. Her cape, always worn for the warmth and protection it provided, draped neatly over her wings. Benediet scrabbled on the floor for his boots.

The old woman glared at Aioffe. "It's not safe out there for the boy, or you. We should all stay here. Together."

Aioffe glanced at the roof above. Through the cracks, daylight filtered through, but also, an eerie silence. The absence of missiles should have alerted her to the difference in this day. "For once, I'd agree with you. It's not safe anywhere though." She advanced towards the door, but the woman stood her ground and blocked the way out.

Benediet, however, had no such politeness. "We've got important work," he said, and barrelled past her skirts.

The woman tusked under her breath. As Aioffe went to move through the exit as well, her wrinkly arm shot out to the door frame, blocking her. Aioffe lightly touched the bare skin on her wrist and met the woman's eyes. As she pushed her will to leave down, she saw the fear of the other, the inexplicable. The different.

"I must go," she whispered.

*****

Jones Jones and Tarl walked in silence towards the gather field. The sky blushed orange, and the air seemed curiously clear, as if all clouds of doubt had been swept away in the few hours they had slept. As they joined their colleagues in their cent, Tarl noticed their number had dwindled again. The voices of Alf, Tom and Will flitted into his mind like echoes. They should have been here, beside him, but their sacrifice was destined to fade into the memory of those who loved them only. For sure, the cost of an individual's life wouldn't weigh on people's minds until the final tally was made, and then, each name would be no more than a footnote in history's records. Read and reconciled by scholars more educated than he.

While they waited, priests mingled, marking foreheads with a holy water cross and proffering absolution. Tarl kept his head dipped. He could not yet seek forgiveness for his sins. If anything, he needed the promise of returning for that blessing as reason to come back alive. He could not die with the killings on his conscience. He would not perish with unfinished business either, he decided. The Bishop of Norwich, who he had not seen for days, he realised, would have to be the priest to grant forgiveness, for he was the one most lied to. What had he been thinking, to claim stolen altar goods were blessed by St Crispinian? That he was from ancient, distinguished blood-lines? Then using the threat of exposure to seal the bargain? All of those lies paled in significance to his offering Aioffe up as a spy - his biggest mistake, he saw now.

The lump in his throat ached as he fiddled with the war-axe hung from his belt. Yesterday's spilt blood had dried, dulling the steel head. He checked and strung his bow and picked up two arrow bags, anything to detract from the strange yearning to grip Aioffe's knife. Despite his desire to caress it, he left the talisman hidden nestled against his calf. The secret weapon with two sides - both saving him and reminding him of his deeds.

He glanced to the heavens, at the forget-me-not blue sky. Perhaps today it would be reunited with its owner?

The thought of Aioffe, her softness and smile, confused him. Worse - distracted him from the horror which doubtless lay before the army now. Tarl rocked his head to dispel the image of her - skin slightly glowing, violet-blue eyes staring at him - from his mind. He must focus. Distraction would cost lives.

Sir Thomas Rempston's face was set with determination as he approached. "Listen up! This day, men, is when we take back what is our King's god-given right to hold." He looked around the assembled soldiers. "Henry leads our attack on this side of the town. The Leure gate is our target while the Duke of

Clarence will approach the other side. No walls can stand in our way, no Frenchman will deter us. We move as one unstoppable force. Trench by trench, we advance until there is only the stretch before us, and by God, we will advance. The men-at-arms will march ahead, archers behind. I want a cloud of arrows to clear the way for the ladders. Over our men's heads, shoot long or shoot your own. If something moves on the walls, they die by our blessed points or by the fire of our steel."

His eyes flashed from underneath bushy eyebrows. "They will pay for last night. For those we lost, we now take no prisoners. By the order of the King, Harfleur and all its residents will pay the debt with their lives by nightfall."

Tarl closed his eyes and prayed that Aioffe wasn't in Harfleur after all.

CHAPTER 43 – REUNION

To delay longer risked the loss of more lives. There was little stealth about the attack. With pageantry and noise, the preparations to march were themselves a statement that this was a final push. Henry's show of force was as much about building spirit and to warn the weakened garrison and people of Harfleur that, finally, the English army was coming for them. For conquest.

They prodded thousands out of their beds - everyone who could walk and hold a weapon amassed on the muddy grass. Tired, ill, armoured or no, this was the attack they had been waiting for and no-one shirked their duty. All elements of the army, all the arrangements and plans, came together with a swiftness which only clear leadership and planning could provide.

Tarl was first sent to a corner of the field, with hostlers and farriers to make last minute adjustments. He'd never shoe'd horses so fast, but someone had thought to bring all the spares from the forge, and between them all, the mounts for knights were readied. He was so absorbed with tapping in nails on a bay who danced with excitement, he almost missed the trumpets announcing the start of the march.

Tarl glanced over at the white-clad backs of the troops leaving the field as he packed up his tools. Most of the jupons were bloodied and muddy from last night, but still brought the disparate band of soldiers together as one. Weapons, with more distributed if people had lost theirs, were drawn or strung. Glinting in the morning sunlight, the wide blades of freshly wiped pole-axes hovered above helmets. A matter of pride perhaps, that blades were cleaned before the next kill. Aioffe's knife rubbed against his ankle as he walked across, reminding him his sins could not yet be so easily rubbed away. The air grew thick with the smell of nervous and sickly bowels, incense and ale.

A vast pile of bundled together branches had already been dropped through the dawn light, onto the still boggy land between the army camp and the walls, or in trenches. This would increase the speed of the thousands of men as they approached. Bringing up the rear, pages followed with supplies, including barrels filled with arrow-bags hung on either side of the horse's bellies, and torches to light pitch soaked parcels for fire arrows.

As he walked across the gather field, Tarl could hear the cries of battle. He picked up his pace. As he dropped down the fields and into the valley below, he could see the white, red and silver swarm trailing towards the pale walls. First to reach the perimeter was a line of men at arms, shields held high against the volley of arrows from above. The Leure gate, with its twin bastions which rose forty feet high two months ago, now stood at half its original height and was patched with wooden pews and planks.

Tarl spotted the standard of Sir Thomas Rempston, not far from Erpingham's, and he headed towards the ranks of longbows. Hundreds, thousands of bowmen spread out in rows behind troops of men at arms and knights. Even more archers were already in the forward trenches, firing over the barriers and beyond. Flaming arrows poured onto the rooftops of the town. At this proximity, spreading panic was as important as a kill shot.

As Tarl jogged along the line, searching for Jones-Jones, Sir Thomas's herald tooted and the commander's arm raised to halt the rain of arrows.

Tarl froze, then he looked across the sea of helmets filling the Lézarde valley and the looming pale walls, to see what Sir Thomas had paused them for. His heart thumped as he recognised ladders, fashioned from tree trunks linked with chains, thrust against the stones. To the left from the expanse of red and white, a beetle of shields rushed forwards.

A thud from the battering ram striking the great gates signalled a renewed flurry of crossbow fire down from the still formidable defences. Englishmen brave enough to climb the ladders screamed as boiling oil tipped over them.

"Forward!" Sir Thomas shouted, and the archers piled out of the trench. Tarl found himself jostled along. Cries of "Come on!" and "Let's finish the bastards," showed the eagerness to advance on their prey.

As Tarl stepped over the wooden bundles, already sinking but still supporting the weight of the footfall, he glanced ahead. The stone and timber walls crawled with soldiers ascending. A cheer went up from his left, and he saw the Leure gate doors had splintered. The surge of archers swerved course and clambered as fast as they could towards the entry point. Hand to hand combat beckoned, and pole-axes dipped for a charge.

But not Tarl. Slinging his bow across his chest, Tarl ran holding only his satchel in his hands. Arrow bags bounced against his back with every footstep. His breathing grew ragged from pulling in great clouds of smoke from the flaming arrows devastation. Ringing in his ears was Sir Thomas's words. No prisoners would be taken. Harfleurians would pay with their lives.

He had to find Aioffe, before the slaughter began.

*****

Within Harfleur, the streets were empty. Muffled noises of battle, English cries and then the thudding barely reached Benediet's ears, but to Aioffe, the danger was all too close. As they walked towards the centre, all she could think of was how to keep the boy safe. A grey ring of smoke hovered around the edges of the town as fires raged on the tinder dry rooftops and barricades.

A reckoning was near. The absence of townsfolk gossiping, eking out their last meal or slumber, told her as much. Although she was confident they could dodge apprehension by the garrisoned soldiers while the attack was happening - after all, everyone should be manning the defences - she doubted the English would stop to ask questions if they got through.

She glanced up, more out of habit now, and wished she could just fly up and search for signs of Tarl from above. Her desperation grew with every thud of her heart. If only she were higher. If only she could escape the threat of capture and leave. With everyone distracted, if she shot straight up, through the circle of fires engulfing the perimeter, perhaps no-one would see? Her wings twitched beneath her cloak, ready for her command.

Her head and heart collided as she almost bent her knees, but caught sight of a pair of tatty leather boots. Too big for a boy, but all that he had to remember his father by.

Benediet still needed her. Until this siege was over, her debt to him remained unfulfilled. His impetuous nature couldn't be trusted. She wondered if this was another phase of his grief, as it was clear his enthusiasm for war had overtaken his earlier fear. Her fist clenched over his as they trotted along the street. The boy must not get swept away by a foolish notion that he could take on a well-trained, armed soldier as revenge for his father's death.

She decided their best hope was to try to wait it out somewhere safe. But where was safe? Her wings fluttered underneath her cape, and Benediet smiled up at her. Sanctuary, that was what she sought. The only common ground between English and French was the Church. She remembered what Tarl had said, just after they had first agreed she would spy for the Bishop, for Henry. 'The Church should be a sanctuary, respected by everyone under any circumstance,' and then Tarl had sighed.

Irrespective of the outcome of the attack, there was refuge inside a Church, surely? She had not felt the presence of a vampire priest in the parish church of St Martin's, so that was where she guided Benediet. It had lost its steeple and bell some weeks ago, but the graveyard there was full of the fruits of her labour. She smiled to herself as they turned to take the riverside path. Unable to leave her charge and find Tarl, there was no better place for her to let him know where she was. She just had to believe he would think to look there, if he still survived, that was.

Forget me knots, she thought, as she glanced to the light blue-grey sky above. There was hopefully time enough for a carpet of them to grow.

As they crossed the bridge, the cries from outside the walls stopped. She slowed, wondering what it meant.

"Why did you stop? What's wrong?" Benediet asked. He looked over the side of the bridge as if trolls lurked under.

"I don't know," she replied, looking around. Shadows from the overhanging buildings had narrowed as the sun reached its apex. Below, the wide riverbed was silent, occupied only now by rats and the odd wild-flower stubbornly clinging to the stone sides. Where once babbled fresh water, flushing away all waste, the French defensive measures diverted the vital river away, before it reached the walls. Blocked inside and, having nowhere else to leave their filth, the residents still emptied their chamberpots into its trench, leaving the water course a rancid cesspit of effluence, a brown muddy snake which poisoned the two halves of Harfleur.

She transferred the bowl of carrots into one hand, so her fingers could rub the tingle at the back of her neck. It didn't ease her disquiet, and Benediet looked at her strangely. "Come, let's get to St Martins." Aioffe pulled her hood down so it covered more of her face, and moved into the slim shade across the bridge.

*****

Tarl's progress into Harfleur was abruptly halted by a wall of standing archers. "What's happening?" he asked another vent.

"The King is parleying with the townsfolk," the archer replied. He nodded his helmet towards the open space in front of the rubble which was all that remained of the Leure gate. There was no way to see over the helmeted heads, even with Tarl's height advantage. "They opened the gate before we could bash it down. No-one's to enter the town yet."

Tarl's heart fluttered. What would the King do now? Kill everyone in Harfleur as he'd directed his men to? Was that why the archers stood, bows drawn? With a heavy sigh, he joined their ranks. Pulled his own bowstave from his shoulders and readied a broadhead arrow. The heart-shape at the end of the shaft reminded him of Aioffe, and of the arrowhead he'd left in the bed of forget me knots. As he pulled the string, Tarl couldn't help but think of the pious, considered ruler he had met in the forest all those weeks ago. But Henry was also a king tired of waiting. Still holding ready, Tarl closed his eyes and prayed that the Lord would show his guidance, his forgiveness, to the young King.

Gradually, the longbows lowered. No arm could hold a pulled string for too long and be sure the curled fingers would release upon signal. The army stood for what seemed like hours, more than enough time for pounding hearts to calm and cooler heads to prevail. Plenty turned around, strolled away from the frontline and relieved themselves.

Sir Thomas wandered along his lines, stopping to talk to the archers and keeping energy levels high with threats about how quickly the negotiations could fall apart. Even now. They had to hold their nerve and be ready.

Tarl mouth dried. Every moment he stood, not searching inside the walls for Aioffe, dragged. Idleness allowed his mind to wander, layering upon his nerves with the expectation of more death to follow. He wiped the sweat from his brow with his sleeve.

Then, the trumpets sounded to retreat. As the men around him lowered their bows, resignation on their faces, Tarl stayed motionless. His feet planted, bow raised as he scanned the horizon of the walls. This was the closest he had moved to Aioffe in weeks, and he could not bring himself to leave. Within minutes, he was virtually alone.

It was the worst of luck when he saw, from the corner of his eye, that Ap Tudor had also not left the battlefield. Several hundred metres away, sword in hand, he dithered from foot to foot as if ready for combat. Tarl gritted his teeth and gazed across to the gate, where members of the King's entourage still lingered, talking with a few Frenchmen. Henry himself cantered slowly away, armed guards surrounded him with their pennants held high.

Tarl's gaze narrowed as he focused instead on the remaining representatives of the council. As if he felt his stare, a black-robed figure with a long gold chain around his neck turned. The Bishop of Norfolk's glare landed directly on him. Tarl quashed the urge to duck.

But, the Bishop looked pale, weak even, with drooping shoulders. He leant against a black horse, barely participating in the animated conversation his peers were engaged in. Tarl blinked then dragged his eyes away. There was something peculiar in that vampire's stare which unnerved him. And he needed all the nerve he had to stand here. Alone, almost, and vulnerable.

Only when Henry had disappeared from sight did Ap Tudor turn and spot Tarl. His sword pointed towards him. In response, Tarl swung his bow around.

Ap Tudor's lips curled and for a minute they stared down their weapons at each other.

"Lord Ap Tudor!" The Bishop's voice wavered across the field. "Return to your quarters forthwith. You are not needed here."

Owain's head snapped around, and he received a glare. After a moment, he sheathed his sword and stalked off.

Tarl held his breath and hoped he would not come back and order his return as well. Or, query why he had not rejoined his unit. Ask after Aioffe. Ask anything. The man was a coward, a thug, but one who played the politics to his advantage. He wondered whether anyone else had noticed the Welshman's absence at the gun pit last night.

Yet, he could ill afford a confrontation when so much rested on getting inside the barricades to locate his wife. The Bishop's head inclined towards Tarl as he turned back to his conversation.

The ditch beneath the walls was just a few feet away. He looked down the barrier, towards the towers near the sea wall. The men at arms had not removed all the ladders from that side, the army having converged on the Leure gate entrance. A plan formed   as   he   crept   forward.

CHAPTER 44 – CRYPTIC CRYPT

The graveyard was silent, save only the rustles of scattered leaves whispering in the breeze. Although it was only mid-afternoon, a chill touched the air and Aioffe shivered. "Let's leave the carrots here, by the gate, then rest inside for a minute," she said to Benediet. The child nodded solemnly and obeyed.

"When will the soldiers be here?" Benediet asked.

"I'm not sure." Nor could she confirm which army.

"But they will come here? Or should we take them to the garrison for when they return?"

The very last place Aioffe wanted to go. She shook her head. "Why don't you see if the door is open? I just want to check on the parsnips."

Benediet wandered down the path towards the chapel entrance. As soon as he was out of sight, she cast about, looking for the most obvious spot for a message to Tarl. If this was to be her last hours before capture, she wanted him to know she thought of him still. She couldn't know, only hope, if he had somehow found her message in the forest, but logic had told her he would need charcoal eventually, and the clearing was the obvious choice of location for that messy business. Whether he went or someone else to burn the coals, a cross shaped bed of forget me knots was likely something which would catch the eye of any believer, and maybe word of it would spread to him.

After the destruction of last night, in her heart, she suspected Tarl would be drawn to lean into his faith, if he survived. He might seek solace and forgiveness in a church, and there weren't that many in town. This centrally placed church would, if Harfleur fell, be the one a leader would choose for any religious ceremony relating to the conquest, as it was close to the administrative buildings and garrison. It's the one she would have chosen, were she in Henry's position.

Selecting a grave which had a Celtic style cross, with a ring around the middle like the one on the church in Wrye, she ploughed her fingers into the soil. Pushing the tendrils down drained the dregs of her energy.

She leaned against the headstone and closed her eyes. Her last rat had been several days ago, and she considered perhaps she should have drawn in those chaotic tendrils the night before, to fortify herself for whatever came next. A fleeting moment of peace was all she sought.

Her nose twitched, a familiar smell reaching her nostrils and alerting her. As her eyelids flew open, she launched herself up and stumbled down the path to the church.

Benediet, who should have been at the doorway by now, was gone!

*****

Tarl tugged off his jupon and, quite literally, ditched it. Replacing his bow over his shoulders and turning towards the sea, he crouched low as he made his way along the deep, boggy trench the French had dug in front of the walls. The English had dropped bound sticks into the ditch to make traversing easier. It didn't help him move any faster though, as they snapped and cracked an announcement of his presence with every mis-step. Where no branches were laid, swamp water slopped into his boots, and they squelched as he stepped through the mud. There was nothing to be done about it though - too risky to climb out entirely and weave around the wooden defensive shields or linger at the base of the wall whilst looking for a suitable foothold to clamber up. His outline would be all too obvious to the cluster of people outside the Leure gate.

After he rounded a corner tower, the ditch stopped, and he had no choice but to clamber up. A few feet away, a ladder still leaned against the wall. Tarl breathed a little easier. He checked above and to the bastions on either side before stepping on the chain.

As he climbed, he kept an eye on his surroundings. As he neared the top, he paused and pulled out his war axe. Doing so sent a shiver of dread through him, but he pushed aside the sudden influx of recollections. His core muscles screamed in protest as he heaved himself up and over the parapet using his battle axe as a grapple. Any moment he anticipated discovery, and anxiety clenched his stomach. His heart fluttered with exertion as he unhooked the string from his bow so it could be used as a spear, then crept along the deserted walkway. Below him in the streets, he heard frantic activity and shouts as townsfolk tried to contain the fires, but Tarl sent a prayer of gratitude up for the smoke cover obscuring his entry.

*****

Aioffe reached the main porch of the church and stopped. Of the thick double doors, one rested ajar by a finger width. Sticking her nose in the air, she sniffed.

A sickly, sweet scent lingered. Not from the flowers she had covered the grave with, for forget-me-not's had little perfume, but of recently burned incense. The musty, smoky smell of Benediet's boots. And the stench of vampire.

Here. That was the smell which had awoken her from her brief respite.

The Bishop of Norfolk, to be precise. His personal odour hung heavy with the sourness of sickness, and the iron tang of metal and blood.

She leaned her ear into the crack in the doorway. Deadened whispers from deep inside the building reached her ears. She recognised the Latin - a prayer she had often heard the priests used to absolve people of their sins. Before they died.

Aioffe chewed on her lip as she thought. Her senses picked up no signs of any other life-forms nearby. No-one to help her rescue Benediet from the Bishop's clutches. Her stomach clenched as she wished she had her knife, or any weapon, but she carried nothing bar her wits. She didn't even have the element of surprise, for surely he must have seen her when he passed her in the graveyard. After drawing in a deep breath, Aioffe opened the door and stepped inside.

The church was dimly lit by the remnants of the daylight filtering through the windows. A fug of incense hung, potent but invisible, close to the altar. A shiver ran through her as she scanned the wide, empty space. At the steeple end, a rough barricade hid the rubble which had fallen when the spire fell, leaving the chapel drafty and open to the elements. Aioffe walked down the central aisle, checking the remaining pews and scanning the recesses of the side altars. Benediet and the Bishop were nowhere to be seen.

Then, a yelp echoed into the room. She dashed towards the altar, noticing a slim doorway at the edge of the rood screen. As she went through, her foot stumbled on the step. Steadying herself on the stone wall, her wings fluttered behind her, but the passage was too narrow for them to extend. She swept her cloak aside, so it hung in front of her and stepped with greater care down.

*****

Tarl jogged through the streets of Harfleur trying to orient himself, as well as look like he should be there. He carried his bow as a staff and set his face with a purposeful expression, hoping no-one would stop and ask his business. He'd had many weeks to think about where Aioffe might be held if she were captured, and become convinced that if she were alive and imprisoned, the most obvious place was somewhere central, like a garrison or a town gaol. As he had entered close to the harbour, he found then followed the dried riverbed until he reached a bridge.

He stopped and looked up the stinking river course, trying to judge how much further he had to go. Across the way, between the overhanging houses, he spotted an open square, with a church to one side. Tarl chewed his lip and thought about the view he had seen of the town when he was on top of the ridge. There had been a few spires dotted amongst the rooftops, and one which had been almost central. He clambered out of the ditch and jogged down the path towards it.

As he approached, he noticed this steeple had been damaged even though it was approximately in the middle of town. The reach of Henry's siege weapons was impressive, and, now he was inside and could see the destruction for himself, he had no doubt that if the negotiations broke down, Harfleur would eventually be flattened beyond repair. He walked across the square and stood at the gate to get his bearings. The cobbles before the entry to the church had a reddish-brown tint to them, and his lips tightened. He swallowed, thinking with sorrow about how many more bodies would be brought here after today, and how many had lives had already been lost in the siege. As he gazed over the graveyard, expecting to see mounds of freshly dug resting places, his eyebrows pinched together. Some of the graves appeared to have vegetables growing on top!

At first he was impressed by the resourcefulness of the town, but then his arms tingled with a chill. He walked over and bent to stroke the feathered leaves of carrots, parsnips and the low stalks of turnip. But that was not all that was growing: forget-me-nots adorned an entire mound beneath a cross-shaped gravestone. His heart faltered. A sign. Aioffe's message, as clear as the one she had left in the forest. He spun around, his hands shaking.

If she could do this, then she might not be captured, but free. Where though?

*****

From below, in the darkness, Aioffe heard a deep moan of satisfaction. Then, the smell of blood. Its metallic tang clogged in the back of her throat. As quickly and quietly as she could, Aioffe crept down the curved stone steps. Part in response to the dry smell of decay, her wings rose as she reached the bottom.

The Bishop stood, hunched over a kneeling Benediet. His head nuzzled the boy's neck, feeding. Benediet seemed absolutely focussed on the small cross which hung from the roof, a carved figure of Jesus gazing down upon him. Aioffe flew across the room, hands outstretched. She shoved the Bishop away from Benediet and he sprawled to the stone floor.

Benediet looked up at her in surprise. His mouth dropped as he saw her wings, but little hint of recognition showed in his vacant eyes.

But the Bishop levered himself up with ease and glared at her. "How dare you!"

"How dare you!" She shouted back. "This boy is under my protection."

"He is food. French. Mine."

As if in a trance, Benediet returned to staring at the cross. His neck seeped blood from two puncture marks. Aioffe hovered between the Bishop and her charge.

"You failed, Mistress Smith." The Bishop lowered his hands and sneered. "I knew I should never have trusted a fae spy to have loyalty."

"I was captured."

With lightning speed, the Bishop rushed at her.

Aioffe had been expecting an attack. As quickly as he ran, her reactions were faster. Copying a move she had seen her brother use in combat training many times, her wing joints rotated, pushing her horizontal in the air. She stuck out her feet. As the vampire collided with her limbs, she kicked upward. Stomping, drumming, up his chest, her body flipped up and over as her feet punched into his throat, jaw, nose and forehead in quick succession.

Her wings beating to drive her closer to him as his body was pounded away by her kicks, the momentum span her heels over head. Once her aerial spin was complete, she saw the vampire's charge had stalled. Buffeted away by her kicks, he landed on his side. With unnatural haste, he sprang back onto his feet. Before she could think about the most effective counter move, he charged once again. This time, his outstretched hands aimed for her waist.

Aioffe was caught off guard as she twisted away from him. His fingers grasped the edge of her cloak. Twirling like a dancer, the Bishop yanked. Dragged out of the air, she hit a long stone box. Her chest bore the brunt of the impact, and she gasped in pain.

He yanked the fabric again, pulling her towards him across the floor. Red saliva dripped from his lips as he grabbed her arm and wrenched it back to the flagstones. "And this is why my kind won before," he panted. As he bent over her, the foulness of his sickly breath turned her stomach. She screamed.

The noise echoed around the chamber and roused Benediet

from his trance. "Non!" he cried out.

"Don't, Benediet!" Aioffe's head whipped around, but he was already crouched to pounce. Ignoring the child, the Bishop's fingers clamped down on her neck and pinned her in place on the cold stone. He bore down and constricted his digits around her throat until she could no longer draw breath.

Despite the darkness, Benediet launched himself towards them. His judgement was poor, and the child banged into and off the vampire's arm instead.

The Bishop whipped his arm around and wrapped it about the child's torso. He then gazed at her and laughed. Aioffe caught again the stench of his illness, soured further by a desperation for fresh blood which drove any rationality from him. Then he drew close the little, limp body as his lips pulled back for another bite.

*****

The scream came from the church, muffled but unmistakable. Tarl ran towards the building. The door thumped as he barrelled through, his war hammer and bowstave in hand.

Empty.

Where was she? Tarl's heart constricted in his chest. He pelted down the aisle and stood in the centre of the high vaulted room. Which direction had the scream come from? His throat tightened as he swivelled around, searching. Listening.

He glanced over to the altar, just as from underneath his boots, it seemed, there was a thud.

He looked at the floor, bewildered. How could she be beneath him? Under his feet, an engraved stone marked someone's life. He stamped, feeling foolish.

*****

The Bishop froze, his eyes rolled up. Hearing the thump above, Aioffe struggled, wheezing beneath his grasp on her throat. Her captor ignored her entirely, even when her fingers scratched against his hand, trying to push him off. He was too strong.

The vampire's other arm tightened around Benediet's waist and he dipped his fangs once again towards the boy's neck. Benediet was already limp, his head hung so close to hers she could see his face whitening, skin thinning as the Bishop drank.

Aioffe's flesh crawled. Unable to breathe, her limbs were losing their strength. Her hope of escape. Before her eyes, the darkness of the vault closed in and her heart slowed. After everything she had done to avoid capture, she had ended up in a gaol after all. A black hole underground. Worse, one which smelled of decay. Human corpses, bones and death. Her eyelids fluttered. Although she writhed, the vampire grew stronger with every gulp.

Benediet twitched, his boot grazing her knee. Renewed in her determination, she could no longer bear to watch the life drain out of him. She screeched with her last remaining air. Without pause, the Bishop's hand moved to cover her mouth. He pushed her head to the side, his fingers dug into her cheeks to keep her pinned down.

As she drew in breath through her nose, she smelled a waft of fresher air enter the black room. A scent of charcoal, ash, sweat and human all too beloved to her.

Tarl!

She heard his footsteps falter on the steps. Why did he not come down? Then she realised - in the pitch black, a human would be unable to see. She banged her heels against the floor, hands slapped on the flagstones. Anything to let him know she was here.

Another step.

"Aioffe?" Tarl whispered.

She screwed her eyes closed, hardly daring to believe he was here. Her fingers reached out into the dark, feeling for what she needed.

His Lifeforce was agitated, tinged with the orange of agitation. She pulled, mentally apologising for what she took. Her mind filled with a mental impression of him, his strength. His arms as they wrapped around her. The touch of his lips as they   ground   into   hers.

CHAPTER 45 - A MISTAKE NOT REPEATED

Tarl saw Aioffe then. Her skin glowed through the darkness and he almost smiled. Lit by love, his eyes widened as he saw the gentle curve of her jawline. But, her body was obscured by another, and another. There were too many limbs to understand how the bundle of bodies fitted together.

A hand, white as if moonlit, curled around a black back. Her finger pointed at his target. A rasp and thump of feet on the flagstones. Without hesitation, he rushed over, axe raised.

Covering the small space in only a few strides, his mind interrupted. The Frenchman's face flashed before his vision. Yet still, his legs continued to move towards her indicated target. A slick of mud, or maybe blood, registered under his feet. Her rasped squeal of pain broke through the fear which threatened paralysis. He brought the hammer down.

The crack of the axe, steel against bone, juddered up his arm, echoing, spinning around his head. He staggered, reeling like a drunkard, and let go of the handle. As he turned aside, unable to bear what he had done, it remained cross-like, embedded between shoulder blades. His stomach clenched as his gaze slid back to his weapon in disbelief.

He had killed again.

And inside a crypt, a holy place of rest.

With a soft thud, the bodies fell from Aioffe. She pushed them away and reached up to him with long, pale arms. Tarl couldn't catch his breath, just drank in her slim body as she unfurled to stand. Her fingers traced his jaw, their tenderness chasing aside those terrible pictures in his mind.

"You came. For me," she whispered.

Tarl, mute, swallowed and nodded. All the things he wanted to say to her if he ever saw her again, and now he couldn't squeak a word. For a moment, he wasn't even sure if she was real, or another fantastical dream. A hallucination.

She glanced down, then crouched over a form on the floor. Not the one which he'd hit, but a smaller body. Dimly lit by the sparkle of her skin, Tarl watched as she bent her head closer to a child's mouth and sniffed.

"He's lost a lot of blood, but he'll live," she said, and turned to face him with a smile so broad his chest ached. He couldn't catch his breath.

"Breathe," Aioffe urged, taking his fingers in her own. A radiance spread through his body and mind. Calming. Trusting. There was no need to fear any more. She was here.

She was here! His eyes flared but he drew in a deep, shuddering breath.

"Out, then in again."

He did as ordered.

Slowly, his fingertips tightened around hers. The mist of his mind cleared as he gazed down into her eyes. Her glow was fading, so in desperation for the lightness to return, he pulled her upright and wrapped her in his arms. His bow, upright and pliant, bent with their embrace and seemed to warm simply from touching her skin.

His cheek laid on top of her soft hair. "I thought I'd never see you again," he whispered. "Thought you had gone."

"I was. But not by choice. I was captured when he," she tipped her head towards the larger body, "sent me away on a mission the day before the siege started. And then I couldn't escape."

He looked down at the stone floor. Aioffe was glowing enough for him to visually to confirm her attacker. Tarl suppressed a shudder. He pulled back from their embrace to study her face, his thumb brushing up her cheekbone and sweeping a strand of hair away. "I should never have put you in danger." His throat tightened.

Aioffe turned his face back to hers. "You didn't endanger me, not at all. I chose to go when the Bishop asked me to. What happened was my fault. All of it. I…" She glanced down at the boy at her feet.

Tarl could barely make out his body, but heard the soft sounds of slumber in the otherwise silent chamber.

After a while, she said, "I stayed because of him. I'm sorry if it defied the orders I was given, and you wondered where I was. Benediet's father was killed, in part because they didn't know what to do with me and we got caught outside the walls when dawn broke and the firing started. There was no-one else to look after him. He was alone, and grieving. I couldn't leave."

Her blue eyes sought his in the darkness and he saw they were filled with tears. He nodded his understanding, his heart aching for a boy who, like him, lost his parents too young.

She touched his hand and continued, "I couldn't come back to you, although I wanted to. If I had, then the Bishop would have killed us both because I hadn't completed the mission he set me. While I was only 'missing', he still had reason to keep you alive. As leverage to use against me. By staying in Harfleur and paying my debt to Benediet for keeping me hidden, I hoped to keep both of you alive."

"I found your message. Messages." Tarl smiled. "I hoped too. Prayed."

"I'm glad."

They stood in silence for a moment. Then both spoke.

"I missed…"

"I'm sorry…"

They laughed.

"I'm just glad you're alive," Tarl said.

Her hand crept over his heart. "I'm glad you are too."

"I… I was worried I would be too late."

"You almost were!"

Tarl wanted to tell her then. Of how frightened he'd been. How foolish. How much he regretted pushing her away because of how different she was, when, in all honesty, he felt more, and was more alive since he had met her than he had ever been. That he knew how much her presence alone must have comforted the child, for he had missed her so deeply it pained him, but he would have gladly borne the pain to save another. Would kill again if it would save her suffering.

But the words wouldn't come out of his mouth. He let out a deep sigh. Of all the people to kill, why did it have to be the Bishop of Norwich? Trusted advisor to the King. Instigator of their enforced separation. Another clergyman injured by his hand. A vampire.

A vampire. His breath caught. The recollection of the last vampire he'd encountered cantered into his mind, then bucked him off balance as he recalled his mistaken assumption those many months past. Was this one actually dead, though? Tarl's eyes narrowed on the possible corpse. Before today, he hadn't seen the Bishop in weeks, and back on the battlefield earlier, he had looked wan and miserable. Weak, as if sickened like half the army was. Despite this, he must have persuaded the officials to permit him entry into Harfleur through the Leure gate, while Tarl had been wasting time clambering through the ditches and scaling the walls.

"Is he safe now?" The Bishop hadn't moved, but that meant nothing when dealing with immortals.

Aioffe's mouth tightened as Tarl wiped the sweat from his

palm on his jacket. "Did I...?"

"It needs to be finished." Her expression darkened. "Or we will have to disappear and hope that he can never find us. Even then, there's no knowing if he informed his kind about my presence with the army, or here."

They both stared at the Bishop. As he'd fallen to the floor when Aioffe pushed herself up, the sharp wedged point of his hammer axe had fallen out. He noticed the hole was bloodied but begun to close. The skin on his face mottled and grey in the dimming light reflected from Aioffe's.

Aioffe's eyes flicked to the boy. Only shallow breaths could be heard, but he showed signs of recovery in the flutter of his eyelids. "We need to act fast," she whispered. "I hate to say this, but it really is him or all of us. There are consequences far greater than you can imagine if we leave him alive."

The glow from her skin dulled, leaving them in almost complete darkness. "I can't see what I've got to do," he said. "Where to aim." His fingers tightened, sweaty, on his bow.

"Let me." She took the bowstave from him before he could say anything further. "He was my enemy, not yours. He would drink the whole town dry and still be afflicted with what sickens him. I tasted it in his essence, and madness lurked in the fringes of his thirst. He would have exposed himself eventually because of his need. Staking is the kindest and quickest way to a release, for his kind." Then there was a squelch.

Tarl jumped as he felt the flutter of something rising into the air brush over his cheeks, then what smelled like molten iron and ash. A sensation of enlightenment and relief swept through his mind, as if the passing of the Bishop somehow freed his soul in its transition. Perhaps there was an afterlife for vampires? A sound of metal clanking onto flagstones told him where his hammer axe now lay, so he bent and felt around for it in the darkness. "What now?"

"We leave. It is done." She squeezed his arm gently. "Thank you for saving me."

"It's you who have saved me." Tarl handed her the war axe, then knelt. With his arms stretched, he felt around the cool stone floor until his fingertips touched the cloth of the boy's clothing. He curled his hands under the thin, flaccid body and pulled him close to his chest as he stood. "You saved him as well. Let's go."

She took his elbow and guided them upstairs, into the light.

CHAPTER 46 - REFUGE AND REFUGEES

Tarl carried the unconscious boy through Harfleur, Aioffe by his side, holding his weapons under her cloak. They blended in, covered in ash and blood like so many others. Just a husband and wife, their sickly son in arms, trailing towards a way out of the mess. A mournful look was easy to affect, and no-one gave them a second glance as they headed for the Leure gate. Everyone was too pre-occupied with their own problems.

They joined a queue of residents passing through the open gate and out, to freedom. En route, they overheard what people said about what had happened, which Aioffe translated for Tarl and whispered to him in English. The Harfleurian council, along with some hundred other citizens, had overruled the garrison commander, and conceded the township in return for a truce. King Henry, in a change of heart which pleased Tarl, had granted the townsfolk the opportunity to go, or become English subjects if a French army did not appear with re-enforcements in two days. After so long held captive, and still with a vein of resistance, many of the few hundred remaining residents chose to leave, their belongings bundled onto shoulders and heads for ease of travel. Any horses or mules had long since been eaten, so carts had to be pulled by hand.

Nobody believed help was coming, for only one ship had appeared with supplies in the last month. Harfleur had been abandoned by its mad King, but they would not stay and suffer under an Englishman with a tenuous claim.

As they passed under the crumbling arch, Tarl turned to Aioffe. "I wish we could go home."

She bit her lip. "I cannot." But her tone was less certain than it had been.

"I can't either."

"You could return to Wrye now that this war is over?"

He shook his head. "I don't know that it is, or will be. There is still time for Henry to gain more ground before winter sets in. The truce may not last, or he may keep us here until spring and carry on." He shrugged. "And, everything is different now. I'm different. And you, well, you are clearly different, but that's not the bad thing I stupidly thought it was."

His mouth dried, but he needed to tell her now, before he lost the chance again. He stopped walking. "Aioffe, I was frightened of your difference." He hung his head, but she touched his arm.

"You are different to me as well. If I had never met you, I would never have known what it is to feel anything other than..." she paused. "A hunger for more." She looked down at the boy in his arms. "If you and Benediet had not shown me what it is like to live in your world, I would never have felt such things. Tasted emotions. Known what it is to live freely, to face death, and then mourn."

"Mourn?" It seemed such a peculiar thing to say, but her words invited Tarl somehow, if he could just find the right words to tell her.

"Benediet lost his family and he suffered. You don't suffer if you have not loved. The person is just absent, no longer present. I had never loved before," her blue eyes flicked to his. "So I never had any reason to fear the loss of something, or to be driven to protect it so much. Even if," she smiled, "for my love, for the one I love, I had to stay away."

His lips rose. "I think... I might love you too," Tarl said, surprised at how easy it was to say those particular words to her. His soul soared as she turned her eyes up to his, her smile matching his own.

Aioffe pulled her hood up over her head so her face was obscured as she leaned towards him. As their lips touched over the boy in his arm, the heat of her surged through his body like warm honey. Tarl could hardly draw breath. His pulse throbbed and he ached to hold her closer.

Yet this was not the place for anything more than sealing what had been said. His cheeks flushed hot as she pulled away from him. Vivid blue eyes burned into his, silently acknowledging the desire, but the kiss itself reminded them both of the danger of public affection.

He lifted his head and whispered, "While you were gone, life felt empty. But I hoped, and when I found the heart arrowhead you left, that hope kept me going."

"I hoped too, even in the darkest of times. Perhaps that is the essence of love?"

They smiled gently at each other, then carried on walking steadily along the track outside of town, not really knowing where it would lead, but, not caring. Aioffe's skin glowed only slightly beneath its chalky ash coating. They kept stealing glances at each other as their stride seemed to fall into synchrony. Aioffe barely stumbled at all, and Tarl's rapid heartbeat eased with every footstep together. As dusk fell, and they put some distance between them and the people trailing behind them, his chest felt less constricted.

"I think," he said, as they reached a dam in the river, "it is your capacity to love which sets you apart from all others. Not your wings, or glow, or anything else which your kind are. But you are open to everything, all human experiences. And all whilst having to hide what you are. You even took care of this lad, without knowing him."

He paused, then laid Benediet down on by the side of the riverbank. The child, barely conscious, turned over in the long grass, nestling himself into a more comfortable position to sleep.

His eyelids fluttered as Aioffe stroked his brow and muttered in his own language, "Rest, Benediet, we are safe."

Tarl continued, "I knew someone who loved that kindly once." He drew in a deep breath. "My mother. She was different. A special healer of sorts. What she did, though, was heal through care. She had potions, and maybe magic of some sort, I don't know. Her main cure for everyone was love."

He gazed out across the battlefield, wisps of smoke still marking the smouldering remains of the siege weapons. "When they accused her of witchery, she tried to tell them. Tried to say her actions were done in the Lord's name. They didn't believe her." He swallowed. "And I couldn't protect her. They wouldn't take the word of a boy, no matter how much I prayed for them to believe me. Those in charge, those who accused her, then cast her out of our village. When she refused, and people shied away from her loving care, she took her own life. As if that would prove she was normal. She walked into the sea, then must have been dragged under by the tide."

A tear fell down his cheek, leaving a white line where it cleaned away the dust. He choked, the memory of it still fresh to him. "They found her body washed up on the beach the next day. But she left us. Left me. I wanted her to be absolved, cleansed, so I had her buried. Which left a debt which I stole to pay off. And I thought, if I could just get her soul blessed, then it might lift the curse of her final sin."

"Her sin was to die?"

Hair fell over his eyes as he shook his head. "Taking her own life was the sin, in the eyes of the Church. There was nothing else she ever did which she had to be ashamed of."

"That was what you wanted the Bishop to do? Bless her soul so she could stay in the graveyard?"

"I didn't know then, what I think now. It was her grave you covered in forget-me-nots, when we first met. I should have said this before. Now, everything is different. When you interrupted me in the act of stealing, I was cross, but I see now that it was a blessing. You opened my eyes to what was real and what isn't, and yet I blamed you. For revealing the truth. For being different, like my mother." He sighed and ran his hand over his face. "My past is a burden you should not have to bear."

"I don't bear the burden. It's you who carries it with you. It is grief, I know that now. I saw it with Benediet. The sadness and loss is like a stone which grows heavier the more you bear it. Until you put it down."

Turning his head sideways to look at her, the knot in his stomach rose into his throat. "I cannot."

But she looked away. "Just as I cannot fly away from my past, I suppose."

The river babbled, filling the silence between them as they sat in contemplation.

"How did Benediet lay down his burden?" Tarl asked.

Aioffe's lips lifted. "Surviving was hard enough. But we found a common purpose, and that distracted him enough for his grief to pass. He needed food, and there was none."

"The carrots I saw?"

She nodded. "He wanted to do more, we both did, to keep the French going. So they could fight for their homes." Glancing up and down the track, a few people plodded ahead of them, yet more straggled behind. "The homes they now leave. But they had that in common, at the time. A reason to continue fighting, even if it was futile."

"Should we have stayed? For him?"

Aioffe shook her head. "It was very hard for Benediet to live in the place where his family lived. I can't go back, and I don't think he would want to either. I wonder if, after a death, everyone needs a fresh start. He wouldn't get one in Harfleur."

"Maybe we should have a common purpose then," Tarl

replied. "Maybe you are right and this voyage was the fresh start I didn't realise I needed. Certainly, we cannot go home, either of us. So we should find a new home. Together."

"I'm not ready to call one place home again. Not yet." She looked at him from the side of her eyes, then her gaze rested on Benediet again. "But he needs stability. Continuity and safety so he can grow up into a man." She sighed.

"We cannot take care of him, not like he needs. A boy needs a family. People more established to give him a chance at life. A trade. Security."

"Perhaps we should be the ones to find that for him?" Aioffe said. "I'd be sad to leave him, but happier to know that he would be taken care of." She leaned back onto the grass, her eyes lifting to the sky. "He should not have to live a secretive life, which mine will always be if I stay amongst humans. It's a challenge too much to ask of a child. I understand now. I placed you into that position, which I should never have done."

Tarl's hand cupped her head as he laid down next to her. "Aioffe, I don't blame you at all. You were forced into exposing yourself to me by Father McTavish. A man. A vampire, who should have known better, but wanted to humiliate you. I kept your secret because of fear, but now I keep it out of love."

She turned in his arms and nestled into him. "I know. And I thank you for keeping it."

"Besides, you keep my secrets too. Who else knows about my murky past? My crimes? But, we do know some people now. Friends who have helped, and might know of a safe place for Benediet."

Aioffe thought for a moment. "Agnes…"

"Doesn't have children."

"Do you think she'd take one in? He's very keen on sheep."

Tarl smiled. "It sounds like the beginning of a plan."

Their smile was interrupted by a loud stomach gurgle. They

turned to see Benediet had awoken. He blinked at them then glanced at his belly.

"He's always hungry," Aioffe laughed. "Did I mention that?"

Tarl stood and held out his hand to help Aioffe up. "I imagine there'd be a feast at the camp tonight. I'd like to see how John and Alf fare as well." This morning's muster felt like an age ago, and he hadn't eaten himself all day.

Benediet sat up, frowned at Tarl who promptly beamed at him. Bemused, the boy turned his face to Aioffe. "Is he an angel as well?"

She shook her head and laughed before she replied in French as well. "No, he's my husband." She knelt beside him and lifted up his hair. The bite marks on his neck had scabbed over, but he was still alarmingly pale. "Let me wash this away," she rubbed at the dried blood. "Then we'll go and find some food for you."

His eyes widened. "Where?"

"You can come with us, to King Henry's camp. Don't worry, you will be safe with us. Harfleur belongs to him now."

He looked downcast.

Aioffe touched his arm. "You don't have to go anywhere if you don't want to. You are free to go back to Harfleur, or come with us to the camp. We might even find some hot food there."

Benediet's eyes widened and his expression showed how torn he was by the decision between food and everything that he knew. Tarl crouched down next to Aioffe and pointed at the stream of refugees leaving Harfleur. Catching the boy's eye, he tightened his lips with sorrow.

"Tarl also knows what it is to leave home because your family has died," Aioffe said softly in French. "But, like you, he has angels to guide him, always."

Benediet's wary gaze wandered over his face, studying the shadows of it in the evening light while he decided whether to trust the stranger.

Aioffe stood, then stepped over to the riverbank and dipped the corner of her cloak in the fresh water. She returned and scrubbed at Benediet's neck. He squirmed away, but she persisted until his neck was clean of blood, then she ruffled his hair so it fell covering the wound.

"Tarl will give you a lift, and you can be our look out soldier? Maybe you'll spot the food before smelling it." He grinned back up at her.

She turned to Tarl. "Can you carry him on your shoulders?" She said in English.

Obligingly, he pivoted on his heels and presented his back to the lad.

Aioffe lifted Benediet onto Tarl's shoulders and up he stood. The boy clutched at Tarl's long blond hair as they loped across the   fields   towards   Henry's   army.

CHAPTER 47 - HARFLEUR IN THE HORIZON

A week and a half later, Tarl and Aioffe stood on Harfleur's harbour wall and waved across the sea to Benediet, who furiously waved back from a ship's deck. They were both delighted, and relieved, at how quickly Benediet had taken to Agnes and John. John's fever had broken almost at the first sight of the child, so the pair doted on him as a lucky charm. Benediet communicated his excitement and relief at new found security and a ready supply of food with in a peculiar mixture of gesture, French, and was picking up Welsh with surprising ease.

Within days of knowing him, the childless couple offered him a home in their rolling countryside, with plenty of animals to enchant. The prospect of fields, plentiful food and an adventure crossing the sea, had enthralled the lad as much as the idea of living near the huge, safe castle at Beaumaris.

Perched on Agnes's shoulders as she leaned against the ship's railings clutching his ankles, he mimed shooting a bow at Tarl, who grinned. The boy, along with Agnes, John and several thousand of the sick English army, were set to return across the channel. Agnes's grey hair whipped around her face as the breeze picked up, filling the sails of a small ship bound for Wales and a new beginning for Benediet.

Tarl had been ordered to stay, still under his indenture to serve the King for a few months yet. Not needed for harvest and, as an able-bodied bowman and one of only a few remaining smiths, he was hard pressed to refuse the order.

After discussion with Aioffe, he agreed to see the rest of the campaign out, even though the prospect of more battles seemed to silence him whenever she talked of combat. As they watched the sails approach the horizon, the very idea of violence paled into insignificance compared to saying goodbye to the boy they had both grown fond of. Although he was bound for safety, he left behind an aching scar on their hearts.

"I wonder how many sheep he'll chase?" Aioffe said as they turned to leave.

"Enough to cause John some trouble," Tarl chuckled. "But they'll need his help on the farm. John would struggle otherwise, even though his wound healed better after your care."

He took her arm as they stepped over the rubble and down to the street. They wandered back towards the English camp, hand in hand. A makeshift road had been created over the swampland, but the landscape, like the town, was permanently scared by the long siege. Forests had been felled, the fields left fallow, and fresh meat was scarce. Once the cannon fire ceased, the gunpowder fog lifted within a few days, unveiling the true extent of Henry's destruction. The river flowed once again through its original course through Harfleur, its clear water washing away the immediate threat of doom and disease which had clouded the town.

"They say the King will leave a garrison of men here," Aioffe said as they neared their tent.

He grimaced. "From what I saw, there's barely anything left worth defending." Tarl's fingers clutched his satchel. "How much longer can Henry fight on with so few?"

She pulled the flap back and crawled inside. Emerging a few seconds later, with the bag of blunt arrowheads and a whetstone, she sat down to sharpen them. He crossed his legs and dropped to the grass beside her, then his shoulders drooped.

Before she could ask what saddened him, he rolled his eyes and said, "Oh no."

Aioffe stiffened as she followed his gaze across the field. Ap Tudor strode straight towards their tent, his shoulders back and positively flouncing. She hoped he would have been aboard the ship and on his way home, but apparently not.

"There you are, Smith!" He clicked his fingers at Tarl. "Hop to. This tent should be down and packed. We leave in an hour."

"For where?" Tarl seemed intentionally surly both in tone and expression.

"The King marches on Calais, and we are to scout ahead."

Tarl shook his head. "We'll travel with the main army."

Ap Tudor's lips twisted. "You are my man. A common thief paid and protected by my good name, and you'll do what I say."

It appeared that Ap Tudor had risen in rank as various commanders fell sick or left for England. Tarl glanced at Aioffe, whose lips pressed together as if she held back a retort.

Ap Tudor swept his arm towards the valley. "We are to ride on and inform my liege of any problems ahead. Scout for crossing points, and alert him to any French troops in our path." He pointed at Tarl's bow, where the tip poked out from the bottom of the tent, then at Aioffe. "I'll need protection, and your wife, I've heard, can now speak the language."

He mock bowed towards her. "After the miracle of her return." His head tilted up to meet Aioffe's stare. He leered. "I wonder how many times you spread your legs to secure that privilege?"

Aioffe gasped, her mouth falling open.

Tarl jumped to his feet, fist already clenched around an arrowhead. He pointed it at Ap Tudor and glared. "You do not speak of my wife, or any woman, that way," he spat.

Ap Tudor's eyes glinted, then he held up his hands and stepped back. "What other explanation can there be? A pretty woman like her…. Did you never wonder?"

Tarl strode forward and jabbed the arrow's point under Ap Tudor's throat. "Because that's the price someone like you would extract?" He grabbed the Welshman's lapel and twisted so it choked.

Squirming against his grasp, Ap Tudor's face flushed with fury. He gurgled, "Get your hands off me."

Aioffe noticed a change in Tarl. The whites of his eyes flared and his head whipped aside. His clenched hand dropped, then he staggered a few paces away. Aioffe pushed herself up and rushed over.

"Tarl, what is it?"

His eyes screwed shut and he brought his hand up, as if to shield them.

Ap Tudor sneered. "That's right, you should be ashamed. Show some respect to your betters."

Aioffe put her hand on Tarl's arm - he was shaking!

"Leave us," she ordered over her shoulder.

"What's wrong with him?" Ap Tudor pointed a wavering finger. "Is he sick? It makes no difference, we must depart." He pulled back from them both then straightened his jacket. "Get yourself together, bowman. Do you think you are the only one who suffers the flux?"

Tarl hunched over, clutching his head in his hands. Aioffe crouched down next to him and rubbed his wrist. "My love…"

He shook her hand off. "Don't. They'll go in a moment."

"But…" Her fingers had brushed the orange in his Lifeforce though, and she knew something had irreparably changed in him. Aioffe swallowed the wave of helplessness which washed over her as she stood. Why did he no longer want her assistance when he suffered so? She recalled that same tinge when he had injured the Bishop. "Just breathe," she said, her voice low.

As his chest dragged the air in, expelling it in uneven gasps, she stayed with him, hoping her presence alone would also calm him. When he reached up to grasp her fingers, she knew he was back with her.

"I'll start packing," she said. The road ahead of them might be long, like the nights he spent calling, shouting in his sleep. Maybe then, under the stars, he would tell her what troubled him.

CHAPTER 48 - AGINCOURT

For two and a half weeks, Henry's army, or what remained of it, quick-marched North, often long into the night. For speed, the lumbering cannon carts, wagons with supplies and those too ill to keep up were left behind. Bowmen, nimble of foot and carrying only what they could strap to their backs or sling over a horse, made up the bulk of the force.

The army's progress up the coastline to re-enforce the sanctuary of English lands around the port of Calais was frustrated by French troops harrying them from across the Somme river. Bridges were destroyed and rain swelled the waters to impassable. Henry and his men were forced to divert inland for many days, to find a suitable fording point to cross. Then, over two-hundred miles from Harfleur, possibly more by Aioffe's calculations, their approach to Calais was blocked again.

The night before last, she had flown ahead of the English while they slept, and discovered what lay in wait for them. After counting fields of tents stretching further than a man on the ground could see, she predicted the Dauphin's forces were three times the size of Henry's. Dismayed by the overwhelming numbers that amassed, she flew further afield, for miles across the countryside, where she spotted more troops. She calculated this second army was only several days' march from the French encampment.

Worse, the re-enforcements brought with them heavy

weaponry, cannons and catapults, similar to those which had battered Harfleur. And Henry's siege weapons were either on a ship or left behind.

All of this information she told Tarl, who relayed it in terse terms to Ap Tudor, who had then claimed the knowledge as his own before the King. Henry was minded to take a stand, to force an engagement before the other French troops could join the Dauphin. The idea initially met with opposition from his advisors, but the King's decision was final.

The English made camp on the outskirts of a small village called Azincourt, close to where the French had made their base. That evening, the men were instructed not to drink ale or make merry, but to rest and pray, in readiness for the morning. Although many wished to fortify themselves with wine and ale, the majority heeded their commander's advice and bedded down to sleep while they could. It was rumoured that the King himself wandered through the tents that night, offering solace and encouragement to those souls still plagued by flux or awake with anxiety.

Overnight, the rain fell heavy for hours, soaking anything and anyone not under canvas cover. By daybreak, the camp's mood was distinctly tetchy. Uncertainty, illness and nerves wrestled against their relief that the ordeal might soon be over, as orders were calmly issued to don armour and ready weapons. The autumn sun hung low in the sky, and a damp chill lingered to stiffen tired bones. While the King awaited the return of his dawn messengers, who again offered the Dauphin a diplomatic resolution, Tarl's cent was ordered to the western woods, which overlooked a large, ploughed field in the gully between forests.

Aioffe helped to strap him into the padded jerking. He left the white jupon off, as instructed, to better his camouflage. Both their faces pinched and pale with nerves. As he pulled on his boots, he tried to reassure her of his intention to come back to her, of the soundness of the King's plan, and of his faith the Lord God would strengthen his bow, but his words sounded hollow. Perhaps he meant for the platitudes to comfort himself, she wondered, but she didn't voice her doubts to him. Instead, she kissed the blade of her bone-handled knife and passed it to him. He tucked it between leather and calf with a smile.

"It saved me before," he said. "I hope I don't have to use it again, but at least I will have a part of you near me."

Her lips trembled. "I want it back, and you. Promise me?"

"I promise to love you for as long as my heart beats, my bow bends and the stars shine." He took her hand and kissed the back of it. "Will you wait for me here, where it's safe?"

Because of the lump in her throat, she could only hang her head and nod rather than meet his eyes. There was no need to say that promises might not be kept. They both knew that. Only destiny knew what the day would bring. While still under the cover of canvas, they kissed goodbye with such tenderness her soul soared.

"Bring back my heart and knife," she whispered, while his face was still close to hers. "And may your Lord God bless you with good fortune today and forever." Her fingers clenched his biceps as he embraced her once again, his hands smoothing down the wings on her back in a soft caress.

When he pulled away, he brushed off the tear which rolled down her cheek with his thumb and brought it to his lips. He smiled crookedly. "An angel weeps for me. That's all the blessing I need."

Yet, as soon as he left, she realised she could not sit and bide time while a battle raged in her absence. She cared little about the overall outcome of the fight over land ownership. Destiny would settle that matter for the humans. But Tarl's involvement made the fight personal. The not knowing of his fate, when she had lived with the same question for so many weeks while trapped in Harfleur, was too much for her to ignore.

With every intention of returning once the battle was over to be here for him, she pulled on her cloak. Keeping her head covered and low, she hurried back to a wooded hill several miles away so she could fly up and watch from above.

"Why do they wait?" Aioffe said to herself, as she stared down at the silver mass of helmets gathered in the mouth of the valley. She estimated tens of thousands of men and horses amassed like a swarm ready to swoop over the countryside and swamp the invaders. They seemed disorganised to her. Clumps of people shuffled around, as if being ordered from one place to another, as if they weren't sure who's lead to follow.

At the other end of the field, the English stood patiently in far lesser numbers. A few thousand bowmen lined up behind the knights and foot soldiers, too far away for even their long range to hit the French troops. But, several thousand more longbow archers hid alongside Tarl in the woodlands.

Her wings tired from hovering on high through the morning hours while nothing happened below. She glanced again, through the low clouds, towards the western woods where Tarl waited. She couldn't spot him from this height. Hidden inside the forests which banked both sides of the muddy field, the tangle of bare branches obscured the true number of English bowmen in their brown jerkins from their enemy. The planned deception made her twitchy. Without much armour, the archers were vulnerable to attack - should the French discover them.

"Hold your fire," the word came down the line. Tarl's hands shook. The hours waiting in near silence played havoc with his attempts to push aside the images from his mind. Here, on the wooded incline, at least there was less chance of him freezing in a face-to-face fight. But the French numbers Aioffe had reported wrapped around his chest, tightening it with fear. He had never before wished so much that his wife was wrong.

He peered out from the trunk he leaned upon and glanced down the field. A wall of armoured horses, chain mailed and blinkered, pranced in front of thousands of suits of armour. Neat lines of crossbows, wound and loaded, pointed skyward. They were pressed together so tightly, he couldn't even make out individual faces. A choppy grey steel sea, which would surge into battle below like a dammed river released. But they hadn't moved either, for several hours.

He breathed out and lowered his bow. Then, a platoon of English footsoldiers, wearing only light armour, were led forward by a commander atop a slim destrier. Tarl's hand gripped the bowstave and raised it once more.

"Wait," the whisper came down the line.

"Tis a j-j-joke," Jones next to him said. "They'll be s-s-slaughtered."

In disbelief, they watched the troop steadily advance across the field, stopping just out of reach of the crossbows. The men at arms lowered their pole-axes and started jeering, cat calling.

By late morning, Aioffe surveyed the French army spread out like a skirt over the countryside. They bunched together tightly as the waist, filling the narrow end of a ploughed field, and flared in a fan over the grasslands behind.

Aioffe's fists clenched as she stared down at the Dauphin's force amassed below. Perhaps she had miscounted? They now appeared nearly four times the number of English troops. Mounted knights, men at arms, and cross-bowmen, arranged in vanguard units, awaited the command to attack. She spotted the colourful hats of pages and servants as they circulated, offering refreshments as if this was a mere pageant.

But it wasn't. It was a day which hung heavy with the probability of many deaths.

It mystified her why the French had not simply swept across the field and swarmed over the far smaller group of lightly armoured English foot soldiers, in front of a paltry few mounted knights who waited patiently and attentively for Henry's command.

Her eyes widened with horror. From above, a platoon of men advanced to the middle of the field and looked like a small, brackish pond, when the lake, dammed by the bottleneck of the landscape at the other end, glinted and looked fit to burst.

"They cannot hope to win," she said to the sun as it peaked in the grey sky. The rain-clouds may have emptied themselves overnight, but the late October day remained overcast. St Crispin's day, she'd heard them call it, after the saint whose shoes and cross Tarl had claimed to own all those months ago. The co-incidence of the personal connection and this day of reckoning did not escape her notice, but she tried not to read into it as she studied the action below.

The French ignored the English jeers. Instead, they sent a volley of crossbow bolts towards them. The Englishmen's laughter reached her as the arrows short range fell far shy of hitting any of them. Several mounted knights, commanders under the Dauphin she presumed, huddled together before cantering back to stand in front of their troops. The prince himself stayed apart from the mass, watching from his white mount and surrounded by priests in their official robes.

The small group of foot soldiers in the battlefield stepped a few paces backward and resumed their challenging taunts. She dipped, just enough to catch the English cusses shouted across the field. The straight ranks of Frenchmen rippled as a few men broke the line and strode forward, brandishing their swords and crossbows as if they couldn't bear the insults any longer.

When they had lurched close enough to shout at the spaced out individuals, the English danced around, mocking and cussing as if they had no fear of their imminent demise. The few crossbow bolts launched were easily dodged as the lithe guards had plenty of warning before the short range shafts landed harmlessly on the ground. The archer then had to take a few minutes to reload and re-crank the weapon. Those with drawn swords were entirely ineffective from a distance, and resorted to waving them around as they stumbled up the boggy field. Few others dared to break rank and advance to support their colleagues without the official order being given.

Aioffe almost smiled. The brave Englishmen refused to be cowed before the overwhelming force which deafened their shouts with curses of their own. After a minute or two, during which time not one of them had been injured, the small band was led away by their mounted officer. They leisurely sauntered back up the field as if without a care they turned their backs on the threat. The English line remained where it was, calm and alert. Silent and… small.

A trumpeted command sounded, and the French raised their weapons. The air filled with noise as the line of knights and foot soldiers, heavy in their armour, clanked forwards in a surging wave of steel.

But then, Aioffe realised why Henry had been so insistent the battle should happen today. It wasn't only because of the threat of another large army joining the French - it was because of the rain and the landscape. The soil, churned and free from plant roots, pulled at the boot. Within minutes, the first swathe of soldiers, and their horses, fell foul of the puddled clay. With their feet clogged by sticky mud, every step grew more tiresome. Worse came with the push from behind, as more and more units entered the field, buoyed up by the release of being sent to fight for their country.

In the woods, the shouts and clanks drifted away on the wind as if irrelevant. Every bowman heeded the order. "Wait…"

Impatiently, Tarl held his bow string by his cheek. He could feel the sweat building in his palms.

Then, finally, the peep of whistles sounded through the trees, rippling through the woodland like a chorus of birds.

"Release!"

Arrow after arrow pelted from both sides of the field. The air a cloud of white goose feathers, whispering death to those beneath. Tarl did not need to take aim, for the plan was for a hailstorm of steel tips to pierce the heads of the French once they were bogged down. He emptied his first and second quiver within minutes, then had to pause to open the lid of the next.

As he fumbled with the leather strap, he glanced through the trunks to the battlefield, awash with silver and brown bumps. The English baiting party had retreated, and a thousand long bowmen were leisurely picking the front wave of French off over their heads from the end of the field. All around him, the air whistled as the fletching flew.

To save time, he unbuckled the lids of all the quivers upright against the tree and piled them up at his feet. Then, he pulled, aimed and shot into the quagmire with a rhythm which felt almost calming.

The carnage below made Aioffe's fingers tingle. Wisps of Lifeforce danced above the battlefield, but she resisted the temptation to pull them towards herself. It was impossible to differentiate between human and creature races. Almost lost amongst the vibrant, crazed strands of daemon and glittering shards of witches were the reds, golds, and orange of humankind.

The expectancy of waiting all morning was finally released into the frenzy of bloodlust.

But so many delicate tendrils were cut short, fizzling into nothing, when the longbows rained havoc. Still more warriors flooded into the killing field. Tumbling, stumbling, over the bloodied bodies of their countrymen. Weapons pointed forwards at first, then flagged as their bearers tired with the effort of movement through the slippery ground.

Henry's battle plan was a triple trap, she saw now. If the first was the pincer-like position of his troops on three sides, two of which were hidden from sight until the moment they fired their fatal shots, then the bottle-neck of entry to the battlefield was the second. Heavy armour which was supposed to intimidate, to protect in hand to hand combat, reduced the French forces to slow-moving targets as they lumbered forward. It offered little to no protection against the piercing power and range of English longbows. The mud itself became the third trap - every knight or horse's step developed into a muscle-wrenching, tiring effort to pull out of. The rain overnight saturated the freshly ploughed earth, and Henry had learned the lesson at Harfleur's swamp.

More and more men at arms rushed onto the battlefield, certain their number would overwhelm Henry's sickened army. Clambering over their comrades, a blanket of arrows from the woods pierced them from the sides. The pile of bodies rose until the middle of the field itself resembled a child's daubed painting, smeared with red and brown.

Someone must have directed the longbows to cease firing because the woodland spray drizzled out.

Barely a moment later, Henry's trumpets ordered his remaining troops to advance. The line of soldiers cautiously advanced. Lighter, and largely on foot, they waited for the lucky few to make it up the field before they cut them down with the ease of the well rested. Sensing victory, they pushed deeper into the field, dealing a swift end to tired French warriors caught in the mud. The thuds and yells of pain, the screams of broken horses - a slaughter began in earnest and it sickened her. As the tendrils which overhung the field blackened, then snuffed out, she could bear to watch no more.

Aioffe twisted her head aside, glimpsed the beaming sun and thought of Tarl, her gentle man. How ill suited his character was to combat of this nature. What if, now the longbows had stopped, the forest bowmen were ordered to enter the fray as well? Her heart raced, wishing she could see where he was. To tell him not to go. He was already crippled by nightmares. Further fighting at close quarters would no doubt afflict him even more. Or fatally.

Her terror at the prospect chilled her blood, stilling her wingbeat. Distracted by the vision of a future without him in it, she felt herself falling. Her wings paralysed when the full horror of the possibility of losing him in the carnage on the field rushed through her body.

She gasped as her eyes spotted flashes of brown brushing through the trees below, moving closer and closer as she dropped. An instinct for secrecy, buried deep within, overrode her frozen panic. Her wings instinctively began to beat against the air, swooping her up again. A cool breeze as she flew soothed her brow, until she dared to glance down anew.

The archers in the woods beneath stalked forward, towards the battlefield. She had to land. She had to know where he was. The sudden yearning to be closer to him was too much to bear, and worth the risk of exposure.

Her eyes scoured the countryside, searching for a nearby place to drop down. She glanced at French camp, across the empty fields where the army had gathered. She blinked, not sure if her sight deceived her, and looked again.

A snake of men, armed with crossbows and swords, stealthily entered the west woodland.

Tarl and Jones ran out of arrows. "W-what are we supposed to do now?" Jones asked. "It's a b-bloody mess down there."

Hammer axe in hand, Tarl's heart thumped as he knew full well what their likely next order would be. Biting his lip, Tarl looked around for their commander.

A blood-curdling scream from behind sent shivers down his spine. He whipped about, axe raised.

From deep within the trees, he heard the crunch of footsteps snapping the twigs. Poised on the balls of his feet, his eyes darted between the trunks.

Then, from out of nowhere, a crossbow bolt slammed through Jones's head. His body crumpled to the ground.

Instinct kicked in and Tarl ducked. Hands reached to protect himself as he curled himself into a ball. Crouched against the trunk, he held his breath and tried not to look at the stubby shaft sticking out of his friend's skull. With a thumping heart, he listened, but his blood rushed in his ears and drowned out any warning he might have had.

The force of the arrow jolted him forwards, sprawling into the leaves. Then, a terrific pain spread, lightening fast, through his shoulder. The breath he had been holding puffed out of him. Cheek to the forest floor, he dared not move as scruffy black boots stepped closer. A grunt as they paused by his still head.

He gazed vacantly ahead. A shadow crossed his eyeline. Tarl's fingers tightened around the axe. The dark gaze of a previous assailant flashed into his mind, taunting him. Daring him to move yet his limbs would not, could not, obey.

A boot disappeared from view. Something smacked down on his skull.

Agony circled his head, clouding his vision. His eyes rolled back.

The boots shuffled off, rustling leaves in their wake.

As his blood pulsed slowly into the ground, a rainbow of bright colours shimmered before his eyelids. Tarl prayed as he slipped into the darkness.

CHAPTER 49 - UNINTENTIONAL GIFT

Aioffe landed by the side of a stone hut on the edges of the forest. She glanced around, but saw no-one. Yet, the dark stench of death hung in the air.

She ran towards the source. Brushing past branches, flying leaves caught in her cloak and whirled in her back draft. Every sense she had was alert and tingling to aid her quest.

Whenever she heard a noise, she dodged, and chose another path between trees. Her gaze swept through the forest, searching as she followed towards the smell.

She encountered a body, an Englishman whose features she recognised, lying face up. An arrow embedded in his chest, white hands clenched around the shaft. Her chest tightened, and she stopped to check the cool skin of his neck. There was nothing she could do for him, but the latent warmth in his body told her he had not long passed.

The enemy was close. She detected sour grape on breath and the leathery sweat laced with garlic lingered in the cool air. Every twig snap betrayed their location.

Stepping carefully over mossy roots, then sprinting between trunks, she brought her breathing under control. Her body felt fluid and alive, at one with the woodland. She was the predator, not they. But her quarry was not the enemy - she hunted her husband. Creeping on, she spotted more bodies. The disturbed leaves splashed with blood signalled a scuffle which had ended badly for both.

The noise of the battle in the field over yonder was harder to ignore: intermittent clangs and curses, gurgles and cries. Her mind tried to filter them out, concentrate on the whispers instead.

She snuck up behind two Frenchmen, who stopped to reload their bows. One urged the other to hurry. The reply was brief, and telling. "There's no point. The day is lost."

Aioffe leaned her head against the trunk and closed her eyes until she heard the soldiers move off. Above her, the branches rustled the few leaves clinging still. She opened her eyes to watch them fall. Yellowed, curled, they drifted on the breeze, and reminded her of the frailty of human life. How quickly it passed. Her heart thudded, overwhelmed for a moment by the task of trying to locate one man amongst thousands. She had to find Tarl. That one life mattered the most to her. If it took all day and night, she must see him again.

As hot, wet tears spilled down her cheek, she brushed them away with the back of her hand. She tipped her head and sniffed in a deep breath. A faint, familiar whiff teased her nose. Was it her knife's handle? She inhaled again. Tarl's distinctive scent, the citrus tinge to his Lifeforce when he feared, embedded in the grooves of the bone grip. Alongside it, notes of heather and fir - her own unique marker.

Allowing the smell to roll around her nostrils, she then opened her mouth a little, and drew in the air. Circling around, she stopped where the taste of him was strongest.

Then, she pushed herself up, gathered her skirts and pelted in its direction.

Tracking his path, she saw first the strands of his Lifeforce. They hovered, orange twisted with black, at the base of a huge ash. His body sprawled over the roots, face down. She gasped, seeing then the bolt sticking out from his shoulder. Then, as she dropped to her knees beside him, she noticed the bloody, muddy wound to his head.

But, he was still alive! Just. She touched his cheek, her fingers sweeping away a strand of hair plastered against it as she felt his aura. Death had already gripped him in its clutches. The pooled blood the reason why. There was no way of knowing how much of his essence had returned to the earth. Black tendrils still wrestled with Tarl's strong orange ones, tugging them down to the earth in a battle for life itself. He had little time left.

She rocked herself over his body, keening as her arms reached down the length of his back as if they would sweep away the pain he bore. His still warm skin reacted under her touch. Leg muscles began jerking, shaking. She blinked as the orange strands seemed to tussle with renewed vigour.

She could not give up on him, not now. Tarl was her truest love. He couldn't leave her!

He groaned, his lips a bluish tint. She stroked his face again, whispering, "My love, I am here. Do not fear." Whether he heard her or not, she couldn't tell, but it calmed her to say the reassurance. A crease of pain whitened his face. The strands wavering around them darkened as death tightened its clasp once more.

Benediet's father had been closer, she recalled, so there remained a chance for Tarl. She must act fast, or lose him.

She reached down to retrieve her knife from his boot and glanced quickly around the woodland. A few feet away, Jones had not been as lucky. His face was white as his murky eyes stared lifelessly between another arrow. No Lifeforce strands hovered over his corpse.

No-one to help her, but no-one to witness what she had to do.

Her hands glowed faintly as she used the blade to cut his jerkin open. Then, she tore the linen shirt beneath, exposing his bare chest. The fabric splayed out over her knees like wings. Although blood seeped from a graze to his forehead, it gushed from the hole in his back. The arrow's shaft had not punctured all the way through and stuck out between spine and shoulder blade. Mindful that with every minute and movement his life dripped away, she had no choice but to haul his torso over so he rested on his side, with the arrow and injury close to her knees. Resting his head on her lap, she examined the wound to his shoulder.

Tarl's eyelids fluttered, as if he sensed her intentions.

Her lips tightened as her fingers parted the wound. With her index and middle fingers, she felt inside him for the arrowhead. As her fingers curled around it, the sharp blade sliced her fingertip. It only hurt a little, nothing to what Tarl must suffer. Her digit wriggled past the slow pulse of a vein and down the side of a tang.

The broadhead's tip was embedded in rib bone.

Her heart hammered as she considered how to remove it. Because the arrow had been spinning as it entered Tarl, to retract the head through his back, she would have to twist it, or the long tangs would catch on the shoulder blade and vein.

Her only alternative was to push the entire arrow and shaft through his chest. Although this would make another cut to his front, she decided it was the safer option.

It took only a small amount of pressure to lift the tip free of its bone trap, but her sliced fingertip throbbed as she manoeuvred the sharp edges to line up with the gap between his ribs. She bit her lip as she pushed on the wood to carefully guide the arrow through his shoulder. He moaned when his skin punctured, then sliced cleanly as the arrowhead emerged. The smooth, short shaft followed, unfettered by fletching. As soon as it was free of him, she tossed the arrow away.

A well of blood gushed out through both holes. To stem the flow at the front and back of his torso, she pinched the skin together with her fingers.

The blood seeped through her grip, no matter how tightly she held the wounds together. She heard his heartbeat slow. The dark wisps greyed, obscuring the paler orange as Tarl's essence oozed into the earth. His body felt heavy in her lap, as if he shrunk from her with every drop of blood lost.

Her ministrations weren't enough. She had to do more, give more.

She had never before restored a life, only bargained a tiny fragment of her immortal life to take the pain from an animal. It was a deal innately and silently made between differing Lifeforces. An endless cycle, a returning of essences necessary for regrowth older than time itself, which Aioffe operated within purely by instinct. Perhaps, if she were to reverse the wheel, though? Rather than take, she could return Lifeforce?

In a heartbeat, she accepted the cost to her which she knew must be paid for his life to continue.

Aioffe pushed down through her fingertips. Such was the pressure, her fingers almost embedded again within his flesh. Tipping her head back, she brought to mind everything pure and good about him. How he had rescued her from the priest in Wrye. His look of awe when he first saw her naked wings. How he held her secure when they rode through the waves from Wales... the gentle way he stroked her... the warmth of his gaze as he gathered her into his arms and held her. With every caress, every touch, his spirit bound himself to her, with care, acceptance and love. Her wings rose, the cloak falling between them, radiant in the early evening light.

Time lost all meaning as she poured her love for him down, into the wound, through his flesh so it might become as one with him, as much as he was now a part of her life. Breathing in, she pulsed as much of her own Lifeforce as she could into him. Her soul sang as she committed her entire being to saving his. She felt the pain and joy of their essences mingling. Her blood replenishing his body through the tiny cut in her finger. As it throbbed, his heartbeat against her palm grew stronger.

Only when her wings drooped and grazed the ground did she stop. Drained, she opened her eyes and looked down at him. In her lap, his eyes were wide open and blue, gazing up at her.

"What are you?" His voice was thick. He coughed, a bubble of blood popping out of his mouth along with red phlegm. "Who are you?"

"Do you not know me?" A smile touched her lips as she wiped the spittle away with her skirt.

He frowned, his head shuffled from side to side in her lap.

She glanced around as her heart sank. How could he not recognise her, after everything? How to explain? Her head span.

But it was not over.

Tarl suddenly jerked, arching his back. His hands shot out, grasping at the dry leaves atop the blood-soaked earth.

Aioffe's face fell. What had she done? Had she made him worse? With gentle hands, she felt around his head to the graze, which had stopped bleeding and seemed fine despite what must have been a heavy blow. She smudged a finger over the arrow site to see what lay beneath and frowned. The wound underneath the dried blood had healed completely. Only a slight and indented scar above his nipple remained to mark the story of his mortal injury. So what was wrong with him? Aioffe struggled to keep her thoughts focussed in her weakened state. Had something else, like a twig or leaf, been trapped inside his chest? Or maybe she'd damaged him when she pulled out the arrow?

His body relaxed as the spasm passed. Absorbed and dismayed as she tried to examine his chest and figure out what had happened, the gentle touch of his fingers against her jaw startled her.

"I do know you..."

Her quick grin split her face almost in two. "I should hope you do," she whispered. The relief was instant, and the band constricting her chest disappeared. "I'm your wife."

"My wife?"

"Well, sort of."

Once again, a shudder swept through him. His hand dropped. "So cold."

He shivered on her lap. She wrapped the remnants of his shirt over him, adding after the heavier weight of his down stuffed jerkin, but the tremors of fever continued.

The grey clouds of the afternoon had cleared overhead, and a chill crept into the air heralding a frost to fall. Only then did she notice the noise of battle had been replaced by the twitter of birds clacking in the branches. She gripped the edges of her cloak and wrapped it around them both like a tent, but it wasn't enough. His teeth still chattered together as he shook.

He was too weak to survive an autumn night. They could not stay here, on the open cold ground. Exposed. Undefended.

"I think, if you can, we need to find shelter. A fire, or something." Laying his head carefully on the leaves, she stood. The trunks wobbled. She pulled in a deep breath and waited for the dizziness to pass.

"Are you al-alright?" His words barely made it out between the chatters of his teeth.

She nodded and took a step. The more she moved, the better her head felt. She hoped the same would be true for him. After retrieving his satchel from where it fell, she slung it over her shoulder and tucked her knife into her belt, then slowly, carefully, helped Tarl to a stand. He brought a hand to his head, weaving slightly.

"Hold on to me," she said, wrapping her arms around his waist. "There's a hut over the brow. Maybe you'll recover faster with some rest."

They staggered through the trees, him leaning on her and gasping with exertion. Despite being so close to her, he still shivered. Every step seemed to torment him. He moaned and held his head as if it would burst. They had to stop frequently for him to catch his breath. At times, she saw he walked with his eyes screwed together, trusting her to lead him to safety. But his heartbeat was strong, and the wisps of his Lifeforce, although pale, wavered glittering about in her vision.

By the time they reached the hut close to where she had landed, the stars above pricked the black sky. The building was faintly lopsided, almost leaning into a tree trunk only a hand span away from the wall. An ivy creeper invaded the gap between a slate roof and rough stone walls.. Aioffe used her knife to lever off the rusty bolt on the door.

They stumbled inside. The windowless shack reeked of dung but was empty of any former inhabitants. Tarl leaned against the door frame while Aioffe took off her cloak and laid it on the ground. The semi-circle almost covered the earth floor, hiding the tree-root which had grown underneath, causing the masonry to crumble.

Tarl collapsed on the thick woollen warmth and curled himself into a ball.

"Rest now," she said, smoothing his brow and adjusting the jerkin so it covered him better. Aioffe darted outside again and rushed around the undergrowth to grab an armful of dry twigs and branches wherever she found them. Rushing back, she piled them in a corner. Her stomach tightened as she noticed Tarl's breathing labour as tremors rattled through his body.

She peeled some dried moss from the wall, then packed it into the base of the firewood. From his satchel, she plucked out the strike-a-light pouch she knew he always carried. Close to the fire, she laid out the kit. She struck the firestick onto the small flint and a spark flickered. Another strike, longer and with more pressure, produced a better spark, which landed on the charcloth square. The burnt linen caught as she blew and she laid it on the moss tinder. Within moments, the flames spread and began to lick around the twigs.

As the fire grew, casting dancing shadows across the stone walls, his shivers worsened. He wrapped his arms about himself, fingers splayed over his shoulder blades, knees drawn up on the cloak. He moaned, clawing at his back. His fingers tore at the linen as if it pained or weighed on him. Mumbling and incoherent, Tarl appeared to have little comprehension of where he was, or of her. He was instead trapped inside his own, delirious mind.

The flames weren't sufficient to burn away whatever ailed him, Aioffe realised, even though she could feel the difference in the hut's temperature. She didn't dare drag him much closer to the fire, but her fears grew as the minutes passed with little change. All around him, the tendrils wavered in an unfamilliar pattern, as if they didn't know which way to move. On his clothes, the blood and mud darkened, sticking to his skin as the fire dried his trauma onto him. Her heart raced as fast as her mind, wondering what else she could do.

His hand actions pinching and jerking at his shirt suggested he didn't want the fabric covering him. Perhaps, if heat could reach his skin more directly, the warmth might have more of an impact? Liberate him. She tugged off his top layers, exposing his chest. She was surprised to feel his skin was cool to the touch, yet he groaned as if he had a fever.

The coldness of his skin concerned her, like the chill of a gravestone. In her mind's eye, she envisaged the human burial grounds. The final and eternal solitude of a grave. Tears welled in her eyes. She could not bear for him to be so cold, so alone. Not when she burned with love for him.

Aioffe stripped. The satchel, wool skirt, jacket, and underskirts dropped to the ground and she emerged from her human disguise. Naked.

She crouched by his head and stroked his hair. Tarl's eyes

opened. His hand shook as he held it up towards her. "Angel," he whispered, his voice hoarse. "My angel."

Her wings beat softly, wafting the heat from the fire towards him. He beckoned her closer with deep blue eyes which glinted with yearning.

"Come," he said. "Be mine."

Although she wasn't certain if it was him or the delirium talking, her soul soared with his acceptance of her. She lay down, as had been her intention, anyway. Her skin's glowing heat felt hot against his chill as she pressed her chest into his back and curled her legs into his. As her arms wrapped around him, her wings fell so they draped over both their bodies in a silken, shimmering veil. She turned her head, pressing her cheek between his shoulder blades as she embraced him.

After a few minutes, when their breathing synchronised and the frequency of his shivers subsided, his hands moved up to clasp hers. He said, "Tell me, wife, how did we meet?" His voice was still hoarse, but behind his words she detected a clarity which had been absent before.

"Do you not remember?"

He shook his head. "I know I love you though," he said. "You are beautiful, strong, and wise." His breath eased out in a long sigh. "I just don't know how I came to be here, with you. Where we are."

Aioffe kissed his back. His acceptance of her, especially as she lay next to him, skin pressing skin, made her feel as if she could melt into him forever. "We met on an island, midwinter just past. It was cold then as well, but we got on a boat and travelled far away."

"Tell me more."

Aioffe held her tongue for a moment. Her heart ached, for to tell him the bare truth might cause him to relive that trauma. The loss of his mother, the shame of his theft, and then the horror he had endured these last few weeks.

Perhaps, if he truly couldn't remember, it was a blessing.

"I had hurt my ankle," she started. "And you helped me." Aioffe swallowed, wondering just how much she should stick to the facts and how much she should soften. "You took me in. I could have stayed there forever with you, just you and I, like we lay here now."

"Then why did we leave?"

The lump in her throat remained, but she carried on skirting the truth, grateful she didn't have to look him in the eye. "I wanted to go. I'm an Outcast from my world. Falling in love with you makes me doubly so. In your world, no matter how much I tried, a person such as I cannot be seen. Truly seen as you see me now. Your village was small. Too small for my strangeness not to be noticed. I needed to be ordinary, and you offered me that. You told me to call you husband, and I your wife. I didn't know what it meant until recently. You meant for me to be protected. Only you were wise enough to see I needed that, even though it feared you at the time."

"I am not scared now," he said. He rolled over in her arms, snaking his up so they embraced each other. "How could I be after you saved my life?" He winced as he bore weight on his shoulder.

As she met his eyes, she saw he tried to spare her feelings, too.

"Where does it hurt?"

His lips pressed together briefly, then he said, "The pain is less when you are close."

Her fingers splayed across his shoulders as she nestled into his broad chest. His heartbeat steadied and she realised his shivers had stopped.

They lay there for a moment, entwined. His hand wandered up to her neck, gently stroking, then his fingers slipped through the strands of her hair. Ever so softly, he tugged her head back, then bent his own down. His breath mingled with hers as his eyes roamed over her face. Then, his lips soft as petals when they met hers.

Her heart raced, answered by Tarl's. The kiss deepened until Aioffe felt herself melting into his warmth. Her body moulded into his; legs and arms twined together. Hands, then lips caressed her skin, leaving tingling trails in their wake. A burning intensity grew in her belly. She felt an unfamiliar and peculiar need to embrace him fully, even though they were as close as two bodies could lie.

She wove her fingers through his hair, stroking back the strands which fell about his face. He grinned, then brought her fingertips to his lips, kissing each. When he reached her middle finger, with the cut still slicing through the pad, the lightness of his kiss sent shivers through her.

Her fingertip throbbed, and a bead of blood burst through the wound. He looked at her, raising an eyebrow. Then, he licked the bead.

Aioffe gasped. Tarl kept his lips on her fingertip, the welling blood colouring his lips. His expression changed as he tasted her essence. Aioffe froze, pulse fluttering. Would the exotic taste of her be too much?

He studied her, eyes prowling, roaming her face, as if he could read her mind. His lips parted. He held her gaze as his mouth closed over her finger once again. Pulling the shaft deep inside himself, his suck bewitched her very core.

Aioffe's head tipped back and she gasped as the sensation swelled inside her. With every pulse, he sucked, until the pressure in her belly, between her legs, then her whole spine built. She arched her back, feeling weightless, like flying. A surge of release shuddered through her; wave after wave of joy flowing through her entire being. When it subsided, rippling away, all that remained was her head spinning. The pressure on her finger had gone.

She opened her eyes as a lazy smile stretched across her mouth. His face was close to hers, breathing heavily.

He glowed.

He was glowing!

"Tarl! Look!"

He sat up as he glanced down, turning his hands over as if he couldn't quite believe it. Flexed his fingers then stared down at his own chest. There too, his skin glowed faintly. The same as hers. "A gift. You have given me…" He said, incredulously, and shook his head in disbelief. His face flooded with joy. He reached for her, then almost immediately, his face crumpled. "Owww…"

His free arm shot up, bent at the elbow and tried to feel behind, to his shoulder blades.

Aioffe sat forward and peered quickly over him. She blinked. Checked again. It couldn't be. How?

Between his shoulder blades, on either side of his spine, twin bumps had risen.

"Wings!" She sat back on her heels, her eyebrows high on her forehead.

"Wings?"

In response, her enormous appendages rose behind her.

"You gave me wings too?" Tarl's voice trembled.

The enormity and consequence dawned on her, and all she could do was nod.

"How wonderful," he said, then strained to see over his shoulders.

Then his eyes widened and he screeched.

The Lifeforce tendrils around him became jagged, splintered. Multiplied. She recognised the pattern in the strands this time though, from centuries of transforming the Lifeforce of an animal into sustenance for herself. Her heart wrenched. To be so close to him, to have given everything to save him, only for her to unintentionally make him something else. Something he once feared. Even though he now fully accepted her, loved her, that didn't mean he wanted to be like her, did it? There is little so fearsome as change itself for human or faekind.

The how and why of his new growth mystified her as he collapsed to the ground. Her hands brushed over his skin as his body jerked, his face contorted with agony. With her touch, she understood these were growing pains, rather than injury. A transition she could not stop, only ease. She didn't sense his life was in danger any longer - his Lifeforce strands were strengthening rather than dissipating, if anything.

Aioffe pulled him into her arms again. "Shhh," she whispered, over and over again, lacing her voice and touch with her energy until he calmed. To grow, perhaps he needed to be stilled to the point of acceptance, only this time, unlike with the animals she fed from, she had no intention of drawing out his Lifeforce to sustain her. She judged the moment of his acquiescence, then laid him down.

He slept soundly, deeply, and seemingly unaware of her presence. His heartbeat steadied and slowed. How long would wings take to grow? She had no idea. He was unique - both human and fae. The transition would certainly not occur overnight, so how could she keep him safe and still for an indeterminate amount of time?

She held him in her arms as her gaze wandered around the hut, up the walls to the roof and back to the fire. The flames dwindled, smoke drifted across the darkened stones, coiling around the ivy leaves. The large green leaves made her think of Naturae, and of how fae pupae matured. She had been the last cocoon to break from a vine, that much her nurses had told her. Her development and growth took many years, decades, because many, many more awaited her. An eternity.

A cocoon. That was what Tarl needed to transform! With reverence, she shrouded his body in her black cloak, leaving only his head free. She sat back on her heels, studying his resting face. Aioffe leaned forwards, brushing his lips with a final kiss. Her fingertips buried themselves into the soil, searching for the strands within. She closed her eyes and called to them.

White threads, as smooth as silk, answered her command. They danced out of the earth, wrapping themselves around Aioffe's lover, shimmering in the light of the dwindling fire. Aioffe wept as inch by inch, they bound him until his form was obscured. Her tears fell onto the fibres, soaking them with her sorrow and loneliness, her hope and love.

Someday he would return to her. Whole. Winged. Until then, she would guard him with her life, as he had protected her.

TARL AND AIOFFE RETURN IN *DISRUPTING DESTINY* BOOK 1 OF THE NATURAE SERIES.

READ ON FOR THE FIRST FEW CHAPTERS!

A HISTORICAL NOTE

Owain Ap Tudor - Grandfather of the Tudor Dynasty

The historically minded reader be familiar with the name Owain Ap Tudor, featured as a character in this novel. Very little is actually known about real Owain Tudor before he came into Henry's court, some time around the campaigns in France. A few years later, Owain Tudor would eventually drop the 'Ap' and go on to marry Henry V's soon to be wife, Catherine, in 1421 after Henry V dies. Ultimately, by this marriage and his connections, he manages to restore his family's name and fortunes, founding the Tudor dynasty via his grandson Henry VI, which would rule England for nearly a century.

The Ap Tudor's could claim a prestigious family heritage and held land in Anglesey. Unfortunately, Owain's father, uncles and many other members of his family were punished in 1406 for their part in Owain Glyndŵr's uprising. Records show that many of his family either were put to death or heavily fined. Please forgive my poetic license in writing that Owain proclaims complete ownership of the lands around Beaumaris - his family did own nearby land on Anglesey but I have been unable to verify if they still owned property in Beaumaris itself at the time (1415), some properties having been forfeited to the crown or church after the uprising.

The character I have written in this work of fiction suggests that Owain Ap Tudor would, seeing how the tide has turned against supporters of Welsh princes, be keen to distance himself from his father's miscalculations. To prove his loyalty to the English oppressors, my Owain Ap Tudor rallies some of the many Welsh archers who could claim part-credit for the success at Agincourt, and thus leads the men of Beaumaris into battle, perhaps encouraged by his countryman, Dafydd Gam. Owain Ap Tudor is listed as serving with Sir Walter Hungerford in other battles later in Henry V's campaigns in France, perhaps where he encounters his future wife, Catherine of Valois. His appearance at Agincourt is not specifically noted - he would have been 15/16 at that time.

If this seems young, remember, a boy officially became a man at the age of 8 in those days. Henry V himself was seasoned 29 by the time he fought at Agincourt, but had already successfully led his own army to quell the Welsh uprising (1403-1408) - from the tender age of 16. He recovered from a near fatal injury with an arrow through his cheek at the battle of Shrewsbury.

Dear Reader,

I've always loved the stories where the odds are beaten. They fill me with hope.

This book would not have been possible without the constant support and encouragement from my family, friends and readers who asked to know more about how the main characters in the Naturae Series got together. This is their tale, of how love can blossom even in the strangest of circumstances and between the most different of people.

Although it took a lot of research to bring the story of the Welsh archers at Agincourt to life with authenticity, I owe a huge thank you to my beta readers who have helped bring colour to the romance side of the tale. These include Clare Meadows, Annette Graham, Jodie Angel, and Avril Mason. Your kind critique has strengthened the story and I am grateful for the time and effort you brought to helping me, a not very romantic person by nature, blush the romance.

A Polite Request:

I am an independently published author and as such, reviews are critical to successfully getting my stories seen by readers like you. It would mean the world to me if you could leave a review on your favourite bookish websites about this book so that others can find it!

If you have enjoyed this book, why not visit www.escapeintoatale.com to find out more about the Naturae Book series?

1417AD – A FOREST NEAR AGINCOURT, FRANCE

The growing pains were excruciating. Tearing his skin, continually stretching as new cells formed, split and formed again. In his conscious moments his body railed against the constraints of the cocoon, ripples of agony searing through his gangly limbs, straining for release yet finding none. He had no concept of how long he had endured the pain, only that it was ever present, peaking until he could bear it no more.

Gradually, he became more lucid as the pain diminished. In those brief moments, he was aware of light filtering through the thin membrane, and a shadow hovering over it. This time, consciousness arrived and with it, a realisation that the agony had gone. His nails unclenched from his palms, leaving bloody half-moons. Working his hands up past his naked chest to his face, his fingers sought instinctively to remove the source of the suffocation. The shadow darkened, and he heard it say a muffled, "My love."

The yearning to join the voice, to be free, drove his panic. A guttural sound came from his throat as he clawed frantically at the suffocating veil. With a squelch, his nails snagged a hole and he pulled, straining with his entire being to enlarge it. Taking a huge gasp of breath, he realised that tender hands smoothed limp membrane away from his face.

"Open your eyes," she said, that gentle yet somehow familiar voice again, as her touch wiped mucus from his nostrils. The panic subsided in him and, for a moment, he was aware only of his heart thumping uncomfortably in his chest, beginning to slow as the breaths came easier. He forced open his eyelids, turning his head in her direction. Focus blurred before clearing, then began to blink from the light streaming through the window behind the shape.

Part of him expected the pain to return when he moved his limbs, yet instead the joints felt lubricated, smooth. Stretching out, he became aware again of the cool, wet membrane, now slipping from his naked body. Feeling it with his toes and hands, it suddenly revolted him. He instinctively jerked away from it, falling towards her.

His knee hit the earthen floor hard as he fell, and the jolt sent a quick wave of pain through his leg. To his surprise, it wasn't the same kind of agony as he had so recently endured - quite dull by comparison. A pale hand clasped his arm, supporting him as he straightened to look up at her properly.

"My love," she repeated, and his eyes finally came into focus on her mouth. Small white teeth peeked through smiling red lips, framed by long silver-blonde hair. He knew her... he knew that voice and he recognised her smell. Lavender, witch-hazel and fir - all mingled to provide a scent that was uniquely hers. His arm reached up to touch her face, still not daring to speak, and in one smooth movement, he stood to his full height, instinctively yearning to be nearer. As he breathed in, her arms joined his and they clasped each other. Their eyes locked together, searching for confirmation that their very souls were still intact.

From the edge of his vision, he glimpsed iridescent wings

unfurling from behind her. He was mesmerised by the light from the window aperture which shone through them like the finest of stained glass, illuminating and shimmering. His shoulder blades quivered and, turning his head, he saw his own newly formed appendages rise up, silvery translucent grey yet with the radiance of hers catching the sunshine. Her eyes filled with wonder as she reached out and stroked the edges of his wings. Her touch tickled as rain falling on cold skin.

His senses exploded at her caress and the immediate surroundings rushed at him, overwhelming him. Almost involuntarily, his toes scrunched away from the vibrations of the worms wriggling through the earth beneath his bare feet. The distant call of a lone seagull circling high above briefly deafened, piercing his ears to the point of painful before fading as it glided away. His heart pounded as the volume of the next noise washed over him. As his gaze darted to the window, he frowned, before his drowsy mind identified the ominous rustling sounds - fir trees creaking in the breeze accompanied by the crackle of pine cones flexing to share their seed.

He turned back to her, wide-eyed and seeking reassurance. His newly sharp focus met a gentle, knowing smile and his grip tightened. Opening his mouth to try to speak, all he could taste was the burnt ashes emitting the last of their woody tang, chalky and spent as they lay in the hearth. Instead, he gulped sour air with a tinge of iron lingering on its edges. He swallowed to clear the mustiness from his throat, hoping the other smells and sounds would stop their assault as well.

Drawing in a deep breath, feeling his chest expand without the anticipated stab of pain, he recalled - he'd needed something, anything, to take away the pain from the injury.

The blood. Running his tongue around his mouth with the lingering iron taste, he remembered the blood. But not just his own. Mingling, warm and salty, rich, red. He had absorbed the long history of her Lifeforce, and she his - a much shorter, human life. He jerked away from her gaze; something akin to shame caused him to study the ground beneath him as he searched his foggy mind for clarification.

Her blood held the only promise she could make him at the time, and neither of them had understood the consequences. But, he would have done whatever it took to stay with her.

Then, the change had begun. Numbing his senses as she had bundled him tightly, suffocatingly. Somehow, she must have known he needed to be wrapped - she hadn't mentioned in their frantic discussion before they shared blood, he was sure. He looked up at her in horror, reeling from the invasion of the memory. Stepping back, his face formed the question before he could speak it.

"I didn't know," she tailed off. Her hand clasping his arm with a wobble in her voice. "I... I'm sorry. I'm sorry for the pain. I've never done this before," she said. "The wings are... unexpected. I thought it would be as it is for animals, you'd just heal. But you were in so much distress, I felt I needed to cocoon you, like a pupae. When I saw the lumps form, I hoped the wrapping would make it easier."

She blinked, but her eyes still pleaded for understanding. Forgiveness even.

Drawing a ragged breath, he took a moment to reply. Should he tell her that it had been unbearable? That he had changed his mind? Was that the truth, or just a remnant of the hurt talking? A childish plea to return to his former self?

He contemplated how best to respond to her unspoken request, searching the depths of her bright blue eyes as he tried to calm his breathing. The familiarity of her shapes, her colours and scent reassured him. And with that comfort, he remembered he had been enthralled by her. That, from the minute he had seen her unclothed and the truth of her revealed, he had been fascinated. The knot in his ribcage eased as clarity returned.

How could he ever have thought to pull away from her when all he wanted to do was be with her? And, if possible, be more like her? Love itself had infused their ribbons of blood, binding their destiny together, for what would now be an eternal lifetime.

He felt a waft of cooler air soothe his neck, rhythmical as a heartbeat. His lips lifted and he felt a rush of unexpected giddiness as he acknowledged her unintended gift. His own wings, beating without effort, as if they had always been there.

He had chosen this. Chosen of his own human free will. He knew what had been done could never be undone.

"No longer Tarl, the smithy's son," he whispered as he stroked her pale face. "Change is upon me." He pulled her closer and searched her luminous blue eyes in wonder and forgiveness.

He did not know, nor could have known, that she had truly changed her own destiny; he only knew the future she now had was with him by her side. "And I, I relinquish Aioffe… She was alone, and now is not," she said, with conviction and hope in her voice.

He had a sense of responsibility for her happiness falling silently from her shoulders onto his, as she took his hand, whispering, "Together, we can be truly free." She tilted her head to one side, eyes flaring as she absorbed the noises outside. "But, we need to go now - before we are discovered!"

CHAPTER 1 – SEPTEMBER 1534

Tendrils of smoke filled the young man's sensitive nostrils with the lingering scent of waxy paper, apples, sea salt and lichen-covered bark, evoking happier memories of the last five years. Tasting the essence of their temporary home as if that would commit it to the past only, he had to subdue the cough tightening his throat. No matter how many times they ran, the thought of starting over again sat on his heart, heavy and full of dread and sorrow. He swallowed down the bitterness, resolving to look to the future. He tried looking up at the clear skies, but the canopy of stars through the array of amber leaves blurred as his eyes welled. Shaking his long blond fringe away, he jabbed at the embers. Bright sparks gracefully leapt into the air and twinkled before vanishing with a quiet pop.

The snap of a branch behind him made him spin around, but his face quickly lifted into a smile as he saw her. Pale in the moonlight, her skin always glowed clearest at night, lighting the shadows with its luminescent tone. She smiled gently at him and held out a slim hand. "Ready?" She said softly.

"Soon," he answered, taking her chilled fingers in his and leading her to the warm log at the fire's edge. In the still, dark forest where they were most comfortable, they sat companionably, slowly pushing in their paper identities nearer the glowing core. The moment of sadness he felt earlier lifted in her company; she was, and always would be, his partner in their long journey to survive. Together they would carve out another future, in another town. It never got any easier, no matter how many times they resettled.

He replayed memories through his mind's eye - the lowered gazes from the once welcoming shop-keepers, a lull in conversation amongst the previously courteous ladies after church when they approached. Then, inevitably, the anger. Always under a veil of suspicion, the striking young couple were ultimately people with no verifiable roots who never truly fitted in.

Often, it started innocently enough with the womenfolk noticing a peculiarity about the newcomers - even after years of living peacefully, side by side, within the community. Talking, gossiping about why they weren't quite 'right'. Then the menfolk joined their wives, voicing their anger, their sense of injustice. Before long, something would happen which wasn't 'usual', and, having nothing more than guesswork and gossip to interpret, sometimes the mob mentality would begin. Despite their efforts to lie low, the couple would find themselves hounded out of town if they missed the warning signs and delayed.

Here, the apples had tasted so juicy, the surroundings so beautiful, they had almost left it too late to move away. Life here had been unexpectedly rich and varied, with its frequent visits from travelling performers and community rituals celebrated with gusto and wine. A temperate southern climate made it harder to resist the temptation to feed from them, especially her - she was trickier to keep sated. The people in this seaside township were generally so happy and full of Lifeforce, it was hard to leave. Some he had counted as friends. Stranger still to have no time to say goodbye or make their excuses for leaving.

The sunlight was just starting to pick through the forests when he heard the voices, faintly at first, then growing closer. Then, the crash of dogs bounding through the drying undergrowth. Picking their way nearer to their hideout, he knew they would have discovered their empty rented house by now and come looking for them in the nearby copse. Maybe even the bodies of the animals they feasted on, desiccated and hastily buried in the dead of night, had been found.

He rubbed her shoulders in his lap, gently whispering, "It's time, my love. We need to go. They are close." She opened her eyes and sat up quickly, blinking in the pinkish light of dawn, her ears suddenly picking up on the sounds as they got closer. The dying embers of the fire would give their location away, and she hurried to pick up the heavy leather sacks she had brought with her earlier.

Without warning, a large, shaggy-looking dog bounded into the clearing. Pulling up and planting its feet wide, it paused to glare at them, judging as it sniffed. Then, it lifted its head and started barking loudly. The clipped yaps ensured that other canines arrived, circling them and noisily declaring their hunting success. Salivating jaws anticipated the reward awaiting them from the men not far behind.

The hounds didn't advance on them, instinct warning them they were not top of the food chain in this instance. But they wouldn't betray their masters and back away. Dark pairs of eyes fixed on the couple, unblinking. Hunter versus hunter. Beast versus beast.

The fae were trapped. He stepped towards one, making to shoo it away, but the dog growled, digging in with its haunches and baring yellowed teeth in a snarl. Fetid breath puffed in the crisp dawn light, surrounding them with a foul-stenched net.

"We will be seen if we leave from here," she murmured, barely audible to most ears over the noise of the barks and snarls. She hurriedly fixed straps behind her, the bag altering her slim silhouette, making her look strangely unbalanced with a protruding pot-belly where it hung.

"Probably, but it's a risk I think we need to take," he said. "I'm willing if you are?" Despite his long cloak, now draped over his chest, he also appeared cumbersome with his front-strapped sack on.

"Over 'ere!" Shouts, sounding close, followed by dull snapping branches as boots crashed their path through the undergrowth.

She nodded and pulled the bonnet from her head to free her hair. Shimmering wings unfurled, the morning light bouncing off them as it streamed through the tree leaves. "Straight up!" he said as he bent his knees to lift off, his darker wings already freed and waving slowly.

They shot up through the canopy and into the bright sunlight. Shrinking below, the fields were dotted with sheep and horses, mottled green and brown hedgerows marking their boundaries. Small thatched dwellings laid low to the ground, their stone chimneys spouting thin wisps of smoke as early morning fires were stoked. Higher they flew, out of the range of the voices shouting, cussing as the enraged and frightened humans found the still-warm ashes of the fire. Higher, to where the birds circled, swirling in formation around them.

Looking up through the trees, one of the men saw their odd-shaped silhouettes, out of reach of arrows, disappearing into the clouds. Shaking his head, the notion that he had witnessed something not of his world was forced from his mind. It did no good to stir up further talk of the devil amongst them. A man would only have to spend yet more time in the confessional and at prayer if he had seen anything sinister, after all. Best not to mention it.

*****

"Who shall you be today, my love?" she called over the clouds. "I like the name Joshua!" He smiled and shook his head, grinning at her. "You like Joshua because you liked the boy, not because you like the name, I think."

"He had the sweetest tasting Lifeforce I have had in a long time," she said, remembering, "but I nearly got carried away. I caused this relocation, and for that, I'm sorry."

"You are insatiable, in more ways than one," he called back, moving closer to grasp her hand mid-air. They slowed, joined hands, then fluttered to face each other. In the brilliant sunlight, they gazed at each other, searching, studying and reconnecting. Together they hovered, hands clasped around the bulky sacks filled with their only belongings, two halves of a lumpy, bejewelled butterfly. In the unfiltered light, high above the clouds, their love glowed through in its intensity. It would be absurd to think that they had ever blended in - no human would have mistaken them for mortals were they to glimpse them now. Fair skin, ash-white hair almost translucent as the sunshine poured through it, and wings rippled with rainbow tones, fluttering as they lingered in the moment.

"I can't promise more boys like him," he said, looking at her lips as he leaned in for a kiss. "And we must try to blend in more next town, and not risk losing control with a human, however much we become lost in their energy. We can survive without them, you know!" He reproached, but still with love in his tone. "We could have stayed longer if only we had been more careful. I think the lad will recover with some rest. The young usually do, then attribute their lack of get up and go to overdoing it, or some sort of malady."

She smiled and nodded, but nevertheless felt remorseful. Her need for sustenance from the unseen joy humans emitted was compulsive, necessary even. The Lifeforce faekind gained from its root source in blood was enough for him, but satisfying her needs was more dangerous and required crowds of people. Keeping control of herself during these times was always a challenge. A moment or two longer in her thrall, and it would have been too late for that poor boy. She sometimes forgot herself in those heady inhalations, but had so far never broken her own rule of not killing a child in the heat of the inhale. But youth, they were so free, so deliciously innocent. Their Lifeforce had no filter and its purity was sublime.

"I just want to build a home with you, where we can live in peace. I don't think that's too much to ask?" Joshua's begging broke through her guilt-laden reminiscing.

She pulled back from the embrace and stroked his face, feeling the boyish stubble along his jawline. "I know, I wish for a home also," she said wistfully. "Maybe this next time."

"You always say that."

"I know."

"Never satisfied," he teased.

He flapped his dark wings and spun her around and around. She leaned her head back and relaxed, allowing him to take the lead in a dizzying spin. They both laughed at the release of the exhilarating action. As he slowed, he lowered his face to embrace her again.

"My head!" she said, breaking off the kiss. "It's still spinny... if this is what death feels like, I could die right now, happy. It's like a little death."

"Believe me, this is not what dying feels like," he said, nuzzling her ear. "I could remind you what a 'little death' feels like if you want though?"

Her grin broadened, "You'll have to catch me first!" She darted upwards, playing. Like dancing dragonflies, they dashed around the skies, giggling and whirling.

"I won't lose you again, minx!" He caught her slender ankle, "I will follow you, find you, hound you down like we are hunted now, even if there were an arrow still jutting from my side!" He paused, hovering up to look her fully in the face earnestly.

Stroking away loose strands of hair from his cheeks, she

whispered, "Never. I'll never truly run from you. Nothing will ever part us." They embraced again, and he gave her bottom a squeeze through her skirts. Squealing in mock outrage, she pushed away from him and dashed off. He followed, of course, and they continued their journey north together.

*****

They slowed after a few hours and dipped down through the cloud blanket, to where it was raining and grey. Flying lower, yet still out of sight, they scanned the ground with hawk-like eyesight for a group of houses - a town, not just a village. The occasional straight Roman road cut gash-like through the landscape. He pointed northeast, and together they gracefully swung around and headed for a small wooded area they noticed, close to a sizable cluster of dwellings. Rough tracks weaving their brown trails around the countryside meandered through fields less enclosed by hedges than they had been in the south. Through the drizzle, the patchwork of leaves turning golden amber enticed them for the cover it could afford.

They landed by the side of the woods and pushed aside undergrowth to enter the forest. Hidden by branches, the couple dropped their packs and loosened their garments, secreting their wings close to skin. Helping each other, they straightened their attire, pushed hair back into caps and tucked smock edges neatly into jerkin and kirtle. A last check before hoisting their belongings onto their backs, a brief kiss for luck, and their windy and unusual travel method was obscured.

Returning to the muddy track, they picked their way through the puddles left by carts and carriages, and headed towards a cluster of buildings ahead.

"How about Annabella? For me. Mistress Annabella Meadows," she said as they approached an inn nestled on the crossroads of the road into town.

"I'm flattered you remember my little treats," he said, glancing down and smiling at her. "And a fitting way to honour her charms. I plan to demonstrate how stimulating I found her Lifeforce, just as soon as we find our next abode." Giggling, they pushed open the faded oak door and entered, hoping to buy a room for the night where they could rest. It was getting dark, and experience had taught them it was best to view a new possible home in daylight. The smell of damp leather and stale ale assaulted their noses as they crossed the threshold, but there was comfort in the humanity within and a warm hearth.

THE NATURAE SERIES

Risking Destiny
Discover a villain's creation in this Viking Age Prequel
Order your copy now **www.books2read.com/riskingdestiny**

Destiny Awaiting
The enemies to lovers Prequel. Escape to Agincourt, where averting a war between their races and their countries, Aioffe and Tarl's battles of the heart are destined to fight with faith and hope itself.
Order your copy now
www.books2read.com/destinyawaiting

Disrupting Destiny
Book 1 – A country torn apart, lovers caught in the middle in the early Tudor age.
Order your copy now
www.books2read.com/disruptingdestiny

Anarchic Destiny
Book 2 – A forgotten heir, a queendom in crisis... chaos will reign as Bloody Mary makes her move for power.
Order your copy now **www.books2read.com/anarchicdestiny**

www.escapeintoatale.com/books

Printed in Great Britain
by Amazon

20211524R00222